THE WAYWARD SON

BY
YVONNE LINDSAY

Published in Great Britain 2012
by Mills & Boon, an imprint of Harlequin (UK) Limited,
Eton House, 18-24 Paradise Road, Richmond, Surrey TW9 1SR

© Dolce Vita Trust 2012

ISBN: 978 0 263 89193 5
ebook ISBN: 978 1 408 97772 9

51-0712

Harlequin (UK) policy is to use papers that are natural, renewable and recyclable products and made from wood grown in sustainable forests. The logging and manufacturing processes conform to the legal environmental regulations of the country of origin.

Printed and bound in Spain
by Blackprint CPI, Barcelona

New Zealand born, to Dutch immigrant parents, **Yvonne Lindsay** became an avid romance reader at the age of thirteen. Now, married to her "blind date" and with two fabulous children, she remains a firm believer in the power of romance. Yvonne feels privileged to be able to bring to her readers the stories of her heart. In her spare time, when not writing, she can be found with her nose firmly in a book, reliving the power of love in all walks of life. She can be contacted via her website, www.yvonnelindsay.com.

To E.M.
—In the immortal words of Casper, "Can I keep you?"

One

She hadn't seen anything quite this beautiful in forever. The exquisitely colored autumnal landscape aside, the figure of the man chopping wood in the distance, shirt off, muscles rippling in the still-warm Adelaide Hills sunshine, was quite enough to remind Anna of every hormonal response her body was capable of. And then some.

Never averse to indulging in appreciation of the male form—even if her busy work-filled schedule meant she rarely did anything about it—she walked a little closer. A tingle of awareness skimmed across her skin, raising goose bumps on the surface, which had nothing to do with the hint of evening breeze that rolled through the hills. It was only when she was about twenty meters from him that recognition hit her with all the subtlety of a bucket of ice water.

Judd Wilson.

Her entire reason for being in Australia.

Although they'd never met, there was no mistaking Charles Wilson's son. Obviously tall, Judd had dark hair and warmly tanned skin stretched over a physique that was the epitome of every woman's fantasy. His sharply sculpted features hinted at a resemblance to his father. She'd hazard a guess his eyes were the same piercing blue, as well.

Anna was surprised when her inner muscles clenched on a purely instinctive female reaction and her heart stuttered a little in her chest. She hadn't responded this strongly to anyone in a while, and she sure as hell never expected to feel so drawn to the son of the man who was not only her employer, but practically a father to her. She drew in a deep breath and forced back the flood of attraction that threatened to swamp her anew—reminding herself that she was here on business. She'd made a promise to Charles—a promise she fully intended to keep.

His instructions had been painfully clear. Somehow she had to persuade Judd Wilson to come home to New Zealand, before the father he hadn't seen in more than two decades died.

Anna took a few more tentative steps through the pathway designated amongst the rows and rows of grapevines that striated the land. Her eyes were fixed on the male figure working ahead of her—the man completely oblivious to the bombshell she was about to drop on his world. She paused for a moment, sudden nerves weakening her resolve.

Judd had been only six years old when his parents' divorce resulted in his and his mother's leaving New Zealand—not to mention leaving Charles, and Judd's baby sister, Nicole—behind for good. Did he even remember his father? Would he be pleased at the chance to reconcile, or would he be bitter over all the lost years?

Anxiety over Judd's potential reaction was swiftly followed by a swirl of familiar anger and defensiveness on Charles's behalf. If it hadn't been for Cynthia Masters-Wilson's deceptions, Charles would never have been separated from his son in the first place. Anna hadn't yet met the woman who had torn apart Charles's very reasons for existence, and she certainly wasn't looking forward to it. No doubt it would prove to be a necessary evil at some stage, but for now her focus was on meeting Charles's son and on gauging what his response to his father's contact would be. Her intense physical reaction to him now promised to make that a little more complicated than Anna had anticipated.

She was here with a job to do, she reminded herself sternly, even as her eyes flicked back toward Judd's sun-kissed torso one more time. She couldn't afford to let herself get distracted. Perhaps right now was not the best time to meet him and try to broach the topic. This was a matter that would require good timing and not a small amount of finesse if she was to be successful, and she owed it to Charles to be successful. Lord only knew he'd done more than enough for her family over the years. The least she could do in return was bring some peace of mind to the man who had supported Anna and her late mother for most of Anna's life. She couldn't just barge in and potentially destroy her one opportunity to bring Judd Wilson home.

She took a turn in a different direction, determined now to create some distance between herself and the very man she'd flown almost five hours to see. There would be time enough during her stay here at The Masters' Vineyard and Accommodation, she reasoned with herself. She had to tread this road very carefully if she was going to succeed.

Despite her best intentions, she didn't get very far.

"Hi, there," a voice as rich and sensual as a classic Shiraz called out from behind her. "It's a beautiful evening, isn't it?"

She couldn't ignore him now—not when it was vital she make a good impression. Anna braced herself as she turned around to face her boss's son.

Must be the new guest for the accommodation side of the business, Judd thought to himself as he watched the woman come closer. His cousin Tamsyn sent an update to all staff at the vineyard at the beginning of each week as to which of the luxurious cottages on the property would be accommodating guests for the coming days. She certainly hadn't mentioned that their newest visitor was so stunning.

Judd narrowed his eyes and tracked the movements of the woman in the blue dress as she approached. She walked with a gracefulness that belied the uneven ground she strolled along, and there was a sensual sway to her hips that sent a jolt of pure male appreciation rocketing through his body.

"Judd Wilson, welcome to The Masters'." Judd shifted the ax to his left hand so he could reach out his right to shake. She smiled in response, a slow movement of her lips that made his groin tighten almost imperceptibly, but the effect when she placed her hand in his was unmistakable. Raw need, hot and greedy, unfurled with latent intent. Interesting. Very interesting. Perhaps he'd found a solution to the boredom that had been plaguing him for weeks. He smiled back and clasped her hand firmly.

"Hi, I'm Anna Garrick," she said, her voice husky.

Her eyes searched his face keenly. As if she was looking for something. Perhaps some spark of recognition from him? No, the instant he thought of it, he eschewed the idea. If he'd ever met Anna Garrick before, he had no doubt he'd have remembered her.

From the top of her burnished dark chestnut-colored hair to her perfectly proportioned body and the tips of her painted toenails, she was his every fantasy. Even her voice—slightly soft, slightly rough—stroked his senses in a way he could never forget.

"Lovely to meet you, Anna. Did you arrive today?"

Her eyes flicked away, as if she was suddenly nervous—or hiding something. Judd felt his instincts go on alert.

"Yes, I did. It's wonderful here. You're so lucky to live in such a beautiful area. Have you...worked here long?" The question was innocent, but he'd caught the slight hesitation, as if she'd started out with the intention of asking something else.

"You could say that," Judd replied, his smile tightening. "It's something of a Masters family business—I grew up here."

"But your name…"

Ah, yes, his name. The reminder of the father who cast him aside all those years ago—and the reason why, even as the very successful head of The Masters' far-flung interests, some of his cousins still never quite treated him like he belonged.

"My mother is Cynthia Masters-Wilson," he replied. No need to go into details. Not when there were so many more pleasurable things he'd like to discuss with this woman.

"And do all Masters chop wood for the winery fireplaces?" she teased.

"But of course," he replied in kind. "Anything at all we can do to make your stay more…pleasurable." That certainly sounded better than admitting that he'd needed the tension release after an incredibly frustrating day of work.

Some days were like that. Bashing at the keys on a laptop didn't quite cut it when you just needed to get physical. And when his choices were either to chop wood or to resort to physical violence against his cousin Ethan, Judd had, reluctantly, chosen chopping wood.

Of course, Ethan really did need someone to knock his head straight. The man might run the winemaking side of the business with undeniable skill—their stock of award-winning wines was proof enough of that—but he was so stuck in his ways, he might as well be cemented in place. Ethan was devoted to maintaining the integrity and superiority of the wines that were synonymous with The Masters' brand. With the current glut of certain wine varieties on the local market, Judd was equally adamant that Ethan needed to diversify. He'd been suggesting it from the day the first projections about the excesses had arisen some years ago. His cousin was like a bear with a sore head on the issue and even more stubborn with it.

Yes, he definitely needed the distraction Ms. Garrick provided.

"And I do hope you'll let me know if there's anything at all *I* can do for you," he added.

"I'll keep that in mind," she replied. "But I can't think of anything I need at the moment. My plan for now is just to enjoy a ramble through these lovely grounds before it gets too dark."

"Then I'll let you return to it. But I'll be seeing you at dinner tonight?"

"Dinner?"

"Yes, we have a family dinner to welcome the new guests every week. There would have been an invitation in your welcome pack when you checked in. It begins with drinks in the formal sitting room of the main house at seven o'clock." Judd stepped closer, taking hold of her hand again. "You will be there, won't you?"

"Yes, I'd like that."

"Excellent," he murmured. "Until then." He lifted her hand, brushing his lips against the back in a soft kiss. She seemed taken aback for a moment, but then she gave him another slow, delicious smile before walking away. Judd leaned on the ax handle and watched her go. Shadows were beginning to creep along the foothills. He looked up to the ruins of the gothic mansion that crowned the nearby peak.

The charred remains were all that was left of the original Masters home. Years after its destruction, it remained a symbol of the family's past glory and their fight to rebuild a world that had been burned to the ground in a devastating sweep of ravenous bushfire. You had to admire a family that had had every marker of their wealth laid to waste, but who had fought back, tooth and nail, to be where they were today.

He was proud to be a part of that heritage. Despite his name, he was as much a Masters as any one of his many cousins and had just as much right to be here. Even so, he'd always felt as if he was an outsider. It had made him work twice as hard to prove his worth, and that work ethic had pushed The Masters' forward and onto a global platform beyond the family's expectations since he'd taken over as head of operations.

But perhaps he'd been too work-focused lately. It had been a while since he'd let loose. His duties here had consumed him for months now. Today, he'd finally admitted to himself that, no matter how hard he pushed himself, he was bored. Life, work, everything lacked the challenge he craved. A little light flirtation with the lovely Anna Garrick could be the perfect antithesis to the frustrations he was facing.

Judd methodically stacked the pile of logs he'd split and put away his tools before heading for his suite of rooms and having a much-needed shower. The prospect of another evening with his family suddenly held a great deal more appeal than it had after his latest altercation with Ethan's inflexible attitude.

Perhaps he'd found the challenge he was seeking after all.

Judd's hair was still slightly damp when he made his way into the formal sitting room, where whichever members of the Masters clan who were resident gathered for drinks with the guests before dinner. It was an old-fashioned habit, one that had its roots firmly linked to the ruins on the hill and a lifestyle long since gone, but one which still held a certain charm and which had no doubt been integral in keeping the family so firmly knit together.

Sunset brought a deeper chill to the air outside, which was offset by the crackling fire in the large stone fireplace.

He cast a glance around the room, giving a grim-lipped nod briefly in Ethan's direction before smiling at his mother, who sat, with her usual supreme elegance, on one of the chairs near the fireplace. No sign of the new guest yet.

He crossed to the sideboard and poured himself a half glass of The Masters' pinot noir. As he did so, he saw the object of his intentions hover in the doorway. He moved toward her immediately, but his mother—ever vigilant—beat him there. As he approached, he could hear her questioning Anna.

"Excuse me for being so forward, but you do look familiar to me. Have you stayed here before?" Cynthia asked.

To his surprise, a swiftly masked look of shock flitted across Anna's face.

"N-no," she replied. "This is my first visit to South Australia, although I hope it won't be my last."

She smiled, but her eyes still held a shadow of the shock he'd seen earlier. Was she lying? His instincts honed to a sharper edge. Ms. Garrick was becoming very interesting indeed.

"Perhaps you have a double out there. They say we all do." Cynthia glossed over any awkwardness with an arch of one expertly plucked brow. "Tell me, what can Judd get you to drink, my dear?"

"A glass of sauvignon blanc would be lovely, thank you. I hear you recently were awarded two golds for your sauvs."

"Yes, we were. We're very proud of Ethan and what he's doing with the wines," Cynthia said with a pointed look toward her son that told Judd his cousin had probably already apprised her of their earlier dispute. "Aren't we, Judd?"

"He's a master, that's for sure," Judd agreed.

His double entendre didn't go unnoticed by his mother, who flung him a silent rebuke with her expressive eyes, before apparently deciding it would be a suitable punishment to him to lead Anna away and introduce her to the other members of the family. Judd was forced to admit that his mother had chosen her chastisement well—Anna was the only one in the room whose company he truly wanted tonight.

He stood with one hand in his trouser pocket and observed Anna's movements as she was introduced to Cynthia's two older brothers and then Ethan. The instant his cousin stood to welcome the newcomer, Judd's hackles rose and every feral instinct inside of him leaped to the fore.

Something must have shown on his face, because he didn't miss the spark of interest in Ethan's eye before his cousin leaned forward to say something to Anna. Something which made her laugh. The sound itself was enough to send his blood humming along his veins, but knowing it was Ethan who had brought that laugh to her delectable lips set his teeth on edge.

Determined not to give his cousin the satisfaction of knowing just how much, and how surprisingly, his action had riled him, Judd turned to welcome Ethan's sister, Tamsyn, as she appeared in the door.

"I see you've already met our latest guest," she commented, removing his untouched pinot noir from his hands and taking a sip. Her brand-new engagement ring flashed brilliantly in the overhead lights. "Mmm, good. Can you pour me one?"

"Have this one, I haven't touched it."

"Thanks," Tamsyn answered with a smile.

"That fiancé of yours not here with you tonight?"

"No, he's still in the city—working." Her warm brown eyes searched his face. "You look tense. Is everything okay?"

Judd forced a smile to his lips. Tamsyn always had the unerring ability to sense when something was wrong with him.

"Nothing that won't be sorted when your brother learns to pay as much attention to market trends as he does to our guests," he commented.

Tamsyn laughed. "Oh, well, good luck with that, cuz. You

know market trends are the last thing Ethan concerns himself with. But I wouldn't growl too much about that." She nodded in Anna's direction. "You know Ethan's partial to blondes. And this particular brunette keeps sneaking glances at you, anyway. Have you met her yet?"

Judd nodded, letting his gaze track back to Anna's slender form and drinking in the smooth lines of her body, allowing a satisfaction-filled smile to cross his face when he realized his cousin was right—Anna's attention wandered in his direction several times. "Did she say what she was doing here in Adelaide?"

"No, I just assumed it was a short vacation. She didn't say much when she rang to make the booking."

"A short vacation?"

"I'm sure you'll have plenty of time to get to know her," Tamsyn teased. "But yeah, she's only here four days."

"I'd better not let her waste any more of her time here, then," he replied. "If you'll excuse me."

Without waiting for Tamsyn's reply he made his way across the room and to Anna's side. She turned and gave him a smile.

"It must be lovely being able to work with your extended family like this," she said. "Ethan's been filling me in on what you all do."

"It has its benefits, certainly," Judd agreed. "Tell me, have you planned any extended sightseeing while you're here? As luck would have it, I find myself with a couple of days with little to do and I'd love to show you around if you're keen."

Anna told herself to remain calm. This was exactly the opportunity she needed. Time alone with Judd Wilson would help her to better find out what he was like. She knew Charles had expected her to simply make an appointment with him and to give him the letter that even now burned a hole in her evening bag, but despite Charles's directive, she wanted to understand her boss's son just a little more before she took that step. God only knew that Charles had borne his fair share of disappointment in his lifetime and, if she had her way, his last years would be quite the opposite.

As much as Charles longed to be reunited with Judd, Anna knew that Charles was braced for his son's refusal. That was why he'd told no one but Anna how crucial it was to him to bring Judd back into the fold. Charles had sworn her to complete secrecy, not allowing her to tell even his daughter, Nicole, who had subtly taken up the reins of the company when Charles first got sick, any of the details of this trip. The cone of silence rankled, especially when Nicole was her best friend and they all not only worked together, but lived under the same roof, as well. Anna couldn't help but feel that she was betraying Nicole by doing all of this behind her back.

It was for Charles's sake, she reminded herself. And Charles deserved her very best efforts to convince his son to come home. If only she knew what the best approach was for her to take!

Instinct told her that Judd might be more receptive if she hid her true purpose for a little while longer and got him to open up to her more before she revealed the truth of her visit. But the purely female part of her worried that the longer she put off her business, the harder it would be for her to resist the powerful draw pulling her toward him. She chose her response to Judd Wilson's suggestion carefully.

"Are you sure? I wouldn't want to impose on you. It's my first visit to the region and I can already tell I haven't left myself enough time to enjoy it fully."

Judd leaned in closer. "Maybe we can entice you to come back again."

His words sent a shiver of anticipation across her skin. If the man got any more enticing she'd need a chillingly cold shower before the night was through. This visceral reaction to Judd Wilson was an unexpected complication she wasn't quite sure how to handle. But at least his reply showed her one thing—he was *definitely* willing to let her get to know *him* better…at least for as long as she hid the truth.

A dinner bell sounded down the hall, saving her from making a response. Judd offered her his arm.

"May I escort you to the table?"

Anna hesitated a moment before tucking her hand in the crook of his arm. "Are you always this formal?" she asked.

He shot her a look, a fierce blue blaze of fire in his eyes that let her know in no uncertain terms that he himself could be very informal, indeed. Her body reacted on an unconscious level. Her nipples tightened, her breasts suddenly full and aching with a desire to be touched. Everything in her body tensed, drawing her into a heightened state of awareness.

"When I need to be," he responded with a smile that was pure wicked intent from the curve of his lips to the light that gleamed in his eyes.

Anna forced herself to break eye contact. The compelling power of his male beauty was quite enough to take her breath away and to addle her wits along with it. Maybe getting to know Judd Wilson wasn't such a good idea after all. As Charles's assistant, she had the opportunity to interact with many powerful and compelling men, but never before had she dealt with a man with such effortless charisma.

The next few days suddenly took on an edge of uncertainty. What on earth had she let herself in for?

Two

The long wooden table in the formal dining room had been set with a dazzling array of china, crystal and cutlery. Anna sent a silent prayer of thanks that her upbringing in Charles Wilson's home meant that such a setting didn't faze her. Charles had insisted she have all the same social advantages Nicole enjoyed, even if—with her mother's position as Charles's housekeeper and companion—she hadn't had anywhere near the same financial background.

Seated near the top of the table, at Judd's right, Anna could observe the family dynamics in action. It was clear that Cynthia was very much the female head of the household. If Judd Wilson physically resembled his father, his estranged sister, Nicole, was her mother personified.

Anna studied Cynthia from her vantage point at the table. This was what her friend would look like in another twenty-five years—without, perhaps, the faint lines of bitterness that bracketed the older woman's mouth. That said, and despite the swish of gray at her temples that contrasted to her thick, dark hair, Cynthia Masters-Wilson was still a striking woman.

She carried herself with an almost regal air—expecting everyone to defer to her wishes and not holding back her disapproval if those wishes were not observed. Anna wondered briefly what Cynthia had been like early in her marriage to Charles, and found herself caught by the older woman's very intent gaze. Giving her hostess a smile, Anna tore her eyes away, mildly horrified that she'd been caught staring. The last thing she wanted to do was attract attention to herself.

There was a strong bond between Cynthia and her son, too, Anna observed. Judd, it seemed, was the only one capable of defusing his mother's rather autocratic attitude and bringing a genuine smile of warmth to her fine features. So why then, when her son was obviously so important to her, had Cynthia left behind her one-year-old daughter, Nicole, when she'd returned to Australia? Had she ever taken a moment to think about the baby girl she'd left behind and what impact her abandonment would have on that infant's life?

Anna had come to Australia full of sympathy for Charles, who had been so hurt by Cynthia's actions during their marriage. But seeing the woman now just brought home how badly Nicole had been cheated, as well.

"You're looking serious. Is everything okay with your meal?" Judd asked softly in her ear.

The gentle caress of his warm breath made her skin tingle, and she forced her concentration back from where she'd let it lead her. Anna shook her head.

"No, everything is wonderful, thank you."

"Is it something else that's bothering you?" he pressed, reaching across the table in front of him to lift a bottle of wine to top off her glass.

Just you, she thought before giving her head a shake.

"I'm perhaps a little tired, that's all."

"We can be a bit overwhelming, can't we?" he commented.

"No, it's not that. Actually, I envy you this. I'm an only child, as were both my parents. To have so many family members all in one place… Well, you're lucky."

"Yes, we are lucky—and equally cursed at the same time," he said with a charming wink that took the sting out of the latter part of his statement.

And Nicole should have had the chance to be a part of this, too, Anna added silently. Not for the first time, she wondered what had happened to drive Charles and Cynthia, and their children, apart. Whatever it was, Charles had flatly refused to discuss it, aside from saying that Cynthia had betrayed his trust—something she knew that Charles considered unforgivable. Whatever it was, Anna knew that it had not only ruined his marriage, but it had led to a major rift between himself and his business partner also. So many lives altered. And here she was, trying to mend a fence. Boy, was she ever out of her depth.

By the time the meal had progressed to coffee and dessert, Anna asked to be excused from the table, pleading tiredness. The gentlemen at the table stood as she moved her chair back, and she found herself completely charmed by the effortless old-world manners.

"Thank you all so much for your company tonight, and for dinner," she said.

"You're very welcome, Anna. Just let housekeeping know tomorrow if you'll be joining us again during your stay," Cynthia said graciously. "Do you have anything special planned for tomorrow?"

"We'll be doing some sightseeing and then I'm taking her into Hahndorf for lunch," Judd interjected.

"Oh?"

Cynthia hid her surprise but not before giving her son a sharp look that gave Anna no doubt that his mother would be grilling him on his choice of companion the minute she left the room. Cynthia composed her features into a bland smile. "Well, then, I hope you enjoy our little taste of Germany. Sleep well."

"Thank you," Anna replied and turned to leave the room.

To her surprise, Judd followed her. As they reached the front door she stopped.

"Why did you tell your mother you're taking me out tomorrow?"

"Because I am," he said confidently. "You can't visit the Adelaide Hills without stopping at Hahndorf, as well. It would be culturally insensitive."

"Culturally insensitive or not, I got the impression she wasn't too pleased about it."

"She thinks I don't work hard enough, but that's my problem, not yours."

He opened the front door and gestured for her to precede him. Out on the narrow road that led to the restored pioneer's cottage where she was staying, Anna felt the night air close in around her with its frigid arms. She shivered, wishing she'd thought to bring her pashmina with her when she'd come across to the house earlier.

"At the risk of being cliché," Judd said, removing his dinner jacket and dropping it over her shoulders, "I think you need this more than I do."

"Thank you," she said softly.

He wasn't kidding. Judging by the heat of his body still held in the lining of his jacket, he certainly had no need of the garment. She instantly felt warmed by it. A faint waft of spice, blended intrinsically with a hint of vanilla and woody notes, enveloped her. She recognized the scent as Judd's cologne and felt her bones begin to melt.

"The nights can be quite cool here from now on. The staff will have lit the fire in your cottage for you. It should be lovely and warm compared to out here."

Anna had an instant and vivid flashback to watching Judd

chopping wood this afternoon. Did he accomplish everything with that much vigor?

"It's still a beautiful night," she said, looking upward at the inky darkness of the sky peppered with dots of light—anything to distract her from the influence of what he did to her.

"Certainly is."

There was something about his voice that made her drop her gaze and meet his. He was looking straight at her. Despite the fact that at least a meter separated them, she felt as if he'd reached out and touched her. Anna swallowed against the sudden dryness that parched her throat. This man was sensuality personified. With only one look, he had her virtually a quivering mess of longing.

She barely knew him and yet she was already on the verge of casting all her careful self-imposed rules to the four corners of the earth and inviting him to explore this overwhelming attraction between them. And she knew her feelings were reciprocated. She could feel the energy and tension fairly vibrating off him. What would he be like when he lost control, she wondered, allowing herself to dwell for only a moment on the idea before slamming it back behind her all too weak defenses.

She broke eye contact before she could do something totally out of character, and began to walk a little more briskly along the path. Judd silently kept pace with her. At the cottage, he waited as she opened the front door. She shrugged off his coat and handed it to him.

"Thank you again."

"You're welcome," he replied.

Why didn't he just turn and go? She felt a flush rise in her cheeks. Did he expect her to invite him in? The cottage came with both a well-stocked kitchen and wet bar complete with a wine chiller, she'd noticed on checking in earlier today. But what kind of message would that send, she wondered, if she asked him to join her for coffee, or a drink? One thing she knew for certain was where it would *lead*—straight to the luxuriously appointed bedroom, and a steamier, wilder night than any she'd had in years.

The thought aroused her as much as it scared her. She wasn't the kind of woman who hopped in bed with a man she'd barely met, and she'd never mixed business and pleasure before in her life. If she gave in to Judd's advances now, where would it leave her when she had to tell him the truth about why she was here?

"You're thinking again," Judd said, his lips twitching with a barest hint of a smile.

"I do that a lot," she admitted.

"Here, think on this, then."

Somehow he'd closed the distance between them without her noticing. His hand snaked around the back of her neck—his fingers warm against her cooler skin. Her face automatically tilted up toward his, her lips parting on a silent protest. She knew the protest was futile. She wanted this as much as he did, and she was helpless to ignore the demand.

His mouth, when it captured hers, was gentle, coaxing, and Anna felt as if he'd lit a fire that ran through her veins. A small part of her had hoped his kiss would be disappointing—something that would make it easier to refuse his attentions. In all honesty, she had known to the depths of her soul that his touch would be like this—*magic*—and she wanted that magic with every cell in her body.

She fisted her hands at her sides in an effort to prevent herself from reaching out and touching him. It would be too much, too difficult to step away from, but the way his lips teased hers invited her closer, and before she knew it, her hands were pressed against his chest, the fiery warmth of his skin burning through the expensive cotton of his shirt and letting her know that he could set other hidden parts of her aflame if only she'd let him.

His chest muscles shifted beneath her hands as he lifted his other arm to curve around her waist, drawing her closer to him. Hip to hip, there was no denying he was as powerfully aroused as she. Tension built in her body, coiling tight as he deepened their kiss and coaxed her lips open with his probing tongue.

He tasted of fine wine and illicit, unspoken promises. Promises that made her clench her thighs together against the swell of desire that rippled through her body before centering at the core of her belly. She rocked her pelvis against him, the movement a futile attempt to assuage the pressure building inside of her. Instead, it only incited her further. Anna kissed him back with a passion she'd never unleashed before, meeting his tongue with her own, letting him know that she was no innocent bystander in this assault on her senses.

She lifted her hands from his chest, sliding them upward, over his shoulders and the strong column of his neck, and burrowed her fingers in his dark hair, holding him to her as his lips devoured hers, as hers did his. She pressed her body against him, her nipples taut and sensitive against the lace of her bra, her breasts aching for his touch.

The call of a night bird punctuated the air, its unfamiliar sound bringing Anna back to her surroundings. Bringing her mind back to the task she'd been sent here to execute.

She untangled her fingers from Judd's hair, and let her hands drop to her sides once more. Their kiss, when it ended, was more bittersweet than she'd imagined, the loss of his caress felt deep inside. Judd rested his forehead against hers, his eyes still closed, his lips moist and slightly parted on an uneven breath. It would be so easy to kiss him again but she knew that if she did, it wouldn't stop there. Not with this conflagration that had ignited between them.

A kiss, a good-night kiss, was all it should have been and yet it had escalated into so very much more. She wasn't in a position to let that happen. She didn't dare explore this further, not without some truths between them, and she wasn't ready to tell Judd exactly what she was here for just yet.

The atmosphere between them was filled with possibilities, yet Anna knew she could choose only one. To say goodnight and to let Judd go back to the main house.

"Is this how you say good-night to all your guests?" she asked, in an attempt to lighten the mood that swirled around them.

His lips quirked in a half smile and he lifted his head. "No, only you."

Three words. So simply spoken. The expression in his eyes so honest it went straight to her heart. She clamped down on the feeling, fighting it back so she wouldn't succumb to the lure of the invitation in his gaze. Or to the physical plea that thrummed through every particle of her body.

Her mouth dried. She had no idea of how to respond to him without it sounding careless and glib.

"It's okay, Anna," he said, as if sensing her quandary. "It was only meant to be a simple good-night, nothing more. Unless you want it to be?"

"I...I can't. I—"

"Don't worry," he interrupted. "I'm nothing if not a patient man. And you're worth waiting for. But I promise you this—sooner or later we will make love, and when we do, it will be unforgettable."

His words left her speechless. Unforgettable? Oh, she had no doubt that sex with him would be off the Richter scale. She'd never been into casual encounters, not that anything about Judd Wilson was casual. For him, though, she might have considered it if he hadn't been Charles's son.

Judd pressed his lips against her cheek, almost at the corner of her mouth. All she had to do was turn her head ever so slightly and she could let this lead to its natural and, no doubt, very satisfying conclusion. But she held firm and felt Judd's unspoken acceptance of her refusal.

"I'll pick you up in the morning about nine," he said, letting her go and taking a step away. "Sleep well."

She watched him leave, his long legs eating up the distance along the wide track that led back to the main house. When he was out of sight, she finally let her body sag against the door frame.

Just hours ago, she'd arrived in Australia with one goal in mind—to convince Judd to come with her to New Zealand and reunite with his father. She still wanted—needed—to achieve that goal, but another need was taking over. A need to make the most of her time with Judd, to follow through on the attraction between them and see where it led.

But she knew she couldn't give in. So much rested on how Judd reacted when he learned why she'd come. If things between them got out of hand and he learned the truth too soon, she could inadvertently ruin all of Charles's hopes for reconciliation. She couldn't bear the thought of letting him down like that. Even if it meant closing the door on any chance to explore the sizzling attraction between her and Judd.

Her fingers fluttered to her lips. She could still feel him, still taste him. And God, she still wanted him. How on earth was she going to get through an entire day in his presence without giving in?

Three

The V8 engine of his Aston Martin Vantage roadster purred as Judd drove slowly along the private road that led toward Anna's cottage. A quiet smile of satisfaction played across his face—a total contrast to the frustration that even now held his body deliciously taut with expectation.

He hadn't felt this depth of attraction to a woman in a very long time. Actually, to be completely truthful, he'd never felt quite this level of need in relation to anyone else before.

Today was going to be interesting, very interesting indeed. And tonight? Well, that had the potential to be even better.

The faint burr of his cell phone distracted him. A quick look at the caller ID saw him ease his car to a halt and press a button on his hands-free kit to respond.

"Good morning, Mother. I didn't expect to hear from you this early."

Cynthia didn't waste any time on pleasantries. "I know where she's from."

"Who? Anna?"

"Who else? I was certain she looked familiar, and now I know why. I knew her mother. She worked at Wilson Wines. She was just an office dolly back then—flirted outrageously with the traveling reps. She left when she married one of them, pregnant of course, but I always suspected your father had his eye on her. About three years after we got here I heard that when her husband died, Charles employed her as his *housekeeper*—like anyone expected that was the truth."

Judd tensed. Every time Cynthia mentioned Charles Wilson there was a tone to her voice that set his teeth on edge.

"Did you hear me, Judd?"

"Yes, I heard you. What do you expect me to do about it?"

"Well, confront her, obviously. Her mother was living with Charles, ergo, so was Anna. Find out what she's doing here, because I'd wager she isn't here on holiday. It has to be something to do with your father."

He hated to admit it, but his mother could be right. Ever since they'd met, he'd suspected that Anna was hiding something. And the way she'd looked at him right at their first meeting was as if she was searching his face for a resemblance to someone. Had she been comparing him to his father? He stilled the curl of anger at that thought and at the possibility that his family might be being used by Charles Wilson again. Instead, he channeled his heated emotions into a tool to hone his thinking.

"I'll deal with it. Don't worry."

"I knew she was trouble the second I laid eyes on her," his mother continued. "She's probably working for him, you know. In fact, I wouldn't be surprised, if she's anything like her mother, if she is warming his bed. He always did prefer younger women."

His mother's words were acid in his ears. Cynthia had never let go of the bitterness she felt toward the man she'd left behind in New Zealand. He could still remember the first day he and Cynthia had arrived at The Masters' and she'd pointed to the shell of the mansion up on the hill.

Their house in New Zealand had been an identical replica of the original Masters home—a wedding present built under Charles's orders for his beautiful bride. Seeing a wrecked, charred ruin of a house that looked so very much like the one he'd always known had been a deeply unsettling experience for Judd, especially when Cynthia told him that the ruin would be a constant reminder of what they'd all lost when his father had rejected them both and banished them back to Australia. And it was to be a constant target for all that he should strive to regain.

His six-year-old mind had been unable to fully understand what she was saying, hadn't grasped the depth of her obsession with the home she'd lost not once, but twice, and every day at The Masters' he'd learned what it meant to be rejected by the man who'd fathered him. Whether it was the pitying gaze of his uncles and their sometimes overzealous attempts to be a father figure in his life, or the overheard remarks made by the staff from time to time when they didn't know he was listening, he knew exactly what it felt like to be a cast-off. He snapped his mind back to the present.

"I said I'll deal with it, Mother. By the end of today we'll know exactly what she's up to."

"Good. I know I can rely on you, Judd. Be careful, my darling."

Careful? Oh, he'd be more than careful. He disconnected the call and guided his car once more toward Anna's cottage. He'd be so careful that Anna Garrick would hardly know what had hit her.

Anna stood waiting for him on the patio of the cottage. She looked deceptively fresh and innocent, dressed in layers of light clothing. He knew she was anything but innocent, especially if her response to him last night had been anything to go by. He hoped she was up to a little heat, because today promised to be warm in more ways than one.

She walked toward his car as he got out and opened the passenger door for her.

"Nice wheels," she commented.

"I was always a James Bond fanatic as a kid." He smiled. "Some things never get old."

She laughed and settled in the red leather bucket seat, its color a perfect foil for her chestnut-brown hair, he thought as he swung her door closed. As he got back behind the wheel she rummaged in her handbag, pulling out a long bamboo hairpin before twisting her long hair into a knot and securing it at the back of her head.

"I can put the top up if you'd rather," he said, his eyes caught on the elegant line of her neck, the perfection of her jaw.

"No, it's a beautiful day. Let's make the most of it," she answered with a smile that hit him fair and square in the gut and reminded him of just how uncomfortable it had been to walk back to the main house last night.

"Good idea," he agreed and maneuvered the high-performance sports car onto the driveway that led off the property. "You mentioned yesterday that it's your first time in Adelaide," he probed. "What made you decide to come here for a break?"

She remained silent for a moment. From the corner of his eye he could see her press her lips together, as if she was holding back her instinctive answer and taking the time to formulate another.

"It was suggested to me," she said, averting her gaze out the side window.

Oh, he'd put money on the fact it was suggested to her, and by whom. Even without the insight his mother had offered, it was Anna's evasiveness that gave her away. He'd known that she had something to hide, and now that he suspected it involved his father, he was absolutely determined to find out what it was before the day was out. In the meantime, there was nothing, absolutely nothing, stopping him from having a good time along the way.

As they turned out the driveway that led from the vineyard and out onto the main road heading toward the hills, he saw her gaze pulled up onto the ridge and to the silhouette of the devastated building that stood there. He waited for her to say something, to ask about what had happened. Everyone did, eventually. But she remained silent. The expression on her face was pensive. Some devil of mischief prompted him to comment.

"It was magnificent in its day, you know."

"I beg your pardon?" She turned to face him.

"Masters' Rise, the house up there." He let go of the steering wheel with one hand and gestured up toward the hills.

"It was your family home?"

Did she really not realize, or was she just bluffing? "Not that one, although I lived briefly in a replica of it back in New Zealand when I was young." When she didn't comment on that, he pointed back up the hill. "Masters' Rise was destroyed before my time. My mother and uncles lived there as youngsters, though. I don't think the family pride ever quite recovered from its loss. I know for a fact that my mother's didn't. And it wasn't just losing the house—a good bit of the vineyard was destroyed, as well."

"It wasn't as if they could have done anything to stop it, though, was there?"

"Done anything?"

"Well, it was a bushfire, wasn't it?"

He shot her a piercing glance.

"At least that's what I think I read somewhere," she added hastily.

Oh, good cover, he thought before slowly nodding.

"They were lucky to escape with their lives," he said. "Unfortunately, they didn't have much else—well, not much else but the Masters' tenacity. Rebuilding the house wasn't an option—not when they had to recreate their entire livelihood, as well. It would have taken everything they had left and they were forced to choose between rebuilding their home or re-establishing the vineyards and winery."

"Tough choices. It's a shame they couldn't do both."

"Yeah."

Judd lapsed into silence. Wondering, not for the first time, how different life might have been if the Masters family hadn't been forced into that decision. It couldn't have been easy for his mother and her brothers, starting over from scratch, seeing the life of ease and plenty they'd enjoyed vanishing in a flash. Was that why it had been so easy for Charles Wilson to sweep Cynthia off her feet? Was the life of wealth and luxury he offered truly impossible for a girl, who'd spent so long struggling, to resist?

"So, what's on the agenda for today?" Anna asked, her voice artificially bright. "Last night you mentioned Hahndorf, right? Where and what is it?"

Judd flashed her a smile before transferring his attention back to the road in front of them.

"It was originally a German settlement, established in the early eighteen hundreds. Much of the original architecture still survives and is used today. It's not far from here, but I thought I'd take you a couple of other places first and then we'll head back into Hahndorf for lunch."

"Sounds lovely, thanks. Really, I appreciate you taking time out of your schedule for me."

Judd reached out and caught her hand in his, giving her fingers a gentle squeeze.

"I want to get to know you better, Anna. Can't do that stuck in my office, now, can I?"

To his surprise, a flush of color spread across her cheeks. She blushed? The ingenuousness of the act was totally at odds with the wanton he'd held in his arms last night. Yeah, there was no doubt about it. Anna Garrick intrigued him, and he liked being intrigued—even if it was by someone with a hidden agenda.

Her fingers tingled beneath his touch and Anna felt heat surge through her body, staining her cheeks. God, this effect he had on her would be her undoing. She gently withdrew her hand, distracting herself by poking about in her handbag for a tissue. Her fingertips brushed against the envelope holding the letter from Charles and she pulled her hand out of the bag so rapidly she elicited another one of those piercing looks from Judd.

"So," she said, forcing her heartbeat to resume a more normal rate with a few calming breaths, "where are you taking me first?"

He gestured to the highest peak ahead of them.

"Mount Lofty. From there you'll see the whole of Adelaide spread out before you."

Judd proved himself to be a very efficient tour guide. That he knew the area like the back of his hand was obvious, as was his love and appreciation of his surroundings. By the time they'd taken in the panoramic views of the city and beyond from the peak of Mount Lofty and then strolled through the exquisitely beautiful botanic gardens below, Anna was having a hard time reminding herself that this was no pleasure jaunt.

Judd's fingers were loosely linked in hers as they walked, and every nerve in her body went on high alert, focusing intently on the scant physical connection they shared. Wishing against everything that the connection could be deepened and intensified.

She fought to regain control of her senses. She'd be crazy to embark on anything physical with Judd Wilson. Totally and utterly crazy. But no matter what her head told her, her body demanded something else entirely.

In her bag, she felt her cell phone discreetly vibrate. The only person who would be calling her would be Charles. Her stomach lurched. Was he okay? He hadn't looked well when she'd left Auckland yesterday. Extracting her fingers from Judd's light clasp, she reached into her bag.

"Excuse me, I need to take this," she said, putting the phone to her ear and turning to walk a few steps away from him.

"Have you met him yet?" Charles's voice sounded strong and healthy.

"Yes, I have," she said guardedly, wishing she'd let the call go to her message service and then phoned Charles back when she had a little more privacy.

"Well, what's he like? Have you given him the letter yet? What did he say?"

Charles's questions fired at her with the less-than-subtle force of a battering ram and she created a little more distance between herself and the subject of those questions.

"It's hard to say at the moment. No, and nothing yet," she answered each question in turn.

"You're with him now, aren't you?"

"Yes," she replied. "Look, it's really not a good time to talk. Can I get back to you later?"

Please say "yes," she silently begged. In response, Charles's hearty chuckle filled her ear.

"Not a good time, eh? Okay, then, I'll leave you to it. But make sure you call me back later today."

"Yes, certainly. I'll do that. Goodbye."

"Anna, don't hang up!"

She sighed. "Yes?"

"I'm counting on you. I *need* my son with me."

"I'll do my best."

"Thank you, darling girl."

He disconnected the call and Anna felt her shoulders sag with the reminder of what he expected of her.

"Bad news?" Judd asked.

"No, not really," Anna hedged.

"Anything I can help with?"

She fought back the strangled laugh that rose in her throat. If only he knew. But no, the last thing she could do was divulge the details of that phone call. Not yet, anyway. She shook her head and pushed her phone back in her bag.

"It was just work, I can deal with it later. I'm starving," she said, trying to shift the conversation onto safer ground. "How about that lunch you promised me?"

"Your wish is my command," Judd said, taking her hand again and lifting it to his lips.

His blue eyes gleamed, letting Anna know in no uncertain terms that he was definitely open to more than just lunch. Again that surge of heat swirled deep inside her, making her body tighten in anticipation. She fought to paint a smile on her lips. This was all going to be so much harder than she had ever imagined.

On the short drive to Hahndorf, Charles's words kept echoing around in her head, *I need my son with me.* An unexpected flash of anger rose within her. Charles was so bent on reuniting with his long-lost son that he'd completely forgotten he had a daughter right by his side. A daughter who understood his wine importation and distribution business better, almost, than her own father. A daughter who'd spent her whole life stepping up in an attempt to fill the near insurmountable gap left when Cynthia had taken Judd to Australia.

Anna wondered again about the contents of the letter that weighed so heavily in her handbag. She knew Charles was planning on offering Judd an incentive to return, but he hadn't shared the details with her. Whatever carrot he'd chosen to dangle, what would it mean to the sister who didn't even remember Judd? The one who worked so hard to please her father, for no reward other than his love and hard-won approval? Anna adored Charles with every breath in her body. He'd been the only father figure she'd ever known, but she worried that he'd overstepped the mark with this obsession with Judd and that he'd damage his relationship with Nicole irrevocably.

"What sort of work do you do that they need to call you when you're on vacation?"

Judd's voice interrupted her thoughts and made her start. She'd been dreading this question and had already decided that a vague response would be her best bet.

"Oh, I'm a P.A."

"You must be pretty important to your boss if he can't keep from calling you."

Anna forced her features to relax into a smile. "I've worked for him since I left school. We're probably closer than most boss/employee relationships."

She caught Judd's piercing look before his eyes resumed their surveillance of the road in front of them. He began to slow the car as they approached a township, and Anna let out an involuntary exclamation of delight as they entered the main road. Lined with massive trees and with quaint tin-roofed buildings, she'd have thought she'd stepped back in time if it hadn't been for the bustle of people and modern vehicles that lined the street.

Judd expertly backed the Aston Martin into a car space and came around to open Anna's door.

"I'm surprised he let you out of his sight, if you're so *close*," he said, his words weighted with something that Anna couldn't quite put her finger on.

"I'm my own woman," she answered.

"I'm pleased to hear it," Judd said in return, taking her hand and tucking it firmly in the crook of his elbow. "Because I don't like to share."

"I've heard that trait was reserved for only children," Anna said with a soft laugh, trying to defuse the heady rush of excitement his words stimulated inside her.

"What makes you think I'm not an only child?"

Oh, Lord, she'd nearly stepped right in it. She scoured her memory quickly, although deep down she knew that no one here in Adelaide had mentioned his estranged family to her.

"Oh, I don't know. I just assumed, since you grew up here surrounded by your cousins, that sharing was a natural part of your life."

She held her breath, hoping he'd be satisfied with her reply. To her surprise, he let out a short laugh.

"Yeah, I suppose that'd be a natural assumption."

"So, are you?" she probed, wanting some insight into how he might feel about the sister he hadn't seen in years.

"An only child?" He shrugged. "It's complicated. My parents divorced when I was young, and they split my sister and me up at the same time. I was six, she was just one year old."

"Isn't that unusual? That your father kept your sister?"

"He didn't want me—my mother did."

Judd's words, so simply spoken, hinted strongly at the hurt that had to lie behind them. Anna wanted to protest. To tell him that his father wanted him very much indeed, but they weren't her words to say.

"Have you ever wanted to see your sister? Get to know her?" she pressed, taking a different tack.

"Why the sudden interest?"

"Oh, nothing. It's just that, as I told you last night, I *am* an only child and I always wanted siblings."

"The human condition, huh? Always wanting what we can't have."

"I suppose so," Anna admitted, sorry that he'd so deftly avoided answering her question.

They walked along the shady sidewalk, stopping every now and then to wander into one of the many galleries before they crossed the road to take an umbrella-covered table outside an obviously very popular inn. Anna pulled the pin from her hair and shook it loose from its temporary restraint. She didn't miss the glow of pure male appreciation in Judd's eyes as she did so and felt her body warm in response.

"Would you like a menu, or would you like me to choose for you?" Judd asked.

"Go ahead and order for me. I eat just about everything."

"What would you like to drink? A glass of wine?"

Anna eyed a nearby patron swigging at a foam-topped beer. "One of those," she said, pointing.

"Beer?"

"Sure. Don't tell me you're one of those people who don't think women should drink beer."

"Not at all." He laughed. "In fact, I plan to join you."

When the waitress came over he ordered their meals and two beers. They didn't have to wait long before the food and drinks arrived. Anna gasped when she saw the size of the platter placed before them.

"It's their Taste of Germany. You couldn't come here without trying it," Judd said.

"I'll take your word for it. I sure hope *you're* hungry, too," Anna replied, taking a sip of her chilled beer. "Mmm, that's good."

She grew so engrossed in the meal and their surroundings that she didn't notice when a family with several children raced by their table. One of the kids lost his balance when his foot hooked into the handle of her bag, which she'd placed on the ground by the table leg. Anna's hands flew to stabilize the beer mugs on the table as it rocked under the impact of the youngster's clumsiness.

"Oh, no! I'm so sorry," his harried mother said, rushing to pick up the belongings that had scattered from Anna's bag.

"Don't worry, it's okay," Anna assured her, reaching for the items the woman had so far gathered and shoving them back in her bag. "Really, it's my fault. I shouldn't have left the strap hanging out like that."

Judd had risen from his chair and was helping to collect Anna's things. Too late she saw the stark-white envelope that had been ejected from its hiding place. His long-fingered hand hovered over it and her heart sank to the soles of her feet as she registered the exact moment he identified the name on the front.

He settled back in his chair, handing most of her things back to her, but holding the envelope between his fingers as if it contained something dangerous inside. The mother and her son moved on, rejoining the rest of their family, but Anna didn't even notice. All she could do was stare at Judd and the flat packet in his hands.

"Care to explain this?" he said, his voice suddenly devoid of the warmth it had contained only moments ago.

Anna took a deep breath. "It's a letter."

"I can see that. It looks like a letter to *me*."

She couldn't maintain eye contact and instead dropped her gaze to her lap, where her fingers knotted in anxiety. This was all wrong. She'd wanted to give him the letter when she was ready, when she was in control and when she could better gauge what his reaction would be. Not in a public place like this, with no warning and no chance to prepare him for the letter's contents.

"It is," she said softly.

She flinched as she heard the envelope tear open. Her stomach tied in a knot of unbelievable proportions as the sound of a single sheet of paper being unfolded overwhelmed the noise of the diners and sightseers around them.

Anna finally lifted her gaze and watched as Judd read the letter his father had written. The letter that had the capacity to change all their lives. When he'd finished, he neatly re-folded the sheet and put it back in the envelope. Still he said nothing. A shiver of fear danced down her spine. He was calm, too calm. She'd seen Charles get like this and she knew that it was only the quiet before the storm. What was coming could only be cataclysmic.

She reached across the table, touching his forearm. He shook off her touch as if she were nothing more than an annoying insect.

"Judd—" she started, but whatever she'd been about to say died in her throat when he met her eyes and she felt the full fury of the glacial fire reflected there.

"Who the hell are you and why are you really here?"

Four

Across the table Anna stared at him in shock. She felt all color drain from her face and a numb coldness settle in the pit of her stomach. She'd done this all wrong. She should have just followed Charles's orders right from the start to make an appointment to see Judd and tell him from the outset why she was there. She took a deep breath before speaking.

"I…I've told you who I am. I'm Anna Garrick. And…" Her mouth dried, forcing her to pause for a moment, and swallow, before continuing, "And I'm here because your father desperately wants to make amends for the past."

"If he's so keen to make amends, why isn't he here himself?" Judd demanded.

His skin had gone taut across his features, lending an implacable hardness to his face, and his eyes burned with a hard blue intensity.

"He didn't tell you in the letter?"

"I want to hear it from you. Why did he not come here himself? Was he too ashamed to face up to me, to face up to the truth that his own pride and his stupid accusations are responsible for having torn our family apart in the first place?"

Anna made a small noise of protest. It wasn't like that. Sure, she'd heard that Charles hadn't been an angel at the time his marriage to Cynthia had fallen irrevocably apart—who ever was when under extreme pressure?—but from what her mother had told her, she knew that Cynthia had done plenty of damage, as well. Charles definitely hadn't been solely responsible for what had happened, no matter what Judd's mother might have told him.

"Well?" Judd demanded.

"He's unwell. His doctor wouldn't clear him to travel." The diabetes that had plagued Charles for so many years had worsened, in part due to his late diagnosis and subsequent reluctance to follow medical recommendations to prevent further damage to his body. His kidneys were showing signs that renal failure could be just around the corner.

"How convenient."

Judd lifted his stein and took a healthy swig of its contents, and Anna felt the initial stirrings of her own anger rise in response to his derision.

"It isn't convenient at all, actually. Look, I'm not privy to exactly what he said in his letter to you, but I have a pretty good idea of what he's asking. He wants to see you again. To get to know you before he—" Suddenly overwhelmed with emotion, her voice broke.

"Before he what?"

"Before he dies," she said shakily.

"You care about him?" Judd's voice was devoid of emotion.

"More than you could ever understand," she said, forcing herself to pull it together. "He is not a well man, Judd. Please, this could be your last chance to get to know him. He's your father, surely you owe him that."

"Owe him?" He snorted a laugh. "That's rich. I don't owe

him anything and I haven't exactly missed out on having him in my life. I don't see why that should change, although he has certainly attempted to sweeten the pot to entice me back to New Zealand."

"Sweeten the pot?" She felt a building sense of dread. Just what kind of incentive had Charles offered?

"You really don't know?"

"If I knew, would I be asking?" she snapped.

"Strange, given that you're his valued *employee,* and given—by your own admission—how *close* you are and how much you care about him, that he didn't see the need to apprise you of his intentions."

She didn't like his unspoken insinuation that there was something unsavory between her and Charles. Sure, she loved him—like a father. But how could she explain that to Judd now? He'd never believe her.

Judd leaned back in his chair and fixed her with his intense gaze. "It seems that your esteemed employer wishes to offer me a controlling interest in the family business."

"He what?"

A controlling interest? Just like that? Black spots swam before Anna's eyes and she gulped at the air. How could Charles do that to Nicole? How could *she* have done that to Nicole? Anna knew her best friend had standards just as high as Charles's when it came to loyalty and honesty. When she found out that Anna had been the messenger who had gone behind Nicole's back to practically hand deliver Charles's company to Judd, would Nicole ever forgive her?

"And that's not all. Apparently, he wants to assign the family home to me, as well." He casually waved the letter in the air. "All to do with whatever I please."

Anna couldn't believe her ears. "He wouldn't do something like that. You have no loyalty to Charles, no loyalty to Wilson Wines. For all we know, you'd just sell off your share to someone who didn't give a damn. Charles would never do something so rash."

Would he? Had he become so desperate to mend the vast chasm between father and son that he was prepared to offer the world on a platter? This would destroy Nicole. She'd grown up in the New Zealand house—it was still her home. And she'd poured her heart and soul into the business— surely not to simply see half of it handed over to her brother? Charles couldn't be so cruel.

But Anna knew full well that Charles was capable of doing such a thing. Single-minded to a fault, his aim was to return his son to his side before he died. When his doctors had confirmed that time might be running out, he'd gone after his goal to bring Judd back into his life with every weapon at his disposal. He'd do whatever it took, even if it meant hurting the daughter who loved him so very much.

Ever since the posthumous delivery of a letter from his former partner and biggest business rival, Thomas Jackson, he'd become obsessed with Judd, with somehow rebuilding a bond between them. Anna hadn't been privy to the contents of the letter but she'd wager her very generous salary that it had to do with the rift between the business partners and Cynthia and Judd leaving New Zealand very shortly after. She'd often wondered if Thomas Jackson and Cynthia had been lovers.

Which begged the question—had Charles believed Judd was not his son?

Judd passed the letter across to her.

"Read it for yourself."

The words blurred before her eyes and she blinked to clear them. It was true. There, in Charles's scrawling black handwriting, was his desperate appeal to the son he'd turned his back on twenty-five years ago. She knew what it must have cost the older man to put his emotions in words like this. Never a demonstrative man, it shocked her to see him pour his heart out onto the page. Ever hedging his bets, though, he'd insisted on Judd undergoing DNA testing to prove he was, without a shadow of a doubt, Charles's child. Ah, so there had been some doubt. Now everything began to make sense.

She finished scanning the letter and neatly folded it before handing it back to Judd.

"I had no idea he had planned this. Will you accept his offer?" she asked.

"He insults my mother, even after all this time, and you think I'm going to leap at his offer?"

"Insults Cynthia?" She didn't follow his reasoning.

"The DNA test. He wants proof she didn't cheat on him when I was conceived. It's obvious, no matter what he says in that letter, he hasn't changed a bit. He still expects to call all the shots. And then there's you."

"Me?"

"What's your role in all this? Did he expect you to also sweeten the deal?"

Anna felt a flush rise in her cheeks. "I don't think I like what you're suggesting."

"Well, you can't blame me. You come to my family's home, you fail to identify yourself or your reasons for being here and you show yourself to be very receptive to attention from me. You certainly didn't object last night when I kissed you."

"That was…"

Words failed her.

"It was what, Anna? Going over and above the call of duty?"

Anna bit back the retort that sprang so readily to her lips and forced herself to calm down.

"I did what I came to do, you have the letter, you've read it. Now the ball is in your court."

And she'd failed Charles, she admitted to herself. The

knowledge lodged like a heavy ball of painful regret knotted tight within her chest. The most important thing he'd ever asked of her and she'd screwed it up.

"Please, I beg of you, don't let what I've done influence your decision in any way. Charles wanted me to be upfront with you. It was my choice to hold back my real reasons for being here."

"Why?"

"I knew he wanted to extend an olive branch, but I was concerned about how you might feel about him and whether you would take advantage of him. He's an old man, old before his time because of his illness. He doesn't deserve any more misery in his life."

"And that's your considered opinion?"

"Of course it is. Look, you don't know him. You probably barely remember him. Whatever happened in the past is past. It can't be undone. Can't you put it aside and consider what it would mean to him to make amends with you now?"

Judd stared at her for a moment, his expression not giving any sign of what he might be thinking. The knot of dread tightened even further.

Put the past behind him? Did she have even the faintest idea what she was asking? Of course she didn't. She hadn't been torn from the father who had adored him one minute and then refused to look at him the next. She hadn't been transplanted into another family, another world, and been told to "man up" because his mother expected him to be strong. He'd lost count of the number of times he'd watched cars arrive at The Masters' and hoped against hope that his father would alight from one of them. That he'd come to say it had all been a mistake.

But what his six-year-old heart had wished for had never happened and, in time, he'd learned not to scan the parents' faces at school events for the man whose features he'd always been told were an older version of his own. He'd learned to inure himself from the hope that one day his life would return to what it had been before.

And it had made him a stronger man. A man who knew that the only person he could, or should, rely upon was himself.

His first instinct on reading his father's entreaty was to ball it up and to tell Anna to take it back to Charles-bloody-Wilson and to tell the old man to put it where the sun doesn't shine. But then rationality overrode the deviation into emotionalism.

Without realizing it, his long-estranged father had actually given Judd the opportunity he'd quietly dreamed of for many a year—payback. Not only for rejecting the son who'd so earnestly idolized him, but for what he'd done to Cynthia.

Judd had heard the story from his mother more times than he could count—after pulling her away from her home and her family, Charles had neglected her. Ignored her. Prioritized every concern over and above his relationship with his wife. And when Cynthia, in her loneliness and frustration, had started spending more time away from home, trying to find friends and activities to fill the void left by her husband's absence, Charles had turned into a possessive monster, constantly jealous and utterly convinced she was cheating on him.

It had all culminated in the fight that had led Charles to kick Judd and his mother out of the house. And that was the last Judd had seen of his father. There had been no phone calls. No letters. No visits. Charles had clearly washed his hands of both of them for the past twenty-five years.

And now, this was Judd's chance to pay him back in kind for all the pain he and his mother had suffered. With the controlling interest in the company, Charles was placing the weapons right into his hands. Everything his mother had told him about the past had shown Charles up for a man who'd always put his business before his family. Judd knew exactly where to strike to cause the most pain, to exact the deepest satisfaction.

He needed time to think, to consolidate the plans burgeoning in his mind, but he had no doubt that he'd shortly be accepting his father's offer. No doubt at all.

He looked over at Anna—his eyes raking over her and taking in the lustrous length of her hair, her exquisite beauty, her enticing feminine curves. She was all woman from the top of her head to the tips of her toes. Even now, as angry as he was, she still had the capacity to excite him, to incite within him the desire to possess her in every manner of the word.

A tug of regret pulled deep inside. His mother's warning had done little to dim his attraction to Anna, but the letter had cast a whole new light on things. Maybe her reluctance to deliver it to him had its basis in something other than what she'd admitted. Maybe she was worried about what his entry back into his father's life would do to affect her position there and what she stood to gain from Charles Wilson after his death. Charles had chosen her as his ambassador in his attempt at reunion, so he obviously trusted her implicitly. By her own admission she said she and the old man were close—that she cared for him *deeply*. How close, exactly? Were they lovers, as his mother suspected? If that was true, it would no doubt give him a double-edged sense of satisfaction when he eventually seduced her.

But as with everything else, it would wait until the time was perfectly right. For now, he wanted her away from The Masters' and somewhere else, where she could do no harm.

He gestured to the food before them.

"Are you going to eat that?"

She shook her head. "I couldn't, not now."

"Let's go, then."

"Back to the vineyard?"

"To get your things, yes, and then to take you into the city."

"The city?"

"To a hotel. It may surprise you, but funnily enough, I don't want you around my family right now. My mother's been through quite enough over the years without adding the insult of your presence."

She flinched beneath his words, her face paling even more.

"Fine," she replied tightly. "When will you let me know your decision about Charles?"

"In good time. You aren't due to return to Auckland for another few days, is that correct?"

"Yes, on Friday morning."

"I'll let you know by then."

Anna paced the terrace of her hotel room, her cell phone to her ear.

"I'm sorry, Charles. I screwed up. I should have just done what you told me to do."

Charles was surprisingly philosophical.

"What's done is done. It's certainly no worse or better than what's gone on before this. Let's just hope he comes to his senses and comes home before it's too late."

Before it's too late. Her heart squeezed. It wasn't like Charles to be melodramatic. She knew he was deteriorating, but had he kept something from her? Was his health worse than even she suspected?

"I still can't believe you're prepared to go to those lengths to bring him home."

"It's his birthright, Anna. You know that as much as I do."

"But what about Nicole? Have you talked to her about this yet?"

"I wasn't going to say anything to her until he's back and we know for certain he's mine. Until then, it's a moot point.

And you're not to say a word, either. You promised me, Anna."

She sighed. "Yes, I know. I won't say a word, but keeping the truth away from her is only going to hurt all of us."

"Let me be the judge of that."

"And the house, Charles. Why the house, too? You're talking about taking Nicole's home right out from under her feet."

"Yours, too," he reminded her with a surprisingly curt note in his voice. "But I will have to trust him to do the right thing and to continue to provide the two of you with a roof over your heads. If I don't do that, if I don't prove to him that I'm prepared to accept him fully, it will never work. Besides, he grew up with the Masters—I know how they feel about the house. Judd is already running their company, so offering him mine might not be enough of a draw. But no one else can give him that house."

"What makes you so sure you have to take such drastic steps?"

"Because that's what it would take to lure me back if someone had done the same thing to me."

If Nicole ever spoke to her again after this it would be a miracle. Anna felt a chill run the length of her spine. She stepped inside her hotel room and slid the glass door closed, but even so, she continued to feel cold. What Charles was doing was wrong, she knew it to the soles of her feet. But it was too late now. The offer had been made. She could only hope against hope that Judd would be man enough to turn it down. That he'd accept his father for who he was without the added enticement of half of Wilson Wines and the home that Charles had built for Cynthia all those years ago.

"So you're not going to give her any prior warning. You're just going to present her with a brother and say this is how it's going to be from now on?"

"They are my children, it's my company and my home, so this is my decision. Don't overstep your boundaries, Anna."

His words stung.

"Of course," she said in reply, even as other more impassioned words filled her mind.

"He said he'll give you his decision by Friday?"

"Yes, he did."

"Let's hope it's the right one. Let me know as soon as you've spoken to him."

"I will."

"Good. I'll look forward to it."

His business done, the call was over, leaving Anna alone to stare at the darkening hills in the distance and to wonder just how all of this was going to end.

Five

"I told you I was right." Cynthia's eyes gleamed triumphantly.

Judd merely nodded. He'd spent the latter part of the afternoon locked in his office, looking at his schedule and seeing where, and to whom, he could apportion his workload. It was one advantage of having several cousins all working within the same family business, he conceded. There were plenty of people just as invested as he was in making sure The Masters' continued to run smoothly. Between his cousins and the well-trained staff they also employed, Judd felt confident he could leave the company in good hands.

Once he had everything worked out to his satisfaction, he asked his mother for a private meeting. Her delight at the enticement Charles was offering was palpable. He hadn't seen her this animated, ever.

"When will you let them know your decision?" his mother pressed.

"On Friday morning. I'll be too busy tomorrow bringing

everyone up to speed with their additional duties to be talking to Anna Garrick."

As soon as he said her name he felt the now-familiar tug of desire. He'd made some inquiries. She lived with Charles Wilson, which confirmed she was indeed far, far more than simply his father's P.A. Stealing her away from him, right under the old man's roof, was undeniably appealing but something he'd have to approach very carefully.

"Do you know how long the DNA testing will take?"

"I believe establishing paternity is a relatively simple process. A few days to a week for the results."

"You know, I cannot believe he would stoop to that. He only needs to look at you to know I never betrayed him."

She injected a note of pathos in her voice, but Judd had heard it all before. When she didn't elicit the response from her son that she obviously wanted, she continued.

"We'll finally have back what should have been ours all along," she said, her voice now stronger, showing her true mettle.

"The house?"

He should have known that would be the most important thing to her. He had to admit to a certain curiosity himself to go back to the place that had been his home for the first six years of his life. But where his mother seemed to want to reclaim the building, Judd was far more inclined to go after it with a wrecking ball…just as he planned to do with Wilson Wines. He'd take his father's legacy apart bit by bit, and when he was done, he'd be back here at The Masters', picking up the reins of his job once again. At that point, his mother could have the darn house for all he cared.

"I'll have to redecorate it, you know. Restore it to its former glory."

"How do you know it's not perfect just the way it is?"

She rolled her eyes at him. "Judd, darling, it's been twenty-five years since I've set foot in there. There will be work to do, I'm sure. I poured my heart into that house—no one loved it more than I did."

"Let's not put the cart before the horse, hmm?"

"Of course. We have to satisfy your father's ridiculous demands first. How long do you think you'll be away?"

"I don't see this taking more than a month."

"That long?"

He thought of his plans for the delectable Miss Garrick. A month? Maybe longer would be better. He wanted to savor this victory.

"Maybe longer. We'll see how it pans out."

After his mother left his office, he sat back in his leather chair and stared out the window at the vineyard and winery that occupied his immediate view. He enjoyed his work here, there was no doubt about that, and he was good at it. But he had become bored in recent months, feeling stifled by the lack of opportunity to make changes. Now, perhaps, even if only for a short time, he'd have the chance to really stretch his mind as he implemented his plans. Plans to dismantle his father's empire and steal his mistress right out from under his nose.

Anna woke on Friday morning in a state of nerves and automatically reached for her cell phone, as she had several times throughout last night. Still nothing from Judd Wilson. Just how fine was he going to cut this? She looked at the time on her phone and raced for the bathroom—the broken night's rest having made her sleep past the time she'd wanted to rise. A car was coming to pick her up and take her to the airport for her flight in about half an hour. She'd already packed her things the night before. All she needed to do was shower and dress in the clothes she'd left out for the journey home.

She was down in the lobby of the hotel and signing off her hotel account when a trickle of awareness filtered through the parting words of the hotel receptionist. He was here. Did that mean she'd succeeded? Was he accompanying her back to New Zealand, or maybe he was merely here to tell her in person that her quest on Charles's behalf had failed.

She knew she had to turn around. Had to face him. It took every ounce of strength in her body to paste a smile on her face and turn away from the reception desk. The moment her eyes lighted upon him she felt the excruciating pull of attraction. How could she still be so drawn to him when he'd been so awful to her? She'd asked herself that question over and over the past two nights, especially each time she'd woken from yet another tormented dream explicitly featuring the man standing directly opposite her.

He'd be a formidable poker player, she thought irrationally. He let nothing show in his expression as to what he was thinking, or whatever decision he'd reached.

"Are you ready?" he said coolly.

"What? No good morning?" she said, unable to keep the acerbity from her voice.

He merely raised one dark brow. Anna grabbed the handle of her wheeled suitcase and headed for the front door.

"Let me take that for you," Judd said, blocking her way and collapsing the extended handle and swinging the case up in one hand.

She'd packed for only three and a half days, and she hadn't packed light, yet he carried the bag as if it weighed nothing. Realizing he was headed for the automatic opening doors and to the dark limousine outside, she propelled herself after him.

"Wait, I've ordered a taxi."

"And I've canceled it. We'll travel together to the airport."

"And then?" she asked, suddenly tired of the game.

Was he coming back to Auckland with her or not? The not knowing was playing havoc with her stomach.

"And then we'll check in to our flight."

"So you're accepting Charles's offer?"

He handed her case to the waiting driver and then opened

the rear door, gesturing for her to be seated inside the dark, leather-filled interior. She halted at the door, not wanting to get inside until she knew exactly where things stood.

"I've consented to undergoing the tests and when my father is satisfied, yes, I will be accepting his offer."

Anna didn't know whether to feel elated or devastated. A hollow emptiness filled her heart. Unable to speak, she nodded in acknowledgment of his words and settled herself in the car. She was grateful when Judd took the passenger seat in the front of the vehicle. She needed some time to gather her thoughts, to prepare herself for what was to come.

The journey to the airport was short, and before she alighted she asked for a moment to call Charles.

"That won't be necessary," Judd said smoothly, offering her his hand to help her from the car.

"Why not?" she asked, reluctantly putting her hand in his and bracing herself for the jolt of electricity she knew would come next.

Sure enough, the merest touch of his fingers was enough to set her heart beating faster. Arousal flared deep inside. Not the type she was used to—the slow, gentle warming of mutual attraction. No, this was far more primal than that. Sharper, more instinctive, and it made her body ache in response. She pulled her hand from his, but the sensation still lingered.

"Because I've already spoken with him."

"You spoke with him?" Anna fought to keep the incredulity from her voice.

"Is that so strange?"

"Well, yes. Especially considering your reaction to his letter."

"As you said on Wednesday, the past *is* past."

She looked at him in disbelief, hardly daring to believe that he actually meant it. A man like Judd Wilson was too intense, too driven to simply put the past in a time capsule and lock it away. He had to have an ulterior motive.

"What? No comment?" Judd gently goaded.

"How was he?"

"He sounded fine. Surprised to hear from me, but I'd say he's cautiously optimistic."

So this thing would play out after all, Anna thought as the driver hefted their cases from the trunk of the car and went to procure a luggage cart. Not waiting for the man to return, she pulled the handle up on her case and headed for the departure check-in area, but within seconds Judd walked at her side, pushing his own much larger cases on the cart in front of him. Basically, everything was out of her hands from here on in. She could only hope that Nicole would forgive her for her part in the machinations of her father. But somehow Anna doubted any of what was to come would be that easy.

Charles's driver and handyman, Patrick Evans, collected them from Auckland International Airport. They were nearly home. Evans drove slowly and inexorably toward the massive gothic mansion Charles had built from the original plans of Masters' Rise—the headlights of the car sweeping the camellia-lined driveway in Auckland's premier suburb of Remuera. Anna had to admit she was relieved to see the house.

Back in Australia, it had shocked her to see the ruins on the hill overlooking the vineyard. Suddenly the home that had always provided her with security didn't seem so permanent after all. Of course, bushfires were nonexistent in the city, virtually nonexistent in New Zealand, really, and nowadays Charles had a state-of-the-art fire detection and sprinkler system throughout the house. But there were plenty of things other than bushfires that could tear a house—and a family—apart.

With the time distance between Adelaide and Auckland, and the flight time in between, it was already dark as they pulled up in front of the house, but clever external lighting showed the property off to its glorious advantage. Anna observed Judd, sitting opposite her in the limousine, and watched his reaction.

"So that's what it looked like," he said solemnly, his eyes raking the two-storied, pinkish-red brick building. "My memories from before we left were…incomplete."

"Apparently it's very true to the original, with extensive modernization, of course. Despite its size, it's still very much a home."

The car rolled to a stop outside the front portico, prominently marked by an ivy-covered, three-storied turret complete with a green-aged copper cupola.

"It's your home."

He made it a statement, rather than a question. A statement she chose to ignore as she stepped from the car and assisted Patrick in removing the luggage from the spacious trunk of the limousine.

The front doors opened and Anna turned, expecting to see Charles, but instead it was Nicole who stood there. Elegant and tall in her well-cut black suit and with her long dark hair pulled back into a ponytail that exposed her pale face, Nicole stared at the man who was her brother.

"I didn't believe him when he told me you were coming," she said, her voice flat—devoid of emotion.

Instantly Anna's defensive instincts went on full alert. Nicole was usually very outgoing, impulsive and generous to a fault. This frozen pale facsimile of her best friend was something she'd never seen before.

Nicole came down the steps and halted near Anna.

"Why didn't you tell me?"

Even as Anna flinched at the question, she found herself internally debating what Nicole was really asking. There was no way to know how much Charles had told her. Had he only announced that Judd was coming back to them—or had he explained all the rest of it, too, all the things Charles had promised to bring his son home?

Either way, her answer was the same. "He asked me not to."

"And your loyalty to him is greater than to me?" Nicole said softly, the hurt in her words flaying Anna like cold winter rain.

"That's not fair, Nicole."

"No, you're right. But there's a lot that's not fair about all this, isn't there?"

Pain reflected in her friend's large brown eyes. Anna put a hand on Nicole's arm and squeezed gently.

"You know I would have spoken to you if I could."

Nicole nodded and turned back to Judd, who'd remained silent as a statue.

"So, brother, I suppose I should welcome you home."

She held out her arms and to Anna's surprise he stepped into her embrace, holding her gently before releasing her and stepping back.

Judd was shocked at the depth of emotion he felt when he saw his sister at the top of the stairs to the house. She'd been a year old when he'd left, and in his mind he'd never imagined her fully grown. Another mark against his father, he thought savagely. All those years wasted.

"We have some catching up to do," he said.

To his surprise, Nicole laughed. "Well, if that's not the understatement of the century. Come inside. Dad's waiting for you."

Judd turned to Anna, who'd watched his reunion with his sister with a solemn expression on her face. "Are you coming?"

"I think this should be just for the three of you. I'll catch up with you all at dinner."

Nicole made a sound of protest. "Don't be silly, Anna. You know Dad will expect you there, too."

Anna looked at him, as if waiting for his approval.

"Sure," he said.

If the stiltedness between her and his sister was any indication, perhaps Nicole didn't entirely approve of Anna and their father's closeness.

Nicole hooked her arm in his. In her three-inch heels they were almost of a height and together they walked up the stairs and into the house that was shortly to become all his. One thing was clear to Judd—Charles hadn't gotten any better about showing consideration to the women in his life. It was obvious Nicole wasn't aware of the full extent of Charles's plans for him. He doubted she'd be this friendly if she knew. That would have to be a bridge to cross at a later date. First, he had to go face-to-face with the man who'd cast him from his home and his country twenty-five years ago, and he had to do it with a civil tongue in his head.

Judd's memories of his father had been of a vital man who exuded energy and bonhomie the moment he stepped in a room. The man who shakily rose to his feet as they entered a large salon was a mere shadow of whom he'd been. Despite Charles's unmistakable frailty, Judd's long-harbored anger at his father's abandonment did not lessen.

"Here he is, Dad," Nicole said.

"Judd—"

"Sir," Judd said, stepping forward and offering his hand.

He watched his father, searching for the man he remembered but seeing little of the vibrancy of his memories. Charles's hair was now steel-gray instead of the black Judd remembered, and his posture was less erect, his figure more portly than fit. But even though his father was obviously unwell, there was a keen intelligence that still gleamed in his eyes as they stood face-to-face. Those blue eyes, very like his own, scoured his features as silence stretched out between them. Something in his appearance must have satisfied the older man, because he gave a short nod and gestured to Judd to sit down.

Anna crossed the room and took the seat on the sofa next to Charles, her hand on his forearm as she leaned closer to whisper something in his ear. A fierce wave of something not unlike jealousy rose from deep inside Judd. Her body language shouted a familiarity between Anna and Charles that screamed loud and clear. A familiarity that Judd silently promised would soon change.

"Don't fuss, Anna. I'm fine," Charles protested, taking her hand and holding it in his for a moment before releasing it. "Now, let's not beat around the bush. You know I want proof you're my son."

Judd felt his hackles rise. "I know I'm your son. I couldn't be anyone else's."

"I'm sure that's what your mother told you," Charles commented, "but you must understand I need to be one hundred percent certain."

"I told you I'm prepared to be tested," Judd said, holding on to his temper by the merest edge.

His mother was no angel, but he knew she told the truth when she said he was Charles Wilson's son. She wouldn't lie about something as vital as that. Not to him.

"Good, good. We can attend to that on Monday and courier the samples to the lab here in Auckland. They offer an express service and promise paternity results within forty-eight hours. It's a shame Anna didn't get you back earlier and that we have to wait out the weekend before we can complete the tests."

He couldn't help it. He had to ask. "Why the sudden urgency? You've waited twenty-five years, surely another two days won't be a problem."

Charles shot him a glance and then smiled proudly. "Well, you certainly sound like me. Straight to the point, hmm?"

"I find it doesn't pay to beat around the bush in important matters."

"No, it never does."

Judd merely looked at him, waiting for him to stop hedging and get to the point. The air in the room became uncomfortable, and in his periphery Judd saw Nicole glance from him to their father.

"I'd like to know, too," she blurted, a tremor in her voice. "Why now, Dad?"

Charles looked at his daughter, a frown of censure on his forehead. "Don't go getting all emotional, Nicole. It's no secret that I'm not getting any younger or any healthier. It's time for me to get everything in order."

"Why did you drag Anna into this? Why send her to do your dirty work?" Nicole persisted.

"That's enough, young lady. I'm still the head of this household and I'm still the head of Wilson Wines. Don't question me."

Nicole slumped in her chair, all the fight gone out of her in a flash. Judd felt a momentary pang of regret for what she must be going through. He'd make it up to her somehow, he promised silently. She deserved something for having put up with the old man all these years without anyone to stand up for her. It was something he'd have done, if given half a chance.

A movement at the door caught everyone's attention.

"Excuse me, sir, but dinner is served in the dining room," a uniformed middle-aged woman said.

"Thank you, Mrs. Evans," Charles said, dismissing the housekeeper and turning back to Judd. "We keep regular hours here for mealtimes—my diabetes, you know."

Charles rose to his feet, refusing Anna's offer of assistance, and led the way through to the dining room. Each room Judd set foot in gave him a weird sense of déjà vu. Although his memories of living here were faded and sketchy, the old photos of Masters' Rise that had been passed on by friends after the fire were imprinted in his mind. This house truly was a complete replica of his mother's old home. No wonder she was so bitter about being made to leave.

He made a silent promise—Cynthia would return to triumph over all this again.

They'd been back one day short of a week. Anna sat at her desk, finding it nearly impossible to concentrate on the work ahead of her. Judd had traveled into the office with Charles this morning, and the two of them had been closeted together for a couple of hours now. Every time Nicole had ventured out from her office, she'd sent a baleful glare toward her father's closed door and the atmosphere had become so tense it was almost palpable.

The arrival of the junior receptionist from downstairs, bearing the morning's mail and courier deliveries, was a welcome distraction. Anna swiftly sorted the mail and then turned to the courier packages. One in particular, slimmer than the rest, stood out. She lifted it and checked the return address. Her stomach instantly knotted. Marked Private and Confidential and addressed to Charles, it had come from the lab he'd engaged to conduct the DNA testing.

She dropped it on the stack of mail she'd already opened for him, as if it burned her fingers. While he'd authorized her, long ago, to attend to all his correspondence, both personal and relating to the business, she had no doubt he'd want to open this particular item himself.

The door to Charles's office opened and she jumped, feeling as if she'd been caught doing something wrong. Judd's ever-intense gaze swept her body and, obviously noticing her reaction, one dark brow lifted slightly in query. She ignored him, something that she'd wished she'd become more capable of in the past few days. Back in Australia, she'd tried to resist her attraction to him because she'd worried about the backlash when he learned the truth. She'd never realized that there was part of the story that even *she* didn't know—that Charles intended for Judd to take over the company. Once the DNA test results verified what they all already knew, Judd would become her boss.

That *should* make him absolutely off-limits. Her brain was sure of it. Her body, though, was much harder to convince.

Just thinking about him was enough to make her body heat with arousal. Being in the same room as him, even under the same roof, was absolute torture. For the past week, work had been her refuge away from him, but it looked like that wouldn't be the case any longer.

"Anna, I want you to take Judd on a tour of our biggest Auckland stockists, introduce him to the store and chain managers. No need for appointments, hmm? Let's catch them on the hop and see how we're faring against the competition."

"Wouldn't you rather do that yourself?"

Anna couldn't think of anything worse than having to spend the balance of the day solely in Judd's company. While she hadn't been able to fault his behavior toward her since their return to New Zealand, there was an undercurrent that remained ever present between them. An undercurrent that kept her nerves wound so tight she was beginning to wonder if she shouldn't request a leave of absence and head away for a couple of weeks, just to be able to breathe again without constantly thinking of Judd Wilson.

"You know I can't drive myself and we can hardly expect Judd to find his way around on his own just yet."

"It's okay," Judd interceded smoothly. "I'm sure that with a GPS I'll be fine."

"No," Charles insisted, his color rising slightly. "I've asked Anna to take you and she will. Everyone knows her already and it will make the introductions much smoother. Isn't that right, Anna?"

Anna pushed her chair away from her desk and stood,

gathering her handbag from the locked drawer at the bottom of her desk as she did so.

"Sure, Charles. Whatever you want."

"Right, then, that's settled." Charles looked at the pile of newly opened mail on her desk. "Is that lot for me?"

"Yes, I was about to bring it through to you."

She saw his eyes light on the courier package and the ruddy color that had begun to suffuse his cheeks faded rapidly.

"Charles? Are you okay?"

"Stop fussing, woman," he blustered. "Of course I'm fine. You two had better get going. And take Judd somewhere nice for lunch, too. I don't expect to see the two of you back here this afternoon. You have a lot of ground to cover."

Resigning herself to Judd's company for the rest of the day, she passed the mail to Charles and took her car keys from her handbag. She watched Charles head back into his office and slam the door closed behind him. So, they weren't to discover the contents of the courier pack until he was ready to share it with them.

"You really don't have to take me around today if you don't want to," Judd said from close by.

"No, it's okay. Charles wants you to have personal introductions, I understand that." *I may not like it, but I do understand it,* she amended silently.

"Do you always do exactly as he says?"

"Why wouldn't I?" she answered, wondering where Judd was leading with his question.

"No reason, I just thought you might stand up to him a bit more."

"He'd never ask me to do something I truly objected to, if that's what you're aiming at," Anna said defensively.

"That's good, then. You don't object to being with me today. Shall we go?"

He smoothly reached out and placed a hand at the small

of her back, guiding her toward the door. She felt its imprint as if she was naked and hastened to create some distance between them. As his hand fell away, her body instantly mourned his touch and she castigated herself soundly for her ridiculous reaction.

Judd didn't speak again until they drove out from the underground staff car park in her shiny dark red Lexus IS 250 F-Sport.

"Nice car," he commented.

"It's a company car, it has four wheels and gets me where I need to go."

"Kind of pricey for a company car for a P.A. You must be *very* good at your job."

There was an insinuation that hung in the air between them that she really didn't like. But she wouldn't give him the satisfaction of biting back.

"Charles likes to show his appreciation to all his valued staff," she replied, choosing her words carefully.

"Some more than others, I imagine."

Again that prick at her relationship with Charles. She knew many people didn't understand it and she'd learned to shield herself from speculation and unkind comments. It was a skill she'd had to develop early when the children at the private school Charles had paid for had discovered she was his housekeeper/companion's daughter.

Growing up with the stigma of her mother's relationship with Charles hanging over her, and the sly innuendo that had accompanied it, had made her a great deal tougher than she looked. It didn't mean that such comments didn't hurt, not at all, but there was no way she would give the person inflicting it any satisfaction at all, nor would she divulge more information than she absolutely needed to. And never, ever would she let herself be a woman who got physically involved with her boss.

She started giving Judd a rundown on the major chains

that Wilson Wines supplied with imported wines as she drove toward their head office. But he interrupted her almost immediately.

"Who is Wilson Wines' greatest competition?"

"Jackson Importers. Why do you ask?"

"In any venture, it always pays to know who you're up against. Tell me about them."

"They were set up just over twenty-five years ago by Thomas Jackson. He died about a year ago and the company is now headed by Nate Hunter. He's about your age and he's been with Jackson since graduating with a business degree from Auckland Uni. That's pretty much all we know about him. He's been working out of one of their overseas offices for most of his career and has only recently come to New Zealand to take the reins from the interim CEO. No one's really too sure what he's like personally. What we do know is that he has a very competitive business head on his shoulders and he works hard to give us fierce competition. He's run their European operations superbly for the past few years."

"Thomas Jackson…I think I remember someone with that name from when I was a kid."

"That would probably be right," Anna commented. "Thomas Jackson and your father were business partners and best friends. They had a disagreement and Charles bought him out."

"Must have been a helluva disagreement."

"I wouldn't know." Anna shrugged, trying to keep her face expressionless. "It was before my time and my mother never spoke about it." True, her mother hadn't spoken about it, and neither had Charles—but Anna had drawn her own conclusions from the rumors that still persisted even years later, and it wasn't difficult to do the math. Charles's divorce from Cynthia and his falling-out with Thomas Jackson had happened at exactly the same time. Those incidents coupled with Charles's insistence on Judd being DNA tested—well, the writing was very clearly on the wall.

Judd sat in his seat, a contemplative expression on his face. Anna wondered what on earth was going through his mind.

"Charles has never said anything to you about it?" he eventually said.

"Not a word, and it's not really something I'd raise with him, anyway. If you want to know more, you'll have to speak to him yourself," she said a little sharply.

Judd chuckled. "And so I'm duly put firmly in my place."

"I didn't mean—"

"Don't worry, Anna. You're right. I should do my own background checks if I want to know things. And I will."

His words made her nervous. Why was it so important for him to dig into the past? Surely it was enough that his father wanted to mend the broken bridges between them. She knew that the death of Thomas Jackson had hit Charles hard. She'd always thought Charles had thrived on the challenge and competition his past colleague presented to him on a regular basis, but now she wondered whether, once the heat and anger had died down, Charles hadn't been suffering regret for the way their friendship had ended.

Either way, the topic wasn't open for discussion as far as she was concerned. She swung her car into a space in the car park at the premises of Wilson Wines' largest customer, grateful for the opportunity to put some space between them. Knowing his opinion of her had done nothing to calm her ever-present awareness of him—of the way her body warmed every time he was in the vicinity, of her hyperawareness of his alluring cologne as it wreathed her senses in forbidden enticement. She resolutely cleared her mind of anything else but what Charles had asked her to do today. She'd get through this, even if it was the last thing she wanted to do.

Six

The minute they set foot back in the house Anna could sense something in the air. There was an energy thrumming through the place that hadn't been there this morning and when she went through to the kitchen for a chilled glass of water, the cook and housekeeper were working flat out on what looked to be very elaborate meal preparations.

"Did I miss something?" she asked the cook, who was busily checking pots on the commercial-size stove top.

"No, dear. Just himself making requests for something very special for dinner tonight—says he has an important announcement to make, and he wants you all to dress up, too. Can you let Miss Nicole know when she gets in?"

Clearly the courier pack he'd received this morning had borne the news Charles had wanted so very much. A vague numbness permeated Anna's body, leaving her confused about how she felt about the news. It was what Charles had wanted, there was no doubt about that. But she knew he hadn't said a word yet to Nicole about his plans. If he had, she knew Nicole would have discussed it with her. Still, Nicole had been avoiding her lately, still stung, Anna was sure, over her not disclosing the reason for her trip to Adelaide. Worried she might miss Nicole, she sent her a text message.

Don't be late tonight. Your dad wants us all dressed up for dinner. He has an announcement to make. —A.

Nicole was quick to reply; a series of question marks flashed across Anna's screen. She swallowed against the knot of disloyalty that tightened in her throat as she texted back.

No idea what it's about, sorry.

On the way to her room she passed by Charles's suite, knocking softly on the door before letting herself in. He wasn't in his private sitting room, so she figured he must be resting. It had become a regular habit of his after a half day at the office—late starts, early finishes and plenty of rest in between. She was reluctant to disturb his nap, but she needed to talk to him about Nicole. Deciding to wait until she heard him up and about in the bedroom, she settled on one of the comfortable sofas he had in the sitting room and popped her feet up beside her.

Some time later Anna stirred at the sound of running water coming from the other room. She blinked to clear her eyes, realizing it had grown full dark outside. She dragged a hand through her hair. It was sticking every which way. Darn, she knew she should have tied it up today. A quick glance at her watch revealed how close it was to the dinner hour. There was no way she'd be able to be ready and talk to Charles this side of dinner. As it was, she'd be pushing it to get ready on time.

She shrugged out of her jacket, tucking it under one arm, and untucked then started to unbutton her blouse as she headed for the door. She opened it and slipped outside into the hallway, only to come face-to-face with Judd. Her nostrils flared, taking in the freshly showered scent of him.

"If you'll excuse me," she said, trying to sidestep past him and get to her room, "I'm running late."

Judd's expression, usually distinctly unreadable, reflected a look of surprise, before a cold, calculating look appeared in his eyes.

"So I see," he said, stepping to one side to let her by.

Understanding dawned with the drenching effect of sub-Antarctic waters. "It's not—"

"Didn't you say you were running late?" he reminded her with that arch to his brow that he used with such great effect.

Without another word she stalked past him to her room a little farther down the hall. She closed the door behind her and leaned against the solid wooden surface, realizing that she was shaking. There was no question that Judd thought he'd caught her *in flagrante delicto.* Anna pushed herself away from the door and forced herself to walk through to her en suite bathroom, peeling the rest of her clothes off on the way. What should it matter what Judd Wilson thought? It wasn't the truth, so as far as she was concerned it shouldn't matter one iota. Even so, as she stepped beneath the spray of her shower, she couldn't help wishing she hadn't put that look of disapproval on his face.

By the time she'd dressed, reapplied her makeup and swept her hair up into an elegant chignon, she'd missed predinner drinks. She joined Charles, Judd and Nicole as they walked through to the dining room. Despite her text to Nicole, her friend obviously hadn't had time to change out of her work clothes—or perhaps had chosen not to, knowing it would rile her father.

"Sorry I'm late," Anna said breathlessly as she entered the dining room.

"You're here in time for the important news," Charles said with a thread of emotion in his voice that put Anna's nerves on edge.

She took her seat, opposite Judd, feeling the blue fire of his gaze upon her as she did so.

"What important news?" Nicole asked.

Anna felt her throat close and her chest tighten. This wasn't going to be pretty. As dependable as Nicole was in a business setting, she wasn't known for deliberation or contemplation when it came to her private affairs. Impulsiveness and impetuosity were more her mark in trade. She wasn't going to take the news of her father's plans happily. Especially not when she'd worked so hard at his side all these years, striving constantly to be everything he needed in business and in family.

Charles seemed oblivious to Anna's distress and to the storm that was brewing. He was puffed up with pride. Anna hadn't seen him this animated in some time. He picked up his glass and gestured in Judd's direction.

"I'd like to propose a toast. To my son, Judd. Welcome home, where you truly belong."

Anna hazarded a look at Judd, watching to see if this open declaration that he was definitely Charles's son would have an effect on him at all. She was disappointed. He merely nodded toward his father and raised his own glass in response.

"Aren't you repeating yourself, Dad?" Nicole asked. "Didn't we already go through this last Friday when Judd arrived?"

"No, I'm not repeating things at all. It is a relief to an old man to be able to acknowledge his family, *all* his family, now that the results have come in. And to that end I have a small presentation to make."

Charles patted a long, narrow envelope that sat on the tablecloth next to his place setting. He picked it up and handed it to Judd.

"You'll find it all in there, son. Exactly as I promised."

Even though he knew there had never been any doubt about his paternity, Judd felt a thrill of exhilaration surge through him. Here it was, the moment he'd been waiting for,

for most of his adult life. His father handing him the tools with which to pay him back for what he'd done to Judd and his mother all those years ago. Tomorrow he would have a solicitor draw up the share-transfer papers in order for him to present Nate Hunter with an offer that the man could not refuse. The controlling interest in Wilson Wines for the princely sum of one dollar. Judd took the proffered envelope.

"Thank you, sir."

"Oh, surely you don't have to call me 'sir,'" Charles blustered. "If you can't call me Dad, then at least call me Charles."

"Thank you, Charles."

He saw the hope in his father's eyes dim a little. There was no way he could call this man "Dad," not after all these years. He scanned the two women at the table. Anna sat there, frozen, as if she was expecting something terrible to happen and she was totally helpless to prevent it. He began to get some understanding of the reason why when he saw his sister's face.

Confusion battled with irritation across her features and it didn't take long before she was demanding some clarity about what had just been passed over to him.

"What did you promise, Dad?" she asked, a fine tremor in her voice betraying her heightened nerves.

"Only what Judd has always been due, Nicole."

She flung a dark-eyed glare at Judd. "And that would be?"

"The deed to the house and a controlling interest in Wilson Wines. The rest will go to you on my death, as you well know," Charles interjected. "Now, shall we have another toast and get down to the business of enjoying the wonderful meal I know Mrs. Evans has prepared?"

"A controlling interest in Wilson Wines?" Nicole's voice rose on a note of incredulity. "Dad, what are you doing? He doesn't know the first thing about the business."

"He has experience with the wine industry in Australia.

And now that he's home, he has time to learn how we do things here," Charles said, as if that was the end of the matter.

"That's not fair. I've given everything to Wilson Wines, to *you*. And you just go and give it all away, just like that. To a stranger?"

"He's your brother, he's not a stranger," Charles snapped back, the color in his cheeks an unhealthy ruddy red.

"He may as well be."

Judd felt he should say something, but he held back. When he followed through on his plans for Wilson Wines, his sister would be glad she didn't know him better and would probably never even want to see him again, anyway. The knowledge gave him a sharp pang of regret. They'd both been cheated of so much by their father's dictatorial decisions. Maybe he'd be able to find her something to do within The Masters'.

Across the table, Nicole laughed, but the sound held no humor in it. Anna reached out and took Nicole's hand in hers, squeezing it tight, but Nicole shook her off, turning on her instead.

"You're just as bad. I suppose you knew about this?"

Anna's expression told his sister all she needed to know.

"I can't believe it. Betrayed by the only two people in the entire world that I love." She pushed her chair back from the table and rose. "I can't stay here and listen to any more of this. It's just wrong."

"Nicole, calm yourself and sit down," Charles interjected. "This is how things should have been all along. You know it as well as I do. I never made you any promises about Wilson Wines. Just you wait, you'll find some young man who'll sweep you off your feet and before I know it you will be married and raising a family. Wilson Wines will just be a hobby for you."

Judd might not know his sister well, but even he could tell that that had been the dead-wrong thing to say. "A hobby?" Nicole's voice rose steadily. "I can't believe this. You can't be serious. Wilson Wines is everything to me. I love the business, love the industry—everything I learned was so I could run the company one day. I've lived under the same roof as you all my life, worked beside you every day I possibly could to try and earn your respect, and yet you don't know me at all."

She made for the door. Anna rose and went after her.

"No, let me go!" Nicole said, tears tracking down her cheeks as she held up her hands as if to ward Anna off.

Judd could see the hurt in Anna's eyes, the guilt she clearly felt for not having given Nicole any warning of what her father had been about to do. Even he felt sick to his stomach that his father could so cavalierly shrug off Nicole's contribution to Wilson Wines in the past few years and denigrate it as a hobby. Another black mark in the increasing collection against Charles Wilson.

"She always was a little high-strung," Charles commented as Nicole slammed the dining room door behind her. "She'll come around, you'll see. She doesn't have it in her to stay angry for long."

"Charles," Anna said, "this is more than a tantrum. Can't you see? You've hurt her deeply."

"Do you think so?" Charles cast her a look of genuine surprise. "No, she's just being overemotional, that's all. She'll calm down soon and see this is all for the best. I've always had her best interests at heart, you know that."

"Do I?" Anna pressed. "Don't you think she sees it as her position within Wilson Wines being undermined, let alone her position here in her home?"

Judd had to admire the way she stuck up for his sister.

"Don't be ridiculous. She'll always be my daughter. In fact, I've probably spoiled her over the years. She'll just have to get used to the idea of sharing with Judd now, is all. Now, come and settle back down. Mrs. Evans is waiting to serve."

"I need to make a call—to make sure she's okay," Anna insisted.

Charles waved a hand. "Fine, then, go ahead. Do what you must."

When Anna returned, Charles rang the small crystal-and-silver bell that stood beside his water glass. Judd watched as Anna resumed her seat, her body vibrating with tension and her distress clear on her features. The call to his sister can't have gone well.

Anna excused herself from the table immediately after dessert, leaving Charles and Judd to talk, but it wasn't long before Charles showed signs of weariness and also left to go upstairs to bed.

Alone? Judd wondered, his mind uncomfortably casting back to when he'd surprised Anna coming from the older man's suite of rooms. She'd clearly been in the process of putting her clothes back on in case someone saw her in the hallway. And someone had. Judd's hand tightened on the stem of the Waterford crystal goblet in his hand, the glowing red wine within it barely touched.

Well, he could certainly find out if she had gone ahead to warm his father's sheets. All it would take would be an inquiry at her door.

Judd barely realized he'd made the decision to check on Anna until he found himself outside of her bedroom. He raised his hand and rapped softly on the door, leaning one shoulder against the jamb as he waited for it to open. To his surprise, it did.

"What do you want? To gloat?" Anna asked him.

For a moment, he was taken aback but he soon recovered his usual equilibrium and took a moment to savor the scrubbed freshness of her face and her hair loose in a well-brushed tumble across satin-covered shoulders. The shadows cast by the soft lighting in her room showed she wore very little beneath her robe. If anything. Instantly he was rock hard, his body clamoring with an urgent need to possess her. He stamped down on the sensation. So she wasn't with Charles now, but she had been earlier this evening. The image of her, fresh from his father's room, still burned in his memory, and he fought the urge to create a new memory— one of his making.

He gathered his thoughts together and expelled a harsh breath before speaking. "Not at all. It should have been handled differently."

She made a sound, a cross between derision and a cynical laugh. "You think? You know you could have asked him to consider Nicole's feelings before making that stupid announcement."

"Mea culpa," he said, straightening from the door frame and holding his hands wide. "It didn't occur to me that he wouldn't have told her privately."

"Well, it's too late now. Hopefully we can sort things out at the office tomorrow, if she's talking to me again by then. What did you come to see me for, anyway?"

"I wanted to make sure that you were okay. You looked upset at dinner."

She looked at him in surprise. "Upset? In being loyal to Charles I betrayed my best friend since I was five years old. Of course I'm upset."

"Why did you do it? Why does he have such an influence over you?" Judd persisted.

"You would never understand," Anna said and started to close the door.

Judd put out a hand to halt its traverse across the plush carpet.

"Try me."

"Look, it's late. I don't want to talk about this now. What's done is done." She stared pointedly at his hand and then back at his face. "Good night, Judd."

He took the hint and removed his hand from the door.

"Sweet dreams, Anna."

But he was talking to a plank of painted wood. So, he thought as he walked back to his room, she didn't want to discuss her relationship with his father. How surprising, not. He was prepared to leave it—for now—but eventually he'd get the truth from her. In the meantime, he'd do his best to imprint his own influence. Whatever her feelings for Charles, the attraction between Anna and himself was mutual—her capitulation would be a sweet success.

The next morning, Anna waited patiently for Nicole to come into the office, but she didn't show. Repeated calls to her cell phone resulted in no response. Charles hadn't come into the office today, either, and according to the household staff, Judd had remained closeted with him back at the house. Anna didn't like the way this was panning out.

She stifled a yawn and decided to take her morning break a little earlier than usual. Maybe a shot of caffeine would help her get through to lunchtime. In the staff lunch room she grabbed her favorite cup from the shelf and headed for the coffee machine. One of the office staff sat at the table, nursing her own cup of coffee and scanning her laptop screen. As Anna passed by she caught a glimpse of the page the girl was on and smiled. The anonymous celebrity-gossip column in the print and online newspaper usually made for a humorous read.

"Anything good in there today?" she asked, sitting down at the table with the other girl.

"The usual, mostly. Oh, wait. Look at this!"

She swiveled the computer around so they could both view the screen. Anna scanned the text, when her eyes were suddenly arrested by a name—Nicole Wilson. The comments about Nicole focused mostly on her being seen letting her hair down in one of the city's bright spots the night before and, in particular, with a certain extremely eligible and wealthy

Auckland businessman who was newly returned to town to take over control of a major company. While his name wasn't mentioned, there was only one person that Anna knew fitted the carefully worded description. Nate Hunter. A photo accompanied the article. While her partner's back was to the camera, there was no mistaking Nicole in fine form on the dance floor.

Somehow Anna managed to say the right things to the other girl and made her way back to her office, her rapidly cooling coffee clutched in her hand.

What on earth should she do? she wondered. She had to get a hold of Nicole and find out what she was up to—but how? She did a quick search online, and found the number for Jackson Importers. Maybe Nate Hunter might be able to shed some light on where Nicole was.

Five frustrating minutes of being stonewalled later, Anna replaced the receiver on her phone. Mr. Hunter was unavailable until further notice. What that meant, exactly, Anna had no idea, but she had the sinking feeling that wherever Nicole was, it was very possibly with him. And given her mood last night and her tendency to be outrageously impulsive, it didn't augur well.

Darn Judd Wilson, she thought, and darn Charles, too. This was all their fault. Anna clenched her hands into fists and fought back the urge to scream. One by one she uncurled her fingers and released her fury on a pent-up breath, then reached for her phone and dialed Judd's number. They needed to swing into damage control before all this blew up in their faces. He'd know what to do.

Seven

"It's preposterous. What on earth is she thinking?"

Anna winced as Charles raged through the office on Monday afternoon after what had been an exceptionally stressful and long weekend waiting for his prodigal daughter to return home. She knew all the anger and tension couldn't be good for him, but there was nothing she could do to calm him down when the bad news about Nicole kept pouring in. The latest update—that she'd turned up for work at the offices of Jackson Importers late that morning—had gone down like a lead balloon.

He continued his rant. "She isn't thinking, that's what. And she wonders why I gave the controlling interest in Wilson Wines to Judd."

"She's hurting, Charles. Give her time, she'll come back." Anna tried to soothe his anger but it was useless.

"Come back? I wouldn't have her back. Not now that she's working for that insufferable miscreant! I've a good mind to cut her out of my will completely after this." Anna wanted to believe he was just blowing off steam, but she had a sinking feeling that he meant every word. Nothing made Charles angrier than what he perceived as disloyalty. No matter what excuse she offered, Anna was pretty sure that Charles wouldn't be forgiving Nicole in a hurry.

"And what are we supposed to do in the meantime, hmm?" Charles continued. "We needed her here to help transition Judd into his duties. Now he's dropped in at the deep end."

"I'm sure I'll cope." Judd interrupted his father's tirade. "I'm not completely unaware of how a business should be run nor am I unfamiliar with the wine industry."

Anna looked at him and felt that familiar tug of attraction she'd fought all weekend to ignore. It was hard enough to resist him under normal circumstances, but over the past weekend, when Anna had felt that her whole world was collapsing around her, Judd had been a rock—stepping right in to make sure everything was taken care of. While Anna had been busy keeping Charles reined in and ensuring that his riled temper didn't prevent him from keeping up with his medical treatments, Judd was the one who'd handled the reporters' phone calls, coordinated with the company's PR team and ensured that all Wilson Wines employees, particularly those who reported directly to Nicole, were reminded of the nondisclosure agreements they had signed.

He'd single-handedly kept the disaster from spiraling out of control. While Anna couldn't help but be grateful to him, she was forced to admit to herself that it was entirely unfair how attractive he was when he was coolly, competently in charge.

Today he looked every inch the high-powered executive, wearing a navy suit and crisp white shirt with a patterned tie. He could have stepped off the pages of a men's fashion magazine, and yet despite the polish, there was still that edge of visceral male that hovered about him.

"Anna?" Charles's voice. "Are you paying attention?"

"S-sorry," she stuttered. "I was woolgathering."

Charles sighed heavily. "I need you to be on your game, young lady. Without Nicole here, I'm appointing you as Judd's P.A. He's going to need the support of someone who knows Wilson Wines from the ground up. You're the only one I trust for that role."

"His P.A.?" Her heart gave an uncomfortable lurch. "But what about you?"

"I'm sure you can draw on one of the girls from marketing to help me when I need it. That redhead who covers for you when you're on holiday, she'll do. It's not as if I'm in here for full days, anyway…although I suppose that will have to change now Nicole's gone."

He suddenly slumped in his chair, his face gray. Anna rushed to his side.

"Are you all right? Do you need the doctor?"

Charles shook his head. "No, don't fuss, Anna. I'm not sick. Not physically, anyway. It just isn't right. I finally get Judd back and I lose Nicole."

Anna fought the urge to tell him she'd tried to warn him that what he was doing would drive a wedge between himself and his daughter. She found consoling words instead to replace the ones that hung bitterly on the tip of her tongue.

"You haven't lost her, she'll be back before we know it, I'm sure."

"In the meantime, you have us," Judd commented. "And speaking of which, I think you should head home and rest and leave the running of the office to Anna and me. We can call you if anything arises that we can't manage."

Anna felt a burst of cold panic at the thought of her and Judd alone together in the office, but still, she found herself agreeing with him. Anything to see to Charles's comfort. After the older man had been driven home by his new temporary P.A., Anna showed Judd into Nicole's office. Charles had stipulated that he should work from there, and while a little voice inside of her had objected vociferously, she accepted the practicality of it. If Judd was to assume Nicole's duties quickly, he needed information to be at his fingertips. Where better than in Nicole's office?

It was lunchtime when he came out and over to Anna's desk.

"I see Nicole had a trip planned to Nelson, leaving on Thursday. I thought Wilson Wines primarily imported from overseas markets."

"We do, but Nicole campaigned to introduce several wines from New Zealand to our catalogue as well, with a view to distributing only to select wine sellers and collectors. She felt it was a strong counter to Jackson Importers' ability to cut prices by dealing through the internet. This way we'd have top-quality wines but without the additional costs involved with importation."

Judd nodded. "Makes good sense. So this project is still in its infancy?"

"Yes, she's already visited a few North Island wineries. This week was to source specific wines from the top of the South Island."

"You'll need to change her tickets to my name and book a set for yourself, as well."

"Me?"

A small frown creased between his eyebrows. "Why not?"

"I don't usually do these trips. My role is more one of support here, at home."

"I need you with me."

"Surely you can—"

"Anna, you're coming with me. We're not departing until early evening on Thursday and will be returning to Auckland on Tuesday morning. The office can survive a few days without you."

"But Charles—"

"Has a new P.A. now. Or had you forgotten that?"

* * *

Judd eyed Anna carefully. He hadn't expected an opportunity to get her alone and to himself quite so quickly but he certainly wasn't going to waste it. Getting her out from under his father's roof and into his own bed had become a task he'd begun to relish. His sister's display of pique had fallen right into his hands. He'd thank her for it one of these days. Probably right about the time he offered his controlling interest in Wilson Wines over to Nate Hunter.

After the weekend's development, he'd shelved his original plans to hand over the company right away. Oh, he still intended to take Wilson Wines apart…but not quite yet. Charles was still reeling from Nicole's actions, and Judd wanted him feeling secure and invulnerable again when Judd struck. Besides, seducing Charles's mistress away from him would be a lot easier when she was forced to work right at his side.

For now, business was the least of his concerns. His sights were very firmly set on the woman in front of him. The woman whose scent, even now, tantalized him. Living under the same roof and not touching her—imagining her with his father—had been torture these past few days. He hadn't seen any overt displays of affection between them, but she'd certainly been hovering over Charles nonstop. Judd also hadn't forgotten her state of dishabille last Thursday evening when he'd caught her coming from the old man's rooms.

Each time he'd had an opportunity, he'd cut her from Charles's attention over the weekend, even going so far as to brush against her from time to time. He knew his touch unsettled her—the faint flush of color on her cheeks had been a dead giveaway—but she'd managed to gracefully extricate herself from each situation and create a distance between them that had left him frustrated both physically and mentally.

This trip to the South Island was a godsend. She would be

his willing lover before they returned, and stage one of his decimation of the things his father loved would have begun.

By the time Thursday morning rolled around Judd felt as if every cell in his body was taut with anticipation over what this trip would bring. He'd done some more research and had personally contacted each of the wineries they were to visit to explain that he was coming in his sister's stead. So far the reception had been promising, as had been the sample wines that Nicole had in her office that she'd received in advance of the trip. He could see why she'd chosen them. They had distinct appeal on many levels. His sister definitely had a strong talent for innovation and combined it with exemplary taste.

The business side of the trip aside, he was looking forward to the concentrated time alone with Anna Garrick. That she very clearly wasn't only made the prospect more appealing and the challenge even more enticing. He still well remembered her response to his kiss that first night at The Masters'. Remembered the feel of her body, her full breasts, the soft curves of her body against his, the taste of her. Damn if he wasn't getting hard just thinking about it.

He walked into the dining room at the house that already felt like home and saw Anna at the sideboard helping herself to cereal and milk.

"Good morning, all ready for the trip?" he asked.

She took her bowl over to the table and sat down before acknowledging his presence.

"Good morning," she said, her voice a little husky as if she'd not long been awake.

The fresh scent of her and her immaculately applied makeup gave lie to the thought that she'd tumbled straight from bed. Add to that the fact that she was dressed smartly in a cream blouse neatly tucked into a pair of taupe-colored trousers that she'd cinched at the waist with a wide black belt, suggested she'd been up for some time. The blouse was made of some sheer floaty fabric that clung to her in all the right places. Beneath it he caught a hint of a lacy camisole. He was going to have to exhibit some control, he decided, if he wasn't to walk around all morning in a state of constant arousal. But there was something so carnally alluring about her, he knew it would be easier said than done.

Anna pushed her cereal around in her bowl, clearly not finding the prospect of breakfast at all tempting. In the meantime, Judd helped himself to some fluffy scrambled eggs and a couple of strips of grilled bacon.

"Are you sure you really need me to come with you on this trip?" she blurted as he sat down and reached for the coffeepot on the table.

"I wouldn't have said so if it wasn't necessary."

She sighed, the action making her breasts rise and fall beneath the gossamer-fine fabric and making his fingers itch to touch it and what lay beneath.

"I really don't think I should be leaving Charles, what with Nicole gone, as well."

Judd felt his resolve harden. "He's an adult and quite capable of taking care of himself."

"But he'll be alone."

"In a house filled with staff? I don't think so. I've spoken with Mrs. Evans already. She'll keep a close eye on him."

"It won't be the same," Anna replied, a mutinous set to her mouth.

He'd just bet it wouldn't be the same. And if he had anything to do with it, it wouldn't be the same ever again. If Anna was going to pay a furtive visit to anyone's room, it would be to his from here on in.

"He'll cope. Mrs. Evans will be staying in and has all the necessary numbers if she needs assistance." He looked at her swirling her spoon in her now-soggy cereal. "Are you going to eat that?"

She looked down at her bowl, a flash of surprise on her features when she saw the mess in there.

"Um, no. I'm not hungry."

"Are you sure? There's no meal service on the flight."

"I'm aware of that. I'll be fine."

"You don't look fine."

She huffed another sigh. "Look, I don't like small aircraft, that's all. But I'll be okay."

"Fifty passengers isn't such a small aircraft. If you're that worried, I can hold your hand for the entire flight. Rest assured, I'll take good care of you, Anna," he said, giving her a look that intimated a whole lot more than hand-holding.

"I think I'll be able to manage without that. Besides, it's more likely that the prospect of being with you for the next few days is what makes me anxious."

She got up and placed her bowl and spoon on an empty tray at the end of the sideboard. Judd stood and blocked her path as she went to walk past him.

"Now, why would that be, I wonder?" He lifted one finger and traced the edge of her lower lip. "Could it be that you're *anxious* to repeat that kiss we shared in Adelaide?"

"N-no, of course not," she refuted.

"Really?" he said softly. "Do you ever think about it?"

She shook her head and he leaned in a little closer.

"I do." He let his hand drop. "And I look forward to the next time."

"There won't be a next time," she said adamantly, nudging past him and heading for the door.

He watched her leave with a small self-satisfied smile on his face. Oh, yes, these next few days would prove very interesting indeed.

Anna shot up the stairs to her bedroom and closed the door firmly behind her as if another barrier could make a difference to the way Judd Wilson made her feel. She rested a hand on her chest, feeling her rapid heartbeat beneath her palm.

He's just teasing me, she told herself. *Playing games like a cat with a mouse. I certainly don't want a repeat of that kiss.*

Liar! her alter ego whispered in her ear. She shook her head to rid herself of the word echoing in her mind and mentally rechecked her luggage for the trip away. She had everything she needed and then some. All of it nondescript and practical, with not a single low-cut neckline or suggestive hemline amongst it all.

Externally, at least, there'd be nothing about her to tempt Judd Wilson. She hadn't been unaware of his presence these past days. In fact, she could almost say she'd been hyper-aware of him. She'd chosen the blandest combinations of clothing she possibly could every single day, and yet, on several occasions, she'd caught him looking at her as if he'd like to eat her all up.

The visual image of him doing just that forced a moan from her constricted throat. The flat of her hand drifted down to her breast, to where her nipple peaked against the fabric. She couldn't deny it. He had a near uncontrollable effect upon her.

Sex. It was just sex. He was a strong healthy male and he hit all her hot buttons. She really needed to get out more, she decided. Meet new people. Maybe when she got back she'd get a hold of one of the guys at work who was always teasing her about a date. Maybe then she would be able to work this aching tension out of her body and inure herself to Judd Wilson's overwhelming magnetism. She'd get onto it the minute they got back, she promised herself. The very second.

Eight

Anna was shattered by the time they made it back to their riverside hotel in Nelson on Thursday night. They'd arrived at Nelson airport just after two in the afternoon and had hopped into their rental car and driven straight out to the first of two vineyards and wineries that they'd visited today.

The visits, and subsequent talks, had gone well. Nicole's dream was being well and truly brought to reality. Anna fought back the pang that her friend wasn't the one actively seeing her idea come into fruition. Still, it couldn't be helped. She'd made it clear that she'd washed her hands of Wilson Wines, her father and, by association, Anna and Judd, as well. It still hurt that her best friend had severed all ties between them so instantaneously, but she had to respect Nicole's decision.

She rubbed wearily at her eyes, feeling as if she had no more control of her life right now than a leaf did, floating on the river outside. Warm fingers closed over her forearm.

"Are you okay?"

Judd. Always Judd. Always right there, in her face, in her space, in her mind. Somewhere along the course of this week she'd begun to depend on him—on his unwavering sense of command and his capable manner. Even Charles had begun to defer to him—something Anna had never believed she'd see in her lifetime. She had to get a grip on herself—to break the spell Judd was so easily waving about her. She opened her eyes and looked pointedly at where his hand made heated contact with the bare skin of her arm.

"You can let go of me. I'm not about to keel over," she said tartly.

"Of course you're not. Here, this is your room key. We have adjoining rooms. I thought we should eat in tonight and then go over the proposals we discussed with John and Peter today."

"And I suppose we *must* do this tonight?"

"It'll pay to iron out any potential kinks early, don't you agree?"

"Sure," she said, resignation in her voice. "I'd like to freshen up a bit before we eat."

"No problem. I'll order for both of us and have it delivered to my room. Just come through the connecting door when you're ready."

When she was ready. That was rich. *How about never,* she thought defiantly. But she knew she would go through to his room to dine with him. She owed it to Charles if no one else. Already rumors had begun to circulate this week about Jackson Importers approaching at least three of Wilson Wines' major European suppliers. They'd had exclusive contracts with those suppliers but they were all coming up for renewal. A fact that Nicole had known only too well. Was she behind this attempt to undermine her own father?

"Sounds good. Give me half an hour."

"There's no big rush. Take an hour if you need it."

"Thanks, I will." Another hour she didn't have to spend in his company was all good as far as she was concerned.

When she let herself into her room, she cast her eyes around, familiarizing herself with the layout. Basic but comfortable, were the first two things that came to mind, until she stepped into the bathroom and saw the spa bath installed against a white-tiled wall. A sound of anticipation mixed with pure pleasure escaped her and, as she ran the bath, she quickly divested herself of her travel-worn clothes.

She lost track of how long she'd soaked until she heard a muffled knocking from the connecting door. She dragged herself from the water and wrapped herself in a towel. A quick glance at the bedside clock confirmed she'd used up her one hour of grace.

"I'll be right there," she shouted at the closed door, and quickly dried herself off.

She unzipped her case and grabbed fresh underwear, the sheer shell-pink panties clinging a little to her skin as she shimmied into them. She hooked up her bra and then padded on bare feet back to the bathroom to apply some moisturizer and to brush out her hair. She wasn't going to the effort of reapplying her makeup, not when she hoped to be in bed— her own bed, and alone—very soon.

Back in the main room she extracted a lightweight, loose-fitting cotton sweater in taupe and a pair of black Capri pants, before shoving her bare feet into a pair of silver leather slides. A long silver chain with a large silver spinner on the end completed the ensemble. There, that should do it, she decided.

Another knock at the connecting door startled her. She reached out and pulled open the door. Her gaze flicked over him as he filled the frame, making her wish she'd waited a few seconds for him to move away before opening the door. He'd obviously had a shower and changed, too, and her nostrils twitched at the light scent of his cologne. His hair was still wet, making it look blacker than black, and his jaw looked freshly shaven. He'd changed into blue jeans and a black T-shirt that clung to his broad shoulders and chest as if it were made for him. Probably was, she thought cynically. He'd never looked anything less than tailor-made this whole time she'd known him.

"You look worth the wait," Judd said smoothly.

"What's for dinner?" she asked, ducking under his arm and moving into his room.

It was the mirror of hers, with the exception of a California king-size bed instead of the queen she had. She swallowed as she tore her eyes away from the expanse of linen, the bed already enticingly turned down for the night.

"I chose two entrées and a shared main from the menu that I thought would complement a couple of the wines we tried today. We can share the entrées or have just one each. Your choice."

The idea of sharing a dish with him, let alone two dishes, was a bit daunting, but Anna reminded herself she was here to work.

"We can share," she said with as much nonchalance as she could muster.

The autumn evening was still surprisingly warm, and the covered dishes on the trolley near the door to the balcony emitted a mouthwatering aroma. A table for two was set on the balcony overlooking the river, a squat white candle burning in a hurricane lamp providing illumination. Altogether it was a shamefully idyllic and romantic setting. She should have insisted on dining in the main restaurant, she thought, as she took her chair and Judd placed the two entrées in the middle of the table between them.

Anna busied herself filling their water glasses, while Judd poured them each a small measure of the pinot gris they'd brought back with them today.

"So, what shall we start with?" she asked, suddenly very hungry.

"Black Tiger Prawns on a bed of noodles with this wine, I think," Judd suggested, lifting the cover off the first plate.

By the time they'd enjoyed their way through the prawns, followed by a sampling of Green Lipped Mussels and then their shared main course of a trio of meats, Anna felt as if she'd eaten enough to feed an army.

"The new Syrah should be very popular, don't you think?" Judd commented as he leaned back in his chair and took another sip of the wine he'd just mentioned.

"Indeed. It's a variety that seems to be growing in popularity here. To get exclusive distribution on this label is going to be quite a coup. Charles will be pleased."

And there he was again, Judd thought. His father, still intruding.

"Why is his approval so important to you?" he asked.

"He's my boss," she answered simply, turning her face away to look at the lights from the marina sparkling on the now-inky dark water that ran alongside the hotel.

"He's more than that, though. Isn't he?"

She sighed. "Yes, he is. He's always been there for me, and for my mother while she was alive. Without him, I wouldn't be where I am today. I owe him a huge debt of gratitude."

He couldn't quite get a handle on it. It was clear by the tone of her voice, and her actions with his old man, that she loved him. But just where did that love lead?

"He's quite a guy," Judd commented, a little of his frustration creeping into his tone.

"The way you say that…" She shook her head. "You don't know him. Not really."

"And whose fault was that?" he said pointedly. "Look, let's not talk about my father, okay? Let's talk about something else."

She stifled a yawn. "I'm sorry, I think I need to turn in. I haven't been sleeping well lately, and we have an early start for the day tomorrow."

"Sure," he said.

She did look tired, he admitted to himself as he rose from the table and walked with her back to the connecting door. But even with the dark rings under her eyes she was intensely appealing. He'd enjoyed sharing dinner with her—her keen insights into the wines had been valuable, and her company had been surprisingly soothing while they ate. But his enjoyment of her companionship hadn't dampened his desire for the evening to end on a far more sensual note. His body tightened as he considered his plans for this time away together, and as she turned to say good-night, he reached out and caught a few strands of her hair between his fingers, twirling them over and over.

Her mouth parted, as if in protest, but the objection never came. He leaned a little closer.

"Don't you ever wonder?" he asked, pitching his voice low and watching her pupils almost consume the hazel irises of her eyes.

"Wonder what?" she asked, her voice that husky whisper that did crazy things to him and sent a heated jolt of need straight to his groin.

Her eyes had fixed on his lips as he spoke. He moved closer still, until there was no more than a hand width separating their faces.

"What it will be like when we kiss again."

"Who said we'll kiss again?"

"Oh, we will. Don't you want to know if what happened the first time will happen again? Whether we could be *that* good again?"

She blinked and drew in a breath, the word *no* beginning to form on her lips. The sound never made it, as he closed the short distance between them, caressing her lips with his—at first gently and then, when she didn't pull away, with more pressure. His fingers tunneled through her hair to cup the back of her head.

The sensation that shuddered through his body was intense. Even more potent than the last time. He stepped closer, aligning his body with hers and wrapping his free arm around her waist, drawing her against him—feeling the heat of her, the softness, and letting her know in no uncertain terms of the strength of his arousal for her. Slow seduction be damned. The contrast between their bodies incited him to want more, to want it all, to want it now.

His tongue traced the seam of her lips, and as she parted them, he stroked it across the tender inner membrane before tasting her deeper. She met his assault with a parry of her own, her hands now clutched in the fabric of his T-shirt, clinging to him, her hips pressed tight against his own. He flexed his pelvis, gently grinding his hardness against her mound. A moan vibrated from deep in her throat and he captured the sound with his mouth.

Her nipples were hardened points against his chest and he knew without a doubt that one kiss would never be enough. His need to possess her overwhelmed everything else—every need, every thought, other than one. He wanted Anna Garrick like he'd never wanted anything in his life before.

Anna fought to clear the fog of desire that clouded her mind but failed miserably. Hot, hungry need clawed through her as Judd kissed her deeply and she kissed him back just as hard. She knew she should pull back, call a stop to this before they went past the point of no return, but somewhere deep inside she acknowledged that they'd passed that point long ago. What would happen now was inevitable. Nothing—not even the vow she'd made to herself for so many years to never have an intimate relationship with her boss—could stop her from giving in. She wondered whether she would still be able to walk away with some pride, with her heart intact, but her feelings for Judd had crossed some unseen line. Even back in Adelaide, she'd been drawn to him in a way she'd never experienced before. She wanted to take this further—to know him better, to *know* him in every meaning of the word.

There was no reason left that was strong enough to convince her that she shouldn't reach out and take what he was offering. No reason at all. And in return she could give in to him. Anna loosened the fists of her hands and skimmed her palms over his muscled chest and down toward the waistband of his jeans. She yanked the cotton fabric of his shirt loose and shoved her hands underneath, desperate now to feel his skin against hers. But it wasn't enough. His skin burned beneath her touch, igniting her to want even more.

The taut coil of desire deep in her womb tightened even more, and between her thighs she felt herself grow swollen and wet with need. Judd loosened his grip on her, using both hands to push aside her sweater. They broke apart momentarily as he swept the garment up and off her body, exposing her to his gaze. He groaned and bent his head to her neck, nuzzling the tender skin behind her ear and leaving a heated trail of kisses along the way to the hollow of her throat.

One hand cupped her breast, his thumb flicking a distended nipple through the sheer lace of her bra. Her legs threatened to buckle beneath her as his mouth traced a beeline for the tightly beaded nub. He tugged the edge of her demi-cup bra down, exposing her to his hungry mouth and sending a sizzle of pure fire to her core. She clutched at his waist, anchoring herself to him, and arched her back, easing his access to her as he alternately laved and suckled her.

"You taste so good," he said against her sensitive skin. "But it's not enough."

"Not enough?" She could barely manage to get the words past her lips.

"No, I want to taste all of you."

Judd straightened and gently pulled her hands out from

under his T-shirt before he led her back into his room and to
his bed. As she watched in silence, he stripped off his shirt
and kicked off his shoes. She reached for him and unbuttoned the top buttons of his fly, her knuckles brushing against
the unmistakably swollen ridge of his penis. He grabbed her
hands with his.

"That's more than I can handle right now," he groaned,
pressing one of her palms against his erection. "Can't you
feel what you do to me?"

Words failed her. Her entire body was on fire, liquid
molten heat that slowly consumed her inside and out. Judd
skimmed his hands up to her shoulders and slid the straps of
her bra down before reaching behind her and unsnapping the
hooks. The garment fell away from her. He stared at her for
so long she began to feel self-conscious, but then he lifted
his gaze to hers, his eyes glittering.

"You are so beautiful," he said, reaching out one finger
and tracing the pink areola that contracted even tighter under
his gentle touch.

He unfastened her pants and pushed them down her legs,
the black fabric swiftly followed by her panties. He knelt
before her, helping her to step out of the wisp of fabric, then
let his fingers glide up her legs, over her trembling thighs and
pausing for a second to let his fingers brush the moisture that
gathered at their apex.

"You feel so hot, so ready for me," he murmured before
pressing his lips where his fingers had been.

His tongue darted against her most sensitive spot, teasing and tasting as if she were some decadent dessert to be
slowly savored. Anna clutched his shoulders as he increased
the pressure of his tongue, as his lips closed over that sweet
bundle of nerve endings, as she was hit with a sudden sharp
wave of pleasure that radiated from her core and out to her
extremities in a crescendo that tore a cry of satisfaction from
deep within her.

She could barely stand another moment. Judd rose swiftly to his feet and guided her back onto the bed. Against her overheated body the sheets were a welcome stretch of coolness, but that coolness was soon swamped by the heat of Judd's body as he rose over her.

He'd said she was beautiful but he was far more so. The symmetry of his body, the strength of his muscles, the golden tan of his skin and the heavy maleness of his arousal—each inch perfection in itself, let alone presented to her as whole.

He'd already grabbed a condom from somewhere and sheathed himself.

"I'm sorry," he grunted as he positioned himself between her thighs. "This is going to be hard and fast, but I promise to take longer next time." He eased his swollen length inside her, his face flushed with concentration. "And the next," he said, his voice strained as he thrust forward, "and the next."

Anna rocked her pelvis to meet his every move, her hands clutching his forearms as they braced at her sides, her legs wrapping around his hips. Her body responded to his fierce possession, a delicious tightening of her inner muscles heralding another orgasm. And then she was there, spasms of pleasure heightening in concentration until she thought she might break apart from the sheer strength of them. Judd lunged within her, his whole body shuddering as he, too, reached his pinnacle of completion.

When he collapsed against her, his breathing was ragged, his body still rocked intermittently by tiny tremors. It was several minutes before he withdrew and rolled to one side. He stroked away several strands of her hair that had settled over her face.

"I'll be right back," he murmured.

Anna nodded, too shattered to speak. A delicious lassitude consumed her body and she lay back on the sheets, barely daring to believe what had just happened between them. Judd came back from the bathroom and slid into the bed beside her then gathered her to him, whereupon he made good on his promise to take longer the next time. And the next.

Dawn was breaking when she awoke. She was sprawled across Judd's chest, her legs tangled in his as if she couldn't get close enough to him. The last time they'd made love she'd been poised above him, and in their aftermath she'd collapsed right where she lay. Their lovemaking had left her nearly incoherent. She'd never felt this close to another human being ever before.

In bed, Judd Wilson was a completely different man. Gone was the underlying tension that always kept Anna on edge in the office, wondering what was really going on in his keenly intelligent mind. No, in bed there had been nothing between them, quite literally. No past, no future—only the present.

Anna carefully loosed her legs from between his and levered herself onto the sheets beside him. Judd barely moved, lost in a sleep so deep his face relaxed into lines that made him look so much more approachable than he did on a day-to-day basis—less driven, less ruthless.

In the gray light filtering through the windows she looked her fill and wondered where they would go to from here. She couldn't be angry with herself for breaking her long-standing rule—clearly Judd was a man who could never be resisted for long. But now that they'd started this affair, she didn't know what came next. She didn't want the kind of relationship her mother had had with Charles, which, while it was a deep and loving friendship, had never given her mother the full security of marriage which Donna Garrick had quietly craved. Her mother's quiet acceptance of everything had made Anna angry with her for just *settling* for a half life.

Charles and Donna had been occasional lovers, a fact that was governed partially by his diabetes-related impotence and by the strictures of Donna being in his employ. There'd always been an imperceptible barrier between them. One that neither of them had fully crossed. Anna had always felt that her mother had compromised her own happiness for the sake of that vague relationship. Perhaps her need to provide a home and a quality education for her daughter had driven her, or perhaps, after her husband's death, she wasn't prepared to risk her heart again for a passionate love.

Anna had been five when her father had died unexpectedly, and her mother had been offered the position as Charles's housekeeper. Anna had grown up under Charles's roof lacking nothing materially. Deep inside, though, she knew that she wanted more—the emotional strength that came with being intrinsically linked with another soul being first and foremost on her list.

Judd was the kind of man she'd always believed she'd fall in love with one day. His looks aside, his intelligence and ability to provide made him an exceptionally attractive mate. But he was more than all that. This past week she'd seen so many of his strengths—his ability to calm Charles in the wake of Nicole's defection being a perfect example.

Could she have all she wanted with Judd? Did he feel the same way about love and marriage and building a life together forever? Did he feel the same way about her? She almost laughed in the early-morning gloom. God, she was pathetic. Here she was after one night of mind-blowing sex and already she was marching him down the aisle. She didn't even know for certain how compatible they were in other aspects of life. All she knew was that the moment she'd set eyes on him she'd reacted to him on an instinctive level she'd never experienced before. Bearing the brunt of his anger when he'd discovered her deception over her reasons for being at The Masters' had been painful to bear. But once they'd gotten to New Zealand, things had changed. She'd seen sides of him she hadn't suspected before. And then last night…well, last night had changed everything. Now she knew for certain that she wanted a future with him. But was that what he wanted, too?

Guilt drove a splinter into her thoughts. And what about his relationship with his sister? What about hers? Nicole already thought she'd gone over to the enemy by having represented Charles in Adelaide. If she knew that Anna was now considering getting seriously involved with Judd, she'd be even more angry—even more hurt. A lifetime of friendship shattered for a man she'd known for only a matter of weeks.

And what about Charles? How would he react to all of this? He'd seemed to encourage the two of them to spend time together, but would he approve of them having a real relationship?

Of course, all of that presupposed that a real relationship was what Judd wanted with her in the first place. Did she dare to even ask? So much was at stake—so much could be ruined if this went badly. Her job, her closeness to the people who meant the most to her, nearly everything she had, including the roof over her head in the house she'd lived in for nearly all her life, could all be lost.

She looked over again at Judd's sleeping form. Even now, the urge to touch him was irresistible. In spite of herself, she curled up closer at his side, feeling a little thrill of pleasure when his arms tightened around her.

For now, he wanted her and she couldn't deny that she wanted him. And away from her friends, from the gossips at the office, from Charles, he was too tempting to resist. Things would change when they got back to Auckland. If nothing else, she certainly wouldn't want to engage in anything inappropriate under Charles's roof. But for now…for now, she'd fall back asleep in Judd's arms. She'd worry about the consequences later.

Nine

Judd felt Anna's withdrawal from him grow incrementally larger as they got closer to home. It started at breakfast on the last morning of their trip, where she'd suggested eating in the restaurant rather than in their room as they had the past few days, and it had continued through their final appointments and for the duration of their plane trip to Auckland. Now, it was dark as Evans drove them up to the house and even though she was sitting right next to him, it felt like she was a million miles away.

After Evans had taken their bags inside the front foyer and gone to put the car back in the multicar garage, Judd turned to Anna.

"Will you stay with me tonight?"

"Judd..." She shook her head, not making eye contact.

"Why not?"

Suspicion roiled inside of him. Was it because they'd be under his father's roof? Or maybe it was because she'd be sleeping in Charles's bed tonight. Anger flared hard on the heels of his suspicions. She'd been his, all his, the past three nights. Those nights hadn't been anywhere near enough to sate the hunger he had for her and he damn sure wasn't sharing her—especially not with his father.

"It just wouldn't be right," she said, picking up her weekend bag and starting up the stairs.

"We could be discreet," he heard himself say. "Although you would have to try harder not to scream when I—"

"Don't. Just, please don't," she said, her voice shaking and warm color spreading across her cheeks.

"I only want to give you pleasure, Anna. Nothing more."

Her hazel eyes locked with his, and for a few seconds he thought he had her, but then she shook her head again and turned away up the staircase.

He watched her retreat from the bottom of the stairs, his whole body humming with frustration. Leaving his bag at the base of the stairs, he turned and went through to the salon, reaching for the brandy decanter and splashing a measure in one of the crystal tumblers he'd swept up off an engraved silver tray on the sideboard. He knocked back a generous mouthful of the spirit and relished the burn as it traversed its way down his throat.

She might have refused him tonight, he decided, but he hoped it would be the last time she did so. Anna Garrick had become an addiction he had no desire to shake. He finished the last of the brandy and headed for his room and his frustratingly empty bed.

The next morning Judd watched Anna under hooded lids as she summarized their trip to the South Island to Charles— leaving out what he felt to be the most important details, of course. For all her poise and aloof elegance, she was neither poised nor aloof in bed. No, in bed she was voracious and generous, two qualities he held in high esteem in a lover. After that first night they hadn't bothered with booking two rooms again, spending their days visiting various wineries and their nights exploring every inch of one another's bodies.

And what a body. Full in just the right places, and firm in others. A man could lose himself in her. And he had, over and over again. It had been difficult to keep his hands off her when they took their business meetings, especially when he'd seen the way other men looked at her—drawn to her beauty, her charm, her sharp mind tempered with such inherent sweetness. She was phenomenal in every respect, and it had been all he could do to keep from crowing that she was his.

Or rather, she *had* been his, until they'd returned to Charles.

Sleep had been a long time coming last night in his large empty bed. She'd well and truly gotten under his skin, he admitted. He wanted her now, even as she showed Charles a swiftly cobbled together PowerPoint presentation showing where they believed the company would make gains on the current market with their new trend of stocking domestically produced wines.

Judd shifted in his chair to ease the sudden tightness in his groin, his movement drawing Anna's attention. Her eyes flew to his face, a question in them—he merely smiled in response and narrowed his eyes just a little. She blushed, a totally delightful quality, and a dead giveaway as to her physical state. He let his eyes drop deliberately to where her nipples left the tiniest peaks through her bra and against the fabric of her blouse. He didn't mistake her sharp intake of breath, nor her very deliberate body language when she turned away from him and wrapped up the presentation.

"So, you see, Charles, all in all, Nicole was on the right track."

"Well, she's not now," he grumbled. "So you're both convinced that this is the right way to go?"

Judd rose from his chair. "New Zealand has long held a

strong position on the world stage for its superior-quality wines. Our clientele deserves to be offered the exclusivity of these labels. We'd be foolish not to. And, I would suspect, if we don't act soon, someone else will."

"Jackson Importers, you mean?" Charles asked sharply. "We can't have them upstage us. How soon before we can get these varieties into distribution?"

As Anna smoothly took over the logistics of the proposal, Judd sat back to watch her in action. Yes, she was the whole package, all right. Intelligent, beautiful and sexy as hell. And she was his; she just needed a little reminding of it.

Later, after Charles had left the office for the day, Judd called her back into his office.

"Close the door behind you," he instructed as she came in.

"Is there a problem?" she asked as she sealed off the outer office, leaving them cocooned together.

"Oh, yeah, there's a problem, all right."

"What is it? Is it an issue with the new wines?"

"No, come over here."

She did as he asked, a worried crease in her brow. The instant she was within reach, he drew her to him, one hand sliding up her back to cradle the back of her head. He lowered his lips to hers and took them in a kiss he'd been waiting for since yesterday. It had been only hours and yet he'd missed this physicality between them with an ache that had plagued him all last night and all day long.

She pulled away from him. "Stop. What if someone comes in?"

"I've already instructed that all our calls be held. No one will interrupt us, but if you're really worried…"

A few steps across the carpeted floor and the door was securely locked. Anna turned, her back to his desk, and faced him.

"What do you think you're doing?"

He smiled in response. "What I've been wanting to do since we got home."

He backed her up to his desk, boosting her up onto its surface, and, hitching her, oh, so sensible office skirt up to the top of her thighs, he stood between her legs.

"If you won't stay with me in my room, we'll just have to make do," he whispered as he bent his head to her neck and lavished the sensitive skin there with alternating nips of his teeth and licks of his tongue.

He felt the quiver of longing that rippled through her.

"But we're in the office, people will know," she protested, but he knew her heart wasn't in it.

Even now her hands were at his waistband, unfastening his belt and sliding his zipper down to gain access to his body. As her hands freed him from his boxer briefs he shuddered in response, relishing the silky softness of her fingers as they closed around his hardness and squeezed with just the right kind of pressure.

"No one will know but us," he groaned into her mouth as he reached between her legs and found her hot and wet already.

His fingers eased behind the fabric of her panties, sliding along her slick crease, back and forth, back and forth. She moaned in response and he kissed her again, flicking his tongue within her, mirroring his actions with his fingers. She rocked against him, trying desperately to force him to make contact with that part of her that he knew would send her flying over the edge, but this time he wanted to extend the torture just a little longer.

Somewhere along the line in the past few days she'd become necessary to him, and sleeping without her last night had been something he wasn't in a hurry to repeat. He wanted her to want him so much, to need him so much, that she wouldn't consider sleeping without him again.

He eased her back down on the desk and took his time

with his free hand flicking open the buttons of her blouse. One by one he worked his way down, his knuckles skimming the soft swells of her breasts as he lingered on those in particular.

"Please, Judd. Let's just do this."

"In good time," he answered, but even as he did so he privately acknowledged that he wouldn't be able to control his desire for her for much longer. Even now he ached to be inside her, his erection at an almost painful level.

She'd given up touching him, so mindless as she was now to his touch. He bent and blew a cool breath across the exposed skin of her breasts, noting with pleasure how the skin raised in tiny goose bumps, how her nipples pressed against the smooth cups of her bra. This one had a front clasp, he realized with a carnal smile, and he wasted no time in squeezing the clasp and letting it ping open. It was like peeling open a luscious, ripe and forbidden fruit.

There she was, on his desk, upon the papers he'd been working on before their meeting with Charles, her hair spread in disarray over his notations, her blouse fallen open together with her bra and her beautiful luminous skin exposed to his hungry gaze. Her nipples, the palest of pinks, were tight nubs of arousal.

He bent down to take one taut peak softly between his teeth, rolling the tip of his tongue against the hard bead of flesh. Beneath him, Anna moaned and squirmed, her pelvis rocking hard against his hand, still striving to make contact with that part of him that now drove him almost to madness. And this was madness. Taking her here, like this, on his desk. It was the ultimate foolishness, and the ultimate fantasy all rolled into one.

It was too much for him. She'd get her wish—he couldn't wait any longer. He reached into his pocket and pulled out a condom then pushed his trousers and briefs down. Sheathing himself took only a moment, but even as he did so she watched him with eyes glazed with such passion he almost lost it right there and then. He eased off her panties and let them drop to the floor and then spread her legs wide. He would never lose this image of her from his mind, he thought as he positioned himself at her slick entrance.

She groaned as he pushed inside her, a guttural sound that made his balls tighten and the head of his penis swell even tighter. He reached for her hands, linking his fingers through hers and bending her arms up so her hands were beside her head. She lifted her legs up to wrap around his hips and he thrust inside her again, watching her eyes cloud with the sensations that spiraled through her. She had caught her lower lip between her teeth and he felt her ripple against him as he increased his pace. Her body began to shake and a soft cry escaped her. He lowered his face to hers, taking her mouth and absorbing the sounds she made as she crested the peak of their passion, the spasms of her body wringing a climax from him that took all his strength not to shout with the sheer power of it.

He collapsed over her, his breathing hard and fast, the slick of perspiration making his business shirt cling to his back. Suddenly the incongruity of their situation struck him, and a chuckle bubbled up from deep inside.

"We must look a sight from the doorway, hmm?" he said, nuzzling her neck before nipping her skin ever so lightly.

"I can't believe we did that," she said, loosing her fingers from his and pushing firmly on his chest. "I won't be able to face anyone in the main office after that."

"You won't need to. Let's go home for the rest of the day."

"We can't, there's too much to do."

Judd allowed her to push him away and stepped away from her, allowing her to slide off the desk and begin to straighten her clothing. She bent to pick up her panties and wriggled back into them, then she grabbed a wad of tissues from the dispenser on his desk and put out her hand.

"Here, let me get rid of that," she said as he removed the condom.

"I wondered why Nicole kept tissues on her desk," he said.

Anna shook her head. "I doubt that's why she had them there."

He smiled in response. "You never know." He adjusted himself and pulled his briefs and trousers back up, tucking in his shirt and straightening his tie. "There, now no one will ever know but us."

"But they may well wonder," Anna said dubiously. "I always swore I'd never…"

"Never what?"

"Never leave myself open to gossip."

He frowned. "What makes you think anyone will gossip about us?"

Was she worried about it getting back to Charles? So let it, if that was the case. He'd even go so far as to start the rumor himself if it meant he had her wholeheartedly.

"Just the nature of people. It was tough at first, starting here while Mum was still alive. Everyone knew she'd worked for Charles before she left to get married and everyone had something to say about us living with him after my dad died."

"How did that come about, exactly?" Judd asked, hitching one hip against the desk they'd just made love upon. God, even the briefest memory of what they'd just done and it was enough to put his blood on a slow burn again.

"A whole string of things, really. Poor financial decisions on my parents' part, a bit of bad luck, as well. Dad was killed on the job. He was driving to a sales call when a tanker blew a tire and hit a bridge abutment. Dad couldn't stop in time and hit the wreckage. They said he died instantly. It was all so sudden. Mum went from being a happy, stay-at-home wife and mother to a single parent with no income, a stack of funeral bills and no prospects of the life-insurance payout until all the paperwork surrounding the accident was taken care of. Charles approached Mum to offer help and when he realized what a terrible position we were left in, he offered her work and a home for both of us. I was only five, and too young, and too sheltered, to remember most of it. All I knew was that I got to live in a big house and that I had a built-in playmate."

Judd began to put two and two together. "So you grew up with Nicole?"

"Pretty much like sisters, really. Charles even sent me to the same school as her. He did far more for my mother and me than was due. I owe him a lot."

"So, he and your mother. Were they…close?"

"Were they lovers do you mean?" she asked bluntly. "Only very occasionally, from what I understand. Once, after a particularly nasty bout of bullying at school, I confronted Mum about their relationship. She tried her hardest to be honest with me and said that theirs was more a relationship based on companionship. Perhaps she was a bit too honest, but she wanted me to understand. Apparently, one of the long-term side effects of Charles's diabetes was a constant struggle with impotence. It had affected him for years, probably since before you and your mother went to Australia. But you know, even despite their closeness, Mum was always still very much an employee. When I was younger I used to hate that she allowed herself to be taken advantage of that way—now I see it was a choice she made to keep us both secure."

"So you and he—"

"Charles and I what?"

"Were never lovers?"

A look of horror passed across Anna's face. "No! Never. How could you even think that? He's always been a father figure to me, nothing more, nothing less."

"So that night I saw you coming from his rooms, half undressed—"

"I'd been waiting to talk to him about Nicole. I fell

asleep—on his sofa, in his sitting room. And then when I woke up and realized how late it was, I was in a hurry to get back to my room and hop in the shower so I could get ready for dinner. I can't believe you'd have thought that of me." She crossed her way to the office door and pointedly unlocked it. "I'm going to the ladies' room to get rid of this, and then for the rest of the afternoon I'll be in my office if you need me."

Judd felt momentarily giddy from the swell of relief that coursed through him. She wasn't Charles's lover. Her devotion to the old man was merely like that of a daughter. Hard on the heels of that thought, he realized just how much he'd hurt her with his assumption, and discovered that he was genuinely sorry to have upset her so deeply. He needed to make amends.

"Anna?"

She hesitated. "Yes?"

"Look, I'm sorry. I jumped to the wrong conclusions. Let me make it up to you. Stay with me tonight and I'll show you just how much."

She shook her head emphatically. "No, whatever you might think of *me*, I won't disrespect Charles that way."

Without saying another word she swung open the door and stalked off. Judd watched her until she was out of his line of sight before crossing around to the other side of his desk and realigning his paperwork. She hadn't exactly embraced his apology, but at least she hadn't closed the door on them both completely, either. It was time to rethink his strategies with respect to his father and to Anna. One thing he remained certain of—he wanted Anna Garrick for himself—no matter the consequences.

Anna spent the rest of the day at work in a state of total turmoil. Was she destined to be her mother's daughter after all? Was this what it had been like for Donna with Charles? That all he had to do, when he wanted to, was beckon his finger and Donna had been his for the taking, just as Anna just had been with Judd? She'd told herself that their interludes during their trip had been a fluke, that once they got back to Auckland, it would be back to business as usual, but when he'd touched her in the office, she hadn't been able to resist.

Her body still thrummed with the aftereffects of her orgasm, making it difficult to concentrate. That, along with the disbelief and shock that she'd allowed herself to be coerced into making love with Judd in his office, and on his desk no less. She'd have a few bruises tomorrow, no doubt. Her own participation in the event had hardly been that of a submissive.

She'd never been incapable of refusing a man before. She'd been selective with her sexual partners—civilized. This thing with Judd was most definitely not civilized. It was earthy sensuality at its most basic level and it had been, oh, so very good. Even now she wanted him again—but at least this time rationality prevailed. Saying no to him had been driven by her respect for Charles. She smiled at herself. Ironic, it was her respect for the very man who'd made her lose a measure of respect for her mother that now governed her choices and decisions. A psychologist could no doubt have a field day with that.

But there it was. It was how she felt. Charles hadn't had to be a mentor for her in her youth, nor had he been obliged to continue to provide a home for her after Donna had died. Yet he'd been a rock for her. Now she owed it to him to be that rock for him, which—for her, at least—meant not sleeping with his son under his own roof.

It stung that Judd could have thought that she and Charles were having an affair. She shuddered. Nothing could have been further from her mind, or Charles's, she had no doubt. But what would have made him think that?

What, or who?

A niggle of doubt emerged from the back of her mind. Something just wasn't right and she couldn't figure out what or why. But there were so many other things on her mind just now that it was easy to dismiss it.

The next few days kept her very busy in the office. Following up with the wineries they'd visited and processing exclusivity contracts with them, making sure every *i* was dotted and every *t* crossed, was the kind of work she welcomed. Right up until four out of the six wineries they'd sent contracts to sent them back with a note saying they'd received another offer of distribution that they had decided to accept.

Four phone calls later and Anna was feeling sick to her stomach. Jackson Importers had apparently aggressively wooed away the business that she and Judd had thought was in the bag. She wasn't looking forward to sharing the news with Judd or Charles.

As expected, Charles was apoplectic.

"How dare she? I can't believe a daughter of mine would stoop so low as to steal business from her father."

"I hate to point this out," Judd said, "but it was her idea all along. By the looks of things, these people's loyalty sat with Nicole rather than with Wilson Wines. It's my fault for not anticipating this might happen."

"Your fault? Rubbish. She's doing this to spite me."

"Maybe," Judd agreed, "but maybe she just followed through with her new boss on an idea she felt had merit. Did you ever give her credit for coming up with this?"

Anna sat back in her chair, stunned into silence. What was this? Judd championing Nicole? Up until now they'd barely discussed Nicole at all. Anna had assumed that Judd felt the same animosity toward her that Charles did, and had been careful not to bring her up. But to hear him supporting her ideas and giving her props for following them through, that was something Anna had never anticipated from him.

"Of course not, it was her job. She did it competently."

"A little more than competently, I would say," Judd observed, a note of censure in his voice that Anna found herself in total agreement with.

Charles had often been strict with his daughter. He had sheltered her, yes—in that respect he'd taken his responsibilities as a father most seriously. But Anna had seen how being the older, single parent of a beautiful, headstrong daughter had left him feeling that he had to be firm, set high expectations and offer limited praise in order to keep her from running wild.

It probably hadn't helped that he had been so busy with business concerns. Anna knew that Nicole had devoted herself so completely to Wilson Wines in the hopes of winning her father's approval, but it had seemed to add even more tension to their relationship. Charles never grew comfortable straddling the line between boss and father, and had been rather too hard on Nicole in his attempts to avoid showing favoritism. Plus, his old-fashioned attitudes about women in the workplace had been a constant source of irritation between them.

The end result was that Charles had stifled Nicole's adventurous spirit to a point where Anna's friend had often complained to her that she felt her opinions meant nothing to him. Charles did love Nicole, but Anna had always felt as if he struggled with how to show it—and frequently made things worse by saying the wrong thing. In fact, as she'd grown older, it had occurred to her that he may even have actively fostered their friendship so that he could use her as something of a go-between with him and Nicole—someone who could understand both of them and carry messages back and forth without causing offense.

"Well, you'll just have to do it better, my boy. I know you can do it. Let's show Jackson Importers that we're made of sterner stuff. Forget about mounting this New Zealand–based initiative."

"And the wineries who have decided to contract with us, what about them?"

"We'll use them as a test on the market. Could be a flash in the pan—who knows. If it's worth developing further, we'll look into it when the figures start coming in. In the meantime, what about expanding our range of Californian wines?"

After their meeting, Anna went back to her office to create a list of potential contacts for Judd to follow up on based on Charles's directives. She was just checking her email when a message came in that she wasn't expecting to see. Nicole. The subject header was blank, giving her no insight into what the other woman wanted. Feeling as if a thousand eyes watched her, Anna opened the message, her eyes scanning the contents quickly. Her friend wanted to see her, was begging her, in fact. She said she'd meet Anna at a waterfront restaurant in Mission Bay at one o'clock. That was in about ten minutes' time. She could make it from their Parnell offices if she left right now.

Anna chewed her lip. She'd missed Nicole terribly, but the choice her friend had made to join Jackson Importers put them on opposite sides, yet how could she refuse her longtime best friend's request?

The accusations Nicole had flung at her before leaving that awful night had hurt—mostly because she knew she'd deserved them. Loyalty to Charles aside, it had always been her and Nicole. She should have found some way to have given her friend prior warning of the bombshell that was about to be dropped on her life. No doubt Charles would be dead set against her seeing Nicole, but bolstered by Judd's clear support of his sister earlier, Anna reached her decision and fired a response back—*I'll be there.*

Ten

Judd sat in his office and realized that the feeling he'd been carrying around with him for the past several days was happiness. Assuming control of Wilson Wines had turned out to be just the kind of challenge he needed. The pressure being put on them by Jackson Importers gave him an appetite to succeed where his father had failed. Strangely, though, handing Wilson Wines to Nate Hunter on a platter didn't hold quite the appeal he had thought it would anymore. He shook his head slightly. Where was that inner fire that had burned deep down inside all these years? Where was the urge to inflict upon his father a measure of the pain the older man had inflicted upon him? He must be going soft.

Of course, there was still the matter of the house. His mother had emailed him, asking when she could visit and put her redecorating schemes into action. He'd put her off for now, but he knew she wouldn't be held back for long. How Charles would handle being under the same roof as his ex-wife was another matter. Judd had noticed his father tiring in the past week. The half days he was spending in the office were taking a toll but, in typical Charles-like manner, the older man had waved aside Judd's concerns and had flat-out laughed at Judd's suggestion that his father cut back to perhaps only three, or maybe four, half days a week until he was feeling stronger. His father was nothing but stubborn—a trait, he acknowledged, he also shared.

He glanced over the report Anna had left on his desk earlier this morning, barely even seeing the words. Stubbornness didn't just run in the Wilson family. Anna Garrick had her fair share of it, as well. While it had given him no small amount of pleasure to know she wasn't his father's mistress, she still refused to sleep with him under his father's roof. She was nothing if not principled, but it was enough to drive a man to rent a hotel room.

Judd flicked back through the report again. Something didn't make sense. Ah, there it was, it was missing a page. It wasn't like Anna to make a mistake like this. Maybe frustration was eating her up inside, too. And maybe he could persuade her that a hotel room at lunchtime was a good idea.

With a smile on his face, he went through to Anna's office. He cursed softly under his breath—it looked like he'd just missed her. Through her office window he caught a glimpse of a flash of red as her car headed out the office car park and down toward The Strand. He'd have to find the page of the report in her computer himself.

He reached for her mouse and brought her flying-asteroid-ridden screen back to life. Uncharacteristically, she'd left her email account open. Judd went to minimize the window but his sister's name caught his eye. What on earth?

He double clicked on the email and read its contents before flicking to the sent-items folder and seeing what Anna had said in return. Without stopping to get the page he needed from the report, he went and grabbed his car keys before heading out the office. They'd suspected Nicole of following up on her earlier contacts in the Nelson wineries debacle, but what if it had been something else entirely? What if it had been Anna who'd fed his sister the information she'd needed to usurp Wilson Wines all along?

A part of him didn't want to believe it could be true. She was doggedly loyal to Charles—but she'd been vociferous in her support of Nicole, too. Wasn't that what she'd been trying to do the night he'd seen her leaving Charles's rooms? Attempting to defend his sister? A sister she was closer to than he probably ever would be, he acknowledged with an unexpected pang of regret. He had to see for himself what they were up to.

The drive to Mission Bay didn't take long and Judd luckily had no trouble finding a parking spot in the first car park area at the city end of the beach. As he strolled toward the old stone building that housed the restaurant mentioned in Nicole's email, he saw Anna's car also parked nearby. He could just wait here in the sunshine, he thought, and ask her when she returned to her car, but a piece of him wanted to watch the two women together.

He stepped inside the restaurant, his eyes taking a moment to adjust to the darker interior from the autumn sunshine outside. He spied Nicole and Anna immediately in the corner near the back of the restaurant and allowed the maître d' to guide him to a table not in their immediate line of sight but from where he could still observe the two women.

"I ordered for us already," Nicole said, as Anna settled in the chair opposite.

"Thank you, I think."

"Oh, Anna, don't look at me like that, please."

"Like what?"

"Like you don't know whether I'm going to hit you or hug you."

"Well, you weren't exactly happy with me the last time we talked to each other," Anna said with a weak smile.

Nicole smiled back, reaching across the table to squeeze her hand. Anna began to relax. There was the friend she'd known and loved since she was five years old. Somehow they'd sort everything out, it would all be okay. The waiter arrived with chicken Caesar salads for them both, and after he'd gone, Anna gave her friend a good hard look.

"How are you, really?" Anna asked.

Nicole was a little thinner than before, and her face was taut with tension.

"I'm doing okay. Things are...complicated right now."

"You're telling me. Why on earth did you go to work for Nate Hunter? Your father is beside himself."

"Pissed him off, huh?" Nicole said, with her characteristic cheek, before a look of regret shadowed her expressive eyes.

"That's one way of putting it."

"How is he? Someone told me they'd seen him the other day but that he wasn't looking so good. It made me worry about him and it's not like I can just pick up the phone and call him to ask how he is."

"He's doing okay. This whole upset has slowed him down a bit, but—and I'm sure you probably don't want to hear this—Judd is picking up the reins pretty capably."

"Figures. The golden child. Even though I was always there, and he wasn't, I could never measure up to him, you know." Nicole's mouth twisted into a bitter line.

"Your father loves you, Nicole."

"I know, but it's not the same. I could never fill the hole that Judd left, and now he's back."

Anna's heart twisted. She was sure that that wasn't the case. Charles loved both of his children—he'd just gotten in such a habit of being strict with Nicole that he didn't know how to show it. Still, she knew how much it had to hurt to see

Charles lavish the affection on Judd that Nicole had always craved for herself.

"So you won't be coming back to us anytime soon?"

Nicole gave her a haunted look and shook her head. "I...I can't."

"What do you mean, you can't? Of course you can. Your home is with us, your career was with us. Come back, please?"

"No, it's not that simple. Not anymore."

"Why? What is it?"

Nicole shook her head again. "I can't talk about it just now. Maybe later, who knows? I just wanted to see you again and to say sorry for the horrible things I said before. I was upset and I needed someone to blame. Unfortunately, you were it."

"So are we all good now?"

"Yeah, we are. I've missed you so much."

"I've missed you, too."

They finished the rest of their lunch while discussing anything and everything other than work, or men. For some reason Nicole was cagey about the questions Anna started to ask her about Nate Hunter, and Anna certainly wasn't prepared to talk about her feelings for Nicole's brother to her face. It was easier to skirt over those issues and just skim the basics. By the time she had to head back to work, Anna felt so much better for having been able to spend some time with Nicole.

"I'm glad you emailed me," Anna said, standing and giving her friend a hug as their lunch together drew to an end.

"I'm glad you're still talking to me. I don't deserve you, you know."

"Of course you do, and more," Anna replied. "I'll settle the bill, okay? Next time will be your turn."

"Are you sure?"

"That there'll be a next time? Of course there will."

"Not that, silly." Nicole laughed.

Anna felt a sense of relief that she'd finally brought a smile to her friend's face, a smile that, however briefly, dispelled the tension that had been there. She watched Nicole head out the restaurant before she went to the cashier to settle their account. To her surprise, it had already been paid.

"There must be some mistake," she said.

"No, there's no mistake," said an all too familiar voice from behind her. "I figured it was worth the price of lunch to find out what you were up to."

Judd caught her elbow in a firm hold and guided her out the door toward the car park.

"What are you doing here?" she asked, hating the panic in her voice.

"More to the point, what are you doing here?"

"Nicole asked to see me for lunch, that's all."

"All? Seems kind of interesting that the week we lose a considerable amount of business to Jackson Importers you should meet her for lunch. Are you sure you weren't discussing anything else, like the Californian wineries on our list, for example?"

"Of course not! I wouldn't dream of doing anything of the sort." Indignation fueled her to add, "I don't know where you managed to form this incredibly low opinion of me, and I really don't care, but don't keep bringing your insinuations to my face. They are, without exception, wrong."

"So why were you together?"

"We're friends. We've been friends for most of our lives. Did we need a reason?"

"I understood that your friendship was pretty much severed over me."

"Don't rate your effect on people so highly. As I said, we've known each other a very long time. It would take far more than someone like you to destroy that. Look, if you feel that strongly that you can't believe me, why don't you just fire me? In fact, forget that. I quit. I can't work for someone who doesn't even begin to know the meaning of the word *trust*."

Anna pulled her arm free of his hand and headed for her car. She was shaking with anger to think that he could even begin to imagine that she'd do anything to deliberately sabotage Wilson Wines. It would be like slitting her throat, both professionally and personally.

She heard his footfall behind her and she dug in her handbag for her car keys, desperate to get away from him. She wouldn't let him know how much his words today had hurt, just like she hadn't shown him how his belief that she and Charles had been lovers had also cut her.

"Anna, wait!" he called.

But she didn't want to wait. She wanted distance and she wanted it now, before he saw the sheen of tears that now glazed her eyes. Damn it, where were those keys? Long, warm fingers closed over her hand as she finally extracted her keys from the depths of her bag and her finger depressed the remote to unlock her car.

"Anna, stop. I'm sorry. I jumped to conclusions."

"You're pretty good at that,.aren't you?" she said bitterly, blinking back the moisture that stung her eyes.

"What can I say, I have a suspicious mind." He smiled back at her, and despite herself she was charmed by his self-deprecating tone. And that was more than half the problem, she acknowledged. He could get under her defenses with no more than a smile.

"I need to get back to the office. Please let me go."

She stared pointedly at his hand, which still captured hers within its warmth.

"Not yet. I want to apologize to you properly. I've been an idiot and I've treated you very unfairly. In my defense I can only say that it started back in Adelaide."

"But surely you can understand why I didn't tell you the truth about why I was there right from the start? For all I knew, you would have just shipped me off the property—which is what you pretty much did anyway after you read the letter."

"I can understand now. And like I said, I am sorry for allowing myself to let that color my judgment about you."

"Fine, I accept your apology. Now let me go."

"Ah, Anna, in such a hurry to leave me?"

He stepped a little closer and Anna felt that all-too familiar thrum of awareness course through her veins. He was like a drug to her, and she was rapidly losing, becoming addicted. She'd let herself become dependent on his kisses, his touch, everything.

"Don't, please."

She dropped her handbag and put up her hand, but he didn't stop moving, not even when her hand became trapped between the wall of his chest and her breasts. He was so close she could see the silver striations that feathered his irises and lent his eyes their particular vivid blue hue. Her heart quickened as she watched his pupils dilate.

"Don't what?" he asked, his voice soft, enticing.

"Don't kiss me."

"Afraid of me, Anna?"

"No," she admitted. "I'm afraid of me."

"I'll keep you safe," he said.

His kiss was short and incredibly sweet. The seal of a promise that offered so very much—perhaps even a chance of a future together that was no longer threatened by the shadows of his family's past. She was trembling when he released her, her entire body screaming for more than just that brief embrace.

Judd bent to collect her bag and handed it to her, then opened her car door, holding it for her as she slid into the driver's seat.

"Will you be okay to get back to the office?"

"Sure," she said, willing her body back under her control.

"I'll see you there."

"Judd? How did you know where to find me?"

He gave a small frown before answering. "There was a page missing from the report you gave me. I went to your computer to reprint it and you'd left your email open."

So for all his apparent mistrust of her, he hadn't been actively snooping. And, he'd *listened* to her—really listened. The thought gave her another little thrill of hope. Anna nodded and pulled her door closed before starting the engine and backing out of the car space. Judd stood to one side, watching her leave. She gave him a small wave and drove out of the car park.

Judd went straight into Anna's office when he arrived back at Wilson Wines.

"About your resignation," he started, closing her office door behind him.

Anna looked up, surprise on her face. "My resignation?"

"Yeah, back at the restaurant. You quit, remember?"

"Ah, yes, so I did."

"Just for the record, I don't accept it."

"For the record," she repeated, a tiny smile on her face, before slowly nodding. "Okay. So we're all good now—I can get back to work?"

"No."

"No? What's wrong?"

"I miss you," he answered simply.

"Miss me? But we see each other every day," she protested.

"Is that enough for you? Really? Tell me, Anna, how are you sleeping at night, knowing I'm just down the hall from you—wanting you as much as you probably want me?"

He watched the muscles in her throat work as she swallowed.

"What? Lost for words?" He moved across the office and

sat in the chair opposite her desk. "Seems to me that we have a pretty good thing between us. Wouldn't you agree?"

"Physically, yes," she finally concurred, although he could see how reluctant she was to admit even that.

"Don't you think we should let that play out? Keep exploring it to its fullest potential?"

To his surprise, sadness seemed to cloud her eyes. Her voice, when she spoke, was flat. "No, I don't. Tell me, Judd, how do you define *potential?*"

Her words surprised him. "Define it? Are you kidding me? You mean you have this level of physical synchronicity with every man you sleep with?"

"And there we have it," Anna said, throwing her hands in the air. "Just how many men do you think I've slept with?"

"Does it matter?"

"No, it doesn't matter, but you continually imply I have loose morals. First you accuse me of sleeping with your father, then you jump to the ridiculous conclusion that I was sharing company information with Nicole." She shook her head emphatically. "There's no way I can even begin to contemplate any kind of relationship with you when you don't trust me at all—over anything!"

"You're right," he admitted, deciding to take another tack on this argument.

He had assumed the worst about her all the way. In the beginning that had partly been her own fault, but he was man enough to admit it had been far easier to remain guarded around her than it was to examine just how much he wanted her, or why. He'd hoped that, as with all his conquests, he'd enjoy the ride while it lasted. After all, he didn't plan to stay in New Zealand forever.

The moment he thought that, though, everything in his mind rebelled. For some reason this had stopped being a temporary fling. He'd gone at this whole exercise looking upon everything as being temporary—expendable even. But somewhere along the line things had changed, and that change started with Anna.

Her voice pulled his attention back. "Of course I'm right. So you'll agree that we should forget about there being any kind of relationship between us, except for at work."

"I can't do that, Anna."

"I beg your pardon?"

"I can't do that. What I can do, if you'll let me, is learn to trust you. To get to know you better and to show you that I'm worth you giving me that chance. Will you at least try with me?"

He watched as her emotions played across her face.

"You want me to try to let *you* trust *me*? You hurt me, Judd—both on a professional level and on a personal one. After we made love down in Nelson and here, in your office—" Her voice hitched and she paused and swallowed before continuing. "Did you honestly think I was so promiscuous as to go from one man's bed to another, and back again?"

"Since we're being honest, I have to admit that it made me furious to think that you could do that."

"But I'm not like that!" Her voice rose in obvious frustration.

"I know that, Anna. I'm learning all the time."

"Fine. Okay, I will try with you. But on one condition."

"What's that?" he asked, knowing the answer before she even verbalized it and hating that, in this at least, he could read her so well.

"I'm not sleeping with you. Not straightaway. We can get to know each other the way normal couples do."

"We've missed a few steps, that's true."

"And I want your word of honor that you won't try to persuade me otherwise. I'm helpless against you. There, I admit it. Show me that I can trust *you*. Don't use that knowledge against me."

Every particle in his body rebelled against the idea, but he found himself nodding in agreement.

"Agreed," he managed, even though his jaw felt tight and his throat barely allowed the single word past it. "A date tonight, then. That'd be a good start. I'll meet you downstairs in the lobby at the house at seven."

What the lady wanted, the lady was definitely going to get. And while it would be a living torment every second until she capitulated to him, he knew that very soon, she'd be his again. And once she was, no matter what his plans for Charles Wilson, he knew she'd stay by *his* side.

Eleven

Anna waited in the lobby at the house and paced the black-and-white-tiled entrance nervously. This was going to be their third date in the three days since last Thursday, when they'd agreed to take things slowly and learn to get to know one another. So far it had been an exercise in pure torture. Judd had been nothing but a complete gentleman. It was driving her crazy.

Today he'd apparently planned a picnic and told her to dress accordingly. Without any idea of what one wore to a picnic these days, she'd opted for a pair of flat navy leather shoes with a peep toe and clear-colored beads embroidered on top, and teamed them up with a pair of three-quarter-length jeans with the cuffs rolled up and a fine-knit pale pink sweater.

Charles came through the lobby.

"Heading out again?" he asked.

"A picnic today, apparently."

He chuckled. "Have to hand it to the boy. He's not only

picked up the business quickly but he hasn't wasted time with you, either. I knew sending you to get him would be a good idea."

A frisson of discomfort spread through her at his words. Had he meant all along for her and Judd to become close? She didn't like the sensation of being manipulated, not even by Charles, who had probably had the greater hand in guiding her life than anyone she knew—even herself. Before she could respond, Judd came down the stairs.

Dressed in jeans and a silver-gray long-sleeved turtleneck, he looked good enough to eat. Anna blinked and turned her head away. She shouldn't be thinking about him along those lines. He'd adhered to her dictates about their dating to the letter. It was contrary of her to wish now that he hadn't.

"All ready, that's good."

Judd flung her a smile that lent his eyes a wicked gleam. He was up to something, she just knew it. Every cell in her body responded to him as he drew closer and put an arm around her shoulders.

"We'll probably be out for most of the day. Will you be okay?" he asked his father.

"Sure, I'm fine. There's always someone around here if I need something." Charles waved his inquiry away.

Anna looked at the older man sharply. His color wasn't good today and there was an air of frailty about him that sent a ripple of concern through her.

"Are you feeling all right today?" she asked. "We can postpone our outing, it's no bother."

"Anna, I've said it before and I'll say it again. Stop your fussing. I'm big enough and old enough to look after myself. Now off you go and have a great day. Don't you worry about me."

"You heard the man," Judd said, steering her toward the front doors. "Besides," he reminded her when they were out of Charles's earshot, "the household staff has our cell numbers. I've already talked to them about calling me if he seems like he needs help."

"So you agree with me, then. He's not looking so good this week, is he?"

"I've noticed. At the beginning of the week I tried to talk to him about cutting his hours down, but he's nothing if not stubborn."

"A family trait, no doubt," Anna commented.

Judd's lips quirked in response. "No doubt," he agreed.

They went out the front doors of the house and down the stairs to the driveway. Anna looked around but there was no sign of a car.

"Are we walking? Maybe I should change my shoes."

"No, don't change a thing. You're perfect as you are. We need to go to the tennis courts."

"Tennis? Then I definitely need to change my shoes."

"No, we won't be playing tennis," Judd answered.

Totally puzzled, Anna walked alongside him. As she did, she became aware of the air-beating sound of rotors coming toward them. A helicopter? Sure enough, a sleek black chopper was coming toward them, stirring up the air and the early-falling leaves as it lowered onto the tennis courts at the end of the property.

Anna turned and looked at Judd. "You said we were going for a picnic."

"And we are. Just not locally."

He shepherded her to the helicopter and opened the rear door, handing her up into one of the seats and passing a headset to her before following her up and settling in next to her. Anna felt her stomach lurch as the chopper slowly lifted off and circled the property before heading out toward the harbor.

"Did I mention that I don't like small aircraft to you?" she asked, her knuckles white as she gripped the edges of her seat.

Judd's hand pried one of hers free from its hold. "I remember, but I was hoping that perhaps I could distract you on this trip."

He lifted her hand to his mouth and kissed her palm. The instant his lips touched her she felt the familiar tug of desire swell through her body. Oh, yes, he could distract her that way, all right. She hazarded a look out the window as Judd stroked the soft inner skin of her wrist, then dragged her eyes back to him again. His clear gaze met hers.

"Trust me, Anna. I won't let anything hurt you."

She nodded and swallowed, his voice soft and gentle as it filled her ears from within the cups of her headphones. He kept up a steady stream of soothing words, and she'd lost track of how long they'd been in the air when the helicopter began to descend and her stomach lurched again. Judd's fingers closed around hers reassuringly.

"You're doing great," he said. "Anyone would think you're an old hand at this."

"I doubt that, but thanks," she managed, feeling a surge of relief as the skids touched down on terra firma. Judd opened his door and hopped down before turning to help Anna out.

"Keep your head and arms down," he warned.

No problem, she thought as the wind whipped her hair around her face. She ducked down and let Judd lead her toward a glass-fronted building not far from where they'd landed. Behind them, the helicopter took off and wheeled away back over the water.

"He is coming back for us, right?" she asked.

Judd laughed, the sound curling around her heart and squeezing it tight. She felt a momentary panic. When did he start meaning so much to her?

"Of course, all in good time."

"Where are we?" Anna asked, looking around her. As far as she could tell, the dwelling ahead of them was the only one to be seen and there were no boats moored at the small bay in front of them.

"Near Kawau Island. I heard about this place and thought we'd enjoy the solitude. Come on, let's go and see what's on the menu."

Anna followed him up to the building and inside, where a spacious lounge/dining area flowed into a well-equipped kitchen. As Anna walked around to get the lay of the land, a small but luxurious bathroom with floor-length clear-glass windows facing back into native bush behind the building surprised her, while another room, a bedroom, saw her closing the door on it quickly. She didn't want to think about that. Not when they were just starting to get to know one another.

In the kitchen, Judd had removed a bottle of chilled champagne from the refrigerator as well as a platter of antipasto.

"Let's take this outside," he suggested. "Grab the glasses, will you?"

Anna reached for a pair of champagne flutes from a shelf over the kitchen sink and followed Judd out onto the wide deck that faced the bay.

"This is beautiful," she said, sitting down next to Judd on the simple wooden steps that led down off the deck and onto a well-kept lawn. "It's like a world within a world."

Judd reached up and smoothed a strand of hair from her cheeks. "It's a great place to get to know one another better, without everything else intruding."

He deftly dealt with the foil and the cage on the bottle before pouring them each a foaming glass of the golden sparkling liquid.

"Mmm, French," Anna commented, sighting the label and then taking a sip. "Oh, yes, there's nothing quite like it."

Judd didn't comment, and her eyes flew to his in the silence that stretched out between them. He was watching her, his gaze intent, the pupils dilated, his lips parted as if he'd been about to say something but the words had fled before they could be uttered. He blinked, breaking the spell that had locked them together all too briefly, and lifted his glass to his lips.

"I agree," he said, putting his glass down and reaching for a stuffed olive on the platter. "The French definitely have a knack for it."

They fell silent for a while, enjoying the wine, the food, the setting, but then Anna turned to Judd to ask, "Do you remember much of your time with your father, before you went to Australia?"

He sighed and for a moment she wondered if she'd trod on some very sensitive memories.

"I remember quite a bit. I was six when we left. I remember him always being larger than life. Always busy, always entertaining, always booming with noise. I couldn't wait for the moment he stepped in the door at the end of a day, and when he was away on business I'd mark every day off on the calendar until he returned. Despite the fact he was constantly busy with work and clients, he always made time for me."

"It must have been hard when you left."

"Hard?" He laughed but the sound held no joy to it. "I was devastated. My mother was angry and hurt, and no one in Australia had a good word to say about him. It was like my life had turned upside down overnight. I had quite a few issues with his abandonment of me—of both of us."

"No wonder you weren't keen to reestablish a relationship with him."

"No, I wasn't. Despite the fact that I know there are two sides to every story, I find it very hard to understand, or forgive, the way he just cut me from his life like that."

Judd's dark brows drew together, lending a fierce cast to his features.

"But he's reached out to you now. You're here, you're working with him. You must have forgiven him."

The expression on Judd's face cleared. "Yes, I am working with him now."

There was something in the tone of his voice that struck a chord of concern deep inside. It occurred to her that he hadn't agreed that he had forgiven his father. Before she could say anything more, he flashed a smile at her and rose to his feet, putting out a hand.

"Come on, let's go for a wander along the shoreline."

Anna put her hand in his and pushed her worries aside. She was probably being oversensitive, a state she was becoming used to around Judd Wilson.

When they returned from the beach, they went inside to gather together the rest of the lunch fixings that had been left in the fridge for them. Judd poured them each another glass of champagne outside on the deck, while Anna made up plates of slices of fresh-baked ciabatta together with ripe wedges of Camembert and slivers of prosciutto. She added a few slices of sun-dried tomato from the leftover antipasto to the open sandwich she'd put together on her plate and lifted it to her mouth to take a bite.

"Oh, my, that's good," she said after she'd chewed and swallowed the mouthful.

"It looks delicious," Judd agreed. "Mind if I have a taste?"

"Sure," she said, offering him her sandwich.

He ignored the offering in her hand, instead leaning over their dishes, and licked the lower edge of her bottom lip. She saw a tiny piece of cheese on the tip of his tongue before he swallowed it.

"Oh, yes, just how I like it. Ripe and soft. Warm and ready to eat."

A heated flush spread through her, a flush that made every nerve ending stand on end. It had been her call to keep the physical side of their discovery of one another out of the equation. A call he'd respected to a degree that had slowly begun to drive her crazy. Crazy for him.

"Would you like some more?" she managed to say, not taking her eyes from his.

"Sure," he answered.

She picked up a small wedge of the cheese between a thumb and forefinger and held it up to his mouth. His lips closed around the morsel, his tongue abrading her fingers as he did so and sending a shudder of longing straight to the pit of her belly. A familiar tingling started low down in her body and spread out to her extremities.

"More?" she asked.

Instead of answering, he reached out to cup one hand behind her head and gently drew her to him.

"More of you," he said simply before his mouth took hers.

His lips were gentle, coaxing, and she felt herself melt into him. She heard the clatter of dishes as he swept them to one side before hooking his arm around her waist and sliding her closer to him. Suddenly she couldn't be close enough. Her arms lifted and hooked around his neck, her breasts pressed up against his chest—and still she wasn't close enough.

She pulled her lips away.

"Um, Judd? About that condition I made? About us not..."

"Uh-huh," he said, nuzzling her neck.

"I was reacting under duress. I—"

"Anna?"

"Mmm?"

"Shut up and kiss me again."

So she did. Judd lifted her up and guided her to straddle his lap, shoving his hands up under her top and across her back. His hands were hot against her skin and she wanted to feel more of him. She reached for the hem of his sweater, pulling it up and exposing his belly and chest before grazing her nails across his muscled torso. Beneath her fingertips she felt the disks of his nipples grow firm and rigid and she gently pushed him back down onto the wooden deck. As she did so, Judd eased the turtleneck off, leaving his upper body completely bare to her touch.

She bent down and placed a kiss in the hollow at the base

of his throat before tracing her tongue across his collarbone. Every now and then she paused to nip at his skin. He felt so fine, tasted so good, she wanted to savor every second she had with him at her mercy. Her fingers traced the muscles that corded his rib cage, feeling his skin react under her feather-fine touch, and she smiled against his skin as she traced ever-decreasing circles with her tongue around his nipples.

Her hands worked their way lower, slowly unbuckling his belt and unbuttoning his jeans before easing inside the now-constricted fabric. She rubbed one hand along the length of his powerful erection, back and forth through the fabric of his briefs, her lips slowly following the path of her hands until her breath warmed his skin at his waistband. She tugged at his jeans and he lifted his hips slightly, allowing her to slide the fabric down to his thighs and tug down the elasticized band of his briefs, exposing the tip of his arousal to her gaze. A tiny bead of moisture gathered at the swollen dark tip of him and she bent her head, tasting it with the very tip of her tongue.

Oh, yes, he tasted so very good. She closed her lips around him, rasping her tongue around his tender flesh again and again before she drew him deeper into her mouth. Judd's fingers pushed through her hair, cupping her head and holding her against him. Not so firmly that she couldn't withdraw if she wanted to, but encouraging her to continue her assault on that most sensitive and responsive part of him.

Anna curled the fingers of one hand around the base of his shaft and moved them firmly up, then down again, all the time taking him deeper into her mouth while stroking her tongue along him with ever-increasing pressure. She felt him begin to shake beneath her and increased the speed of her movements, one hand still stroking him, the other clutching at the bunched fabric of his jeans. A groan tore from his throat as he began to come, and she took it all with a sense of power that vied with her own arousal to see him so undone beneath her ministrations. She might be helpless in the face of her desire for him, but he was equally so for her, she realized, and the knowledge gave her a sense of control and power she'd never known before.

Spent, Judd relaxed back on the deck, his fingers still tangled in her hair as she slowly released him, first with her hand, then with her mouth. She slid up his body, peppering the surface with tiny kisses all the way, swirling her tongue inside the indent of his belly button—the action making his penis twitch in response against her.

She rolled to his side, letting the fingers of one hand stroke softly over his belly and chest as his breathing slowly returned to normal.

"When you change your mind, you really change your mind, don't you?" he said.

"I like to do things thoroughly, or not at all," she replied in kind.

"Then you won't object if we go inside, where we can *thoroughly* explore the aspects available to us?"

In reply, Anna rose to her feet and held out a hand to Judd's supine form. He took her hand and levered himself up, straightening his briefs and yanking his jeans up to his hips, but leaving them undone. She had never seen anything so sexy before as the man standing in front of her. His hair was mussed, his eyes still glowing with the residual pleasure she'd given him. And his body—he was muscled but not heavily, strong but not overpowering. And he was looking at her like she was the only woman in the world. He was everything she'd ever dreamed of, and more. Judd lifted up the champagne bottle and their glasses, and together they walked back into the cottage.

He hadn't been kidding about being thorough. By the time the helicopter returned for them, it was dark and Anna had never felt more sated on every level. Together they'd made love, eaten, bathed, made love and eaten again. If she could ever repeat a day in her life over and again, it would be this one and it was with this thought that Anna acknowledged the truth of her feelings. She was in love with Judd Wilson.

Twelve

Judd woke to a Monday morning heralded by rain and gusting winds. The flip side of autumn had arrived, and with it Anna had capitulated. Last night she'd come to him, breaking what she had insisted was her hard-and-fast rule about respecting Charles and refusing to sleep with Judd under his father's roof. Strangely, he hadn't felt the smug satisfaction he'd expected when he'd felt her slip naked in between the sheets of his bed.

Something had changed during the day while they'd been alone together. Something that made her body curving around his, within the expanse of his bed, the most natural thing in the world. Something he didn't want to deal with. Later would be soon enough, he decided, as he rolled out of the covers and padded on bare feet across the thick carpet toward his en suite bathroom.

By the time he'd completed his shower, Anna had left his bed, and when he got downstairs to the breakfast room she was already there, looking her usual serene and unruffled self and talking to Charles. No one would have dreamed she was such a vixen in bed.

"Good morning," he said with a smile.

To his delight, she blushed. "Good morning to you, too."

"Sleep well?"

He couldn't resist provoking her. He, better than anyone, knew how well she had slept in those tiny snatches when they were both so exhausted they finally left one another well alone.

"Thank you, I did," she replied before lifting her morning coffee to her lips.

Lips that had done wild things to him yesterday. He slammed the door on his wayward thoughts. There was a time and a place for everything. For now he needed to concentrate on Wilson Wines. He felt like he'd reached a crossroads in relation to the business. While he'd come here with the express intent of undermining everything his father had worked for, and delivering his share of the business on a platter to his father's strongest competitor, there was a part of him now that hesitated.

Growing Wilson Wines in a new direction excited him, but did he really want to throw away the revenge he'd longed for ever since he'd accepted his father would never come to get him? It was a difficult decision, and one he would have to face soon.

As an added factor, his mother had started to email him regularly, asking for updates on the house and pestering him to allow her to visit. Right now, Cynthia was the last complication he needed. Her bitterness toward Charles had only grown over the years, and the prospect of seeing the two of them under one roof again was enough to make the milk in his cereal curdle.

He shot a look across the table at Charles. The older man looked gray and tired. Judd had no doubt that following through on his initial plans would see his father into an early grave and that thought clenched tight in his chest. Some-where along the line, he'd developed respect for Charles and particularly for his business acumen. He'd held it together through stock market crashes, recession and more. Wilson Wines, while not reaching its fullest potential, was still doing extremely well in what had been a difficult and competitive market.

Judd still bore a grudge over the way Charles had handled his personal life, and the way he had treated his wife and son, but he felt a little more sympathy now. He'd seen how deeply angry and hurt Charles could be at what he perceived as dis-loyalty from someone he loved. Even though he'd jumped to conclusions and judged unfairly, the suspicion that Cynthia had been cheating on him must have hit him hard.

Additionally, the challenges for Charles of running a company—by himself, since the split with his business part-ner had happened around then, hadn't it?—and dealing with a marriage that had been falling apart must have taken its toll on his behavior. And according to Anna, Charles was already struggling with diabetes-related health issues then, which couldn't have helped. None of that justified his actions, but taking everything into account did help to put them in per-spective.

He looked again at Charles, watched as he picked up his knife to butter a slice of toast and saw the way his hand trembled, then looked away as a sharp spear of concern shot through him. He didn't want his father's further deterioration to be on his hands.

A loud clatter of cutlery on a plate, followed by Anna's gasp of shock, dragged his attention back to Charles, who now leaned to one side in his chair, his color even worse than before, his eyes closed and his breathing laboring in his chest.

"Quick," he said to Anna, "call an ambulance."

Anna raced out the room and Judd shot to his father's side, loosening his tie and the top button of his shirt before lowering Charles to the floor. Charles's skin was cool and clammy to the touch, and Judd felt a surge of genuine fear pour through him.

Charles slipped in and out of consciousness, oblivious to Judd's voice as he repeatedly fired questions at him in an effort to keep his father awake. By the time the ambulance arrived, Judd was beginning to worry that the older man wouldn't make it.

As Anna gave the paramedics a rundown of Charles's health and medications, he began to understand just how fragile his father's life was.

"I'll go with him in the ambulance," Judd said as Charles was lifted onto a gurney and carted out toward the waiting vehicle.

Anna nodded and squeezed his hand. "I'll see you at the hospital. I'll just need to make a few calls first. Let people know we won't be in to the office."

"Thanks."

Judd followed the medics out to the ambulance and was directed into a passenger seat in the front of the vehicle. The ride to Auckland City Hospital was short, although for Judd it felt as if it took hours. Craning his head to see in the back, he watched as the ambulance officer attended to his father and took stats, which he then radioed ahead to the hospital emergency room. Seeing Charles so helpless made the seriousness of his father's state really hit home.

At the hospital there was a blur of activity, and Judd was forced to wait as a medical team took over his father's assessment and treatment. Finally Anna arrived, her face pale and concerned but lightening a little when she saw him. The instant they made eye contact, Judd began to feel some of the tension within him unwind just a notch and he took Anna into his arms, relishing the feel of her and soaking up the comfort her embrace provided.

"How's he doing?" Anna said as she pulled away.

"They're still doing tests."

A sudden flurry of activity at the emergency room door dragged his attention in that direction and he saw his sister striding through the door.

"Where is he? I want to see him."

Anna interceded before he could speak.

"He's with the doctors. They're still assessing him."

"What happened?" Nicole demanded, turning to Judd, her eyes snapping fire.

"He collapsed at breakfast," Judd replied.

"I thought your being here was supposed to make him feel better, not worse," Nicole fired back before promptly bursting into tears.

Judd bit back the response that flew to his tongue, that perhaps if his sister hadn't left the way she did, Charles wouldn't have been pushing himself so hard with work when he should have been taking things easier. But he could see Nicole was fighting her own demons.

A nurse came toward them. "Mr. Wilson, you can see your father now."

Judd reached for Anna, who shook her head. "No, take Nicole. She needs to be with him more than I do."

With a shrug, Judd turned to Nicole. "Are you coming?"

"Of course I'm coming. He's *my* father."

Together they followed the nurse. Charles was conscious but still looked terribly ill. Lines ran into his arms and monitors were beeping around him.

"What's she doing here?" he rasped, staring at Nicole with a mixture of surprise and anger.

Judd felt his sister stiffen at his side.

"I came to see if you were all right, but obviously you're just fine. You won't be needing me here," she said with a quiet dignity that didn't quite mask the hurt in her eyes.

Judd watched her walk back the way she'd come. Anna

went to intercept her but was brushed away as Nicole kept walking straight toward the exit.

"Was that really necessary?" Judd asked his father, going to stand next to his bed.

"She betrayed us. She made the decision to leave us—that means that this isn't her place any longer, here with us. You'd do well to remember that, my boy." The strain of forcing the words he'd had to say took its toll, and Charles's eyes slid closed again.

A bitter taste flooded Judd's mouth. Betrayed, yes, like his father had betrayed the love and trust of his only son by sending him away—banishing him with his mother to another country. Judd couldn't believe that only an hour ago, he'd been halfway convinced he should forgive his father's actions. The man didn't deserve Judd's compassion, or his forgiveness. Look at how he'd just treated his daughter—banishing her with the same ease he'd banished Judd and his mother so long ago. The concern he'd felt for his father diminished as it was replaced by the old familiar anger, and with it, his resolve to continue on his original course hardened.

Anna straightened up the last of the paperwork she'd been collating and put it in her briefcase, ready to bring home and discuss with Judd this evening. She and Judd took turns at the hospital during the allocated visiting times—today was his turn while she covered at the office.

Charles had slipped into a coma after his admission and things had been touch-and-go over the past five days. If he recovered, it was clear that dialysis would be a regular part of his life from here on in. There was no word yet on when he would be allowed back home, but Anna had already made inquiries with private nursing bureaus to ensure he had the care he would need when, God willing, that eventually happened.

While Judd went through the motions of visiting with his father, Anna was certain there was a new distance now between son and father. Something had happened on the day Charles was admitted to hospital, which had created an intangible wall between them. Judd wouldn't be drawn on the subject and Nicole had also retreated back behind her curtain of silence. Well, there was nothing for it but to be there if they needed her, Anna had decided and, as far as Judd was concerned, being where she was needed meant that she was in his bed at night and by his side during the day.

Rain swiped at her windscreen as she drove home. It was already dark and she was bone weary as she pulled her car into the multicar garage at the back of the house. What she needed most right now was a long, relaxing soak in the bath, followed by dinner and maybe a good movie. She wondered if Judd would be up for that, too. A bath together would be just the distraction they both deserved after the past working week. She already could feel herself relaxing by increments as she imagined it.

Anna felt the difference in the house the moment she set foot inside. It wasn't anything she could immediately put her finger on, but something had changed and it was more than the fact that the hall flowers were arranged on the left-hand side of the hall table, rather than the middle where they normally stood.

She made her way to the front of the house and the main stairs but her feet arrested on the tiled surface of the lobby as a vaguely familiar voice greeted her from halfway up the stairs.

"I should have known you'd be living here," Cynthia drawled with an expression of distaste on her elegant features.

"Cynthia? I didn't know you were coming," Anna managed through lips that felt stiff with shock.

"I'm sure Judd doesn't find it necessary to tell you *everything*, my dear," Cynthia replied as she continued down the stairs and came to a halt one step up from the bottom—a position that continued to force Anna to look up at her.

"I trust Mrs. Evans has made you comfortable."

"Mrs. Evans? Oh, yes, that housekeeper. She'll have to go when I'm back here permanently, you know. No idea of etiquette whatsoever."

"What do you mean, when you're here permanently?"

"When my ex-husband dies, of course. I came as soon as I heard he was ill. So sad for you all, but only to be expected."

"Charles is improving every day. I don't know where you got the idea that he's dying," Anna replied staunchly. "And I'm not that certain he would like you under his roof."

"I think you're forgetting a vitally important point," Cynthia said with a smile that was as cold as the expression in her eyes.

"And what would that be?" Anna asked, feeling the hairs on the back of her neck rise in response to the woman's attitude.

"That this is Judd's house now and, very soon, he'll be giving it to me."

With that, Cynthia swept past Anna in the direction of the salon. All thoughts of a relaxing bath now banished from her mind, Anna went upstairs to her room to change and try and clear her head. Of course the house was now Judd's. How could she have forgotten that? Had he planned to install his mother back in here all along? And what of Charles? What would happen to him when he was well enough to come out of the hospital?

She rushed through a shower and changed into a more comfortable pair of wide-legged black trousers and a long-sleeved tunic top, also in black but chased with silver threads that broke the starkness of the garment. Once she was dressed and had reapplied her makeup, she felt better able to cope with the perfectly coiffed woman who was downstairs. During her shower she'd all but talked herself into believing that Cynthia was sadly mistaken and that Judd transferring the property into her name was a possibility so remote it was laughable.

But a tightening low down in her gut told her it was entirely possible. The doubts that she'd had for the past few days surged up to remind her of what Judd had told her about his mother's obsession with Masters' Rise.

Anna drew in a deep breath and tried to summon the courage she knew she'd need to face Cynthia downstairs. No, it was no good. No amount of breathing would make her feel right about this. She'd just have to haul on her big-girl panties and get it over with. She descended the stairs with a knot in her stomach the size of a boulder, and headed for the salon. Inside, Cynthia sat upon one of the love seats, a glass of wine in her hand and a disapproving look upon her face.

"I'll need to do quite a bit of upgrading," she commented. "Charles has really let this place slide."

Anna felt her back stiffen in response. Not only had Charles done everything *but* let the place slide, Anna's mother had enjoyed a free hand in redecorating and refurbishing as and when required.

"It's a home," Anna answered carefully. "Charles felt it was important that we be comfortable."

"Well, you've certainly been comfortable here, haven't you? I imagine it was quite the come up in ranks from where you and your mother used to live. Tell me, how is dear Donna these days?"

"My mother passed away several years ago," Anna responded uncomfortably. She'd bet Cynthia never called Donna Garrick "dear" anything to her face the whole time she'd known her.

"I am sorry to hear that." Cynthia took a sip of her wine before continuing, "And yet, you're still here. Why is that?"

"Charles said it was to be my home for as long as I wanted."

"But it's no longer his place to offer you that roof over your head." Cynthia shook her head, an expression of sympathy on her face that looked as false as the tone of her voice. "I'd suggest you begin looking elsewhere for your accommodation, although I doubt you'll be as lucky as to find anyone as...*accommodating* as Charles."

"I really don't think it's quite your place to suggest where I should be living," Anna snapped back, suddenly angry where before she'd only felt apprehension. "Judd wouldn't dream of putting me out from under his roof."

"Ah, so the kitten has claws. How charming." Cynthia laughed—the sound grating along Anna's last nerve. "Although you may not feel quite so inclined to leap to Judd's defense when you understand what Judd's plan was all along. Ask yourself, with everything he has in Adelaide, why else would he have come back if not for some well-aimed revenge? It's not as if Charles was ever a father to him.

"You look shocked. Poor dear, I suppose Judd has taken you to his bed and now you've gone and fallen in love with him." Cynthia shook her head and tsked softly. "He's only using you, you know. Despite everything, Judd's a lot like Charles. He won't marry you. Do you really think you're worthy of a place like this when your mother never was? Like father like son, like mother like daughter. My son will ask you to leave soon enough. Wouldn't you rather save face and go before that happens?"

Anna reeled under the onslaught of Cynthia's words. "Judd wouldn't do that," she said woodenly.

Or would he? Her fingers curled in her palms, her nails biting into the skin—the pain an offset to the pain that now squeezed her heart tight. She really didn't know Judd Wilson beyond what he'd presented to her. She knew he was determined and had an edge of ruthlessness lingering beneath the surface at all times. Could Cynthia's words be the truth? She didn't want to believe it. She loved him. He wasn't that kind of man.

Anna felt an arctic chill shiver through her body. Despite her instinct to protest Cynthia's words, they held all too much of a ring of truth about them. The older woman had given voice to Anna's greatest fear—that she would never have the wholehearted love of the man she loved in return.

Thirteen

Judd was exhausted as he got out of his car and climbed the front steps into the house. Funny how it had so rapidly begun to feel like home, he realized, when before it had always been nothing more than something to be acquired and used. Perhaps it was the thought of the woman waiting inside for him. He knew Anna had already left the office and would be waiting for his report on Charles's condition.

He felt like a hypocrite attending the old man at the hospital, but today hadn't been a good one for his father, with his health deteriorating further. Even unconscious, Charles didn't make a good patient. In fact, Judd suspected the word "patient" was totally lacking in his vocabulary. Still, he'd seemed more settled when Judd had left him.

It had been a tough day all around, really. He'd battled with his decision to go ahead and test the waters with Nate Hunter but, in the face of Charles's treatment of Nicole at the hospital, eventually he'd decided to go ahead. He'd spent the better part of the morning trying to set up a meeting with

Hunter, but the man was as elusive as quicksilver. Judd hadn't wanted to leave a message with Nate's staff—all too aware that Nicole could easily intercept it and somehow block him reaching the other man altogether. Maybe tomorrow would see success.

Judd considered the paperwork inside his briefcase. He hadn't dared to leave it in the office in case Anna saw it before he'd completed his plans. Everything had to be lined up just so for all this to work. She wouldn't be happy, and he hoped their burgeoning relationship would weather the fallout once it all went ahead. Her place was with him now; surely she'd see he had no other choice.

He waited for the sense of satisfaction that usually infused him when he thought of his plans coming to fruition, but instead he felt oddly flat. Must just be tired, he rationalized. Between nights with Anna, demanding days in the office and even more demanding time at the hospital, he was definitely not operating at his peak.

As he entered the front lobby he could hear women's voices from the salon. He dropped his briefcase near a hall table and walked through, gritting his teeth as he tried to force a welcoming smile onto his face. The last thing he felt up to right now was company, but appearances had to be maintained.

He could barely believe his eyes as he pushed open the salon door.

"Mother?"

Cynthia rose from her seat and put out her arms to her son. Automatically, Judd crossed the room and allowed his mother to embrace him.

"My boy, I've missed you."

"Why are you here?"

Cynthia pouted. "What? Didn't you miss me, too?"

"Of course," Judd said, brushing her words aside.

She was the last person he wanted to deal with right now.

His plans for Wilson Wines needed to be carefully executed and he didn't need the distraction of worrying if his mother was about to preempt his weeks of carefully layered construction—or *de*construction as the case would be.

He cast a look in Anna's direction. She was pale and sitting with her spine rigid. Her hazel eyes were clouded with an emotion he couldn't quite put his finger on. His protective instincts rose to the surface—surprising him with their intensity. Anna had been fine when he'd spoken to her at the office before he'd headed off to the hospital, which meant that whatever had upset her had happened between then and now. That only left one person who was likely to be the cause, which begged the question, what had Cynthia done to upset Anna?

"Everything okay at the office?" he asked.

"Of course," Anna replied. "I have some papers in my case for you when you have a moment."

"Surely you two can leave work alone for one evening. I've just arrived and I want to hear everything about what you've been up to while you've been gone," Cynthia interjected.

"Let me leave you two to it," Anna said, rising coolly from her seat. "I have plenty to attend to while you catch up."

"You don't need to go," Judd said, wondering why Anna seemed so keen to create some distance between them.

"Let her," his mother said, her long fingers tightening around his forearm. "It'll be lovely to be just the two of us over dinner, don't you think?"

He didn't think anything of the kind. Something was terribly wrong and he had no idea what it was.

"I'll speak to you later, then. If you're sure you won't join us?"

A crooked smile twisted Anna's lips. "Oh, I'm sure. You two enjoy catching up. I'll leave the papers in your room."

He watched with narrowed eyes as Anna left the room, closing the salon door with silent precision. Something was very wrong and the minute she'd gone he felt the exhaustion of earlier tug at him again.

"I wish you'd told me you were coming to visit," Judd said to his mother as they assumed their seats.

"I was hoping to surprise you."

Judd felt a flare of anger burst inside. Surprise him? She had to be kidding. When everything hung so carefully in the balance it was the last thing he needed.

"You certainly succeeded at that," he said ruefully. "How long are you planning to stay?"

"A week, maybe," Cynthia replied. "Longer, if necessary."

"Longer?" The word slipped out before he could prevent it. He was more tired than he thought.

"What's the matter, Judd? You know what we planned."

"Yes, and I also know you were supposed to wait until I told you to come over."

"But I heard that your father was gravely ill—not from you, I might add."

"He's ill, Mother, not dead."

"Well, either way," Cynthia said airily, her hands fluttering in the air, "if you want him to be aware of your revenge, then you're running out of time. You've got to get to work on taking it all over and doing with it what you want to—which is to give the house to me, right?"

That was what they'd planned, but Judd felt himself reluctant to commit to agreeing with her. The whole time he'd grown up at The Masters' he'd always felt as though he didn't fully belong. Strangely enough, he felt as if he fitted here.

He redirected his mother's conversation to the family back at The Masters' as they went through to dinner, but all the while he was acutely conscious of Anna's empty chair at the table. When he was finished with his meal he excused himself, citing business he urgently needed to attend to, and he went back to the lobby to retrieve his briefcase.

He was surprised to see a stack of suitcases by the front

door. They hadn't been there when he'd arrived home, and they couldn't be his mother's. She would have complained long and hard if the airline had lost her luggage, however temporarily. A sound on the staircase behind him made him turn to see Anna, an overnight bag in one hand and her handbag slung over one shoulder.

"What's this?" he demanded, his hand flung out toward the cases at his feet.

Outside, he heard a car pull up on the driveway and give a toot.

"My stuff. I'm moving out. That'll be Mr. Evans with my car." She stepped past him to open the front door and hefted one of her cases onto the front porch. "Thanks for bringing my car around. I hope we can fit everything in," she said to the handyman as he came up the stairs to get her cases.

"What do you mean, you're moving out?"

"Just that." She turned to Evans and gestured to the rest of her things in the lobby. "All of these, too, please."

"Hold on a minute. Where are you going and, more important, why?"

Anna shook her head. "I think you know why. Tell me, did you really come back to wreak revenge on your father? Did you mean to give this house to your mother all along?"

He stood in silence. A silence that damned him in her eyes. Eyes that were now hazed with pain and a sorrow that went so deep he wanted to do anything and everything to make it go away.

Her voice was hoarse when she spoke. "You always thought the worst of me, but it never occurred to me to think you were capable of something like this. I didn't want to believe you could be so calculating, but it seems I was terribly wrong. I really don't know you at all, do I?"

Evans had collected the last of her bags and was now waiting by her car. Anna started to head out the door. Judd wanted to call out to her, to physically restrain her from leaving, but he knew he had no right. He *had* meant to give his mother this house all along and he had meant so much more harm to Charles, as well. Right now, though, none of that seemed important anymore as the woman he suddenly realized had come to mean so much to him walked out the door.

A slow burn of anger started deep inside of him. He had never lost control of a situation ever before, and right now everything he'd worked hard for these past weeks, his whole lifetime, in fact, started to crumble. He rubbed at his eyes, unable to dislodge the picture of the misery on Anna's face no matter how hard he tried.

"It's for the best, Judd." His mother's voice came from behind him and he whirled around to face her.

"For the best? What makes you say that?"

"She had ideas above her station and she'd have eventually dragged you down to her level. You know that, don't you? After all, look at what her mother did for Charles. Nothing. She was a convenient mistress and a passable housekeeper. No doubt Anna's been riding on her mother's abilities to sneak her way into Charles's wealth through his bed, too." Cynthia stepped closer, placing one hand on his arm and closing her fingers around it in a hold that surprised him with its strength. "Trust me, Judd. You're better off without her."

He stared at his mother's fingers and their clawlike grip, the physical manifestation of her hold on him the perfect analogy for how she'd tried to direct him all his life. As her words ran through his mind—words that he knew, in this case, to be totally untrue—he wondered what else his mother had told him that had been twisted and distorted away from the truth to suit her own manipulations.

"Did you tell her?"

"About the house? Of course I did. She needed to know, Judd. She doesn't belong here any more than her mother ever did."

"She was an *invited* guest under this roof."

His mother's face paled beneath expertly applied cosmetics. "I don't like your implication, Judd."

"Like it or not, it's still my name on the deed to this property."

"A mere technicality. You know what this place means to me."

"More than anything or anyone else, yes."

Weariness swamped him with the awareness that Cynthia's obsession with this property was outside normal perceptions. Clearly she felt it was owed to her for all she'd lost when she was younger, and for all she'd endured during her marriage to Charles and her subsequent banishment back home to Australia. It was unhealthy and Judd was annoyed with himself that he'd never seen it before now.

Cynthia was Cynthia. She'd never pretended to be anything else but what she'd presented to the world. Subterfuge had never been her style, ever, which was why he'd always assumed that she'd never been anything but honest with him. Only now did he realize that while she didn't lie, per se, her accounts on matters that affected her deeply were twisted by her bitterness into something that only vaguely resembled the truth. Accepting that, and the fact that as an adult he should have seen it sooner, filled him with a fury at himself that he could barely contain.

She'd always be his mother, and he'd always love her as such, but right now he didn't like the person she was very much at all. He needed some distance between them before his anger bubbled over and he said something he might regret.

All his instincts urged him to follow Anna, but with that he was forced to admit he had no idea where to go to look for her. Frustration rose within him anew. Even if he did know where to find her, he doubted she was in the mood to listen to him. He pulled himself free of his mother's clasp, the movement as metaphorical as it was literal.

"Look, it's late and I have work to get through. I'll see you in the morning and we can discuss your return to The Masters'."

"My return? But I've only just arr—"

"We'll talk in the morning," he said firmly, and grabbing his briefcase he went upstairs.

Anna didn't know how much longer she could take this. Working with Judd and feeling about him the way she did, yet knowing just how ruthless he really was, was making her feel sick inside. She had hardly slept over the weekend. The cheap motel she'd discovered on Friday night was hardly in a secluded area and the constant traffic noise and the racket from a nearby bar and club had ensured her nights were punctuated by the kinds of sounds that had dragged her from her restless sleep with a start more than once.

When she'd left the house on Friday she'd been too distraught to think carefully about where she was headed. In the end, to avoid creating an accident, she'd pulled into the motel thinking that it would be for only a night before she found an apartment in the city. But the weekend had passed in a blur of visits to the hospital, timing them to avoid Judd, and spending the rest of her time wallowing in a blend of self-pity and self-disgust that she could have been so foolish as to lose her heart to a man as cold and unforgiving as Judd Wilson.

After a lifetime of promising herself she deserved so much more than her mother had settled for, she'd just gone and found herself falling into the same pattern. Falling in love with a man with whom she would never be an equal—a man who would never offer her more than a job and his bed to sleep in.

She wished she could turn her feelings off as easily as Judd had appeared to do. He'd come into the office this Monday morning with nothing but a professional attitude and a driving work ethic. She should be grateful for that, at least, she thought as she brought his mail in to him.

He was on the phone and she made to put the opened correspondence on the desk in front of him and walk away, but when she did, he reached out and clasped her hand in his, preventing her from walking away. The instant he touched her she flinched, and saw the corresponding frown that crept between his brows as she did so. Anna gave an experimental tug but he continued to hold her firm.

The touch of his fingers on her skin was torture. How many times had those same fingers traversed the length of her body and wrought pleasure from her such as she had never known before? She bit back the sound that threatened to rise in her chest at the memory. The memory of the passion and the betrayal.

Finally, Judd finished his call and relinquished his hold on her.

"Get your bag, we're going to the hospital," he said in a voice that brooked no argument.

"Is Charles all right?" she asked, fear clawing at her throat at the serious expression on Judd's face.

"He's come out of the coma and he's asking for us. Both of us."

The journey to the hospital seemed to take forever, or maybe it just seemed that way because she was bound in this small space inside Judd's car. She was intensely aware of him, from the grip of his hands on the steering wheel to the set of his jaw. And his scent—the scent that insidiously reminded her of dark nights when all she knew was the feel and smell of him, and the sensation of her own pleasure, as he made love to her all through those nights.

She let out a sigh of relief as they pulled into the hospital parking lot and strived to keep her distance from Judd as they walked together to the elevator bank that would take them to the intensive-care unit.

"Only one at a time and only for five minutes," the nurse instructed.

"You go first," Judd said to Anna. "I know how important he is to you, how worried you've been."

She silently examined his words, searching for a hidden meaning behind them, but there was nothing about his expression that suggested his words meant anything other than what was said. She nodded her acquiescence and went into the room where Charles was hooked up to all manner of equipment. He opened his eyes as she entered, a shaky smile on his lips.

"Oh, Charles," she said, sinking onto the visitor's chair beside his bed, tears filling her eyes, "we've been so worried about you."

"Ah, Anna, still fussing?"

He reached for her and she gave him her hand, surprised at the strength she felt in his fingers as he squeezed tight.

"Of course I'm still fussing. I wouldn't be me if I didn't, right?"

He sighed and smiled a little wider. "That's my girl. How are things between you and my boy? Before this little incident I was beginning to hope there was something special growing between you."

Anna didn't want to talk about her and Judd, not now. "Hardly a little incident, Charles. You have to take better care of yourself. In fact, when you go home I've arranged for nursing care for you until you're back on your feet."

Her voice trailed away as she realized what she'd just said. If Cynthia Wilson had her way, Charles wouldn't be returning to the home he knew and loved. In fact, if what she'd said last Friday night held any truth to it, Charles had nowhere to call home at all. The news would shatter his chances at recovery. Somehow she had to persuade Judd to allow his father to live out his years under the roof that had been his home for over thirty years. She felt sick at the prospect but fought to keep her fears from her face. As ill as Charles was, he'd always been pretty astute. He'd know something was wrong if she didn't control herself.

"Pshaw!" he scoffed. "Nurses. I've only been awake a few hours and I've already had my fill of them. But you're not answering my question. You and Judd. What's happening there?"

"We're working well together," Anna hedged.

"Working well together." He said the words as if they tasted like something nasty. "Sounds like you've had a lovers' spat, hmm? You know, I hope you two can work out whatever it is that's keeping you apart. I know you haven't exactly had the best of role models for long-term commitment—Lord only knows I didn't treat your mother as well as I ought to have. She stood by me, you know. She held me together and loved me even when I didn't deserve it. I owed her more than companionship, but I wasn't capable of offering her more."

"Mum was happy, Charles, really." Tears pricked at Anna's eyes.

"Ah, always the mediator. You deserve more than I gave her, Anna. It's your due. Remember that."

Out the corner of her eye she saw the nurse gesture to her. "Look, my five minutes is up and I don't want to use up Judd's time with you, too. We can talk about this later."

Much later, like never, she hoped as she leaned forward to give him a chaste kiss on his cheek.

"Seemed like a very quick five minutes to me," Charles grumbled.

"I'll be back tomorrow, okay?"

"Tonight. Come back tonight."

"If I can," she promised. "Now do as you're told while you're here. Promise me?"

He merely grunted. As she passed Judd in the doorway

she took care not to brush against him, a fact that wasn't totally lost on Judd, judging by the expression on his face.

"I'll wait for you downstairs," she said, desperate for some air.

"Sit, sit." Charles gestured to the chair beside his bed.

Judd did as he was told. His relief at seeing Charles alert again was palpable, but even he couldn't answer himself as to why. Was it because he wanted his father to be fully aware of the payback he had coming to him, or was it something else?

"What, nothing to say?" Charles asked with a bark of laughter.

"I'm glad to see you're feeling better," Judd said stiffly.

Charles snorted. "I'll accept that, it's probably all I deserve. There's one thing about facing your own mortality. It makes you want to clear away the messes you've made of your life—and believe me, I've made a few."

"It's how we deal with the messes that's most important," Judd replied, fighting to keep his voice neutral. Did his father plan to apologize? Did he think that saying "sorry" would make everything okay?

"That's why I needed to speak to you now. You need to know the truth about your mother and me."

"I think I know enough," Judd said, stonewalling.

"No, you don't know the half of it. I will admit it was my fault our marriage failed. I knew what I was getting into by marrying someone so much younger than me, I knew she deserved more than an older man could offer." Charles sighed and lapsed into silence.

Judd shifted uncomfortably on his chair, waiting for the older man to finish what he wanted to say. He didn't have to wait too long.

"I won't beat around the bush, my boy. I wasn't man enough for her. Now don't go getting all embarrassed. I know kids don't want to hear about their parents' sex lives." He made a self-conscious grimace. "I promise to keep it PG. Do you know much about diabetes?"

"Not a huge amount, no."

"Mine went undiagnosed for many years—part of the reason I'm here now. But one of the issues I suffer with the disease is impotence. I was thirty-five when I married your mother and I was already beginning to have problems. She was only nineteen when I met her and such a beauty. I wanted to offer her the moon and the stars. I was prepared to give her anything just to keep her. But when I started having problems in the bedroom I was ashamed. I didn't want to talk to anyone about it—not her, not my best friend, not my doctor, no one. I just threw myself into work. By the time Nicole came along we were barely sleeping together anymore.

"I just kept on working, kept on providing for Cynthia. She had the house, she had you and your sister. I just went on, hoping against hope it would be enough to keep her. She wasn't happy, but I didn't know what I could do to change that anymore. Your mother and my best friend always did get on, and Thomas seemed to be hell-bent on cheering Cynthia up. I got jealous. Started to suspect them of having an affair, of both of them cheating on me.

"One day I came home from work early. Thomas had already left the office and I found him in your mother's room, holding her, as if they were about to make love. I accused them of all sorts of things. I didn't listen when they tried to explain. Turns out she was desperately unhappy and he was consoling her, but I didn't see it that way at the time. I lost a helluva lot that day. My wife, my best friend, my son."

"You didn't have to send us away," Judd said bitterly. "She wasn't unfaithful to you, was she?"

"No," Charles acknowledged, his voice so soft Judd had to lean forward to hear him clearly. "She wasn't. But she let me believe she had been. She told me you were Thomas's child.

That she and Thomas had been having an affair for years and how much he satisfied her. She knew exactly how to hit me where it would hurt the most.

"You know the rest. I could barely see, I was so angry. I told her she could go and take you with her. I never wanted to see either of you again. When Thomas heard what I'd done, he tried to reason with me, to get me to believe the truth, but Cynthia's lies were already rotting my heart and my mind. I wouldn't listen and we never spoke again.

"He died just over a year ago. He'd arranged for his lawyers to pass on a letter to me, should he predecease me. A letter where he told me what an idiot I'd been and how he'd never touched Cynthia, ever. I knew that if he was telling the truth I'd wasted twenty-five years on a hatred I'd had no right to feel. I had to know the truth, but it took a warning from my doctors about my health before I actually found the courage to reach out to you—to admit I was wrong. It wasn't an easy thing."

Judd didn't know what to say. Everything his father told him made sense. Instinctively he knew, even though he didn't want to believe it was the truth, that Cynthia was quite capable of being so spiteful as to spin out a lie of such enormous proportions. But why had she allowed it to go on for so long? Why had she been prepared to walk away from her marriage? And had she never considered, ever, what it had meant to him to be rejected by his father—for his sister to grow up without a mother?

"Judd." Charles shifted and reached a hand toward him. Judd took it, intensely aware of the papery texture of his father's hand and remembering a time when it was strong and warm as it guided him the first time he'd ridden his bike without training wheels. "I want you to know I'm sorry, son. So very sorry for everything I put you through. I was an inflexible, prideful fool. I can't get back what I threw away, but I hope that now you know the truth you can find it in your heart to forgive me and that maybe we can start anew from here."

Judd felt unexpected moisture prick at his eyes. Every wish he'd ever had was here before him. His father was reaching out, wanting to make amends for the past. Charles had talked about his own bitterness being a waste of the last twenty-five years, but what of Judd's own? Channeling his own anger against his father for so long had been just as destructive as his father's toward Cynthia and Thomas Jackson.

"Is that why you offered me the controlling share in the company as well as the house? To make it up to me? Did you really think that would be enough?"

Charles nodded. "I hoped so. I knew you were already successfully running The Masters'. I had to sweeten the bait to bring you home—where you belong. I thought that once you were here that we could start to build a bridge between the past and now. To learn to be father and son again."

He'd come so close to throwing it all away. To destroying everything his father had worked so hard to build.

"Thank you for telling me. It's a lot to take in after all this time. I've been very angry at you for most of my life."

"I deserved that. Are you still angry?"

"Yes, but it's different now—there's more regret than anger. Frustration, too. I just wish things could have been different."

"They can be. We can make it so."

"Yes," Judd said, squeezing his father's hand gently. "Yes, Dad. We can."

By the time Judd joined Anna downstairs she felt as if she had herself back under control, externally at least. He'd been with his father for quite a while longer than she'd expected.

"What did you think?" she asked as they walked back to the car.

"He's a tough old bird. I reckon he'll be around for a few more years yet."

"Did the nurse say anything to you about when he could go home? Supposing he has a home to go to, of course."

Darn, she could probably have handled that better, she thought. But it was too late now. The words hung between them like an invisible challenge.

"What makes you think he doesn't?"

She looked at him in disbelief. "You're kidding me, right? Cynthia and Charles under one roof? She'll never allow it."

"What she will and won't allow isn't an issue," Judd said firmly as they reached the car.

"She seems to believe it is."

"Well, there's a lot that people believe at the moment. Not all of it is true," he said.

His vagueness pushed Anna to speak again. "Are you saying that Cynthia lied to me on Friday night? That it wasn't your intention to turf Charles out and install your mother back where she so supremely believes she belongs?"

"I'm not admitting or denying anything. Charles will have a home to go to—that's all you need to worry about for now."

Anna lapsed into silence, frustrated by Judd's stonewalling tactics. They were nearing their office block before she spoke again.

"I'm going to look for another job. I can't work with you. Not now. Not knowing what you're really like."

"That's your choice, but do you really think the timing is right to leave just now? Without Charles and Nicole, you're pretty much it for historical knowledge and continuity around the place. Anyone would think you want to see Wilson Wines collapse into dust."

"That's not fair. You can't expect me to keep working with you, not now that we—"

"Not now that we what, Anna?"

"Nothing."

"And your resignation?"

"I will wait until Charles is better. That's all I'm promising for now."

The thought of leaving Wilson Wines, the only job she'd ever known, terrified her. But she couldn't continue there, working for Judd, seeing him every day. Wanting him every minute.

Fourteen

Judd's head was reeling. The last thing he needed to deal with right now was Anna walking out on him. If anything, he needed her back home where she belonged as well, but he knew he had some hard work to do in that department before she'd even consider it.

What occupied his mind first and foremost now was something else. Something that challenged every belief he'd grown up with. Logically he'd always known there were two sides to every story, but he'd never dreamed his father's side of things could be so different to what he'd always been told. He'd wanted to refute the words that had poured from his father's mouth, but the man was virtually on his deathbed. Charles had no reason to lie and even with what Judd had always held to be the truth, there was a ring of honesty to what his father had said that demanded he give his old man full justice.

He couldn't concentrate on his work in the office and surprised Anna by telling her he was leaving for the day.

"Call me at the house if you need me."

"I won't," she said bluntly.

He could only give an ironic smile in response. Tough to do when what he really wanted was to lean across her desk and kiss her so thoroughly she would forget what day of the week it was. He'd save that for another time, though. Right now, he had more pressing business to attend to.

Fifteen minutes later, as he pulled into the driveway, he stopped and stared at the massive stone structure that dominated the property. He shook his head. It was only a building—yet it was so coveted, and at what cost? He eased his foot off the brake and slowly drove up the driveway. A van was parked near the front door and he pulled up alongside it, frowning as he read the lettering on the side. Decorators? He shook his head as he got out of the car and let himself in through the front door.

He could hear Cynthia in the salon and the softer murmur of another woman's voice answering her. When he opened the salon door, both women looked up, his mother's face wreathing in a smile of welcome.

"Judd, you're home early! What a lovely surprise. Here, you can tell me what you think of these." Spread before her were a stack of open books of decorating samples and she picked up a selection from the top, handing them toward him. "I think these will be perfect in here, don't you?"

"No, I don't," he said grimly before turning to the other woman. "I'm sorry, but it seems my mother has wasted your time. We won't be needing any decorating advice at the moment. Let me see you out."

The other woman looked shocked, but to her credit she hastily gathered her samples in her arms, shooting worried glances between Judd and his mother as she did so.

Cynthia sat in mutinous silence, her dark brows drawn in a straight line—a harbinger of her temper. She would never argue with him in front of a stranger but he had no doubt that her blood pressure was rising to monumental proportions right now. If there was one thing his mother hated, it was being thwarted in her goals.

Let her be angry, he thought. It was nothing compared to how he was feeling right now. By the time he'd shown the decorator out and returned to the salon, his body was rigid with tension.

"How could you do that to me, and in front of a total stranger?" She rose to her feet and demanded the instant he'd closed the door behind him.

"You're getting ahead of yourself," he said calmly. Strangely enough, in the face of her fury, he began to feel himself settle down by degrees. "The house is still mine."

"Don't you dare tell me after all this time you're changing your mind. This house is mine by right, it always has been. I just bet it's that upstart, Anna Garrick. Has she been poisoning your mind all morning? That type will always try, you know. They cloud your judgment with sexual favors and then they try to pull your strings for the rest of your life."

"Is that what you tried to do with Charles?" he asked pointedly.

Slap! In all his life his mother had never struck him, but it appeared he'd crossed a line with her today. Judd tested his stinging jaw and locked his gaze with hers.

"Now that's out of the way, perhaps you could answer my question."

"How dare you!"

"No, Mother, how dare you lie to me all these years. What kind of mother lies about her son's paternity and deliberately keeps a boy from his father?"

"Whatever I did, I did for you, Judd. *I love you.*"

"Inasmuch as you're capable of loving anyone more than you love yourself, and this house."

"You don't understand."

"Oh, I think I do. I understand you were young and foolish when you met Charles and that you saw in him a chance to relive the former Masters glory that you had pined for all your life." He shook his head. "Why did you lie to him, Mother? Why did you let him drive us away? Was it really worth hurting him so badly?"

"We'd grown apart. After I had Nicole it was as if he lost all interest in me as a woman. At first he said he was having to work longer hours and didn't want to disturb me, but then it became another excuse, and then another until we weren't even sharing a room anymore."

Judd knew his mother better than probably anyone else, and he knew that, for Cynthia, losing Charles's attentions would have been a dreadful blow to her self-esteem. For a woman who appeared so strong, she was more fragile than others knew. She measured herself by the success around her. If the physical side of her marriage was failing, then *she* was a failure.

"Why did you lie to him about Thomas Jackson?"

"You know about Thomas?"

"Only Charles's side. Now I want to hear yours. The truth this time."

His mother began to pace the room, every now and then stopping to finger one ornament or another.

"You don't know what it was like. Charles was such a dashing man when he came to visit us at The Masters' that time. And he was clearly smitten with me. The age gap didn't seem ridiculous to me—he was such a charismatic and *vital* man. He promised me everything I'd ever wanted. He promised me this." She flung her arms out wide before wrapping them tight around her middle. "He made me feel as if his entire world revolved around me. But then, he started pulling away.

"I didn't know what to do or where to turn. I had no other family here. He was my everything, and suddenly he didn't want me anymore. I just wanted to make him jealous. To make him want *me* again. So, I turned to someone else for attention, to show him that if he didn't want me, another man would."

"But his best friend? What were you thinking?"

"I wasn't thinking, that much is quite obvious. Thomas could see there was a growing rift between Charles and me. He loved us both and wanted to do whatever he could to help us over our rough patch, as he called it. I, shamefully, took advantage of his friendship and used it against him. I just wanted to hurt Charles any way I could at that point. I didn't realize then just how much I would end up hurting everyone else. When Charles threatened to send me back to Australia alone, I overreacted. I couldn't lose you and Nicole as well as my home and my marriage. I lied to him about Thomas being my lover and I led Charles to believe it was Thomas who was your father."

Cynthia sighed deeply and sank into a nearby chair. A glance at her face told of the toll her honesty had taken on her after all these years of perpetuating a lie.

Judd chose his words carefully. "They never spoke again, did you know that? Charles refused to see or speak to Thomas for the rest of his life, despite his best friend's repeated entreaties. You destroyed their friendship as thoroughly as if you really had slept with Thomas Jackson. It was only when Thomas died recently that Charles began to wonder if Thomas had really been telling the truth all along."

She nodded and wiped an errant tear from one eye. Judd wasn't moved by her unexpected emotional display. He wasn't even convinced it was genuine until she looked up and met the censure in his eyes. For the first time she showed every one of her fifty-one years and then some.

"I've been such a fool. I was so angry and so bitter it was easier to perpetuate the lie than it was to tell the truth. Besides, once Charles had it in his head that you weren't his, he couldn't wait to see the back of us. I hit him where it hurt the hardest, and he got me right back."

"You could have told him the truth at any time."

"I couldn't. I wanted him to hurt, to know what it was like to be rejected."

"He never rejected you, Mother."

"Really?" She shook her head at him. "Then what do you call him removing himself from my bed, my whole life, the way he did? If that's not rejection, then what is it?"

She stood opposite him, so proud and defiant and yet still hurting inside after all these years.

"Charles is diabetic. At that stage his illness was undiagnosed and untreated. He had no idea that's why he'd become impotent until years after, but he was too proud to seek help for the problem."

She drew in a shaky breath. "You mean it wasn't me all along?"

Cynthia's voice broke as genuine tears began to fall down her cheeks. Despite her focus still being so self-oriented, Judd felt his earlier anger toward his mother defuse entirely. He could begin to understand how her need for payback had molded her ambitious nature into one of harshness—even cruelty. She hadn't been solely responsible for what had happened; both his parents had their crosses to bear, but maybe now they could begin to heal some of the hurt they'd caused. It was going to be a monumental task. So many years and words lay like an echoing chasm between them all. He'd had enough of it. It was time for change—for all of them. Charles, Cynthia, Anna and himself.

He took a step toward his mother and drew her into his arms. Forgiveness had to start with a first step; he only hoped that he could begin to make things right before it was too late.

Judd and his mother talked for hours. When she was finally spent, he saw her to her bedroom with a light meal on a tray and went to his own room to change. She'd agreed to go back to Adelaide in the morning. She would definitely be back, but at a time when emotions weren't so fraught and when Charles was better. Who knew, perhaps between the two of them, his parents could finally lay old ghosts to rest and find some peace between them.

What a freaking day it had been. Exhaustion pulled at every part of his body. Whoever said that the truth will set you free never once mentioned the high emotional toll that could take. Today's revelations had taught him a very important lesson. Life was too short to let go of what mattered to you, especially of what you loved. He didn't want to live the rest of his life plagued by bitterness and regret over relationships he'd allowed to fall apart, as his parents had. He grabbed his cell phone from on top of his briefcase on the bed and punched in Anna's number.

She didn't pick up. No problem, he decided as he descended the stairs and headed for his car. He could ring her and ring her until she eventually gave up and answered. He knew she wouldn't turn off her phone altogether because she was one of the emergency contacts for the hospital.

"What?" she demanded as he called for the ninth time.

"Where are you? We need to talk."

"We have nothing to say."

"Yes, Anna, we do. We have everything to say to each other. I won't give up, you know. I will call you and call you until you give in."

"Look, I'm tired. Can't this wait until tomorrow at the office?"

"I need to see you now. Please? It's important."

He heard her sigh before she answered, "Fine, then."

She rattled off an address that he rapidly keyed into the GPS of the late-model Mercedes he'd bought so Evans would be free to drive Charles whenever he needed him.

"I'll be there in half an hour," he said, checking the ETA on the screen.

"Don't rush on my account," she answered before severing their connection.

By the time he pulled into the budget motel at the address Anna had given him, he felt a knot of anticipation grow tight in his gut. He parked beside her Lexus, which was outside one of the motel units that formed an L-shape just back from the road. Her door opened as he got out of his car.

"Why here?" he asked as he walked the short distance to her door.

"Clean, cheap and close to the motorway. Is that all you wanted?"

She didn't so much as budge from the doorway, nor did she seem to be in a hurry to invite him inside.

"No, that's not all I wanted."

"Then please say what you wanted to say and leave."

Anna's grip on the edge of the door made her fingers ache but she had to hold on to something, anything. If she didn't, she was afraid she might reach out to Judd, to touch him, and then she'd be lost. As much as he'd hurt her, she couldn't deny her body's response to him.

"I'm not doing this outside on the forecourt of some tacky motel, Anna. Let me in."

He spoke quietly but she had no doubt that he meant every word he said.

"If it means I'll be rid of you sooner, then, sure, come on in," she said with false bravado.

She pushed the door open wide and held her breath as he stepped over the lintel and into the compact unit she'd inhabited for the past three nights.

"Can we sit down, please?" Judd asked.

She gestured to the saggy two-seater sofa and settled herself on one of the scarred wooden chairs from the small dinette. His rangy body filled the sofa, making her all too aware of his presence in the shabby room.

"Well?" she prompted, really wanting to get this over with as soon as possible.

"I had an ulterior motive when I came to New Zealand. For years my father had spurned my mother and me, and for years I'd dreamed of what I would do if I had the opportunity to pay him back for all the heartache he'd caused when he sent us away." He paused and rubbed his jawline with a thumb and forefinger of one hand. "I should have known as I grew older that nothing is as straightforward as it seems."

"Nothing ever really is," Anna agreed, wondering where he was leading with this.

She knew he had an ulterior motive for coming to New Zealand, a motive that included turning his own flesh and blood out of his home and installing a woman whose vitriol had flayed strips off Anna's soul. Well, for all Cynthia's subtle viciousness, she'd opened Anna's eyes to the man Judd really was. She should thank her for it one day, she thought with self-deprecating irony.

"No, you're right. Nothing ever really is. My plans were originally twofold. One, to give my mother back the home she deserved, the other to ruin Wilson Wines by selling my shares to its biggest competitor."

Anna gasped. "You can't be serious! It will break Charles's heart. How could you even think of doing such a thing? How could you be so calculating?"

"Calculating? Do you have any idea of what it was like to grow up knowing your father *hated* you so much he sent you away forever? I was six years old!"

Anna recoiled as he abruptly rose to his feet and paced the small room, pushing a hand through his hair. On seeing her face, he sat back down on the sofa.

"Anna, relax. I've already begun to question what I'd planned to do with the business. Aside from the fact that I'd been bored with my work in Adelaide for some time, working at Wilson Wines has provided me with new challenges within the industry that make me very excited for the future of the company—not to mention valuable insights into how hard Charles has worked to keep the business running all these years. If nothing else, I learned to respect him for that.

"Look, I don't expect anyone to think that my plans were honorable—revenge very rarely is. But I've both learned and been forced to face some home truths about my parents and myself that have turned everything upside down."

"I don't see what any of this has to do with me. Why are you telling me?" Anna clenched her fingers together in her lap.

"Because you were part of that revenge."

Fifteen

A bitter taste flooded her mouth. She'd heard as much from Cynthia, but hearing the words directly from lips that she'd kissed in deepest passion, lips that had caressed her entire body and brought her ultimate pleasure, made her stomach lurch. She shot up from her seat.

"I think I've heard enough. I'd like you to go."

Judd stood and reached for her, his fingers closing around her upper arms and gently encouraging her back down on her chair.

"No, you haven't heard nearly enough, and I won't leave until you know it all."

"I don't want to hear it, Judd. You hurt me so much it pains me to see you at work every day. I can't keep putting myself through this. I don't deserve to be made to feel this way."

"No, you don't, and that's why I'm going to make it up to you. Look, when I met you I was instantly attracted to you. That attraction was definitely mutual, as we both established on your first night at The Masters'. But it wasn't until the next morning when my mother told me that she'd figured out who you were that I made a decision to use that attraction against you.

"You see, I had no reason to believe that you weren't there as Charles's puppet. You were so loyal to him, so defensive. It made me wonder just how deep the relationship between the two of you went. I assumed, wrongly I know, that the two of you were lovers, and to add to my revenge plans I wanted to win you off him. To show him that he didn't deserve to be loved the way you obviously loved him."

A tiny sound of pain emerged from Anna's mouth. She'd known that Judd had thought she was Charles's lover, but to hear him put in words what he'd been thinking hit her like a physical blow. She wrapped her hands around her stomach and hunched over as if by doing so she could protect herself from what he insisted on saying.

"Anna, I'm so sorry I treated you like that, and I hope that you'll be able to forgive me. I based my need for vengeance on a life that was as orchestrated as what I'd planned to do to my father. Granted, he's no angel, but he didn't deserve what I had planned to do."

A difficult silence fell between them, a silence punctuated by nothing more than the overloud hum of the old refrigerator and the ticking of the cheap plastic wall clock. Finally, Anna summoned up the courage to ask him the one question that now burned inside her.

"So what changed your mind?"

"You."

He looked up and his eyes burned a hole straight to her heart. Anna swallowed against the fear that formed a lump in her throat.

"You'll forgive me if I say I find that hard to believe."

He gave a humorless laugh. "I don't blame you, but it's true. In everything around me, you are the only thing that's good. You're the only one who remained true to the people you love. I learned today that the truth I'd always believed growing up was nothing but a lie fabricated by one person's need for attention and another's pride standing in the way of giving it."

"What do you mean?" Anna asked, suddenly confused.

A stricken look of pain settled on Judd's face. "My mother lied to me for most of my life. Forcing the truth from her today was one of the hardest things I've had to endure."

"But how did you know she'd lied to you?"

"Charles told me his side of their story today at the hospital. It was the bare-bones version, given how weak he is and how much time we were allowed together, but it made me stop seeing him as the villain in the piece and start to see him as he is. Faults as well as strengths. I knew he had accused my mother of having an affair. She told me that much when I was about fifteen. What she didn't say was that she'd deliberately led him to believe it, then told him I wasn't his son." He shook his head. "And to think I was prepared to crush him without knowing all of that.

"I can't believe I almost threw everything away. Everything—everyone—I'd ever wanted in my life were mine all along, if only I'd had the courage to fight for them. Learning the truth was a real eye-opener for me."

"What you were going to do was despicable. What you did, to me, was despicable."

"I know, and I'm more sorry for that than you'll ever know. It seems betrayal runs in the family. My mother lied to Charles about my paternity in retaliation for what she saw as his indifference to her. She had no idea that what she perceived as his coolness toward her masked a bigger problem."

Anna caught on quickly. "His diabetes. My mother said he'd probably had it for years before he was diagnosed."

"Yes, he was too proud and too embarrassed to seek help, and so frightened that he would lose his beautiful young wife because of it that he poured himself into work so he could at least keep her in the lifestyle he'd always promised her.

"I learned some awful truths about my family today, Anna. Not least of which were the truths about myself. Truths I'm so bitterly ashamed of. I want to make it up to you, if you'll allow me. Everyone deserves a second chance, right? A chance to put things back the way they should have been all along?"

"I don't know if I can do that, Judd. All my life I watched my mother be treated as an afterthought, appreciated to an extent but never really given the love she craved. She deserved more than that—so much more—and so do I. From an early age I told myself that I would only be with someone who loved me completely and put our relationship first.

"When I realized what you thought of me, why you had sex with me," she said bluntly, because no matter how engaged her feelings it could only have been sex, not lovemaking, "I felt second-rate. Your revenge came first, not me. I don't know if I can forgive you that. I really don't."

Judd reached across the short distance between them and took her hands in his, his thumbs stroking across the tops of hers.

"I love you, Anna. I never thought I'd want to trust another person the way I want to trust you. With my mother's lies about my father poisoning the way I saw love, I never wanted to go through what I thought was the greatest weakness in the world. Allowing yourself to become vulnerable to another person, to hand to them the means to hurt you so much, alters the entire course of your life. But I want to be that vulnerable to you. I trust you. I know you. You are loyal and loving and everything I was never taught to be. I would do anything for you, and I swear that from now on I will always put you first. Please, let me show you that I love you."

Anna lifted her head and met his intense and pleading gaze. Her heart wanted to say yes to him, but her head cautioned her to take care. She'd suffered so much these past weeks. Yes, she'd experienced the highest of highs in her life, but along with those came the lows to which she never wanted to descend again.

She took a deep breath. "So, if I asked you to show me you love me by leaving me now, by never talking to me again, by never making another attempt to see me, you'd do it?"

She saw the pain that speared across his features, the light in his eyes dim as he saw all hope of their reconciliation being dashed against his mistakes of the past. Judd let her go and stood up.

"Yes," he said. "I will do that for you."

His hands were trembling and it shocked Anna to her core that his emotions affected him so deeply. Judd Wilson, the ice man, vulnerable to her.

Before he could reach the door of the unit, she flew to her feet.

"Judd! Stop!"

She ran toward him, throwing herself against his back and flinging her arms around him as if she could physically stop him from leaving her.

"Don't go, please don't go. I love you, Judd. Don't ever walk away from me again, please?"

He turned in her arms, wrapping his own around her and holding her close. As she looked up at his face she saw tears tracking down his cheeks. She lifted shaking hands to wipe the moisture away.

"Oh, Judd, don't."

She drew his head down to hers, sealing his mouth with her lips and putting her heart into her kiss, telling him how much he meant to her with actions rather than words.

"God, don't do that to me again. I couldn't survive it another time," he groaned against her mouth.

Suddenly she understood just what it had cost Judd to walk away from her like that. He'd been a confused little boy when at first slowly and then with increasing rhythm, never once losing focus.

Pleasure began to build inside of her but it was different than before. This time they were so much more connected—mind, body and spirit. And when she began to shake with the intensity of her orgasm, she felt him tremble also until with a raw cry he spilled himself within her. Making love had never felt so right or so perfect. A tear slid from the corner of her eye as emotion overwhelmed her.

He was her man, her love, her forever. And she was his.

* * * * *

A FORBIDDEN AFFAIR

BY
YVONNE LINDSAY

New Zealand born, to Dutch immigrant parents, **Yvonne Lindsay** became an avid romance reader at the age of thirteen. Now, married to her "blind date" and with two fabulous children, she remains a firm believer in the power of romance. Yvonne feels privileged to be able to bring to her readers the stories of her heart. In her spare time, when not writing, she can be found with her nose firmly in a book, reliving the power of love in all walks of life. She can be contacted via her website, www.yvonnelindsay.com.

Published in Great Britain 2012
by Mills & Boon, an imprint of Harlequin (UK) Limited,
Eton House, 18-24 Paradise Road, Richmond, Surrey TW9 1SR

© Dolce Vita Trust 2012

ISBN: 978 0 263 89193 5
ebook ISBN: 978 1 408 97773 6

51-0712

Harlequin (UK) policy is to use papers that are natural, renewable and recyclable products and made from wood grown in sustainable forests. The logging and manufacturing processes conform to the legal environmental regulations of the country of origin.

Printed and bound in Spain
by Blackprint CPI, Barcelona

One

Nicole's hands shook uncontrollably as she tried to fit her key into the ignition. Damn, she dropped it again. She swiped the key ring up off the floor of her classic Benz, and gave up driving as a bad joke. If she couldn't even get the key in the ignition, how on earth did she expect to drive?

She got out of the car, slammed the door hard and swiped her cell phone from her bag. Thank goodness she'd had the presence of mind to grab the designer leather pouch from the hall table after her grand exit from the family dinner to end all family dinners.

Her high heels clipped a staccato beat as she marched down the well-lit driveway of her family home to the street, calling a taxi service as she went. Fine tremors shook her body as she waited for the car to arrive. The chill air of the autumn night made her glad she hadn't had a chance to change out of her tailored wool suit when she'd arrived home from work earlier.

Her father had requested that she dress up for dinner in honor of a special announcement he'd planned to make, but by the time she'd gotten home, there just hadn't been enough time. She hadn't thought her father would mind that she'd chosen to put in the extra time at the office instead of rushing home to get ready. After all, if anyone should understand her drive to devote her time and energy to Wilson Wines then surely it would be Charles Wilson, founder and CEO. Her father had invested most of his life into the business he had built, and she'd always intended to follow in his footsteps.

Until tonight.

Another rush of anger infused her. How dare her father belittle her like that, and in front of a virtual stranger, as well? Who cared if that stranger was her long-lost brother, Judd. Two and a half decades after their parents' bitter divorce had split their family in half, what right did he have to come back and lay claim to the responsibilities that were supposed to be *hers?* She clenched her jaw tight and bit back the scream of frustration that threatened to claw its way out of her throat. She couldn't lose it now. Not when she had just discovered that she was the only person she had left to rely on.

Even her best friend, colleague and life-long confidante, Anna, had shown her true colors when she'd arrived home in New Zealand from Adelaide, Australia, late last week with Judd in tow. Sure, she'd tried to convince Nicole that she'd only been following Charles's orders to find Judd and bring about a reconciliation, but Nicole knew where Anna's loyalties lay, and they certainly weren't with her. If they were,

SAVE UP TO 25%

Subscribe to Desire today and get 4 stories a month delivered to your door for 3, 6 or 12 months and gain up to 25% OFF! That's a fantastic saving of over £30!

MONTHS	FULL PRICE	YOUR PRICE	SAVINGS
3	£32.94	£27.99	15%
6	£65.88	£52.68	20%
12	£131.76	£98.88	25%

As a welcome gift we will also send you a FREE L'Occitane gift set worth £10

PLUS, by becoming a member you will also receive these additional benefits:

- 🌹 FREE Home Delivery
- 🌹 Receive new titles TWO MONTHS AHEAD of the shops
- 🌹 Exclusive Special Offers & Monthly Newsletter
- 🌹 Special Rewards Programme

No Obligation - You can cancel your subscription at any time by writing to us at Mills & Boon Book Club, PO Box 676, Richmond. TW9 1WU.

To subscribe, visit
millsandboon.co.uk/subscriptions

MILL
BOO

D2G

Anna wouldn't have kept the truth from her about what Charles planned to use as Judd's incentive.

A painful twist in her chest reminded her to draw in a breath but despite the fact she obeyed her body's demand to refill her lungs, the pain of betrayal by her best friend—the woman she loved like a sister—still lingered. How *could* Anna have known what was going to happen and not given her prior warning?

In her bag, her phone began to chirp insistently. Thinking it might be the taxi company calling back to confirm her details, she lifted it to her ear and answered it.

"Nicole, where are you? Are you okay?"

Anna. Who else? It certainly wouldn't be her father calling to see if she was all right.

"I'm fine," Nicole answered, her voice clipped.

"You're not fine, you're upset. I can hear it in your voice. Look, I'm sorry about tonight—"

"Just tonight, Anna? What about your trip to Adelaide? What about bringing my brother home for the first time in twenty-five years, so he could take everything that was ever mine away from me?" Even Anna's gasp of pain at Nicole's accusations didn't stop Nicole's tirade or do anything to lessen the hurt of betrayal that rocketed through her veins right now. "I thought we were friends, sisters by *choice,* remember?"

"I couldn't tell you what Charles had planned, Nicole. Please believe me. Your dad swore me to secrecy and I owe him so very much. Without his support of me and my mum...you know what he was like...even when she was dying—"

"His support, huh?" Nicole shut her eyes tight and squeezed back the fresh round of tears that fought to escape. "What about your support of me?"

"You always have that, Nic, you know that."

"Really? Then why didn't you give me a heads-up? Why didn't you tell me that he was going to bribe Judd to stay by giving him my home as well as the business?"

"Only half the business," Anna's voice came quietly over the line.

"A controlling share, Anna. That's the whole business as far as I'm concerned."

The shock of her father's announcement had been bad enough. Worse was the way he'd justified the decision to give everything to Judd instead of her. *Just you wait,* he had said, *you'll find some young man who'll sweep you off your feet and before I know it you will be married and raising a family. Wilson Wines will just be a hobby for you.* Years of hard work, of dedication and commitment to the business and to further her father's plans and dreams dismissed as just a *phase,* a passing fad. The thought of it made her blood boil.

"Dad made it quite clear where I stand in all this, and by aligning yourself with him, you've made it quite clear where you stand, too."

Nicole paced back and forth on the pavement at the end of the driveway, filled with a nervous energy that desperately needed an outlet. Anna's voice remained steady in her ear; the sound of her friend's voice was usually a calming influence but tonight it was anything but.

"He put me in an impossible position, Nic. I begged him to talk to you about this, to at least tell you that Judd would be coming home."

"Obviously you didn't beg hard enough. Or, here's something to consider, maybe you could have just told me, anyway. You could have picked up a phone or fired me an email in warning. It's not that hard to do. You had to know what this would mean to me, how much it would hurt me. And still you did nothing?"

"I'm so sorry, Nic. If I could do it over I'd do it differently, you have to know that."

"I don't know anything anymore, Anna. That's the trouble. Everything I've worked for, everything I've lived for, has just been handed to a man I don't even know. I don't even know if I have a roof over my head now that Dad's given the deed of the family house to Judd. How would that make *you* feel? Have you asked yourself that?"

A sweep of lights coming down the road heralded the taxi she'd summoned, and not a moment too soon. She had enough dander up right now to march back on up the driveway and give her father a piece of her mind all over again—for whatever good it would do.

"Look," she continued, "I've got to go. I need some space right now to think things over."

"Nicole, come back. Let's talk this out face-to-face."

"No," Nicole answered as the cab pulled up alongside the curb. "I'm done talking. Please don't call me again."

She disconnected the call and switched off her phone for good measure before throwing it into the bottom of her bag.

"Viaduct Basin," she instructed as she got into the taxi and settled in the darkened interior with her equally dark thoughts.

Hopefully the vibrant atmosphere at the array of bars and clubs in downtown Auckland would provide her with the distraction she needed. Nicole repaired her tear-stained makeup as well as she could with the limited cosmetics in her bag. It annoyed the heck out of her that anger, for her, usually resulted in tears, as well. It was an awkward combination that plagued her on the rare occasions she actually lost her temper, and it made it hard for her to be taken seriously.

She willed her hand to be steady as she applied a rich red lip gloss and gave herself a final check in her compact mirror.

Satisfied she'd done her best with her makeup, she sat back against the soft upholstery of the luxury taxi and tried to ignore the echo of her father's words, the faintly smug paternal tone that seemed to say that she'd soon get over her temper tantrum and realize he was right all along.

"Over my dead body," she muttered.

"Pardon, miss, what was that you said?" the neatly suited taxi driver asked over his shoulder.

"Nothing, sorry, just talking to myself."

She shook her head and blinked hard at the fresh tears that pricked in her eyes. In doing what her father had done he'd permanently damaged his relationship with her, fractured the trust between her and Anna, and virtually destroyed any chance of her and Judd building a sibling bond together. She had no family she could rely on anymore—not her father, her brother, her sister and certainly not her mother. Nicole had not seen or heard from her mother since Cynthia Masters-Wilson had taken Judd back to her native Australia when he was six and Nicole only one year old.

Nicole had long since convinced herself she'd never wanted to know her mother growing up. Her father had been everything and everyone she'd ever needed. But even as a child, she'd always been able to tell that she wasn't enough to make up for the wife and son that her father still missed. It had driven Nicole to work harder, to be a top student and to learn everything she could about the family business, in the hopes of winning her father's approval, making him proud. Goodness only knew running Wilson Wines was all she'd ever wanted to do from the moment she'd understood just what held the balance of her father's attention every day.

Now that Judd was back, it was as if she didn't exist anymore. As if she never had.

Nicole reached up to remove the hair tie that had held her hair in its no-nonsense, businesslike pony-tail all day, and shoved her fingers through her hair to tousle it out into party mode. She would not let her father's actions beat her. Once she'd worked this upset out of her system she'd figure out a way to fix things. Until then, she was going to enjoy herself.

She alighted from the taxi and paid the driver then undid the top button of her suit jacket, exposing a glimpse of the gold-and-black satin-and-lace bra she wore beneath it. There, she thought defiantly, from business woman to party girl in one easy step. Squaring her shoulders, Nicole headed into the first bar on the strip. Oblivion had never looked better.

Nate leaned against the bar and watched the pulsing throng of bodies on the dance floor with disinterest. He'd only agreed to come along tonight for Raoul's sake. Hosting the guy's stag party was small recompense for the work Raoul had done holding Jackson Importers together after Nate's father's sudden death last year. Knowing the running of the business was in Raoul's very capable hands until Nate could return to New Zealand to pick up the reins had been a massive relief. Extricating himself from Jackson Importers' European office and appointing a replacement there had taken time, and he owed the guy big for stepping up to the plate.

His philanthropy didn't assuage his boredom, however, and Nate was on the verge of saying his goodbyes and making his way home when she caught his eye. The woman moved on the dance floor with a sensuous grace that sent a spiraling swell of primal male interest through his body. She was dressed as if she'd come from the office, although he'd never seen any of his staff look that good in a suit. Her jacket was unbuttoned just enough to give a tantalizing view of creamy feminine swells of flesh supported by sexy black satin and gold lace, and while her skirt wasn't exactly short, her long legs and spiky heels certainly made it look that way.

He felt a familiar twinge in his groin. All of a sudden, heading out to his home on the ocean side of the Waitakere Ranges wasn't his top priority anymore—at least not immediately and, hopefully, not alone.

Nate cut through the throng of seething bodies to get nearer. There was something familiar about her but he couldn't place it immediately. Her long dark hair swung around her face as she moved to the beat of the music and he imagined it swinging in other areas, gliding over his body. Oh, yes, definitely gliding over his body—or even spread across the starkness of his Egyptian cotton sheets while he glided across hers. He clenched and unclenched his jaw as every cell in his body responded to the visual image.

He let the beat of the music infuse him and eased in beside her. "Hi, can I join in?" he asked with a smile.

"Sure," she replied, before flicking her hair from her face and exposing dark eyes a man could lose himself in, and a delectably red-painted mouth that was made for pure sin.

They danced awhile, their bodies moving in synchronicity—close, but not touching. The air between them was incendiary. Would they move in such unison alone together, too?

Another dancer jostled past, knocking her against his chest. His hands whipped up to steady her and she looked up into his eyes with a smile that started slowly before spreading wide.

"My hero," she said, with a wicked gleam in her dark eyes.

He found his mouth curving in response. "I can be whatever you want me to be," he said, bending his head slightly and putting his mouth to the shell of her ear.

She quivered in his arms. "Anything?"

"Anything."

"Thank you," she said, so softly he almost couldn't hear her over the noise around them. "I could do with a dose of *anything* right now."

She draped her arms over his shoulders, the fingers of one hand playing with his hair where it sat at the nape of his neck. Her touch did crazy things to him. Things that made him want to do nothing more than take her out of here and transport her to his home, his bed.

Nate wasn't into one-night stands. Aside from the fact his mother had drilled respect for women into him from an early age, he'd never been that kind of guy. Nate liked to plan, to calculate all the angles—spontaneity wasn't really his strong suit, especially in his private life. He knew how important it was to be cautious, to keep people at a distance until you were sure of their motives. But there was something about the girl in his arms that made him want to take a chance.

He looked down into her face and recognition began to dawn. Suddenly he knew why she'd seemed familiar. She was Nicole Wilson—none other than Charles Wilson's daughter, and the second in command at Wilson Wines. Her picture had been in the dossier of information he'd asked Raoul to gather on the competition's business—and most especially on the man who had once been his father, Thomas's, closest and oldest friend. Charles Wilson, who had—after an angry row, rife with false accusations—subsequently become Thomas's bitterest rival.

Once, when he'd been a turbulent teen, Nate had promised his father he'd seek revenge for what Charles Wilson had done. Thomas, ever the peacemaker, had told him he was to do no such thing while Thomas still drew breath. Sadly now, his father was dead—not so sadly, all bets, in relation to Charles Wilson, were off.

Nate wasn't normally one to deliver on the sins of the father, but tonight's potential now took on a whole other edge. He'd been biding his time with Charles Wilson. Accumulating information, and planning his strategy carefully. But even if it hadn't been part of his plans, he wasn't about to ignore the opportunity that had just dropped into his arms.

A waft of Nicole's fragrance drifted off her heated body and teased his nose. The scent was rich and spicy, very much, he suspected, like the woman he held— their bodies moving in unison, undulating to the beat of the music that thrummed around them.

Nate didn't hide the arousal he felt for her. What was the point? If this didn't work out, then there'd be no foul. His plans would carry on regardless. But if it did, if she was responding to him the same way he reacted to her, his plans for revenge against Charles Wilson would take a very interesting turn indeed.

Nicole knew she'd had too much to drink tonight, and she knew full well that she should call another taxi to take her home. After all, it was only Thursday and she still had work tomorrow. At least, she thought she still had work tomorrow.

Thinking about work made her head hurt and the idea of returning to the house tonight just tied her stomach in knots and reminded her again of her father's low opinion of her. Earlier, she'd blocked out that reminder with a shot, and then another, egged on by a group of acquaintances she'd barely seen since she'd graduated from university and whom she could hardly call friends. Still, their lively and undemanding company tonight had been just what she sought. No questions, no answers. Just being lost in the moment. And right at this moment she was feeling very lost indeed. Lost in the undeniable attraction between two healthy young people in their prime.

Very little separated her and her dance partner and as her lower body brushed against him again, a classic Mae West line ran through her alcohol-clouded mind. She couldn't stifle the giggle that bubbled up from inside.

"Care to share the joke?"

She pressed her lips together and shook her head. There was no way she was sharing that little snippet.

"Then you have to pay a forfeit—you know that, don't you?"

"A forfeit?" she asked, her lips spreading into a

smile once more. "Surely you can't punish a girl for being happy?"

"I wasn't thinking of a punishment," he said.

She should be laughing at the line he'd just uttered, she told herself, yet, for some reason, a wicked coil of lust tightened inside her.

"Oh?" she managed through lips that she suddenly felt the urge to moisten with the tip of her tongue. "What were you thinking of?"

"This," he said.

She didn't have time to think, or room to move had she even wanted to dodge him, as he lowered his lips to hers. Lips that were unexpectedly cool and firm. Lips that sampled, tasted and teased her own.

The tight sensation inside her spread, tingling through her body like a slow-building charge of electricity, sensitizing her hidden places, draining her mind of any awareness of her surroundings. All she could think of, all she *wanted* to think of, was the touch of his mouth on hers. Of the delicious pressure of his body as his hands on her hips gathered her closer.

They continued to move to the music—her pelvis rolling against his, her awareness of his arousal becoming a hunger for more than the illicit touch of bodies through clothing. A moan built deep in her throat, a moan she fought to keep inside as he lifted his mouth from hers.

She swallowed and opened her eyes. In this light it was difficult to tell what color his eyes were, but they were definitely unusual and their hooded stare captured her and held her mesmerized. Didn't certain beasts of prey do the same? Was she about to be devoured? The thought didn't upset her as much as it should. God, she had to pull herself together.

"So, that's a forfeit, huh?" she asked, her voice thick with desire.

"It's just one of many."

"Intriguing."

Intriguing wasn't the word. His kiss had totally fried her synapses. It was all she could do to prevent herself from dragging his face down to hers again and repeating the experience. Once more with feeling, she thought, although she certainly hadn't been devoid of feeling while he'd been kissing her. For that moment in time she'd forgotten everything. Who she was, why she was here, what she had left to look forward to.

She'd liked that. She'd liked it a whole lot. She wanted to do it again.

"Hey, Nic!"

One of her acquaintances, Amy, appeared at her side and her dance partner released her. She instantly rued the loss of contact.

Her friend shouted to be heard over the music. "We're off to another club, you coming?"

Nicole's usual prudence screamed "safety in numbers" at the back of her mind, but tonight she wasn't in the mood to be prudent at all.

"No, I'm fine. I'll get a taxi home later."

"Okay. Hey, it was cool catching up again. Let's not leave it so long next time."

And then Amy was gone with the crowd she'd been hanging with.

"Are you sure you didn't want to go with your friends?" her dance partner asked.

"No, I'm fine. I'm a big girl, I can look after myself," Nicole answered.

"I'm pleased to hear it. I'm Nate, by the way."

"Nicole," she answered shortly, happy to keep their

introductions brief as she threw herself back into the thrum and energy of the DJ's latest sound selection.

She was distracted by the flash of someone's camera, no doubt someone's shenanigans would be broadcast on some social networking site tomorrow, but before long her focus was solely on the man in front of her. Boy, but he could move. Some guys just looked as if they were trying too hard on the dance floor but for him, movement came very naturally. And he was so good to look at, too.

His hair was dark, but not as dark as her near-black tresses, and his face was both masculine and had a refined elegance at the same time. And those lips—she was very keen for a repeat of what they had to offer.

"Do I pass muster?" he asked, one corner of his mouth twisting upward.

She smiled in response. "You'll do."

He laughed and the sound went straight to her toes, making them curl in delight. Was there anything about him that wasn't gorgeous?

The crowd around them had begun to thin and Nicole started to become aware that eventually this night would have to end. At about that point she'd be feeling the pain of dancing in high heels for several hours, along with the aftereffects of too much to drink. She hated that reality had to intrude again, especially when she was having such a good time. Nate said something, but over the frenetic pulse of the music she didn't quite make it out.

"What was that you said?" Nicole asked, leaning closer.

Mmm, he even smelled great—like a cool ocean breeze.

"I said, would you like a drink?"

She'd probably had quite enough for one night but an imp of mischief prompted her to nod her head.

"Here? Or we could head back to my place if you'd rather."

She felt a frisson of excitement. Was he suggesting what she thought he was suggesting? She'd never done this before—gone back to some random guy's house for a drink, at least not without a posse of friends with her. But for some reason she felt as if she could trust Nate, and then there was that amazing energy between them. She deserved to find out if those sparks were real, didn't she? Wouldn't it be some solace for the night she'd put up with?

"Your place is fine."

Actually, anywhere but home was fine.

"Great." He smiled, the action sending a sizzle of anticipation thrilling through her veins.

Sore feet and the prospect of a hangover were the furthest things from her mind as Nate took her hand and led her toward the exit. And if thoughts of "danger" or "risk" occurred to her, she brushed them aside. Tonight was a night for taking chances.

And besides, what was the worst that could happen?

TWO

Nate caught Raoul's eye as he led Nicole away, giving his friend a nod. He briefly saw Raoul's answering wink before the expression on the other man's face changed to one of shocked recognition. Nate fought back the smug smile that pulled at his lips.

In all the years he'd spent imagining how he would bring Charles Wilson to his knees, he'd never once imagined this scenario. But then, he'd never imagined taking Charles Wilson's daughter in his arms and feeling such a searing sense of attraction, either. With such a ripe opportunity before him, he'd be a fool not to make the most of it—in every way possible. Still, he had to be careful. It wouldn't do to put the cart before the horse. He could just as easily be calling a taxi to take Nicole home after their drink, but something inside him told him that was very unlikely.

He reached in his pocket and pressed the remote to

the low-slung silver Maserati that waited for them at the curb.

"Very pretty car," Nicole commented as he held open the passenger door for her and she folded her delicious long legs into the passenger bay.

"I like to travel in style," he answered with a smile.

"I like that in a man," she answered, her lips curving in response.

He just bet she did. She'd never wanted for anything and every part of her life had been to the highest standard. It stood to reason that Nicole Wilson's demands of her men would be high. It was a gauntlet he relished picking up.

Unlike Nicole, Nate knew what it was like to struggle—his father had been a living example of the concept for most of Nate's childhood. After Charles Wilson had kicked him out of the business they'd built together, it had taken years for Thomas to reestablish his credibility and build a company of his own. Nate had watched as his father poured his everything into his fledgling business in an attempt to provide something, anything, to the woman he'd accidentally gotten pregnant and the son their liaison had borne. And while Thomas had done his best to shield his only child, the experience had left its mark, resulting in two rules that Nate had lived his life by ever since. Rule one: be very careful who you trust.

Rule two: all's fair in love and war.

Nate slid into the driver's seat and started the car, maneuvering it smoothly toward Hobson Street and the entrance to the North Western motorway.

"You're a Westie?" Nicole asked.

"After a fashion," he answered. "I have a couple of

places. Karekare is where I call home. You still want
that drink at my place?"

His challenge hung between them in the dark interior of the car. He shot her a glance and saw her press
her lips together and swallow before answering.

"I'm all good. I haven't been out to Karekare in
ages."

"It's still pretty much the same. Wild and beautiful."

"Like you?" she asked, her eyes gleaming as she
shot him a glance.

"I was thinking more along the lines of you."

She laughed, the sound filling the cabin of his car
and making his gut tighten in anticipation.

"Oh, you're good. You know all the right things to
say to salve a wounded soul."

"Wounded?" he probed.

"Just family stuff. Too complicated and too boring
to bring up now," she hedged.

Was all no longer well in the Wilson household?
Nate wondered. He'd made it his business to know
what happened within Wilson Wines and he'd heard
of the return of the prodigal son. Had Judd Wilson's
arrival served to uplift the mantel of golden child off
Nicole's shoulders?

"We have a long drive," Nate pointed out as they entered the motorway and his car picked up speed. "I'm
willing to listen if you want to talk about it."

"Just the usual," she said with an attempt at flip-
pancy. An attempt that failed judging by the tone of
her voice.

"Sounds serious," he commented, keeping his eyes
looking forward out the windscreen.

She sighed, the sound coming from somewhere deep

down inside her. "I had a fight with my dad. At the risk of sounding clichéd, he doesn't understand me."

"Isn't that a parental prerogative?"

She laughed, a short, sharp sound in total contrast to the last time she'd done so. "I suppose so. I just feel so used, you know? I have spent my whole life trying to measure up, to be the best daughter, the best workmate, the best—well, everything. And he thinks I should settle down and have *babies!* As if. You know, I think he values a paper clip on his desk more highly than he does me. I've spent the past five years helping him to keep our family business thriving and he tells me it's a nice *hobby* for me."

"I suppose this argument is what led you to the club tonight?"

"Too right it is. I couldn't stay under his roof another second. Oh, no, wait. It's not *his* roof anymore, nor mine. He's gone and given it all to my dear long-lost brother." She expelled an angry huff of air. "I'm sorry, I'm always letting my mouth run away with me. I shouldn't have said that. Just pretend you didn't hear that last bit, okay? I think we should change the subject. Talking about my family is just going to spoil my mood."

"Whatever the lady wants, the lady gets," Nate replied smoothly, even though his curiosity burned to know more about the Wilson family home situation.

"Now that's more like it." Nicole laughed in response. "A girl could get used to that attitude."

"What, you mean that isn't always the case?"

Nicole swiveled slightly in her seat and stared at him. "You say that as if you think you know me."

"You misunderstand me," he said smoothly. "I just

would have thought that a woman like you would have no trouble getting what she wanted."

She gave an inelegant snort, then change the subject. "Tell me about your home. Are you overlooking the beach?"

He nodded. Partly in concession to her change of subject and partly in answer to her question. "I'm on a slight rise looking out onto Union Bay."

"I've always loved the West Coast. The black sand beaches, the crazy surf. There's something so, I dunno, untamed, unpredictable about it all."

"You surf?"

She shook her head. "No, always been too chicken."

Somehow she didn't strike him as the type of woman to be afraid of anything, and he said as much.

"Some boundaries I just never pushed. I grew up as an only child with a parent who could be pretty strict. Sometimes my dad took overprotectiveness a little far."

"Only child? You mentioned a brother?"

"He lived with our mother up until recently. And how on earth did we get back on that awful topic again?"

She pushed a hand through her tangled long hair, exposing the sweep of her high cheekbones and the determined set of her jaw. His fingers itched to trace the fine bone structure, to taste the smooth skin that stretched over it. Nate tightened his grip once more, dragging his eyes back to the road and his mind back to the goal at hand. Yes, he wanted her. And yes, he had every intention of having her. But he couldn't let himself lose control. He had to keep the endgame in mind.

"What about you?" she asked, turning in her seat to look at him. "What's your family like?"

"Both my parents are gone. My mother while I was

in university, my dad more recently. I never had any brothers or sisters."

"So you're all alone? Lucky you." She gasped as if she realized the potentially pain-filled minefield she'd just trodden into. "I'm sorry, that was insensitive."

"No, it's okay. I miss them but I still count myself lucky to have had them both in my life. And my dad was a great role model. He worked his heart out, literally, to provide for us, and I got to repay that once I graduated and started working in the family firm."

Nate deliberately kept things vague. He wouldn't, for a moment, begin to elaborate on exactly why his father's health took such a beating as he strived to build a new business from the ground up. Or who was responsible for that.

"So, surfing?" he asked, very deliberately changing the subject as he took the exit he needed that would eventually lead them out toward the beach.

"What about it?"

"Want to try it over the weekend?"

"This weekend?"

"Sure, why not stay. I have spare boards, spare wetsuits."

"Spare clothes, underwear?" She gestured to her voluminous bag on the car floor. "It might be a big bag but it's hardly *Doctor Who's* TARDIS, you know."

Nate laughed. Her sharp wit was refreshing and appealing at the same time.

"Let's play it by ear then, hmm? Trust me?"

"Sure. If I didn't think I could trust you, I wouldn't be here."

He reached across and took her hand, caressing the soft skin of her inner wrist with his thumb.

"Good."

He let go and placed his fingers firmly back on the steering wheel. From the corner of his eye he saw that she stroked her wrist with the fingertips of her other hand. He allowed himself a small smile of satisfaction. This night was going perfectly.

So why *did* she trust him, she wondered as she lapsed into silence and looked idly out the passenger window. It's not as if she knew him. She'd acted purely on instinct, a fact that—despite her earlier assertion about being a chicken—had gotten her in trouble many a time before.

She gave herself a mental shake. She deserved this night. She had it coming to her after the crap she'd put up with at dinner on top of everything else this week. And everything in her body told her that this was the man to take all her problems away—at least for the night.

Her skin still tingled where he'd touched her, the sensation a delicious buzz of promise hovering just beneath the surface. Did he expect to make love to her tonight? Just the thought of it sent a thrill of longing through her body, making her womb clench tight on a swell of need that all but knocked the air from her lungs. She'd never had this intense a reaction to anyone before. Just sneaking a glance at his hands on the steering wheel, at the way his long fingers curled around the leather, made her want those fingers on her, in her. She pressed her thighs together and felt the swollen heated flesh at her core respond. Just thinking about him touching her was nearly enough to make her go off. What would it be like when he did?

She cleared her throat against the sudden anticipatory lump that lodged there.

"Everything okay?" Nate asked.

"Sure. It's quite a drive from the city to your place. Do you work in town?"

"Yeah. I keep an apartment there for the nights I'm too tired to make it back out to Karekare, or if I have an early run to the airport or early meetings. I sleep better with the sounds of the sea and the rainforest around me, though."

"Sounds idyllic."

"You'll see soon enough for yourself."

She fell silent as they entered Scenic Drive, letting her body sway with the roll of the car as they wound on the narrow ribbon of road higher into the ranges, before winding back down again on the other side. She must have dozed off a little because the next thing she knew the Maserati was driving up a steep incline and pulling into a well-lit garage. A glance at her watch said it was almost 2:00 a.m. The drive had taken nearly an hour. She was miles from anyone she knew, miles from home. She should find the fact daunting—she didn't. In fact, she welcomed it. Knew that with her choice to come home with Nate that she'd thrown her cares to the wind.

"Home sweet home," Nate said, coming around to her side of the car and opening the door for her.

Nicole accepted his hand as he helped her out the car, her senses purring at his touch. To her surprise he didn't let go, instead leading her to a doorway which, when opened, revealed a short set of stairs leading down into a massive open-plan living/dining and kitchen area.

The furnishings were comfortable but spoke plainly of their price in the elegantly simple designs and top-quality fabrics. A large, open fireplace, bordered with gray slate, occupied space on one wall. Even the art-works on the walls and small sculptures on the occasional shelving were beautiful and no doubt expensive. What he surrounded himself with said a lot about him and, so far, she liked it.

"Still feel like that drink?" Nate asked, lifting her hand to his lips and pressing a kiss against her knuckles.

"Sure, what are we having?"

"There's champagne in the fridge, or we could have a liqueur."

"A liqueur, I think."

Something potent and heady, just like him, she thought privately. Nate let her hand go and moved toward a built-in sideboard on the other side of the room. She gravitated toward the wall of glass that faced the inky darkness outside. Beyond the floor-to-ceiling windows she could hear the sound of waves rolling heavily into shore.

In the reflection of the glass she saw Nate come to stand behind her, one arm coming around to offer her a small glass of golden liquid.

"A toast, I think," he said, his breath warm in her hair and making her scalp prickle in awareness.

"To what in particular?" Nicole asked, accepting her glass and raising it toward Nate's pale facsimile mirrored before her.

"To wounded souls, and the healing of them."

She nodded and raised her glass to her lips, her taste buds reacting instantly to the smooth, sweet tang of aged malt whiskey. She allowed the liquid to stay on her tongue for a moment before swallowing.

"Now that is pretty fine," she said, turning to face Nate. Her breath caught in her chest as she saw the look in his eyes. Eyes that were only a shade darker than the deep gold fluid in their glasses.

"Only the best," he answered before closing the distance between their faces.

Nicole felt her heart race in her chest. If this kiss was to be anything like the one at the club she couldn't wait to experience it. Her lips parted expectantly, her gaze focused solely on the shape of his mouth, on the sheen left there by the liqueur. Her eyelids slid closed as she felt the warmth of him, as his lips took hers, as his tongue swept gently across the soft fullness of her lower lip.

He made a sound of appreciation. "Now that's what I call the best."

His lips pressed against hers once more and she curved into his body as one arm slid around her back and drew her closer to him. He was already aroused, a fact that triggered an insistent throb in her veins— a throb that went deeper into her center. She pressed her hips against him, feeling his length, his hardness. Feeling her body respond with heat and moisture and need.

She could taste the liqueur on his lips, on his tongue—its fusion of flavors intrinsically blended with his own. When he withdrew she felt herself move with him, toward him. Drawn as if by some magnetic force.

Nate put his liqueur glass on a shelf nearby before also taking hers and doing the same again. He then lifted his hands to her hair, pushing his fingers through the long mass until his fingertips massaged the back of her scalp, gently tilting her face to his once more. This time his kiss held a stronger taste of hunger, a promise of things to come.

Nicole tugged his shirt free of his waistband and

shoved her hands underneath, her nails gently scoring his back as she traced the line of his spine, up, then down. Logic tickled at the back of her mind a final time, telling her she shouldn't be here, shouldn't be doing this, but need and desire overcame logic with the same inexorable surge and release of the waves that echoed on the darkened shore outside.

He wanted her. She wanted him. It was basic and primal and it was all she needed for now. That, and a whole lot of satisfaction.

Nate's hand shifted to the buttons on her jacket, swiftly loosening them from their button holes and pushing aside the fabric, exposing her to him. His hands were broad and warm as they swept around the curve of her waist before skimming her rib cage and moving up toward her bra.

He released her lips, bending his head lower, along her jaw line, down the sensitive cord of her neck and across her collarbone. She felt her breasts grow heavy. Her nipples beading tight, almost painfully so, behind her expensive lace-covered satin bra. When the tip of his tongue swept across one creamy swell she shuddered in response, the sensation of the point of his tongue electric as it traced a fine line across the curve of one breast. He awarded the same attention to her other breast, this time sending a sharp spear straight to her core.

His tongue followed the edge of her bra before dipping in the valley between. Her breath came in quick pants, her heart continuing to race in her chest. She felt his hand at her back, felt the freedom of the clasp of her bra being released, the weight of her breasts falling free as he slid her jacket off her shoulders and pushed her bra straps down to follow. With scant regard for the designer labels of both garments, Nate let them drop to the polished timber floor.

Nicole was beyond caring as his mouth captured one extended nipple, pulling it gently between his teeth, laving it with the heat of his tongue. Her legs began to tremble and she clung to him, near mindless with the pleasure his touch brought her. When his hands went to the waistband of her skirt she barely noticed, and then, with a slither of silk lining, her skirt joined her bra and jacket on the floor at her feet.

Dressed only in a scanty pair of black-and-gold panties and her high-heeled, black patent pumps she should have felt vulnerable, but as Nate pulled away, his eyes caressing every inch of her, she felt powerful. Needed. Wanted.

"Tell me what you want," he demanded, his voice a low demand that vibrated across the space between them.

"I want you to touch me," she replied softly.

"Show me where."

She lifted her hands to her bare breasts, her fingers cupping their smooth fullness, lifting them slightly before her fingertips abraded the distended tips, sending another shudder through her.

"Here," she said, her voice thicker now.

"And?"

One hand crept down, over her flat belly, and to the top band of her panties.

"Here." Her voice trembled as she felt the heat that pooled between her legs, felt the moisture that awaited his touch, his possession.

"Show me what you like," he said, his hand sliding over hers.

"This," she replied, letting their hands push beneath the scrap of fabric.

She led his fingers toward her opening, dipping them in her wetness before sliding them back up toward the budded bundle of nerves that screamed for his touch. She circled the sensitive spot first with her fingers then with his, increasing the pressure then slowing things down before repeating the cycle once more.

"Keep touching yourself," he commanded, even as he slid his fingers out from beneath her hand, dipping them lower until they played within the soft folds of her flesh.

He hooked his other arm around her, supporting her weight as he stepped in a little closer. She felt the fabric of his trousers against her bare legs—a fleeting awareness only before all concentration went when he stroked one finger inside her body, then another. Her muscles clenched against him as his fingertips glided in and out, caressing with careful and deliberate pressure against her inner walls.

Sensation swirled throughout her body, drenching her with heat and pleasure. The combination of both their touches filled her with an overpowering awareness of him, his strength, his power over her. She'd never felt anything this deep, this intense. Had never been this reckless.

Nate bent slightly, capturing one nipple with his mouth, drawing the sensitive bud into his heat, his wetness, and suckling hard. As he did so, she felt the pressure of his fingers inside her increase and with that subtle change, her body splintered apart on a wave of satisfaction so intense, so immeasurable, that her legs buckled beneath her and tiny pin pricks of light danced behind her eyelids.

Her whole body shook with the intensity of her orgasm as ripple after ripple of pleasure coursed through her. She felt Nate withdraw from inside her, even as her inner muscles continued to pull and tighten against him, heightening the sensations and sending her into another short, sharp paroxysm of bliss. He slid one hand behind her knees and, with his other arm still supporting her back, he swept her into his arms and strode across the open plan area toward a darkened room.

His bedroom, her shattered senses finally recognized as he placed her on the bedcovers. In the fractured blend of moon and starlight that shone through the massive picture window, she watched as he stripped away his clothing. Exposing every inch of his silver-gilded male beauty to her gaze. He reached for her feet, removing the shoes she only just now realized she still wore, then his hands slid up the length of her legs. When he reached her panties he slowly removed them from her before lowering himself to the bed and gently kneeing her legs apart, settling between them.

He leaned across her and ripped open a bedside cabinet drawer and removed a box of condoms. Extracting a packet he made short work of ripping away the wrapper and rolling the protection over his jutting erection. Her hands fluttered to the breadth of his shoulders, his skin burning beneath her touch. Despite his clear and evident arousal, his movements were smooth, controlled and deliberate as he positioned himself at her entrance and looked up to meet her eyes, even now giving her the chance to change her mind, to decide for herself what she wanted. In response, she instinctively tilted her pelvis to welcome his invasion.

Nate lowered his face to hers, his lips a heated seal against her own, his tongue gently probing her mouth even as he eased his length within her. She felt her body stretch to accommodate his size, felt an unmistakable quiver deep inside. Nicole lifted her hands to his head, her fingers lacing through his hair as she held him to her and kissed him back with all she had left in her.

Her body swept to aching life as he began to move, his thrusts powerful and deep, so deep it felt as if he touched her very soul before she plunged into the abyss of sensual gratification once more. In answer, his body stiffened, buried to the hilt, and a nearly stifled cry of release broke from him as he gave over to his own climax, shuddering as her body clenched rhythmically around him. His lips found hers again as he settled his weight on top of her, and she welcomed him. It was real, he was real. His heart thudded in his chest and hers beat a rapid tattoo in answer.

What they'd done together was something unsurpassed in her experience and finally, as she drifted to sleep, the cares and worries of her life wafted away into oblivion.

Three

As Nate woke, he slowly became aware that he'd fallen asleep not just on top of Nicole, but still inside her, as well. He silently castigated himself for his inconsiderate behavior as he carefully supported his weight without waking her.

He ignored the unfamiliar urge to settle closer to her rather than pulling away. After all, certain precautions had to be observed, he reminded himself. He reached between them, feeling for the edge of his condom and cursing when he couldn't find it. He pulled farther away from her, his body instantly lamenting the lack of contact with her lush warmth. The condom was still inside her. In a moment of panic he wondered if she was on the Pill but that fear was quickly assuaged. A woman like Nicole wasn't the type to leave things to chance. It was highly unlikely that pregnancy was something either of them needed to worry about just now.

No, now was a time to concentrate on pleasure. They'd had sex once and he couldn't wait to repeat the experience.

He eased his hand between her splayed legs and found the condom, removing it carefully before disposing of it in his bathroom. As he eased his body back onto the bed beside her he safeguarded them once more by rolling on another sheath and gathered her to him. She curled instinctively against his body, her softness pressing against the hard muscled planes of his chest, her inner heat already beckoning to him.

Her eyes flickered open, a slow smile spreading across her face. He cupped one cheek in his hand. It was one thing to know from Raoul's report that Nicole Wilson was an attractive woman with an incredibly sharp business mind, but it was quite another to discover that she was also a warm and generous lover. The knowledge skewed his vision of how this would ultimately play out.

Sending Nicole back to her father was no longer an option. With a little luck, her anger against her father and her brother just might be deep enough and strong enough to make her willingly defect to Jackson Importers...and to Nate's bed. With Nicole at his side he could take Jackson Importers to the ultimate heights of success, while ensuring his nights were equally, if not more, satisfying.

Of course, there was always the possibility that loyalty to her family would win out. Nate would be a fool not to plan for that contingency. If that happened, he'd have to be more...creative in the methods he used to keep Nicole. He didn't want to hurt her—Charles was his only target—but if upsetting her a little was the price to get his revenge *and* keep Nicole in the bargain, then that was a price he was willing to pay.

Sooner or later, she'd thank him for it. He'd already known her father hadn't utilized her intelligence to his best advantage. But Nate would. And she'd know she was appreciated while he did it. Every glorious inch of her.

"You're so beautiful," he said, meaning every syllable.

"It's dark," she replied, a teasing note in her voice. "Everyone is beautiful in the dark. You can't see their bad side."

"You don't have a bad side," he said, leaning forward to kiss her.

"Everyone has a bad side, Nate. We just don't always show it."

There was a painful truth in her words. A truth he knew related directly to him and his intentions but he didn't want to think about that right now. More pressing matters were most definitely at hand.

"Sometimes it's better not to see, then, isn't it?" he asked before leaning across the short distance between them and kissing her.

Their lips touched in a burst of heat and desire, his every nerve striving to attain the heights of fulfillment he knew he would reach in her arms. This time the fire inside him burned steadily, not threatening to overwhelm him as it had before, but his hunger for her had not lessened despite the change in his appetite. This was to be savored, slowly, completely.

Time faded into obscurity and nothing mattered right now except the giving and receiving of pleasure. Each touch destined to bring a sigh or a moan from its recipient, each kiss a seal of the promise of what was yet to come. And when she positioned herself over his body and lowered herself over his straining flesh he gave himself over totally to her demands.

Their peak was no less intense than that first time together, and this time, when Nicole fell into his arms lost in the aftermath and falling rapidly into sleep, he made certain the same accident with the condom didn't occur a second time.

The next time he woke, sunlight was filtering through the native bush outside and into his bedroom window. He reached across the bed. Empty. Where was his quarry now, he wondered as he swung his legs over the side of the bed and stood, stretching as he did so.

"Nice view," a voice said from behind him.

He turned slowly, a smile on his face. A smile that widened when he saw that Nicole had found the camcorder he kept for filming some of the more wild surfing antics on the beach.

"Do you have a license to drive that thing?" he asked.

"I'm the kind of girl who likes to learn as she goes along," Nicole answered in response.

She was wearing just the shirt he'd worn last night, the fine cotton covering her body but leaving her long legs exposed to his hungry gaze.

"So you're more of the hands-on kind?" he said, feeling his body stir and his blood pump just a little faster.

"Oh, yes, definitely hands-on," she said, her voice a little rough around the edges.

"I've always thought practical experience to be vastly underrated, haven't you?" He was fully hard now. Every cell in his body attuned to her, to the camcorder she held, to the idea that now blossomed in his mind.

"Definitely underrated. And the value of visual aids, too."

Oh, God, he thought. She had just read his mind. "I have a tripod for that thing, you know."

She laughed, a deep throaty chuckle that made him clench his hands at his sides to stop himself from reaching for her.

"More than one, I'd say," she said, dropping the lens of the camera down, then slowly back up again to his face.

She was wicked. He liked that in a woman. He liked that a whole lot. "I'll go get the other one," he said with a slow wink.

Before she could say another word he brushed past her, dropping a kiss on the curve of her lips as he went by. "Why don't you get yourself comfortable on the bed? I'll be back in just a minute."

It took less than a minute before he was back in the bedroom and setting up the stand diagonal to the bed. She passed him the camera, her cheeks flushed with color, her eyes bright with anticipation. Beneath the fabric of his shirt he could see the sway of her breasts as she moved on the bed, not to mention the sharp peaks of her nipples that told of her excitement. She passed the camera to him and he carefully positioned it on its mount, ensuring the whole bed was square in the frame.

"You're sure about this?" he asked.

"Oh, very sure. And later, when we review it, we can see where we can improve."

He didn't think it was possible to get any harder but at that moment he did. It was one thing to know they were videoing themselves, another to know she wanted to watch it later.

"Where do you suggest we begin?" he asked, fighting to keep a lid on the carnal urge to simply have at her, to let her have at him and to hell with finesse.

"I think I need to get to know you better, don't you?" She patted the edge of the bed beside her. "Why don't you sit down?"

He sat and watched her as she slid off the tumbled linens and knelt between his legs on the rug beside the bed, placing her hands on the outside edges of his thighs, scratching lightly with her fingernails.

"It seems to me," she continued, "that last night was all about me. So this time, it's going to be all about you."

A fine tremor ran through his body and he watched as her hands stroked up his thighs and down again, each time working a little closer to the inside.

"Do you like that?" she asked.

He was beyond words and merely nodded.

"How about this?"

His mind nearly exploded as she bent her head and flicked the tip of her tongue over the aching head of his arousal. His penis jumped in response to her touch, a bead of moisture appearing only to be licked away just as quickly. Nicole's hair brushed against his inner thighs, obscuring her face. He reached down and pushed her hair aside, holding it against the back of her head with each fisted hand. He wanted to see this, all of it. And, just in case, he wanted the camera to see it, too.

Nicole felt an unaccustomed sense of possession as she lightly stroked her tongue along the length of

Nate's erection, painstakingly following the line of each vein from tip to base and back again. Heat rolled off him in waves as she did so and she felt him tremble as he fought to maintain control. But that control shattered the instant she took him fully in her mouth. He groaned, a guttural sound that came from deep in his belly, and she knew the exact moment he was going to climax. She increased the pressure of her mouth, her tongue, increased the rhythm of her movements until he spent himself. She slowed her pace, taking the last drop of his essence as he groaned again, his hands falling to his sides and his body falling back onto the bed behind him.

She pushed herself up onto the bed and lay propped on one elbow alongside him, letting her fingers trail up and down across his belly and chest as he caught his breath once more. His recovery said a whole lot about his fitness and stamina, she thought as he reached one arm up to her and dragged her down to kiss him. Already he was stirring again, and the knowledge gave her a wonderful feeling. It was all because of her.

"Mmm," she said, her lips bare centimeters from his. "Must be time for breakfast."

"Not yet," he said. "I think we should work up a bit more of an appetite first. And I think you should take that shirt off, too."

He deftly flicked open each button and slid one hand inside, cupping one breast and flicking his thumb across its hardened crest.

"I'm very hungry already," she purred. "I may take some convincing."

"You want convincing? I can be convincing," he said, pushing the shirt off her shoulders and then pressing her onto the bed.

What followed was an education in how someone could deliver a lifetime of hedonistic delight in very short order. Nate applied himself to her with assiduous intent, showing her just how artful he could be with the merest accessories—the tip of a tongue, a feather of breath, the stroke of a fingertip.

She was on the verge of begging, no, screaming for release when he finally sheathed himself with a condom and took them both over the edge of sanity and into a realm where only blithe elation resided.

The camera caught it all.

Their morning set the tone for the next three days. From time to time they would rise, bathe or eat—once taking a long stroll along the beach, Nicole wearing ill-fitting borrowed clothes—before the draw of their fascination with one another would take them back to bed again. By Monday morning Nicole was spent. Physically and emotionally, happy just to curl up against the hard male body beside her and revel in the intimacies they'd shared. Last night Nate had burned a DVD of their video and they'd viewed it while attempting to eat a civilized meal in the main room of the house.

The clothing they'd only recently donned—him in a pair of jeans and T-shirt, her in a sweatshirt of his with the sleeves rolled up and its length skimming the back of her thighs—had soon hit the floor. Their food cooling on their plates as the on-screen activity had incited a new hunger for one another all over again.

Nate still slept beside her and she watched his chest rise and fall on each breath. She was amazed at how natural it felt to be with him, especially considering how little they actually knew about one another. She'd heard the girls at work talk and giggle over their occasional one-night stands—guys they never expected, or in some cases even wanted, to see again—but she'd never believed she'd indulge in something quite so illicit herself. She felt as if the past few days had been a vacation, not just from work and responsibility, but from herself—her own fears and anxieties. On Friday she hadn't even given a care to the fact she had probably still been expected at the office, nor that over the course of the whole weekend she hadn't so much as told anyone where she was, nor checked her cell phone for messages.

It wasn't as if they cared, anyway, a little voice said from deep down inside. Her father didn't believe she had a valid contribution to make to the company, her best friend had turned on her and her brother? Well, he didn't even know her, nor she him. So what difference would it make if she walked away from all of them for good?

A whole lot of difference, she realized. She'd been angry on Thursday night. Really angry. And she'd acted completely out of character. Deep down she knew her family, including Anna, loved her and had to be worried about her having been out of touch for so long.

This person in the bed with a stranger, that wasn't her. Sure, it had been a great time, but all good things had to come to an end sometime, didn't they? Nothing this good ever lasted for long.

A wave of guilt for her behavior swamped her, driving her from the bed and into the bathroom where she gave in to the sudden well of tears in her eyes. She'd behaved irrationally. Stupidly. She had no idea of who she was really with. Everything that had anchored her these past twenty-six years lay on the other side of town—with her family, in her home. So what if her father had signed the property over to Judd? Her brother wasn't about to summarily eject her from the only home she'd ever known, surely. Judd was as much a victim of her father's shenanigans as she. So was Anna, who was far too grateful for all that Charles had done for her and her mother to ever tell him no.

And as for her father... It would be difficult for her to forgive or forget his words on Thursday night. But she couldn't forget twenty-six years of him sheltering and protecting her, either. For better or for worse, he was still her father. They'd just have to find a way to reach an accord. She was willing to take the first step, and come back home.

Nicole dashed her face with water and dried it before quietly letting herself out of the master bathroom and padding quietly across the bedroom floor. As she closed the door behind her she let go the breath she hadn't realized she'd been holding. She gave herself a mental shake. For goodness sake, she was an adult. Her decisions were her own, her choices were her own. The weekend had been great, just what she'd needed, there was no need to sneak around like a thief in the night.

She squared her shoulders and made her way to the laundry room where she'd hand washed and hung her underwear to dry during the course of the weekend. Her suit was on a hanger and had been brushed and steamed to get the creases out after being summarily left on the living room floor for several hours after Thursday night. She slid into her underwear and put on her suit. It felt strange to be dressed so formally after a weekend where clothing had been minimal.

She picked up her bag from in the living room and brushed out her hair before heading back to the bedroom to retrieve her shoes. She'd have to call a cab to get herself into work, she thought as she twisted her hair up into a knot and secured it with a clip she'd found in the bottom of her bag.

Nate was awake when she pushed open the door.

"Going somewhere?" he asked, his eyes unreadable as he watched her slide her feet into her shoes.

"Yeah, time to get back to reality." She sighed. "This weekend has been great. Better than great, thanks."

"That's it?"

"What—" she laughed nervously "—you want more?"

"I always want more, especially of what we've had."

"I never said I didn't want to see you again."

"But you implied it."

Nicole shot him a nervous glance. Was he going to get all weird on her now?

"Look, I need to get home and then head into work."

"No."

She shot him another look, this time the curl of fear in her stomach unfurled to bigger proportions.

"What do you mean, no?"

"What I mean is, you're coming to work with me."

Nate pushed aside the bed sheets and rose to his feet, calmly picking up the jeans he'd discarded last night and sliding them on. Nicole struggled to avert her gaze from the fine arrow of hair that angled down from his belly button to behind the waistband of his pants. She'd followed that path, and more, several times this weekend. A hot flush of color rushed to her cheeks. She couldn't let herself get distracted by sexual attraction. What on earth did he mean when he said she'd be working with him? She didn't even know what he did for a living. And he didn't know anything about her... did he?

"You've got it wrong, I have a job. A job I love, with a family I—"

"Don't tell me you love them, Nicole. Not after what they've done to you."

Instantly she rued the way she'd mouthed off in the car when he'd brought her here, and the truths she'd shared over a bottle of red wine as they'd curled naked beneath a blanket on the couch in front of a burning fire, late on Saturday night.

"They're still family. At the very least I need to clear the air with them."

"Oh, I think that's a bit more than they deserve. Besides, the air will clear soon enough."

Nicole crossed her arms across her stomach. "What on earth are you talking about?"

"When they learn who you've just spent this past weekend with, I very much doubt they'll be welcoming you home with open arms. I'm pretty much persona non grata with your father."

Nate's lips lifted in a half smile, as if he was laughing at a private joke.

"You're speaking in riddles. Why should they care who I spent the weekend with?" she snapped.

Nate came to stand in front of her. "Because I'm Nate Hunter—Nate Hunter Jackson."

Nicole's mind reeled on his words. Nate Hunter? *The* Nate Hunter? The reclusive billionaire who was the new head of Jackson Importers, her family firm's arch nemesis? Her father had never had a kind word to say about Thomas Jackson, or his staff.

Hang on a minute. Nicole replayed his words in her mind. Had he said Nate Hunter *Jackson?*

"I see you've made the connection," Nate said coolly. "And, yes, I am Thomas Jackson's son. Sweet, isn't it? All that time your father accused my dad of screwing around with your mother, he was actually with mine."

Nicole looked at him in horror as his words slowly sank in, leaving her mind reeling. She hadn't just been sleeping with a stranger over the entire weekend— she'd literally been sleeping with the enemy!

Four

Nate watched the shock and dismay play across Nicole's features as understanding clouded her beautiful brown eyes.

"So you knew who I was all along? This weekend has all been about you getting some twisted revenge on my family?" she asked. Her voice shook, betraying just how much his words had upset her.

It might have started that way, Nate admitted to himself, but now he'd been with Nicole so intimately he knew that for the better part of their time together, revenge had been the last thing on his mind. At least, revenge on *her*. Her father, of course, was another matter entirely.

"Did you hunt me out?" she demanded, her voice stronger now.

"Our meeting was by chance," he said smoothly. "A happy chance from my point of view." He stepped forward and reached one finger to her cheekbone, tracing the smooth feminine contour to the corner of her lips. "And I don't regret a second of it, Nicole."

She jerked her head away. "Of course you don't," she said angrily. "Well, your little game is over now. I'm heading back into the city to my family and my job."

"I don't think so," Nate responded smoothly, crossing his arms in front of him.

"You can't possibly be serious about me working for you."

"I'm serious, all right."

"No." Nicole took a step back from him, putting one hand out as if she could physically prevent his words from holding any truth. "There's no way in this lifetime that I'd do such a thing, even if my father didn't want me at Wilson Wines. It would destroy every last vestige of our relationship together. He may not understand me as well as I'd hoped for, but he's still my father. I won't do that to him. I just won't."

Why couldn't she have stayed angry at her family? That would have made this so much easier, Nate thought to himself. Was there any way he could stoke that anger again?

"You *are* talking about the man who said that Wilson Wines was a nice hobby for you, aren't you?"

She shook her head, more in frustration, he imagined, than to negate what he'd just said. Nate pursued his advantage in the face of her silence.

"And you're talking about the man who, without a word of discussion with you—his right hand at Wilson Wines—gave away a controlling interest in his business to someone who is essentially a complete and utter stranger to both of you."

"Stop," she moaned, wrapping her arms about herself and holding them tight. "I know that's what he's done, you don't need to repeat it. He's my father. No matter what, he'll always be my dad. I'll always be loyal to him."

"Really? Why? He's even given away your family home, Nicole. Again, without any prior warning to you, nor any assurance for you that you will have a roof over your head anymore. Haven't you asked yourself yet what kind of man would do that to his daughter?"

Nate was angry, furiously angry. Not at Nicole, who seemed determined to forgive her father anything, but at the man who was at the root of all Nate's unhappiness. The man whose brutal rejection of his best friend had crushed Thomas Jackson's spirit and had forced him into dire financial straits. And the man who had withheld his encouragement and support from his daughter for so long that she'd forgive any insult for the chance to earn his approval.

He pressed on as she stood there silent and pale.

"You deserve more, Nicole. You deserve so much more. You're a strong, intelligent and incredibly capable woman. You should work somewhere where you're valued and appreciated. Think about the team we'll make. We'll be the best the business has ever seen."

She raised tear-washed eyes to his face and he fought to ignore the spear of regret that penetrated somewhere in the region of his chest. He knew his words hurt her but he couldn't afford to be soft, not now. If she didn't give in soon, he'd have to hurt her a lot more. He didn't want to, but he would, if it came to that. All was fair in love and war. And this was war.

"Nicole, your loyalty to Charles Wilson is commendable, but sadly misplaced. Work with me. Help me grow Jackson Importers to its fullest potential. Be a part of something special."

She swallowed before speaking. "And what's in it for you? You can't expect me to believe you're doing this out of the goodness of your heart."

He laughed, a short humorless sound that hung in the air between them for only a second or two. "No, I'm not doing it out of the goodness of my heart. I'm a businessman. I play to win, at all times and," he hesitated a moment for effect, "at all costs."

She shook her head again. "I won't work for you and I'm leaving right now. You're not the man I thought you were, Nate. I can't do what you're asking of me."

"Nicole, I'm not asking."

"I still have some say in this, don't I?" she demanded, turning and heading for the front door.

"Sure, you still have a say," he said, his words halting her in her tracks. "But so do I, and there's still a card left for me to play."

"I wasn't aware this was a game," she said coolly.

"Not a game at all," Nate said, smiling, even though his voice held no warmth anymore. "But all the same, I *will* win." He gestured toward the video camera still on the tripod in the corner of the room. "Ask yourself this, how would your father feel if he saw our amateur movie? What would hurt him more? Seeing you work for me, or knowing that you'd spent this past weekend in my bed?"

"Th—that's not fair," Nicole stammered, struggling to keep her balance. It felt as if the floor had been knocked out from under her. "I didn't know who you were then."

"I never said I play fair, Nicole. Your father already

hates the Jackson name. Already believes your mother slept with my father—it's what tore Charles and Thomas's friendship apart, what divided your family and what destroyed mine. I'll be sure to include a note with the DVD, explaining my parentage. How do you think he'd feel about seeing his daughter intimately engaged with Thomas Jackson's son?"

"You wouldn't!" Nicole uttered the words even though her throat felt as if it had constricted with shock and fear.

"Oh, believe me. I very much would. I want you, Nicole. I want you in my boardroom, in my office, in the field as well as here—in my home and in my bed."

Her skin tautened as his words fell upon her ears. Her nipples hardening even as a rush of warmth spread through her lower belly and her inner muscles clenched involuntarily in reaction to his words. Stop it, she told herself. He wasn't simply talking about sex. He was talking about her betraying her father. About her walking away from the company she'd hoped all her life that she would eventually take over. The job that was so much more than a job. It had been her way of life— her dream. It had been everything to her father and, ergo, everything to her, as well.

What Nate was suggesting was appalling. If she quit her job at Wilson Wines to work for Nate, her father would never understand, never forgive her. But could she take the risk that Nate would follow through on his threat and send her father a copy of their illicit weekend? Even as the thought presented itself in her mind, she knew without a shadow of a doubt that Nate would do exactly what he said. Men like him didn't always play fair or clean—and they rarely bluffed. It would hurt her father if she worked for Nate but it would probably kill him if he saw that video.

"You're a bastard," she said quietly.

"Oh, yes, no question about that," Nate answered, a thread of bitterness in his voice that she hadn't heard before.

She racked her memory. Her father had rarely spoken about the man who had been his best friend from school, but when he did it had been in scathing terms. Thomas Jackson had never married. Never even publicly acknowledged he had a son. Was Nate even telling the truth about his relationship with the man?

She was hit with a sudden wave of hopelessness. Did any of her conjecture even matter when right now Nate held all the cards very firmly in those dexterous hands of his? Hands that had done wickedly delicious things to her over the past seventy-two hours. She clamped down on the thought before it took her over again. She had to forget the man she thought she'd grown to know a little these past few days. Had to remember, instead, the hardheaded businessman who had so mercilessly embarked on their time together knowing full well who she was and what being with him would mean to her family.

Her family. They were what had gotten her into this mess. Them and her blasted impulsiveness. She could see the lines of disappointment carved into her father's face even now.

"So, Nicole, what's it to be?"

Nate stood opposite her, his hands loosely on his lean jean-clad hips, his chest still bare, his shoulders still showing evidence of their passion where she'd clutched him tightly—her nails imbedding in his skin, lost in the throes of yet more pleasure. Even now, with his intentions out in the open, she still had to fight her desire for him. What did that say about her? She didn't even want to begin to examine that question.

She couldn't do it. She couldn't let her father see her wanton behavior, especially with the man who epitomized everything her father had fought against in the past twenty-five years. She had no other choice. She had to do as he said.

"You win."

"There, that wasn't too difficult, was it?"

She flung a fulminating look at him. "You have no idea."

She was damned if she did as he'd demanded, and she was damned if she didn't. At least this way she could protect her father from seeing the full extent of her own stupid behavior. Her face burned with shame as she remembered that she had been the one to pull out the camcorder in the first place. Furious and embarrassed, she pushed the thought away.

Nate Hunter Jackson might have won this round but he wouldn't win them all, she silently vowed. One way or another, she'd get her own back on him.

"This doesn't have to be a bad thing. At least with me you won't be taken for granted, Nicole," he said.

She ignored him. Being taken for granted was the least of her immediate worries. "I need to go home and get my things, and pick up my car," she said with as much control as she could muster.

"That won't be necessary."

She gestured to the suit she'd put back on this morning. Despite her attentions to it, the garment still looked a little the worse for wear and in need of a professional dry clean.

"Sorry to disappoint you, but I need my clothes. I can't wear this forever."

"Personally, I kind of like the idea of you not wearing it."

"Personally, I don't care what you like," she retaliated. She may have been forced into agreeing to his terms but she'd take a long walk off a short pier before she'd take her clothes off again at his behest. "I need my things—my car, my cell phone charger, everything. And I'll need to tell my father and brother that I won't be working for them anymore."

"I'll arrange for your car to be collected. As to your clothes, we can take care of that on the way into work. And, as to your father and brother, I'll take care of letting them know. There's no way to break it to them gently, and being blunt would be a miserable experience for you, but will be quite a lot of fun for me. Now, give me five minutes to shower and change. We can have breakfast in the city before we shop."

He turned and headed for the bathroom.

"I'm not hungry," she said to his retreating back.

Nate stopped and turned around, his hands already at the button fly of his jeans and exposing his lower abdomen to her gaze. "Not hungry? That's a shame. I'll have to have enough appetite for the both of us, then, won't I?"

Nicole dragged her eyes from the half open fly of his jeans and up to his face. His eyes burned with a heat that sent an answering response coursing through her body.

"Yes, you will," she said through teeth clenched so tight her jaw ached. She forced herself to relax the tiniest bit before continuing. "Because I have absolutely no appetite at all."

There, she thought, take that. She spun on one high heel and stomped through to the massive picture window facing the sea in the living room. Even there she was destined for disappointment, she thought. Instead of the rough roiling ocean she'd come to expect from the wild west coast beach ahead of her, there was nothing but a clear-blue autumn sky, rolling deep green water and foaming white crests of waves caressing the sparkling black sand shoreline. It was a complete contrast to the storm of emotion that tossed around inside her.

She was going to work for the son of her father's biggest business rival. He'd never forgive her this. Not in a million years. She shouldn't care, she told herself. He was the one who had summarily dismissed all her years of hard work for Wilson Wines and along with that dismissal had put aside her business and marketing degrees, not to mention the years of after-school and school holiday work experience she'd doggedly labored through so she could understand his business from the ground up. He'd never realized how important the business was to her because he'd never grasped how important *he* was to her.

Somewhere along the line, and from a very early age, Nicole had understood that her father's business was his everything. It was what he poured his heart and soul into every waking hour of every day. She'd thought that if she did exactly what he did, she'd earn his respect. And still he thought it was no more than a dalliance for her. Something to fill in her time before the more important matters of marriage and making babies filled her life.

Her hands tightened into fists, her perfectly manicured nails biting into the skin of her palms, as all her latent frustration built deep inside her. Getting angry at her father all over again would make it easier to walk away from Wilson Wines…but deep down, she knew the anger wouldn't last. She loved her father, and she knew that he loved her, even if they'd both fallen short on finding a way to connect. But even now, she refused to believe that it was too late. She closed her eyes to the perfection of the view outside and forced herself to draw in a steadying breath, and then another. Somehow she'd work her way through this. Somehow she'd work her way back to her family again.

"You ready?"

Nate's voice came from behind her. She opened her eyes and turned around. In a tailored charcoal-gray suit, with a crisp white shirt and flame-colored silk tie, he was a world away from the sensual creature who'd filled her weekend with sybaritic delight. A world away, but no less appealing. She ruthlessly pushed aside the admission.

"I was waiting for you, remember?" she said, scathingly.

He smiled, the action making something inside her tug hard. She silently cursed him for having this effect on her.

"Let's go, then."

The drive into the city was interminable. Nicole checked her cell phone for about the sixteenth time since they'd started out on the road. She hadn't had her phone on all weekend but even now the thing was down to only one bar of battery left. One bar and no blasted reception. Just as they crested a hill, she saw she finally had a signal and, with that, her phone began to vibrate in her hand as one message after the other poured in. By the time it settled down she saw she had six missed calls, an equal number of voice messages and more texts than she cared to count. Before she could do anything about them, though, her phone died—all the beeping and vibrating having drained the last of its charge.

"Argh!" she growled in frustration.

"Problem?" Nate asked, infuriatingly calm.

"My phone just died."

"No problem, I'll get you a new one. It'll be better that way—start over fresh."

"I like this one," she said doggedly. "It already has everything I need in it."

"It has what you needed for your old life—not for your new one. You've got a whole new list of people you'll be working with, communicating with. Besides, that was probably a company-subsidized phone—and you're not with that company anymore."

To her surprise, Nate took one hand off the steering wheel and reached across to take the phone from her hand.

"Needs updating, too," he said, giving the technology a cursory glance. "The one I get you will have better programming—and better access, too. I can't have you out of range whenever you're at the house."

"There's noth— Wait! What the hell are you doing?"

His driver's window rolled down smoothly and he lobbed the phone out onto the road where, to her horror, it was promptly run over by a truck coming in the opposite direction.

"How dare you? That was mine."

"I told you, I'll get you a new one. That one's no good anymore, anyway."

"No thanks to you."

She fought back the tears that suddenly came into

her eyes. This was a complete nightmare. Did he have to control everything? Maybe it would have been better to bite the bullet, after all, and suffer the consequences of her father seeing the DVD. Even as she thought it, Nicole pushed the thought from her mind. Her father's health had been declining in recent years. He'd ignored his diabetes for too long and the damage it had wrought on his system was beginning to tell on him, making him look much older than his sixty-six years. She didn't even want to imagine the impact a major shock to his system would have on his health.

No, she was in this for the long haul. No matter what it took, no matter the toll on her.

"The replacement had better be top of the line," she said, putting as much steel into her voice as she could.

"Of course. Nothing but the best for you, I promise."

"That's quite a promise. Do you really think you can meet it?"

Nate flicked a glance in her direction before returning his gaze to the traffic ahead.

"I'm a man of my word."

"That remains to be seen," she muttered, focusing her attention out the passenger window.

The way he'd said it, it held more threat than promise, and for some reason that, more than anything, chilled her to the bone.

Nate watched as Nicole was taken through to the fitting room of the third designer store they'd been to so far this morning. She'd insisted on getting a new wardrobe before eating, which now left him starving—but not for any food. He was hungry for her. For the feel of the texture of her skin beneath his touch, for the taste of her on his lips, for all the little sighs and moans she made while they explored one another's bodies with intimate precision.

Part of him wanted to say to hell with work—and clothes—and just head back to the house for another day in bed. Only two things stopped him.

The first was the office. Jackson Importers was his father's legacy in so many ways, and when Nate had taken up the mantle as CEO, he'd promised himself that he would invest every energy, every effort, into making the company the absolute best it could be. He didn't balk at long hours or working weekends, and even when he'd been stuck at home with a stomach bug, he'd still checked in through email all day long. Calling in sick on Friday had undoubtedly raised a few eyebrows. If he missed work on Monday, too, his staff would probably send an ambulance out to his house.

The second reason was Nicole, herself. Yes, he wanted her badly—both in bed and out of it. She was more than he'd ever dreamed of. He already knew she had a very smart mind—the dossier Raoul had prepared on the Wilson family had been thorough. If Nate could have found a way to headhunt Nicole Wilson for Jackson Importers after his father's death, he probably wouldn't have even needed to come home from Europe to take over the business. Her misplaced loyalty to her father was well documented, however, and he hadn't even bothered trying to steal her away.

That loyalty was the problem he was dealing with now. He supposed it had been too much to hope that her frustration with her family would lead her to welcome the chance to enact a little revenge along with him.

But her dedication to her father wouldn't be an obstacle forever, he rationalized. Sooner or later, she'd have to realize that Nate treated her better, and appreciated her more, than her father ever could. When she accepted that—and when she realized that the passion between them was impossible to ignore or deny—she'd turn her loyalty to him. She didn't know it yet, but he would be the best thing that had ever happened in her life. He just had to be patient until she came to terms with that—and watch her closely.

Yes, watch her *very* closely, because if the glares she kept giving him were any indication, any hand he reached out to touch her would come back to him bleeding. She was furious with him for forcing her into this position—and a smart, capable woman with a grudge was a dangerous creature, indeed.

So he'd have to be on his guard. Nothing new there—he was always on his guard. And he knew, far better than his father ever had, to be very careful before giving a Wilson his trust.

"Miss Wilson is finished now, Mr. Hunter," the store manager said, coming through with an armful of clothing and a smile that told of the sizeable commission she'd no doubt be earning today.

"So soon?"

"She has very specific tastes and was quick to decide on what she needed."

Nate gave the delivery address of his inner-city apartment for the clothing and handed over his platinum card, then looked back toward the changing rooms. Nicole was walking toward him in a new outfit, one that made his breath still in his lungs and all the blood in his body race to a very specific part of his anatomy. The ruby-red dress, while probably perfectly acceptable office wear on anyone else, skimmed every curve of her graceful figure. The scooped neckline offering a tantalizing hint of the swell of her full breasts. The three-quarter-length sleeves exposing her slender forearms. Forearms that led to delicate wrists and elegant hands. Hands that had gripped him and teased him and delivered all kinds of pleasure.

"All done now?" he asked as she drew alongside him.

"I just need some underwear and sleepwear."

"Sure. Do you want to eat first or keep shopping?"

"Still got that appetite?" she said, with a hint of an acerbic humor.

He looked her up and down very deliberately before meeting the unspoken challenge in her dark-eyed stare. "Always."

His reward came in the sudden flush of color that suffused her cheeks.

"We'd better get some food, then," she said sharply, breaking eye contact and giving her attention to the store manager—thanking the other woman for her assistance.

They stopped at a café in Vulcan Lane where he consumed Eggs Benedict while she played with a mixed berry muffin on her plate. While lingering over his coffee, Nate picked up the complimentary newspaper the café provided. He flicked through the pages, emitting a long slow whistle when he reached the society page.

"Looks like I might not have to make that call to your father's office, after all," he said, folding back the page and showing it to Nicole.

Five

They danced together, right there in black and white. Caught in time forever. Their intense absorption in one another as clear as day on their faces. Opposite him, Nicole paled and drew in a sharp breath.

"Did you orchestrate this?" she demanded.

Nate laughed. "I'm flattered you think I have that much power but, no, I didn't."

She looked at him as if she didn't believe a word that came from his mouth.

"Obviously you want to hurt my dad, but why go to all this trouble with me over something that happened so long ago? Our fathers fell out. Their friendship broke up. It happens."

Nate looked at her over the rim of his coffee cup. Did she really think it was that simple?

"Your father accused mine of something he didn't do. He wouldn't listen to reason nor would he ever accept he was wrong. He broke my father's heart, broke the man inside him, destroyed his honor. And thanks to your father's actions, my father had to work himself to the bone just to make ends meet as he got Jackson Importers off the ground, ruining his health and making him die before his time. My father deserved better than that and so did my mother."

"And will hurting mine bring them back? Will it make it all better again?"

"No, but it will give me the utmost satisfaction when Charles Wilson is finally forced to admit he was wrong."

Nicole shook her head. "You're the one who is wrong, Nate. Let this go. Let *me* go."

Let her go? Before her father had learned his lesson? Before Nicole had accepted how good they could be together? Oh, no.

"Not going to happen." He picked up his cup and drained the last of his coffee. "If you're finished playing with your food, we should get the last of your shopping done before heading into the office."

They walked together up Queen Street toward Auckland's oldest department store. It amused Nate that Nicole maintained a clear foot of distance between them at all times. Not easy to do in the throng of business people, shoppers and tourists who congested the footpaths. When they reached the department store, Nicole lingered awhile at the cosmetics counters on the ground floor leaving Nate to hand his card over again as she purchased skin care, fragrance and cosmetics.

"You don't need to do this," she objected, her own credit card in her hand already.

"Humor me," he said, taking her card and examining it. "This in your name or under your father?"

"It's all mine, paid for by my very own wages. Is that okay?" She snatched it back from him and pushed it back into her wallet before gathering up her bags from the shop girl and heading toward women's wear upstairs.

"I'll get you another one."

"This one is perfectly fine."

No it wasn't, he thought. Anything that led back to Charles Wilson in any way was, in his book, tainted—and her previous earnings definitely led back to Charles Wilson. Nate had every intention of paying her a generous salary, and until that began, he intended to take care of things. Take care of *her*. Nothing but the best for her—he'd promised her that, and he'd meant it.

Upstairs in the lingerie department he was again relegated to a chair while Nicole browsed rack after frothy rack of underwear. When she'd finally made her selection and gone through to the changing rooms he got up from his chair and paced the floor. As he did so, his eye latched onto a stunning ensemble on a floor mannequin. The ivory lace-and-chiffon nightgown and matching peignoir was both innocence and pure sin in one simple package.

Attracting the eye of the sales clerk he gestured to the ensemble.

"Include one of these in Miss Wilson's size with her purchases, thank you. And, please, keep it as a surprise."

He flashed the woman a wink and a smile and the blushing clerk hastened to fulfill his request before Nicole returned from the changing rooms. Already he could imagine peeling the diaphanous garment from Nicole's lithe body, but not before he'd tormented both her, and himself, with touching her through its silken texture first.

It would be torment enough for him waiting for her to come back to his bed. But the waiting would pay off sooner or later. It would all pay off in the end.

It was well past lunchtime before they made it into Nate's offices in a high-rise overlooking Auckland's Waitemata Harbor. He settled his hand on the small of her back as they exited the elevator and directed her toward a set of glass doors emblazoned in gold leaf with "Jackson Importers" and its stylized logo of a bunch of grapes.

He reached forward and opened the door, holding it for Nicole as she walked through and into the reception area. His receptionist looked up and smiled. He introduced Nicole immediately.

"April, this is Miss Wilson, she'll be working with us from now on. I'd like you to call all the staff into the boardroom to meet her in about fifteen minutes."

"Surely that won't be necessary," Nicole protested. "I can just—"

"I want everyone to know who you are and why you're here," he said in a voice that brooked no argument. "Tomorrow I'll introduce you to the staff at our warehouse and distribution center."

She pressed her lips together, clearly biting back whatever it was that she wanted to say. He guided her down the corridor and pushed open the door that led into the boardroom. Seeing her there, in his offices, in that stunning dress, his self-control cracked. The instant the door closed behind him, he couldn't stop himself from sweeping her into his arms, drawing her against his body and lowering his head to capture her mouth. The second their lips touched he felt electrified, the charge of energy he got from her sizzling a slow burn all the way to the pit of his stomach.

"I needed that," he groaned against her lips when he'd sated his need, however temporarily.

"Well, I didn't. I'd appreciate it if you kept your hands, and all your other body parts, to yourself," Nicole answered, moving out of his reach and smoothing her dress in a gesture that spoke more of nervousness than any real desire to stay out of reach.

Well, he couldn't say he hadn't expected that. But still… "You can't deny you enjoyed it," Nate said, observing the brightness of her eyes, the rapid rise and fall of her chest.

"How I might respond to you physically is one thing. Whether I actually want to, is another. Don't touch me again."

"Ever?" he asked, narrowing his eyes.

"Ever," she adamantly replied.

"So you're telling me that if I did this," he touched a fingertip to the slight swell of her breasts visible above the neckline of her dress, "that you don't *want* more?"

Nicole fought to control the wave of need that trembled through her body. She couldn't show him any weakness, not for a minute. Men like Nate Jackson capitalized on weakness and she could not afford for him to get any more leverage on her than he already had.

"There's a name for what you're doing," she managed to finally say. "I believe it's called harassment."

To her surprise, Nate laughed. Genuine pleasure at her words making his eyes lighten and shine.

"You're priceless," he said through his good humor.

"Harassment. Would you have said it was harassment at about 3:00 a.m. this morning, when I—"

Nicole was saved from the torture of hearing him repeat what they'd been doing in the small hours of this morning, and saved, thank God, from giving him an answer when the door behind them opened.

"Ah, Raoul, please meet our newest addition to the team, Nicole Wilson. Nicole, this is Raoul Benoit. Don't be fooled by his name, he's just as much a Kiwi as you or I."

Raoul inclined his head in acknowledgement of Nate's introduction and gave Nicole a shy smile.

"Miss Wilson, it's a pleasure to meet you, and even more of a pleasure to have you on our team."

"I…" What on earth could she say? She couldn't exactly tell Raoul she was here under duress. That she'd virtually been kidnapped and forced to come here. "Thank you."

Raoul looked at Nate and she didn't miss the question in Raoul's eyes as he did so. The expression of supreme satisfaction on Nate's face told her everything she needed to know. Raoul Benoit knew exactly who she was and exactly what Nate was up to. It made her feel alienated, as if she was completely alone in this horrible situation.

Nate's voice broke into her thoughts. "I've asked April to get the staff in here to meet Nicole. I think it's a good idea to let everyone know she's going to be with us from now on."

His words made her feel like nothing more than a trophy, but before she could utter a word of protest, the door opened again. A steady stream of people came into the boardroom, sitting where they could and standing, lining the wall, when all the seats were taken. She was surprised Jackson Importers carried such a large staff in their Auckland offices, and Nate had spoken of a warehouse and distribution staff, as well. It rammed home the reality of what he'd coerced her into doing— working with the thriving and very competitive enemy. The next quarter hour passed in a blur.

By the time Nate showed Nicole to his office, her head was spinning and she was beginning to regret not having eaten that berry muffin at breakfast.

"And this is where you'll be working," he said as he closed the office door behind them.

Nicole looked around the sumptuously appointed office, at the amazing view of the harbor beyond and then back at him.

"This is your office. I can't work here."

He shrugged. "I'm prepared to share my space with you. All my space, Nicole. Together we're going to head up the most successful wine importation business in the country. Why would I want you anywhere else but at my side?"

That all sounded very impressive—but what did it really mean? "Is that a fancy way of saying that you want to keep an eye on me?"

He smirked. "I'll always enjoy having my eyes— or anything else—on you." Nicole huffed in frustration, and Nate continued, "If you're asking if I'll be watching your work, then the answer is yes. I know that right now, you don't want to be here and you're angry with me for forcing your hand. I think that'll change. I think that once you understand the opportunities for you here, you'll see that this is where you belong. When that day comes, you can have any office you want. Until then, you'll understand if I prefer to keep you where I can see you. After all, I'll certainly enjoy the view."

"What about privacy for phone calls and things like that?"

"Worried I might overhear your conversations?"

"Do you plan to follow me to the bathroom, as well?" she demanded, her temper finally fraying. Since his very unwelcome revelation this morning, he'd been controlling everything about her except for how she drew breath—and even that was under deliberation. Every time he brushed past her she got a tightness in her chest that was all his fault.

"Do you need me to?"

"I don't *need* you for anything," she said mutinously.

"Like your father doesn't need you?"

He knew exactly how to cut to precisely where it hurt. Nicole turned from him and tossed her handbag onto his desk.

"Well, if this is where I'm supposed to be, I'd better get to work, then, hadn't I?"

He smiled and gestured to the laptop and cell phone on the desk that he'd arranged to have delivered while waiting outside her dressing rooms. "They're all yours, have at it."

"Mine. Already?"

"I told you I'd take care of you, Nicole. I meant every word I said."

She swallowed against the lump that suddenly filled her throat. He said it like he meant it. As if she was something—no, some*one*—important to him. She didn't want to believe it. Couldn't believe it. They'd had a weekend of great sex. Okay, it was off the scale great sex. But that was all. There couldn't be anything more between them, especially not now he'd made his intentions toward her father explicitly clear.

"Where do you want me to start?" she asked, crossing behind the desk and opening the laptop, determined to keep this on a professional level even if it was likely to destroy her.

"How about you spend some time on coming to grips with our new internet-only business? It's taken off far quicker than we anticipated and reaches beyond our existing New Zealand market and allows us to trade overseas, as well. It cuts overheads considerably as, in many cases, we've been able to coordinate shipping direct between the vineyard and the buyer, thus cutting freight and storage costs to a minimum."

Nicole felt the thrill of excitement at learning a new business model ripple through her. For years, she'd been urging her father to consider an online ordering system rather than solely relying on hands-on distribution. True, hand selling often gave wine-store customers a chance to try something new that they might not have considered before, but to hope that would continue to buoy the market forever was professional suicide. The world changed at an incredibly fast pace. The wine distribution industry no less so.

Another thought occurred to her. Nate's approach to supervision had thrown a spanner in her initial plans to use her access to sabotage some of Jackson Importers' business, but there was still a chance to come out ahead here. Deep down she knew this situation couldn't last. Eventually she'd find a way to return to Wilson Wines, and Nate was giving her the perfect opportunity to learn as much as she could of their successful business practices and think about how Wilson Wines could im-

plement them, or use them to create something even
better.

Remaining focused on business was easier said than
done as Nate pulled up a chair next to hers and brushed
against her as he keyed in the URL that would take her
computer onto the Jackson Importers portal.

"You'll need your own password. I'll get IT onto
that immediately. While I go and sort that out, why
don't you cruise around the website and make a list of
questions you want to ask me?"

She merely nodded as he stood again, sucking in
a deep breath of relief when he left the office. She'd
thought her anger and resentment toward him would
allow her to cope better with his close presence here
in the office. The opposite couldn't have been more
true. She'd found her eyes riveted on his long fingers
as they'd flown over the keyboard of her new laptop,
and had been forced to quell the memory of what those
fingers had felt like as they'd flown over her body.

Nicole leaned back in the high-backed, leather
office chair and swung around to face the view out
over the Waitemata Harbour. Even on a workday the
water was scattered with yachts making the most of
the autumn sunshine and the strong breeze. How she
wished she could emulate their freedom. But freedom
was something that would remain in limited supply for
her until she could work a way out of this mess. Somehow, someway, she'd find a way to get her own back
on Nate Jackson, and, like his father before him, he'd
be sorry he'd ever tangled with a Wilson.

Six

Nate spent the rest of the afternoon with Nicole, discussing the wines they imported and the systems that Jackson Importers had in place both in New Zealand and overseas for distribution to their worldwide network of buyers. By the time the sun was dipping below the Waitakere Ranges in the distance, they were both looking pretty exhausted.

"I think it's best if we stay in town tonight, at my apartment," Nate said as he stood and stretched out the kinks he'd gathered in his back from sitting at his desk so long.

"Whatever you say," Nicole muttered.

"Would you rather head out to Karekare? We'll have to swing by the apartment and collect your new things first."

"I'd rather go home—to my home—but since that's

not going to happen, I don't really care one way or the other where I sleep tonight."

Her dark brown eyes met his in a silent challenge—as if she was daring him to contradict her. Nate knew full well when to pick his battles and she'd be disappointed if she thought he was going to rise to her bait this time around.

"Good then, it's settled. The apartment it is."

A flush rose in her cheeks. Annoyance, perhaps? Irritated or not, she gathered her bag and followed him out the office. She remained silent until they reached the undercover parking below the apartment complex.

"Is that my car?"

While she'd been interested and had plied him with questions about Jackson Importers all afternoon, this was the first sign of genuine animation he'd seen in her face since the weekend.

"Sure is. I have two spaces here. It makes sense for you to have your own wheels easily available, but we'll probably commute together most of the time."

She hastened out of the Maserati and he watched as she checked over her vehicle, examining every panel.

"It's a Roadster, right?" he asked.

"Yeah," she replied, finally satisfied the vehicle had come to no harm. "A '58 300 SL, to be precise. Good to see your people didn't do any damage."

"I only use the best," he replied.

Nicole eyed him over the soft top of her car. What would he do, she wondered, if she just jumped in, started it up and gunned it out of here? The instant the thought blossomed in her mind she knew she'd never carry it through. Not when he held such damning evidence over her and especially not now that the photo of the two of them last Thursday night had probably been brought to her father's attention.

"I'm pleased to hear it," she finally managed.

"Come on up to the apartment. You must be starving by now."

Now that he mentioned it, she was pretty hungry. She'd only had a nibble of the muffin at breakfast and had refused to stop and eat lunch.

"Sure, it's not like there's anything else to do," she said with a touch of defiance.

For some reason he gave her a look that she could only describe as approving. What? She'd subtly insulted him and he beamed back at her? The man was a conundrum, all right. A very powerful and sexy conundrum with an inordinate amount of control over her life right now. She may not like it, but she would just have to get used to it, she told herself. Even so, she didn't have to make him positively happy about the situation.

The trip in the elevator was smooth and swift and the doors opened to a corridor lined with expensive artwork. Her heels sank into the thick carpet as they walked to the end of the corridor where Nate swiped a key card and then pushed open one of two massive double doors and gestured her inside. Her breath caught in her throat as she took in the vista in front of her. She'd thought the view from his office was stunning, but this was something else. She could see over North Head and Mt. Victoria, out to Rangitoto Island and beyond.

"You certainly like your sea views," she said, dropping her bag on one of the wide and comfortable-looking leather sofas that faced out to the balcony.

"I do."

His answer was short and succinct and came from

right behind her. Suddenly she was aware of him. Painfully aware. Every nerve in her body attuned to the knowledge that right now very little space separated them. After that one kiss in the boardroom, he'd kept his distance. She hadn't realized up until now just how much she'd craved his touch. But she wouldn't give in. Couldn't. She had some pride left.

Before he could do anything, she stepped away, creating a void between them as she turned and faced him. A void that left her body silently screaming but which she refused to acknowledge, because that would only have her fall very firmly exactly where he so obviously wanted her, again. She might not be able to control much else in her world right now, but she could have some mastery over herself—however hard fought for.

"Where is my bedroom?" she asked.

"The master suite is right through there," he said, pointing down a wide hallway.

"No, not your bedroom," she said pointedly, "mine. I agreed to work for you. I never said anything about anything else."

"Anything else being?"

"You know exactly what I mean."

"Oh, you mean this?"

Nate traced the neckline of her dress with the knuckle of his forefinger, smiling approvingly when her skin reacted with a scatter of goose bumps. Nicole didn't move, she could barely breathe. One touch from him was about enough to send her up in flames. Already her entire body was invested in that tiny point of contact. She steeled herself for more, knowing she daren't so much as betray another measure of reaction.

"Are you going to force me, Nate?" she asked, her

voice deadly calm and at total odds with the swirl of
desire that fought for dominance.

"Force you? No, I don't think so."

"Believe me, I don't want you."

"You don't want me—or you don't *want* to want
me?"

She held her ground, refusing to answer, still not
moving so much as a muscle. Eventually Nate let his
hand drop.

"There's a guest bedroom and en suite second on
the right. I'll move your things in there."

"Thank you."

Nicole allowed herself to breathe again. It was a
small victory but an important one. She felt as if she'd
conquered Everest.

It was Thursday evening, a week since they'd met,
yet it felt as if it had been a lifetime. Nicole shut down
her laptop and grabbed the overseas market reports she
planned on using as her bedtime reading tonight. Sleep
had been elusive these past few days. Knowing Nate
was only meters down the hall from where she slept
each night was unnerving. *It was your own choice,* she
reminded herself sternly.

She'd been surprised to find Nate appeared unper-
turbed by her insistence on separate rooms, and it made
her wonder whether she was alone in believing their
lovemaking had been way outside the usual realm of
experience. Maybe he was like that with all his women.
She was surprised at the bitter taste that formed in the
back of her mouth at the thought. How many other
women lay in their bed each night reliving, caress by
caress, the exquisite beauty of his touch against their
skin, the possession of his body as it filled theirs?

She closed her eyes as a surge of need billowed through her body. It was just sex, for goodness' sake, she reminded herself as she shook her head slightly and opened her eyes. She could live without it. *Liar,* an insidious voice in the back of her mind whispered.

The office door swung open and the object of her thoughts filled the doorway. Her eyes roamed his body, taking in every aspect of his perfection from the hand-tooled leather of his Italian shoes to the sharp line of his tailored suit jacket. Slowly she raised her eyes to meet his, cursing the flush she knew colored her cheeks.

"I'm glad I caught you," Nate said, dispensing with any social pleasantries.

He was like that, she'd noticed. Charming as all get out when necessary, but straight to the point when it wasn't. Clearly she fell into the "not necessary to be charmed" pile now, Nicole thought with an internal grimace. *Or maybe,* that little inner voice whispered again, *he's just as frustrated as you are and this is how he shows it.*

"What's up?" Nicole answered, forcing a nonchalance into her voice she was far from feeling.

"Your brother and Anna Garrick headed down to the Marlborough region today."

"Judd and Anna? Why?"

"I was hoping you'd be in the position to answer that. We all know it's one of New Zealand's major wine producing areas but Wilson Wines has only ever sold imported product for distribution before."

"Oh, no!" Nicole lifted a hand to her mouth.

"You know why they're there?"

She shook her head. "I can't be certain. Dad pretty

much dismissed my study as being a waste of time and energy."

"Study?" Nate's expression became intent, every muscle in his body drawn tight.

"With the rising cost of international freight and the fluctuation of the New Zealand dollar, I thought it would be a good time to explore the internal distribution of a solid range of New Zealand wines. Wines not already being sold through major liquor retailers and supermarkets. The kinds of wines people might find in upmarket restaurants, bars and hotels. But make those wines a bit more accessible to the average consumer," she explained.

"Makes sense." Nate nodded. "Why did your father dismiss the study? Was it not feasible?"

Nicole laughed. "You think my father explained his decision to me? You don't know him as well as you think. No, he just told me we weren't pursuing it any further and not to waste any more of my time on it. So I didn't. Judd or Anna must have found my reports and somehow persuaded him the idea had merit."

"They've gone down to solicit new suppliers?"

"I'd say so."

Nicole fought to hide the hot rush of anger she felt toward her father for his about-face on her recommendations.

"You must have put a lot of work into this. It pisses you off, doesn't it, that your brother is getting to see through what you started?"

"That's a polite way of putting it," Nicole said. She was angry and hugely disappointed that she hadn't had the opportunity to see it all through. "I'd already approached several wineries whose management teams were very keen to come on board."

"Then I'd suggest you stop wasting time," Nate said, a half smile on his face.

"Time?" She felt like an idiot. What on earth was he talking about.

"Yeah, get down there and win back your business. Show me you can go at this with everything you've got."

Nicole looked at him in amazement. Carte blanche to progress her idea? Just like that? What if it failed? There were already so many wonderful and inexpensive New Zealand wines on the market, could it support more? Would there be a demand for the more exclusive vintages? And what about the upmarket imported wines they already sold? Would they be eating into their current business instead of growing new opportunities?

Her market analysis and research had borne out a definite niche of demand. Maybe she'd been too quick to let her father quash her idea. Maybe she just should have fought harder for what she believed in, what she knew to have great potential. Excitement began to bubble through her veins.

"Right, I'll get right on it," she said, reaching into her handbag for one of the backup memory sticks she always carried with her and powering her computer back up. She'd show Nate, all right. Success or fail, she'd show him, and maybe—just maybe—somewhere along the line she'd get to show her father her true worth to him, after all.

"Need any help?" Nate offered.

"No, I think I'll be okay. I'll start making calls first thing tomorrow and plan to head down on Sunday. I'd rather not bump into Judd and Anna while I'm down there so if I can work out who they're likely to be seeing first, and when, I can follow along behind and make an offer the wineries can't refuse."

"I like the way you think. I take it you have those reports on your drive?"

She nodded, automatically pulling up the files even as he spoke.

Inside, however, she alternated between disbelief that Nate believed in her ideas and the sheer joy of being told to implement them. She hesitated before sending the print command, waiting for him to reveal the catch or to shut her down, but, to her surprise, it didn't come.

"If you print me off a set we can go over them together. I'll order some dinner up for us while you do that."

Nicole nodded again, forcing her focus on the screen in front of her as Nate left the room. He was really going ahead with this. She'd reprinted her list of contacts and her feasibility study by the time Nate returned to the office.

"I've asked a few others to stay back in case you need them," he said as he grabbed a chair and pulled it next to her.

"Really?" she said, trying to control the sudden acceleration in her heart rate as his large body filled the space next to hers.

"We're a team here, Nicole. I wouldn't expect any of my staff to do this all alone. Besides, when it comes to you making an offer your clients can't refuse, I think it would be best if that offer came from a brainstorming session among us all so that it is completely unbeatable."

Nicole murmured her assent and concentrated on her computer screen as unexpected tears sprang to her eyes. A team. Even though she was here under duress, Nate still trusted her with all the resources of his company, backing her play and giving her room to develop her plan collaboratively, with all the help she needed. It was quite a change from Wilson Wines, where an idea of hers would have had to be fully formulated, presented and approved by her father before any backup was given.

It was a system that had probably worked well when the company first began, and it had been so crucial to have a clear chain of command to keep the business stable and the employees on track. But even when the company had grown past that stage, the management style had never changed. At Wilson Wines she'd had to fight for change tooth and nail, losing more often than not to her father's dictatorial management style. When she had her emotions in check she asked Nate a question.

"Has Jackson Importers always done everything by committee?"

She aimed to keep her tone light, teasing even, but she knew she'd come off as sounding critical when Nate shot her a dark glance.

"For the very important stuff, yes. When we succeed, and we do tend to do that a whole lot, we succeed together. When everyone has a hand in it, everyone works harder and feels far more satisfaction on an individual level. Why, don't you think that's important?"

"No, no, it's not that. I've just...not really come across that before."

"Well, you have only ever worked at Wilson Wines, right? Even on your school holidays? You never took any other kind of after-school job, did you?"

She was surprised he knew that information. He

seemed to know a terrible lot about her. Just how much? she wondered, feeling a little as if she was under a microscope—pinned, as she was, by his intent gaze.

"No, I didn't. All I ever wanted was to work with my father."

Nate's expression softened and, if she wasn't mistaken, his eyes gleamed now with something more akin to compassion.

"I know what you mean. From when I was very young and I knew that Dad was working all the hours that God sent so he could provide for me and my mother, I knew that I wanted to help him. I couldn't qualify soon enough. If he'd have let me, I'd have started with Jackson Importers straight from school, but he insisted that I complete university first, and that I take jobs and internships with other companies while I was a student, so I could be sure Jackson Importers was where I wanted to be. At the time, I was upset that he thought I didn't know what I wanted, but now I can appreciate the experience I gained. It helped me have more insight than I would've had if I'd only ever worked here."

"And then you went overseas?"

"Yeah, first of all for a bit of a holiday—again, at his insistence—then, while I was there I just saw so many opportunities for our company if they had a man on the ground right there in the heart of our major European suppliers."

"Your father just let you do that without any experience in the company? You must have been so young."

Nate shrugged. "What can I say? He liked my proposal and he felt we had nothing to lose by it. I worked my butt off on my own for the first few years and then, over time and as we continued to grow, we built up our staff."

Nicole fought back the pang of envy that struck her fair and square in the chest. What would it be like, she wondered, to be able to just pitch an idea and then have a free hand in following it through? Suddenly it occurred to her that that was exactly what Nate had done for her here and now. He'd heard her out, he was now examining her report and making notations on a pad of paper on the desk in front of him, and he'd assembled a team to support her in it.

Her mind reeled with confusion. He was forcing her to stay here—blackmailing her. Why, then, was he basically handing her the chance to see her idea through—an idea that her father had rejected—without any question?

There was a knock at the office door and it opened. Raoul stood there, his tie loosened at his throat and his shirtsleeves rolled up as if he meant business.

"Dinner has been delivered. We're setting up in the boardroom. You guys ready to join us?"

"We'll be through in a minute," Nate said. Once Raoul had gone, Nate stood and gathered up his notes and Nicole's papers. "Are you all set?"

"Sure," she said. "Just one thing."

"What's that?"

"Why are you doing this?"

"This?" he asked, holding her report up in one hand.

"Yeah. Why? It could just as easily fail and cost you a whole lot of money."

Nate shrugged, an eloquent movement of his broad shoulders beneath the fine wool of his suit. "I trust you, and I know you're onto a winner here. I can see it already in the work you've done to date. Why waste it? Besides, I can't wait to imagine the look on your father's face when we win."

"You think we will?"

"Don't doubt yourself or our team, Nicole. We're invincible when we put our minds to it." Nate crossed the room and held the door open. "Shall we?"

She nodded decisively and picked up her handbag and laptop and followed him through to the boardroom. Invincible. It should scare her that he was so supremely confident, but for some reason it gave her strength, instead. Strength and a belief that she could do this.

Hard on the heels of that thought she realized how much she was enjoying working with Nate. Too much, in fact. As an employer, he was the antithesis of Charles Wilson. She didn't have too much time to dwell on her thoughts, though, because once they entered the boardroom they were full-on. Nate invited her to explain her concept to the group in summarized format and then gave them his overview of her report. Over a selection of Chinese takeout they brainstormed ideas back and forth until Nicole barely recognized the idea as her own anymore. Even so, there was one thing she knew for certain. She was really excited about the direction this was taking and the fact that she'd been integral in instigating it.

By the time she and Nate went back to his apartment she was shattered, and yet incredibly buoyed up at the same time. They had a solid plan in place and she had all the ammunition she needed for when she went to win over any business that Judd and Anna might already have secured.

As she went to turn in for the night she paused in the hallway leading to the bedrooms.

"Nate?"

Nate was almost at his door and he stopped the instant she called to him. "Yeah?"

"Thank you for today."

He walked back up the hallway toward her. She couldn't read his expression in the dim lighting but as he drew nearer, she could see the half smile on his face.

"You're thanking me?" he asked.

She nodded. "For believing in me."

He shook his head slightly. "You're worth it, Nicole. I don't know why your father kept you under a bushel the way he did but, with your mind, the whole world should be at your feet. I'm just letting you use what is your own natural talent."

"I—I appreciate it," she answered, unused to receiving such direct praise. "I hate to admit this, but I really enjoyed this evening."

"Hey, there will be many more of those," Nate said.

"Well, like I said, thanks."

She hovered outside her door, her mind still humming with all the excitement of seeing her brainchild grow and expand into a working business plan. A plan she'd be implementing the moment her feet touched Marlborough soil.

It only seemed natural to brush her lips against Nate's cheeks and then, when that wasn't enough, to kiss him on the lips. He remained still for a moment but then his arms were around her and his mouth was hungry against hers. Her heart rate accelerated as she accepted the inevitable. They were going to make love. A part of her was glad of it, glad she no longer had to fight her instinctive and constant response to Nate's presence. But deep inside she knew she was, in part, surrendering to him. Giving a piece of herself that she'd held back. A piece she knew she'd be lucky to get back whole, ever again.

Seven

Nate backed Nicole against her bedroom door and relished the taste of her as they consumed one another with their kiss. He'd known it would only be a matter of time before Nicole capitulated to him again. With a passion as incendiary as theirs, it was bound to happen. Knowing that hadn't made the waiting any easier, but having that advantage over her—making her stay with him—had tempered his desire just enough to take the edge off. Just enough so that he could wait patiently and let her come to him as he'd planned. And now, at last, everything was falling into place.

It had been exhilarating seeing her in action today. There was nothing sexier than a woman with confidence and intelligence, and Nicole had both in spades. That she was perfectly assembled with features that could make even an angel weep was a welcome bonus, in his mind.

But now it was most definitely time to stop thinking and start doing. Doing and feeling. He reached behind Nicole and eased her bedroom door open, walking her slowly inside before closing the door behind them. Cocooning them in darkness only vaguely punctuated by the lights across the harbor that were visible through her bedroom window. He continued to guide her backward into the darkened room. At the edge of the bed he stopped, reaching for the zipper at the back of her dress and easing it down carefully before working the fabric away from her delectable body. For a split second he wished he'd taken the time to turn on a light, so he could feast his eyes upon her as he planned to feast with his mouth very shortly. But compulsion overcame his need to see what he was doing to her, to see her reaction to it. Instead, he would rely on his other senses.

His body craved urgency, but he held on to enough reason to know that he wanted to take his time, to stretch this out for as long as humanly possible. To give and to receive over and over again until neither of them could stand another second of the torment.

Nicole made a little humming sound in the back of her throat as he bent his head and traced a fine line from the edge of her jaw and down the cord of her neck with his tongue. Her hands gripped his shoulders as he moved lower, following the very top of the swell of her breasts inside the expensive lingerie he knew she wore. Lingerie he had paid for. Lingerie he'd tortured himself with all this week by picturing—wondering whether she was wearing the sapphire-blue ensemble, or the ruby red. Or maybe it was one of the other myriad feminine provocations he'd seen delicately wrapped in tissue before being placed in the store's shopping bag and handed over to her.

Here and now, in the darkness, he knew color didn't matter. All that mattered was sensation and, oh, God, she felt amazing in his arms, beneath his lips. He reached behind her, unsnapping the clasps of her bra.

He dispensed with the garment in an easy movement and reached with both his hands to cup the fullness of her breasts, testing their weight and lifting them slightly so he could bury his face in their softness before laving at the crease he'd created between them. He stroked the pads of his thumbs over her nipples, delighting in the straining peaks and the knowledge that his touch was making them harder, making her want him more.

Her hands let go their grip on his shoulders and moved to the collar of his shirt, unknotting his tie and sliding it free before her fingers were at his buttons, unsteady yet determined in their mission. He bit back a growl as her nails scraped across his chest, across his own sensitive nubs. Her hands shifted to the buckle of his belt and then, mercifully, eased down his zipper and pushed his trousers to pool at his feet. His erection strained at the restriction of his boxer briefs, strained for her silken touch, but instead, she scraped her nails softly along his length and he almost lost all control.

Nate eased her back onto the bed before bending to swiftly kick off his shoes and peel off his socks so he could step out of his trousers. He slid his briefs away, allowing his swollen flesh to spring free, and joined Nicole on the bed. Waves of heat rolled off her body, heat that intensified as his fingers roamed inside the fabric of her panties—sought, and found, the slick core of her. He played his fingers across her cleft, reveling in the heat and wetness of her body, knowing it was like this in readiness for him and him alone. She gasped when he brushed the tip of one finger across her clitoris, her gasp turning into a moan as he increased the pressure ever so slightly before easing it off again.

She pressed up into his hand, the movement making him smile. She'd been so controlled all week and now here she was. Her movements uninhibited. He gently slid her free of her underwear and then tugged it away from her body completely before settling himself between her legs. He felt her thighs tremble as he ran his palms across their silky smoothness. Tremble and then tighten as he lowered his mouth to her damp heat. He rolled his tongue across the bead of flesh hidden at her apex. Over and over until her body was so tense he knew she was seconds away from completion.

Completion he would give her. He closed his mouth around that special place and sucked hard, the action sending her over the edge.

Nate waited until the spasms that rocked her body eased off, then rose over her, reaching for the bedside cabinet where, as a good host, he knew there was a stock of condoms. He eased open the drawer and reached inside.

"They're not there," Nicole said from beneath him.

"They're not? Then—"

"I cut them up and threw them out. I didn't want to be tempted."

He'd have laughed if he wasn't so hard he was on the point of agony. Instead, he pressed a kiss to her lips.

"Don't move," he said, "I'll be straight back."

He covered the distance between their bedrooms in record time, then came back with a handful of condoms that he dumped into the still-open drawer, with the exception of the one that he ripped open and swiftly used to sheath himself.

"This time when you come," he continued, as he reached for the beside lamp and switched it on, "I want to see you."

She made a sound as if to protest but the noise cut off as he eased his length inside her. He gritted his teeth together, clenching his jaw tight as he fought to restrain the urge to take her hard and fast. To bring them both to a crashing climax within the shortest time possible. Instead, he moved slowly, painstakingly. She met his rhythm and he smiled down at her as she tried to hasten him in his movements.

"It'll be better this way," he said. "Trust me."

He knew it had been worth the wait as he felt her inner muscles begin to quiver and tighten around him. Nicole's eyes were glazed, her lips parted on a panting breath and her cheeks flushed. A fine dew of perspiration gathered at her temples. His own climax was only seconds away, and in the instant her body began to ripple around him he let go, letting her body wring his satisfaction from him. Giving himself over to the pulse that spent itself all the way from the soles of his feet.

Nicole lay beneath him, waiting for her heartbeat to return to normal, if such a thing were possible. It seemed that from the moment she'd laid eyes on Nate Jackson, she'd been in a constant state of hyperawareness. Colors were brighter, scents stronger and pleasure so much more intense than she'd ever known. She had no idea where this was all going to lead. She only knew, deep down inside, that she would probably never feel this much again with another man. The thought terrified her, because she knew this couldn't last.

She'd never been enough for anyone before. That's

why she hadn't been able to make her mother love her, or to make her father proud. And now she had Nate, who made her feel as if she could do anything…but she knew better than to rely on that. Because she wasn't enough for him, either—not on her own. He was only with her now to enact revenge on her father—once that was complete, she'd go back to being not enough.

Nate shifted above her, pulling from her body before rolling away. Despite the sternly chiding voice in her head telling her not to get too comfortable or too attached, she still made a sound of protest as his warmth left her—right before she froze at his next words.

"Let me get rid of this, we don't want another near miss like last weekend."

Every last vestige of afterglow fled her body as her blood ran cold. "What do you mean 'near miss?'"

"Didn't I mention it? We went to sleep like this that first night. The condom came off. But you're on the Pill, right?"

She wasn't. But that wasn't the issue. He should have told her straightaway so she could have gone to a pharmacy and gotten the morning-after pill. Being with Nate was bad enough but how on earth would she explain a baby to her father?

"Nicole? You *are* on the Pill, aren't you?"

"No, I'm not," she told him, a panicked flutter beginning in her chest. "Why didn't you tell me? What if—"

"I'll deal with it," he said firmly.

He'd deal with it? What about her? Didn't her thoughts or feelings on the matter count at all? And just how would he deal with it? Would he insist on a termination, or would he use a pregnancy as another tool to hurt her father? It occurred to Nicole that while

Nate had given her all the freedom in the world when it came to the workplace, he gave none in her personal space whatsoever. When Nate came back into the bed she had already rolled onto her side and was feigning sleep. She had a lot on her mind—and she knew she wouldn't be able to think if he was touching her.

By the time Wednesday morning rolled around Nicole had everything in the bag. Four out of the six wineries Judd and Anna had visited had jumped ship to Jackson Importers, due in part to the relationship she had already built with them during her feasibility study. And along with them she'd also picked up at least three additional contacts, who were excited about the prospect of widening their distribution.

Her days had been full-on. Judd had done a very good job of selling Wilson Wines to the contacts she'd had on her list, but she'd done a better one and it felt good to be on top. As she awaited her luggage at the baggage carousel at Auckland's domestic airport, she allowed herself a smile of satisfaction.

"Well, if you don't look like the cat that got the cream, hmm?"

Her pulse leaped in her veins as Nate's voice surrounded her in its velvet softness. She turned and faced him, willing her heart rate back under control. Willing her body to calm and cool down just a notch so he wouldn't know just how much she'd ached for him each night she'd been away.

"It went well," she said smoothly. "I didn't expect you to be here to pick me up. I could have taken a taxi."

"I wanted to see you," he said simply.

He bent and kissed her on the lips, a hard press of skin against skin and then he was gone again. She fought the urge to press her fingers to her lips, to hold him there for just a moment longer. Nate constantly surprised her. On the one hand he could be so over-bearing and yet, on the other…

"Oh, there's my bag," she cried, seeing the distinctive iridescent red case coming through on the carousel.

She'd been delighted with the set of luggage when Nate had had it delivered to the apartment before her departure, even if it was a little brighter than anything she'd owned before. Still, it was distinctive and cheerful.

Nate moved to collect her bag, appearing nonplussed about carrying such a feminine item as he placed one hand at the small of Nicole's back and guided her out to the parking building.

"Are we heading straight into the office?" she asked as he directed the car up George Bolt Memorial Drive and toward the motorway interchange.

"No."

"Oh, I thought—"

"I told them we wouldn't be in until after midday."

Nicole was surprised. She'd thought he would have wanted her to debrief the team and keep the ball rolling. Losing momentum with this could be disastrous, as Judd and Anna would shortly find out, to their cost.

Judd and Anna—that was a combination she'd never considered before. And yet the representatives from the wineries had told her that her brother and her best friend had worked quite well together, and had, moreover, seemed…close.

She sighed. There was a time when she would have been the first to know if there was a new man in Anna's life. The two of them had shared everything, and there had never been any secrets between them, until now. They'd been friends from childhood, her father's new housekeeper bringing an inbuilt playmate when she'd taken on the role.

They'd even attended the same private schools, with Charles picking up the tab for Anna's fees so his daughter would never be without her best friend. Thinking about it, she could see why Anna was so fiercely devoted to her father. Charles Wilson had given her the world on a platter. A world her mother couldn't have provided alone on a housekeeper's salary. If Anna hadn't done what Charles had asked of her, it would be like saying she didn't appreciate everything the old man had done for her over the years, and Nicole knew without a shadow of doubt that he would have held his own loyalty to Anna over her head in some subtle way.

She desperately wanted to reach out to Anna again. To mend the breach that had been caused by the conflict of loyalties. To rebuild their friendship if they still had that chance.

And while she longed to talk to Anna about Judd, and the rumors she had heard about the two of them, she also wished for a chance to talk to someone about her relationship with Nate. Nicole snuck a glance over at the man beside her and had to resist the urge to squirm in her seat. Just looking at him drove her crazy—she needed a good dose of Anna's gentle practicality to get her thoughts and feelings in order.

Nicole knew she *wanted* Nate—that was impossible to deny. Yet she still resented what he was doing to her, the leverage he held over her head. And underneath it all, she worried about what would happen next. How long would she spend as a pawn between her father and her lover, and how would it all end?

Nate was surprisingly quiet as they journeyed into the city and he handled the car with very deliberate movements, staying at the upper limit of the speed restrictions. By the time they pulled into the covered car parking at the apartment building she could feel tension rippling off him in waves. What on earth was wrong?

He stayed silent as they traveled in the elevator to his floor but the instant they were inside the apartment, she got her answer.

Nate pulled her into his arms and kissed her, really kissed her this time. Hot, wet and hungry. Her body bloomed with heat, moisture gathering at her center in rapid-fire time. Barely breaking contact with one another, they shed their clothing in a heap on the tiled entrance floor and Nate lifted her onto the marble-topped hall table. She gasped at the cold surface against her bare buttocks, but the marble didn't feel cold for long. She was on fire for him, resenting the time it took him to sheath himself with a condom. And then, thankfully, he was sliding inside her, stretching her with his hard length and driving her to the point of distraction as his hips began to pump.

Her orgasm took her completely by surprise. One moment she was accepting him into her body, the next she was flying on a trajectory that led to starbursts of pleasure radiating throughout her body. She clutched at Nate's shoulders, her heels digging into his buttocks as wave after wave consumed her, barely hearing his cry of satisfaction as his own climax slammed through his body.

It took several minutes for her to come back to reality, to realize just what they'd done and where. Nate rested his forehead against hers.

"I told you I wanted to see you."

Nicole laughed. "Well, you're definitely seeing all of me now. I was beginning to think something was wrong. You were so quiet in the car."

"I wanted to concentrate on getting here as quickly as possible. Believe me, the airport hotels were looking mighty good there at one stage."

He withdrew from her and caught her mouth with another deep kiss. This time with the sharp edge of passion assuaged, and with a tenderness she hadn't sensed in him before. It confused her, but then he was constantly doing that. In some respects he seemed to want to dictate every part of her life, yet in others he let her have her head. She could never predict how he'd react. She wanted to push back at him, verbally and physically sometimes, just to get a bit of space and control back in her life, and then he'd go and literally sweep her off her feet and do something like this. Something that transcended reason and gave her an insight into just how she affected him on a personal level. Or did it? Was she still reading him wrong—seeing what she wanted to see? There was no way to know for sure. She doubted she'd ever have him figured out completely.

Nate lifted her from the tabletop, allowing her body to glide against his as her feet found her footing. She shuddered anew at the skin-against-skin contact. There was nothing she wanted more right now than to prolong the physical link they had between them. In that, at least, they were in perfect harmony.

In their earlier eagerness they hadn't noticed the enameled brass vase had toppled off the surface of the table—its fall to the floor leaving a sizable chip in one of the tiles. Nicole bent to lift the vase back into its place.

"That's a shame," she said, gesturing to the floor. "Will you be able to get it repaired?"

"I won't bother. I like the reminder of how it got there," Nate said with a smile that sent tingles through her body all over again. "Come on, let's go take a shower."

It was well after midday by the time they made it into the office and Nicole was feeling the effects of making her 6:45 a.m. flight and the vigorous lovemaking she and Nate had indulged in before going into work. She made it through her debrief without making any mistakes or leaving any glaring holes in her rundown of who had come on board with them and why, and what she had negotiated in their individual contracts.

The meeting was just tying up when she overheard Raoul mention her father's name to Nate.

"…he wasn't looking all that good. Are you sure you want to keep this up?" Raoul said in a voice that was meant for Nate's ears only.

Nate flicked her a glance before turning his back to her and saying something to Raoul that saw the other man glance her way also before giving Nate a slight nod. Raoul gathered his papers and left the room, signaling the exodus for the rest of the staff. Nicole waited until everyone else had left the boardroom before fronting up to Nate.

"What's wrong with my father?" she demanded.

"Nothing more than the usual," Nate responded flatly.

"So what were you and Raoul talking about?"

"Look, he just mentioned he saw your father at a function over the weekend and that he looked more tired than usual. He hasn't been well, has he?"

Nicole shook her head. No, he hadn't been well. And her leaving Wilson Wines and working for Jackson Importers would be exacerbating that. Responsibility struck her fair and square in her chest as she realized the further ramifications of the business she'd just secured and what it would mean to her father on a personal level. She'd been so focused on beating Judd to the finish line, on winning the business away from *him,* that she'd lost sight of her father's stake in all this. Wilson Wines had been holding on to its market share by the skin of its teeth in recent years. She knew that better than anyone. And yet, with her usual impulsiveness, she'd just made matters worse for them. In particular, worse for her father's already weakened health.

"Nicole, it's not your fault he's not well." Nate's voice broke through her fugue of guilt.

She raised her eyes to meet his. "No, but my being here won't be doing him any good, either, will it? Did you know about his health problems all along? Was that a part of your plan, to take a sick man and make him sicker?"

"What, you think I want your father dead?"

"An eye for an eye, a life for a life. Isn't that what revenge is all about?"

"Nicole, you misjudge me if you think I'm capable of something like that. I'm angry at your father, yes, I'm very angry for what he did to mine. I'm furious that he's never admitted, ever, that he made a mistake in treating his best friend the way he did. But it's not his state of health that I want to change—it's his state of mind. Your father needs to stop thinking of himself as the one on top who is always right, and who can never be questioned. Don't tell me you haven't realized that about him, or that his autocratic ways haven't hurt you, too. *That's* the revenge I want—for him to realize that the world doesn't run on his terms. That he's made mistakes, and people have suffered as a result. Then he can finally start to take responsibility for the damage that he's done."

"Can't you leave it in the past?" Nicole pleaded. "Yes, he made mistakes, but he's paid for them, too. For twenty-five years, he didn't even know if Judd was truly his son!"

"You think that's enough to make up for what he did?" Nate sneered. "He *destroyed* my father. Do you know what that means? He sucked every last bit of joy out of him, every last bit of pride. With his accusations he tainted my father for life. Dad lost more than a friend and a business partner over your father's twisted blame. He lost the respect of his peers, as well, not to mention his income. The roll-on effect to my mother and myself was huge. Don't ever underestimate that. Life became very hard for us all. While you were still in that gothic monstrosity you call home, eating hot meals every night and wearing your designer labels, my mother and I were reduced to being reliant on food parcels and hand-me-downs."

Nate's words rained down on her like hail from a black cloud and, through it, all she could hear was the hurt in his voice. The pain of a boy whose father had changed and withdrawn from him. A boy who'd spent his whole life driven by the dispute between two men.

"But do you see what you're doing to him now?" she asked softly, all her earlier anger and defensiveness having fled. "You're the one in the position of power this time," she reminded him, "and how much damage are *you* doing by refusing to forgive?"

"Look, we're never going to see eye to eye on this and I'm not prepared to discuss it any further."

"Well, that's a lovely cop-out," she pushed back, not ready to let things go just yet. She deserved answers. "You think you were the only one affected? I lost my mother and my brother over the whole situation. Isn't it enough for you, now, that my brother is back? That my father knows that *he* is Judd's father and your father isn't?"

Nate shook his head. "It's not as simple as that."

"Yes, Nate. It is," Nicole insisted. "Judd's DNA testing proved he is Dad's natural-born son. The argument between our fathers was just that. Between *them*. Why let that keep affecting us now?"

"Because he's never apologized. Charles Wilson has never admitted he was wrong," he said stubbornly.

"And if he did, would that make it all go away? Would that change the fact that you and your mother suffered while your father found his financial feet again?"

"You don't understand."

"No, you're right," she said sadly. "I'll never understand. Too many people were hurt back then, Nate. Don't carry on the feud. It's just not worth it."

"I'm not letting you go back to him, Nicole."

"I don't think you can stop me."

"Aren't you forgetting something?"

"No, Nate, I'm not forgetting that you can still hold that DVD over me. I'd just hope that you'd be man enough not to."

Eight

They went back to Karekare that night, their journey completed in silence, and once at the house Nicole said she was turning in early. She woke in the early hours of the morning to find the bed still empty beside her, a faint flicker of light coming from the main room down the hall. She got up from the bed and pulled on the peignoir that matched her ivory chiffon nightgown. The floor was cold against her bare feet, yet she made no sound as she padded along the polished wooden floor.

The room was in darkness, the only light coming from the massive LCD television screen mounted on the wall. Nate was sitting on the couch opposite the TV, a glass of red wine on the coffee table in front of him. Even though the sound was off on the television, he hadn't heard her enter the room, his attention fixed on the screen.

Nicole hazarded a look and instantly wished she'd

stayed in bed. There, in all their glory, were the two of them—making love. At the time she'd thought it would be a bit of fun. After all, she'd been the one to instigate it. Again, her rashness getting her into a situation she'd have done better to avoid. She closed her eyes for a moment, but behind her lids she could still see the images of their bodies entwined. Of the expression on her face as Nate did things to her she'd never allowed any other man to do. Of how she'd trusted him and loved every second of it, never for a moment thinking there could possibly be any consequences.

Opening her eyes, she turned and left the room before Nate could sense or hear her there. In the bedroom she yanked off her peignoir and threw herself back into the bed, closing her eyes tight once more—but not tight enough to stop the flow of tears that came from beneath them.

Nate sat alone in the dark, staring at the screen in front of him, at the evidence of the incredible connection he had with the flesh and blood, passionate woman sleeping in his bed down the hall.

He'd threatened her now twice with the DVD. The first time he'd meant it. The second? Well, he'd thought he'd meant it. Until now. Until he'd started to watch it again and had realized that he could never use this against her.

He still wanted his revenge against Charles Wilson. But he wouldn't—couldn't—hurt Nicole to achieve it. Her words today had struck deep inside him. Logically he knew she was right, but emotionally he was still that determined little boy who'd wanted to make his father's eyes smile again.

Nate had always understood his parents' relationship

was an anomaly amongst his friends' parents' bonds. Deborah Hunter and Thomas Jackson had never married. Never even lived together. Yet they were united as one on the upbringing of their son. He'd asked his mother once, when he was still small, why his daddy didn't live with them, and his mother had had such a sad expression in her eyes when she'd told him that Thomas simply wasn't like other daddies. Nate had never wanted to see that sorrow on his mother's face again, had never pushed for more answers.

It wasn't until he was older that he'd realized what it was that made his father different, and it was something that had made him even more determined to teach Charles Wilson a lesson. Thomas Jackson was gay. His sexual orientation had been misunderstood and even feared by others when he was a young man— if it had been public knowledge then he would have been touched by a stigma that might have seen him lose friends, not to mention business.

Nate himself was the result of a last-ditch attempt on his father's part to disprove the truth about himself. Thomas had explained it to Nate during his last visit to Europe before he'd died. How he'd met Deborah Hunter and, desperate to deny his own sexuality, had embarked upon an affair with her. It was a short-lived fling, but it had resulted in Nate's conception—a fact that had bound both Thomas and Deborah together as close friends for the rest of their lives. Nate didn't doubt that his mother had loved Thomas deeply, nor that he loved her in return. Just not in the way his mother needed.

The knowledge had explained a lot to Nate. Had answered so many questions he'd had but had never put into words. Nate knew his father could never have had the affair with Cynthia Masters-Wilson that Charles had accused Thomas of. It was something Charles Wilson should have known from the start—*would* have known, if he'd truly been a good friend to Thomas. But the man was known for his up-front, old-fashioned and often righteous attitude. In itself that was probably the reason why Thomas never confided his homosexuality to him. He had been afraid that he would lose Charles's friendship—and he had, even if it wasn't in the manner he'd anticipated. But Charles should have trusted Thomas, and the loss of that trust had decimated his father.

Yes, Nicole had been right when she'd said he couldn't change the past. But the little boy inside him still suffered. Charles Wilson had to pay. Nicole, on the other hand, had already paid more than enough, having to walk away from her home, her friends and her family.

Nate reached for the remote and snapped off the television. No, he wouldn't use the DVD against Nicole. The content of it was theirs, and theirs alone. But if he told her he had no intention of using it against her anymore, how could he ensure she would stay? Now that he had her, he didn't want to let her go.

Sure, knowing she was a pivotal member of the Wilson Wines hierarchy, he'd wanted to use her to hurt their business—and if her recent trip was any indication, he'd succeed quite well in that goal. And he'd relished the thought of staking his own claim on someone who Charles Wilson took for granted would always be there. But keeping Nicole with him was no longer just about pulling her away from her father. Now he just *wanted* her, for reasons that had nothing to do with anyone but him and her.

It was more than desire, he admitted, although that was in itself an itch he found he couldn't scratch hard enough, or often enough with her. No, he wanted Nicole in a way he didn't fully understand, and could never describe. A way that had nothing to do with his plans.

And the truth of that scared him.

She was still alone when she woke in the morning but through the bathroom door she could hear the shower running. She lay between the tangled sheets that were the evidence of her restless night and wondered what Nate had been thinking while he'd watched the DVD last night. Was he imagining her father's anger and disgust? Would he send it with a letter accompanying it, explaining that he, Nate, was Thomas Jackson's son? A son Thomas Jackson had raised while Charles had sent his own away in a fit of pride and anger?

The very thought of her father opening such a letter, or even beginning to watch the DVD, made her feel physically ill and she dashed from the bedroom to the guest facilities, heaving over the toilet bowl until her stomach ached with the effort. She flushed the toilet and leaned both hands against the basin, willing her body back under control. With a shaking hand she turned on the faucet, letting the cold water splash over her hands and wrists before rinsing out her mouth and vigorously scrubbing at her face.

She felt like death warmed over. In fact, when she thought about it, she hadn't felt physically fit in days. Was this all the toll of the days she'd spent in Nelson and Blenheim and the emotional demands of living and working with Nate every day, or was there something else she should be worried about? She didn't want to think about the night Nate had said his condom had come off inside her as they'd slept. She didn't want to believe that she could have been vulnerable to falling pregnant for even an instant.

Pregnant? Her stomach clenched on the very thought and she stared at herself in the mirror, noting the dark shadows under her eyes, the lankness of her hair, the pallor of her skin. It had to be the stress, it just had to be. She was worried about her father and under immense strain with Nate.

Nicole wondered again about Charles. It worried her to think that his health had worsened, and she wished she could get a fuller report. Short of visiting him, though, where she had no doubt she would be told in no uncertain terms of how unwelcome she was, she had only one other option. She had to ask Anna. Her friend would know the truth about Charles's health. She'd email Anna today when they got into the office, arrange to meet for lunch if the other woman was willing. And then maybe, just maybe, Nicole would begin to get her life back on track again.

Sharing an office with Nate hadn't bothered her before but today it most definitely did. She had to wait until almost lunchtime, when he headed out for a meeting, before she could compose the email she wanted to send to Anna. By now Wilson Wines would know that she'd wrested their new business from them. Would Anna even respond to her email? There was only one way to find out. She typed in the short missive and hit Send before she could change her mind.

She waited, drumming her fingers on the desk to see if Anna would respond. Maybe she was away from her desk, or maybe she was just ignoring the request to meet at Mission Bay for lunch. She couldn't stand it. She powered her computer down and grabbed her handbag. She'd wait at the restaurant. If Anna showed up, she showed up. If she didn't, well, then Nicole would just find out about her father some other way.

Nicole couldn't get over the relief that swamped her body as Anna made her way through the tables to where she was sitting at the back of the restaurant. Even so, the relief was tempered with a generous dose of apprehension as Anna sat in the chair opposite.

"I ordered for us already," Nicole said, hoping that Anna wouldn't mind she'd gone ahead and done so.

"Thank you, I think."

Dread clutched her heart. Was there to be no reconciliation between them, after all? If the look on Anna's face was anything to go by, twenty-odd years of friendship was about to go down the tubes.

"Oh, Anna, don't look at me like that, please."

"Like what?" her friend said, giving nothing away.

"Like you don't know whether I'm going to hit you or hug you."

Anna smiled, but it was a pale facsimile of her usual warmth. "Well, you weren't exactly happy with me the last time we talked to each other."

No, she hadn't been. She'd been feeling betrayed at the worst level possible, and she'd felt angry and trapped. A situation which she'd only made worse by yelling at her oldest friend, and running off. Nicole forced a smile to her lips and reached across the table to squeeze Anna's hand, the tension in her body easing just a little when the other woman didn't pull away. The waiter arrived at that moment with their Caesar salads and she let Anna's hand go. Once they were alone again, Anna asked her how she was doing. How she was really doing.

Nicole ached to tell her the truth, to tell her she'd gotten herself into an awful situation and that she couldn't see her way out of it, but she held it all inside, instead skating across the reality her life had become. But, she reminded herself, meeting with Anna today hadn't been about her. It was to find out how Charles was doing. She wasn't surprised when Anna told her he was less than impressed with her working for Nate. And, of course, Charles still had no idea that Nate was Thomas's son.

She asked about Charles's health, and was partially relieved when Anna told her he was okay. Anna wouldn't lie about something as important as that. What did hurt, though, was hearing about how easily Judd had picked up her side of things at Wilson Wines. She'd never been able to measure up to him, even though he'd grown up in another country. Always, she felt as if she'd been found lacking, and when Anna began to beg her to come back to Wilson Wines, to come home, she felt as if her heart would fracture into a million tiny pieces.

"I...I can't," she said, shaking her head, wishing the opposite was true.

"What do you mean, you can't? Of course you can. Your home is with us, your career was with us. Come back, please?"

If only it was that simple. Even if she told Anna about the blackmail, how could she admit the deeper truth—that she actually liked working for Jackson Importers? That she felt more valued and appreciated there than she had in her father's own company.

Nicole was ashamed of herself for even thinking it. She skirted around the issue and focused instead on the much-needed apology she had to deliver to the woman who had been her best friend for as long as she could remember. To her relief, Anna accepted the apology with her natural grace and they turned their discussion to anything and everything other than work, or men. How she felt about Nate was too raw and complicated for her to share with Anna just yet. She didn't even fully understand it herself, and until she did, talking about him was off limits. By the time their lunch was over, it almost felt as if everything was back to normal. As normal as it could be without them both returning to work in the same office.

"I'm so glad you emailed me," Anna said, standing and giving her an enveloping hug.

"I'm glad you're still talking to me. I don't deserve you, you know."

"Of course you do, and more," Anna replied. "I'll settle the bill, okay? Next time will be your turn."

"Are you sure?" Nicole had issued the invitation, lunch should have been on her.

"That there'll be a next time? Of course there will."

"Not that, silly." Nicole laughed, happy, on one level, that they were back to their usual banter.

But her joy was short-lived. Being with Anna had just reminded her of all she'd walked away from. All she'd thrown away with her reckless behavior. And now she had another problem to consider—that her impetuosity had possibly gotten her pregnant. That sense of fear and nausea she'd experienced this morning swirled around inside her again. Before Anna could notice she wasn't feeling well, or say another word that might see Nicole blurt out the whole ugly truth of what she'd gotten herself into, she gave her friend a farewell hug and left the restaurant.

The sunshine outside did little to dispel the coldness that dwelled deep inside her. Seeing Anna was an all-too-painful reminder of all Nicole was missing— her father, despite his recent behavior to her, her best friend. Even the opportunity to somehow carve a new relationship with the brother she'd never had a chance to know, and work with him to help stabilize and protect the family company. Instead, she was working against them all—and enjoying it. Shame swamped her. Somehow she had to make things right for what she'd done. Anna hadn't mentioned how the Nelson and Blenheim wineries business loss had been taken in the office, but Nicole knew it must have hurt. She had to find a way to make that up to them.

It was during the short drive back to the city that Nicole's mind began to work overtime. There was most definitely a way she could continue working with Nate and yet remain loyal to her father and Wilson Wines. It would be tricky, but hey, no one had made her sign a confidentiality agreement. She could feed information to Anna on Nate's current development plans. Not enough that it would immediately point a finger at her when it came to light—and it most definitely would come to light, she had no doubt about that at all—but hopefully enough to give Wilson Wines an edge against Jackson Importers. After all, in very many cases they were competing for the same business, anyway. It would only be natural to assume they'd continue to cross swords in the marketplace.

Satisfied she'd finally found a workable answer to her situation, Nicole continued to the office, steadfastly ignoring the conflicted sensation that what she was about to do would hurt the very people who'd welcomed her into Jackson Imports with open arms. She swallowed against the lump that formed in her throat. If she could make this work, Charles would have to see her in a different light. Would have to value her worth to him. Wouldn't he?

Nate came from the 7:00 a.m. Monday morning meeting with his head of IT undecided about whether he was furious with Nicole or filled with admiration for her audacity. Over the weekend, while he'd thought she was sulking in her room, she'd been emailing information to Anna Garrick at Wilson Wines. Information he could well do without them knowing. At least, thanks to the tracking software he'd had installed on her laptop right from the beginning, his team had been able to find out exactly what information she'd passed on. Between the software and the team he had tracking her laptop activity, keeping an eye on Nicole had been an expensive investment, but well worth it if it made him aware that this was the tack she was taking.

But why was she doing it? She'd seemed satisfied with her success with the Marlborough district wineries. Then they'd had that blasted discussion, which had turned them back into silent ships that passed in the office, and in the night. Even at the Karekare house, she'd moved into another bedroom. He couldn't understand it. She was just as strongly attracted to him as he was to her. He knew it to his very bones. Knew it in every accidental touch from the ache it created deep within him and in the clouded look of suppressed need he saw in Nicole's eyes immediately afterward.

And it wasn't just physical. He was making every effort to satisfy all of her needs—including her need to feel valued and appreciated for her work. He was giving her every opportunity to excel at what she did best and yet it still wasn't enough. What more could he possibly give her? And why was everything he'd already given her not enough to make her happy? Was it truly that necessary to her to please her father, to the point where she'd throw away everything else he'd given her for the chance to make Charles Wilson proud?

He could cope with the collateral damage this time, but what she was doing had to stop. For his sake, for the company's sake, and for *her* sake, too. If there was one thing Nate knew, it was that Charles Wilson was a stubborn bastard who never forgave. Not his best friend, or his daughter. Nicole couldn't buy her way back into her daddy's heart with Jackson Importers secrets—she could only sabotage her own chances of succeeding with them. And he wasn't about to let her do that.

He pushed open the door to his office and felt a jolt of satisfaction when she jumped in response to his presence.

"I thought you were in a meeting," she said, swiftly covering her discomfiture.

Rain battered at the office window behind her as autumn's weather finally did an about-face and delivered on its usual wet and windy promise. The weather suited his mood.

"I was," he replied, his voice short as he chose his next words very carefully. "A very interesting meeting, in fact. It seems someone from our office has been feeding information about our latest initiatives to Wilson Wines. I don't suppose you'd know who that was, would you?"

To his satisfaction, she paled visibly under the onslaught of his words.

"How...?"

"How I know isn't relevant. But it's going to stop right here and right now, Nicole."

"You can't stop me," she said defiantly, rising from her chair and lifting her chin. "If you're going to make me work here and I'm privy to certain information, you can't prevent me from sharing it. I haven't signed any confidentiality agreement."

"No? I would have thought that the DVD was enough of a substitute, wouldn't you?"

She wavered where she stood and he fought to control the urge to comfort her. To take her in his arms and assure her he would never dream of using the DVD against her anymore. But he had to stop her in her tracks. Had to keep her where she belonged, where she could be appreciated and valued—*with him*.

"Remember, Nicole. I can just as easily give you access to bad information as I can to good. Ask yourself this—how would you feel if what you were so merrily passing onto your friend at Wilson Wines was enough to turn very strongly to their *dis*advantage? What if it was the straw that broke their financial back?"

She sat back down in her seat, her face drawn into harsh lines of worry. "Have you?"

"Not this time, but don't be so sure I won't in the future. Now, let this be the first and last time you do this, or I will take punitive action, Nicole. Don't think I won't."

"I—"

She was interrupted in her response by the chirp of

her cell phone. He watched as she glanced at the screen and, if it were possible, paled even further.

"Your friend, I assume?" he sneered.

In response, Nicole snatched the phone up and dismissed the call, only to have it start ringing again a few seconds later.

"You'd better take it," Nate growled, "and while you're at it, tell Ms. Garrick that they can expect to have to do their own research and development in the future."

He turned and stalked out the office.

Nicole watched the door close behind him before answering the call. In the face of what she'd just been through with him she really didn't think her day could have gotten any worse, until she'd seen her home phone number come up on her screen. Try as she might, she couldn't fight back the feeling of dread that suffused her.

"Hello?"

"Nic, it's Anna. Charles collapsed this morning at breakfast. Judd's gone with him in the ambulance. You should meet us at Auckland City Hospital's emergency department as soon as you can. It doesn't look good."

"But you said he was doing okay," Nicole protested, at a complete loss for anything else to say.

"He has obviously been feeling worse than he let on. Look, I must get going. I'll see you at the hospital."

Anna severed the connection before Nicole could say another word. Shaking, Nicole grabbed her handbag and headed straight for the elevator bank. She slammed her hand against the call button several times waiting for the car to arrive at her floor.

Finally the elevator doors slid open and she dashed inside, punching the ground floor button as she did so.

The doors began to slide closed but suddenly an arm appeared between them, forcing them to bounce open again.

"Going somewhere?" Nate asked, entering the car and standing close beside her.

"It's my dad, he's collapsed. I need to see him. Please don't try and stop me."

Nate's expression changed rapidly. "How are you planning to get there?"

"I don't know, taxi, something!" A note of sheer panic pitched her voice high.

"I'll drive you."

"You don't n—"

"I said, I'll drive you. You're in no state to be left on your own." He reached forward and pressed the button for the level below ground.

"Thank you," she said shakily, watching as the car slid inexorably down to the basement parking floor.

She couldn't have said later on how long it took to get to Auckland City Hospital. The journey should only have taken about ten minutes but, as with everything since she'd received Anna's call, it seemed to take forever. The second Nate rolled his car to a halt outside the emergency department she shot out the door and headed inside, not even waiting to see if he followed her or not. Ahead of her she could see her brother and Anna. She strode across the floor, her high heels clicking on the polished surface.

"Where is he? I want to see him."

"He's with the doctors," Anna said quietly. "They're still assessing him."

"What happened?" Nicole demanded, turning to Judd, more than ready to lay blame for their father's current condition firmly at his feet. Life had been simple before he arrived. Not necessarily always happy but certainly less complicated.

"He collapsed at breakfast," Judd replied.

"I thought your being here was supposed to make him feel better, not worse," Nicole fired back before promptly bursting into tears.

God, what was it with her these days? So overemotional. She needed to hold it together, especially if she wanted them to let her in to see her father.

A nurse came toward them, "Mr. Wilson, you can see your father now."

Nicole didn't notice that Judd had reached for Anna until she heard her friend say, "No, take Nicole. She needs to be with him more than I do."

What was with that between the two of them? Were they a couple?

"Are you coming?" Judd asked with thinly veiled impatience.

Her tears dried instantly. How dare he act and speak to her as if she didn't belong. It wasn't her fault her father was in there, possibly fighting for his life. "Of course I'm coming. He's *my* father."

Nicole was horrified when she saw her father. Lines ran into his arms and monitors were beeping around him. He looked so ill, so frail. So very old. Guilt assailed her anew.

"What's she doing here?" he rasped, turning his head away from her.

But not before she saw the anger and rejection in his eyes. Nicole stiffened and halted in her tracks. The words of love and care that were on the tip of her tongue drying on her tongue like a bitter pill she'd been unable to swallow. She reached down deep and found what dignity she had left.

"I came to see if you were all right, but obviously you're just fine. You won't be needing me here."

She turned and pushed past Judd, desperate now to get out of the cubicle. Desperate to get anywhere where her father wasn't. He hated her. That much was all too clear. As far as he was concerned, she'd burned her bridges when she'd walked out on him and straight into Nate Hunter Jackson's arms. He'd never stopped to listen before, why should he start now? Well, two could play at that game, she decided, ignoring Anna who was still waiting outside, and kept her gaze fixed on the exit ahead of her.

Nate waited outside in the chilled morning air.

"How is he?" he asked, stepping forward as she came out through the main doors.

"He's about as much a bastard as he ever was. Take me home, please. I can't face going back to the office today."

Nate gave her a searching look before nodding. He wrapped one arm across her shoulders and gathered her to him.

"Sure, whatever you need."

The Maserati ate up the miles that led them back to the beach house and the instant they were inside she turned into his arms, wrenching away her clothing and then his, and pouring her energy into setting his soul on fire for her all over again.

She dragged him to the bedroom and pushed him onto the bed, sheathed him with a condom and then straddled his body. There was no finesse, no whispers of passion. Her movements were hard and fast and before he gave himself over to her frenetic love-making, he made her a silent promise. Charles Wilson would never hurt her again.

Nine

Nate watched Nicole as she slept beside him. She'd been like a madwoman exorcising a demon. As if she was desperate to fill all the loss and pain inside her with something else. While he didn't regret that whatever had happened at the hospital had driven her back into his bed, he hated that she was hurting so much inside. Throughout the day she hadn't said a word about her father's condition or whatever it was that he'd said or done that had upset her so deeply. Even as they'd walked along the beach during a break in the bad weather, wrapped up tight against the bracing wind that streamed across the sand, she'd adroitly steered their conversation away from work and anything associated with her family.

Throughout their talks he'd begun to get a clearer picture of what her life had been like growing up. It hadn't all been a bed of roses, as he'd assumed. For a start she'd only had her father, and while he'd lavished his extensive resources upon her and given her every childhood heart's desire, including a live-in friend in the shape of Anna Garrick, he hadn't been able to atone for the fact that her mother had essentially abandoned her. Mostly, he hadn't tried.

After the collapse of his marriage and his family life, Charles had dedicated himself to his work. When he'd spent time with Nicole, it had mostly been in the role of stern authoritarian, making sure she did her homework, got good grades, behaved well in school. She'd worked hard to excel, hoping to win his approval, but his praise was sparse and hard to gain. And when she fell short of his expectations, well...

Little wonder that right now, Nicole felt as if she'd been cast adrift by both her parents. He knew she was in pain but he didn't know how to make it any better. He also knew that he was responsible for some of the scars she bore right now, and the knowledge carved at his chest with relentless precision.

He could make this all go away. He could destroy the DVD and release her. Even as he thought of it, everything within him protested. She murmured in her sleep as he gathered her against his chest. No, there was one thing these past few days had taught him and that was he never wanted to let her go. Ever.

Charles Wilson didn't deserve her. In contrast, Nate would do everything in his power to make sure Nicole wanted for nothing while she was under his roof. Surely someday, that would be enough.

Nicole poured her energy into two things for the rest of the week, work and Nate. By Friday evening she was shattered. Lack of sleep and the concentration her work demanded as she finalized every last contract for the Marlborough wineries had culminated in a thumping headache by the time she and Nate drove back to the apartment. She wished they were heading out to Karekare. The sounds of the waves and the birds in the bush that surrounded the house were just the kind of tranquility she craved right now. They would drive out there late Saturday evening, though, and she was looking forward to the time-out. Perhaps she'd even take Nate up on that earlier offer to learn to surf, she thought, as they waited for yet another change of lights before they could get closer to their final destination.

Her cell phone chirped in her bag and she ignored it. She should have turned the damn thing off before they'd left the office. After all, any calls she got tended only to relate to work—or Anna, who had been giving her unwanted updates on her father's medical condition.

Things were looking pretty bad for Charles Wilson but Nicole refused to let herself think about that. Refused, point-blank, to acknowledge that the one biggest influence on her entire life could soon be gone if things didn't improve. He hadn't wanted her there at the hospital. He'd made it abundantly, and painfully clear on Monday morning.

Was she so unlovable? Her chest tightened on the thought. Her mother abandoned her, her father now hated her. Even Nate only wanted her because of what it would do to her father and her brother. Nicole had never felt more adrift in her entire life. The pounding in her head sharpened and she must have made a sound of discomfort because Nate reached across to take one of her hands in his.

"Are you okay? You're looking really pale."

"Just this darn headache. I can't shake it."

He shot her a look of concern, his hand lifting from hers and touching her cheek and forehead before returning to the steering wheel.

"I don't think you have a fever, but do you think you should see a doctor? You haven't been looking well all week."

"Look, it's been a stressful week, you know that. I'll be fine. I just need a couple of painkillers and then about a month's worth of sleep."

"Well, I can't promise a month but I have no objection if you want to stay in bed all weekend."

She gave him a weak smile. No, she had no doubt he'd be happy to spend that whole time in bed with her, too. It was about the only time she could dismiss everything else and just concentrate on the moment, on how he could play her body like a finely tuned instrument. But right now, forget-the-rest-of-the-world sex was the last thing she felt like.

"Hey, I can change my plans for tonight. I don't feel so good about leaving you alone if you're not well."

"No, no," she protested. "Raoul's wedding rehearsal is important. You must go."

"If you're sure?"

"Of course I'm sure," she told him. Right now the only thing she craved was maybe a warm bath, those painkillers she'd mentioned a moment ago and then sleep.

In the apartment, Nate went straight through to the master bedroom to get ready for the wedding rehearsal and subsequent dinner that was being hosted in one of Auckland's premier hotels. Raoul had extended both a dinner and wedding invitation to Nicole, as well, but she'd refused, saying she'd feel like a gate-crasher. The wedding was tomorrow at midday, and she'd planned to go into the office in an effort to get ahead for next week.

Half an hour later she was on her own. She roamed through to the master bathroom and ran a deep bath, treating the water with lavender-and-rose-scented bath salts. Already she could feel the tension in her head begin to ease. She took a couple of headache tablets just before she undressed and lowered herself into the soothing water.

In the living room, she heard her phone begin to chirp again. She sighed, and gave herself a mental reminder to check the thing before turning it off. There was no need to rush to check it right away. If Nate needed her, and couldn't get through, he would ring the apartment, and who else would need to reach her right away? She closed her eyes and leaned her head back against the edge, letting the water and the pain relief weave their magic.

The water was cooling by the time she dragged herself out and dried her body before wrapping in a luxuriously thick bathrobe. There was no point in putting on a nightgown. Nate would only remove it the minute he got home, she thought with an anticipatory smile. Besides, her headache was completely gone now and she was ravenous. Maybe she'd watch a movie on cable while she had something to eat, she thought, abandoning her earlier idea of having an early night. And then, by the time Nate got home, maybe she could meet him at the door, dressed in nothing but a smile. The idea began to sound better and better.

First, though, she had to check her phone. Two missed calls, both from the same caller, and one voice mail. Nicole immediately identified her old home number and her blood ran cold. Had Charles's condition deteriorated again?

She punched the numbers to listen to the voice mail, and was surprised when the well-modulated tones of an unfamiliar woman's voice sounded through the speaker.

"This is Cynthia Masters-Wilson and I'm calling for Nicole Wilson. I'd like to meet with you for lunch tomorrow, one o'clock if you're free." She mentioned the name of an inner-city restaurant before continuing, "I think it's time we got to know one another, don't you?"

The call disconnected but Nicole still stood there, staring at her phone. Her mother? After all this time? She sank to the sofa as her legs weakened. Why now?

All her life she'd told herself she never wanted to meet the woman who had so callously abandoned her one-year-old daughter, never to look back, never to contact her or attempt to see her ever again. While she was growing up she'd told herself it didn't matter. She had her father, she had Anna and Anna's mother who was more Charles's companion than housekeeper in the massive gothic mansion Nicole had grown up in. Yes, it had always been easy to dismiss Cynthia Masters-Wilson as entirely unnecessary in her life.

But what did she have now? Nothing. Absolutely nothing. All week she'd been frantically trying to fill the emptiness inside her—working hard and playing twice as much so. If she was completely honest with herself, neither activity had managed to assuage the hollow feeling her father's rejection had left her with.

Reason told her to be cautious, though. This was the first ever, active contact her mother had made in twenty-five long years. As far as Nicole was aware, the woman had never spared her a second thought.

But what if she wanted to make amends? What if her reasons for leaving Nicole motherless for all those years were justified, her remorse for her absence in her daughter's life genuine? Surely she had to have a reason for finally getting in touch with Nicole after all this time.

Curiosity won out over caution as Nicole made up her mind. She would meet with Cynthia—she couldn't ever imagine calling her Mum, or Mother—and she would be seeking a few answers of her own.

Butterflies battled in her stomach as she entered the restaurant located in the historic Auckland Ferry building. She'd chosen to walk the short distance from the Viaduct, but with each step she'd come to dread her decision to attend. What on earth could they possibly have to talk about? And if her mother wanted to offer an olive branch, maybe even try to establish some form of mother-daughter relationship, why do it in such a public place? Surely a private meeting would be more appropriate for a mother and daughter reuniting for the first time in a quarter century.

"You must be Miss Wilson," said the immaculately attired maître d' as she hovered in the entrance, in two minds about turning around and walking back to the apartment. "Your mother is already seated. Please, follow me."

Too late now, she realized. The restaurant hummed with activity and most of the tables were occupied. The sun shined through the windows that looked out over the water, casting a solitary figure seated at a table there in silhouette.

Nicole swallowed back the lump that formed in her throat and focused on placing one foot in front of the other. She smiled at the maître d' as he held out her chair, not wanting to immediately make eye contact with the woman who had summoned her there. She kept her eyes downcast, fiddling with her bag before setting it on the floor beside her chair. Then, with a steadying breath, she raised her eyes.

It was as if she was looking at herself in another twenty-five years. Same eyes, same hairline, although Cynthia's hair now bore wings of gray, and while her features mirrored Nicole's own, there were lines around her mouth. Regret? Bitterness? Would she ever know the truth about that?

"Well, my dear, this is going to be interesting, isn't it?" Cynthia said with a tight smile.

Of all the things she'd imagined her mother first saying to her, that was most definitely not on the list. Nicole bristled.

"Why now?"

"What? No, hello Mother, pleased to finally meet you?" Cynthia gave another of those artificial smiles. "I don't blame you for being angry, my dear, but you have to realize that I'm as much a victim of your father as you and your brother."

A victim? Somehow Nicole thought that was stretching the truth. Her brother had already been proven to be Charles's natural-born son. Why would he have thought otherwise? Charles had believed his wife had an affair with Thomas Jackson. She couldn't imagine Nate's father having been the one to put that idea in her father's head, which only left one other person in that particular triangle.

"Ah, I see you don't believe me." Cynthia sighed. "I feared as much. Come, let's order, and hopefully we can talk."

Even though she didn't feel in the least like eating, Nicole placed her order with the waiter who'd materialized at Cynthia's request. Once they were each settled with a glass of wine, Cynthia began again.

"You're quite the beauty, aren't you? I'm so sorry that I didn't get to see you grow up. It was the hardest thing I've ever done in my life, walking away from you, leaving you with your father. But I knew he loved you, would protect you. Judd deserved the same, with me."

"How could you leave me like that?" Nicole blurted out the question. Goodness only knew she'd waited all her life for the answer.

To her surprise, Cynthia's eyes swam with tears. "Oh, my darling girl. Do you really think I wanted to leave you? Your father wouldn't let me near you. Once he'd come to his ridiculous conclusions about Thomas and me he wouldn't even let me *see* you. He had Judd and me out of the country before I could so much as blink."

She sounded genuine enough, and the grief on her mother's face certainly appeared real. Nicole found herself wanting to believe her, but an inner caution still held her back. Without being able to talk to her father, or her brother about this, she had no way of knowing if her mother was telling the truth. The waiter interrupted them with their lunch order and Nicole picked up her fork, playing with the mushrooms in her salad while her mother daintily tasted a sliver of scallop that had come with her dish.

"You could have written," Nicole said, still not willing to give an inch.

"I did. I wrote to you so many times over the years, but all the letters came back. I can only assume that your father had given the staff orders to return any mail addressed from me."

It was the sort of thing her father would have done, Nicole conceded, but there were still means around such a thing. After all, twenty-five years was a very long time. Nicole was an adult now—approachable in ways that were outside of her father's control. To never have been successful was a bit of a stretch of the imagination. Cynthia could obviously sense her skepticism and waved her hand in the air between them.

"That's all in the past now. We can't change that. But surely we can get to know one another now? Tell me about where you're living. Judd tells me you moved out a few weeks ago. I have to say I was very sorry to hear that you two haven't had a chance to get to know one another. I'm staying at the house now. I was hoping we could all be together again, the way it should be."

"Judd didn't tell you why I left?"

Cynthia gave her a sharp look before shaking her head and placing her fork down on her plate. She took a sip of the mineral water in her glass before speaking.

"He did mention something, but I'd prefer to hear it from you."

Nicole gave an inelegant snort. She'd just bet Judd would prefer their mother hear it from her. No doubt he'd already fed Cynthia a sanitized version of what had happened that night.

"My father and I had a disagreement about his plans for Judd. I felt it better that I be away from them both for a while."

"So where are you staying?"

"I'm living with Nate Hunter." She didn't want to let on about Nate's relationship to Thomas Jackson. As far as she was aware, no one at Wilson Wines knew him by his father's surname. Even at the office he was known as Mr. Hunter. "He's the current head of Jackson Importers. I'm working with him, too."

She watched her mother pale beneath her carefully applied makeup, her pallor making the lines around her mouth stand out even more.

"Would Jackson Importers be connected to Thomas Jackson at all?"

"It was his company before he passed away," Nicole confirmed cautiously.

Cynthia's brow furrowed for a moment. "Hunter? Would Nate's mother have been Deborah Hunter?"

Nicole stiffened. Had Cynthia made the connection? "That might have been his mother's name, yes."

"So, it was true. There were rumors that Thomas and Deborah were an item, but nothing was ever substantiated. Charles, of course, pooh-poohed the notion. He said if Thomas was having an affair he'd be the first to know about it." She made a sound that almost approximated a laugh. "As if he paid attention to anything but Wilson Wines. Anyway, I heard that she had a son out of wedlock, but since she didn't move in the same circles as I did when I lived here, I never really gave her another thought."

Nicole didn't know what to say. It hadn't been her secret to divulge and yet Cynthia had put two and two together so simply. If that was the case, why then had her father never reached the same conclusion?

Cynthia suddenly reached across the table, her slender fingers wrapping around Nicole's wrist and gripping tight.

"My dear, you have to get out of there. No one associated with Thomas Jackson can possibly be trusted. Who do you think lied to your father about me, ruining our marriage? Think of the damage that man's lies have done to our family. You have to realize, there's a lot of bitterness between those men. If you're with Thomas's son there can only be one good reason behind it—he's trying to get at your father."

Her words rang too true, as Nicole knew to her cost. Hearing it from her mother's lips only made her situation worse. She knew full well what had been on Nate's mind when he'd taken her back to his home that first night. She had no reason to believe his vendetta against her father had altered in any way. She was still his greatest weapon, even if through her own distress at her father's treatment of her she'd recently become a more willing one.

"Nicole, tell me, is Nate Hunter holding something over you? Is he forcing you to be with him?"

Her mother's astuteness shocked her and she bit back. "Is it too hard to believe that I might actually want to be with him for no reason other than that he treats me well and appreciates me?" Even as she said the words she was sure her mother would see them for the lie they were.

Cynthia shook her head gently, a look of pity on her face. "You love him, don't you?"

"No!" The single word of protest fell from Nicole's lips even as she questioned the truth of her rapid denial. Did she love him? How could she? She was his lover, his captive, his colleague. His tool for vengeance against her father. How she felt about him was far too complicated to examine in front of her mother. Instead, she settled for a middle ground, saying, "Our relationship—it's convenient for us both."

"Well, I certainly hope that's true, because I'm sure, if he's anything like his father, he has an agenda and that would probably be having some kind of revenge against Charles for when he kicked Thomas to the curb."

"Can we change the subject, please? I'd rather not talk about my relationship with Nate, if you don't mind. Besides, I thought you wanted to get to know me."

"You're so right. I'm sorry." Cynthia smiled, one that almost reached her eyes this time, and skillfully shifted their conversation onto other matters.

By the time Nicole walked back to the apartment she was in a quandary. When they hadn't been talking about Nate, or her father, Cynthia had been excellent company. She'd talked a great deal about her family home—The Masters, a vineyard and accommodation on the outskirts of Adelaide—and Nicole's cousins who lived there. Cousins! She had an extended family. One she'd never had the chance to know. And Judd had enjoyed the benefit of that, as well, on top of her father's total attention, her home and the job she'd loved. While she, even now, had absolutely nothing.

Ten

Nate knew something was up the instant he let himself into the apartment. Nicole was nursing a frosty glass of white wine in one hand, her gaze fixed on the twinkling lights of the Viaduct Basin below, her body language shrieking a touch-me-not scream. Every part of her was tense, a far cry from the languorous woman he'd left in their bed this morning before heading out to Raoul's wedding.

He knew she saw his reflection in the massive window in front of her, yet she didn't so much as acknowledge his presence. A flare of concern lit deep inside him.

"What happened? Is it your father?" Surely he would have heard if Charles had passed away. That kind of information would still have filtered through to the guests from Jackson Importers who were at the wedding.

"No." she huffed a short sigh. "My mother, actually."

"Your mother? I thought she lived in Australia."

"Apparently not. Apparently she's moving back to my old family home. Seems like everyone has a place there—but me."

Despite her attempt at nonchalance, he could hear the pain in her voice.

"Did she contact you?"

"We did lunch together. Such a normal thing for a mother and daughter to do, don't you think? Except we're not a normal mother and daughter, are we?"

He was shocked when she turned to face him, her eyes awash with tears. Instinctively he reached for her, enveloping her in his arms and ruing the fact that he hadn't been here for her when she so clearly needed the support. His father had never said as much in words, but Nate had always suspected Cynthia of being behind the lies that had torn apart Thomas and Charles's friendship. Her poison had tainted the lives of so many people, and now she was here, poisoning Nicole, as well.

"You know," Nicole said, her voice muffled against his chest, "as soon as I was old enough to realize that I didn't have a mother, I wanted answers. Even after I convinced myself I didn't need her in my life. I still wanted to know why I didn't have unconditional love from her the same way all my friends had from their mothers. She wants us to get to know each other. Now. After twenty-five years. Can you believe that?"

Nate remained silent, knowing she wasn't looking for an answer. At least not from him.

"And underneath it all, I don't think I can believe it. I don't know that I can believe *her*. And in spite of that,

I still *want* to believe her, because what girl doesn't want to think that her mother loves her?"

Nate set her away from him a little, so he could see her face. "I don't think you should trust her motives, Nicole."

Nicole laughed. A sharp brittle sound that was nothing like the usual humor in her he'd come to know. "Funny. She said exactly the same thing about you."

He stiffened. "She did? Why?"

"Oh, she had you pegged from the start. Said you were probably just like your father. And she knew your mother apparently. Not well, of course." Nicole lowered her voice. "We didn't move in the same circles, you know," she said, in a parody of her mother's tone.

A chill went through him. "I mean it, Nicole. The way she's come here, after all this time and while your father is so ill—something's not right. She could have reached out to you any time in the past. I don't think you should have anything to do with her."

Nicole pulled free from his arms. "Well, that's my judgment call, isn't it?"

Nate knew he'd overstepped the mark with his last comment but he couldn't take it back now. He'd been speaking his mind and he knew he was right. Cynthia Masters-Wilson was not a woman to be trusted. And he didn't want to see Nicole hurt ever again. But he didn't want this to turn into a fight.

"Yes, it is," he finally agreed with Nicole. "Do you still want to head out to the beach?"

Nicole shrugged and took a long sip of her wine. "Whatever."

"I think we should go, it'll do us good to get out of the city."

"Sure," she agreed, but without any enthusiasm.

He watched as she finished her wine and took her glass through to the kitchen. She rinsed it and put it in the dishwasher and then went through to the bedroom they were sharing again. Her actions were wooden, automatic, as if she'd retreated somewhere in her mind. To a place he knew he couldn't reach. The knowledge chilled him to the bone.

Being at Raoul's wedding today had struck something home to him. It had been a happy, relaxed affair, full of people Nate liked and valued—and yet he'd spent the whole time counting down the minutes until he could leave, wanting to come home to Nicole. Being with her had long since stopped being about having his revenge on her father. What was past, was very definitely past. What he wanted now—Nicole—was very much in the present—and he wanted her to stay that way.

Nicole sat quietly in the car, mulling over her meeting with her mother. It certainly hadn't been the reunion she'd always imagined. Cynthia was a piece of work, all right. Coming back into her life after all this time and then thinking she could tell Nicole what to do. It seemed that all around her everyone was telling her what to do these days. And she was letting them. Everything in her life had become topsy-turvy. Even her period was late and she was never late.

Cold fingers of fear squeezed around her heart. Could she be pregnant? *Oh, please, no,* she thought fervently. *Please just let it be stress.* She wasn't ready for this on so many levels it wasn't even funny. She and Nate hardly had the kind of relationship that could sustain a nurturing environment for a child. Not to mention, she had no idea how to be a mother. She'd always been so professionally focused, so determined to excel in her work at Wilson Wines that she'd never given much thought to building a home and family. Even if she wanted such a thing, she didn't know if she could pull it off. And she couldn't bear the thought of proving her father's prophecy about becoming a mother and downsizing her responsibilities in the workplace.

Suddenly it was all the more important that she know, one way or another. With everything else in her life spiraling out of control, surely fate couldn't be so cruel as to throw her a curveball like that, as well?

"Could we stop at the shops in Titirangi on the way?" she asked. "There are a few things I forgot."

"Sure," Nate said.

When they got to the township he pulled in off the road.

"Do you want me to come with you?" he asked, shutting down the engine.

"Oh, no. I'll be fine. I won't be long," she said, getting out the car as hastily as she could. "Really, I'll only be a minute or two."

Please don't come, she chanted in the back of her mind. *Please don't come.* Thankfully, he stayed in the car and she walked briskly toward the bank of shops near where he'd parked. Where to go now? she wondered. If she went into the nearby pharmacy he'd probably see her and he'd no doubt ask her what she'd been in there for. He kept a full stock of over-the-counter medicinal products at both his homes so she couldn't say she'd needed any painkillers or anything like that. And if she said she was after sanitary products, and she didn't need them, that would just open up a whole new can of worms.

Think! she exhorted herself. The grocery store.

Sure, it was smallish, certainly not on the scale of a full supermarket, but surely they'd carry pregnancy tests, as well. She ducked inside the store and scanned the aisles, praying she'd find what she needed. Finally, there it was. She grabbed a test kit and made her way to the counter. On the way she also pulled some moisturizer and a lip balm off the shelf to add to her purchase. The kit, she'd ferret away in her bag. The other items would be camouflage in case Nate asked what she'd bought.

She was back at the car in under five minutes.

"Get everything you needed?" Nate asked her as she buckled her seatbelt.

"Yes, thanks. I'd just run out of a couple of things."

He gave her a studied look, one that made the hairs on the back of her neck prickle. She'd never been an effective liar. Never had to be. She felt as if the test kit in her bag was emitting some kind of beacon. As if any second now, Nate would be giving her the third degree.

"Right, we'll be on the way, then."

She sagged back into her seat with relief. She was overreacting. He had no reason to suspect her of anything, although he had to realize that she should perhaps have had a period by now. She counted back. It was just over three weeks since she'd met him. Only three weeks and they'd been through so very much. She felt as if she'd lived through a lifetime with him. Even so, it gave her a window of at least another week before he might start to ask questions. Questions to which she hoped to have the answer very soon.

The rest of the journey to the house seemed to take forever, even though it was only just over twenty minutes. Nate kept her attention occupied by talking about Raoul's wedding and the people who had been there, often drawing a quiet laugh from her as he mimicked some of Raoul's older and more eccentric family members. She detected a note in his voice, though, that she identified with.

Neither of them had grown up with a large family group supporting them. No uncles, aunts, curmudgeonly great-anythings. No cousins to play or fight with. Just a tight unit of parent and child.

"Some people are lucky, aren't they?" she said, as Nate's voice trailed off as they neared the driveway to the house.

"Lucky?"

"To have the richness of all those people in their family lives."

"I don't know whether Raoul thought it was particularly lucky when his great-uncle got up to make a toast to absent friends. Fifteen minutes he went on."

She laughed again. She should have gone to the wedding rather than have lunch with her mother. By the sounds of it she would have been in a much happier frame of mind right now if she had.

"Still, it would have been nice, growing up..." Her voice faded on the thought.

Nate's hand came across and grasped hers, squeezing tight. "Yeah, I know what you mean."

They were both silent as they went inside the house. Nicole made her way immediately to the bathroom, locking the door behind her and carefully removed the test kit from her bag. Her hand trembled just a little as she opened the box and withdrew the instructions. It seemed straightforward enough. She extracted the test stick and followed the instructions to the letter.

If she'd thought the trip in the car had taken forever, this felt as if she was aging threefold with every second. She counted silently in her head, refusing to look at the stick until she'd counted over the time the instructions said. She could hear Nate in the bedroom. She needed to get this over with before he decided to check on her.

Nicole forced herself to look at the stick. Stripe in one window…the other window clear. A negative result! A rush of exhilaration coursed through her. She shoved the test back into its packaging, and scrunched the whole thing up as small as she could make it before shoving it into the waste bin in the bathroom, and throwing some crumpled tissues on top of it. That would have to do until she could empty the waste bin into a trash bag later on.

She flushed the toilet and then washed her hands at the basin. Her hands were still shaking with the aftermath of the adrenaline surge she'd felt at the confirmation. She was relieved, immensely relieved, but hard on the heels of that sense of relief came a vastly contradictory spear of loss. Would it have been so very bad to have Nate's child? While they didn't have a normal relationship, maybe something good could have come from all of this. Something that could have healed the rift that had been driven between Thomas Jackson and her father all those years ago.

Babies brought with them their own very special brand of implicit trust and love. At least if she had a child, wouldn't she then have its unreserved love? A love that didn't come with tags and conditions. A love she could return wholeheartedly.

Nicole looked at herself in the mirror over the bathroom vanity and shook her head at her fanciful thoughts. She had worked damn hard to establish her career and she wasn't about to walk away from that now. Not even for some pipe dream of a perfect family life. A dream that would probably go horribly wrong if she ever tried it in reality, just like her long-anticipated meeting with her mother.

No, things were definitely better this way. She had no time or space in her life for a baby, not when everything was so horribly complicated—not now, maybe not ever.

Nate had begun to hate Sunday afternoons. In the past it had never been an issue. He loved his time here at the beach house, even more so since he'd been spending it with Nicole. But for some reason the coming week filled him with foreboding. Something was off with Nicole, too. She'd been different all weekend. He'd tried to put it down to her dealing with her feelings about the meeting she'd had with her mother, but he sensed there was far more to it than that.

Even when he'd reached for her in bed last night, he couldn't help feeling as if she was just going through the motions. He knew she'd climaxed, that wasn't the problem. No, what worried him was the mental distance she'd maintained from him. With the roller coaster they'd been through in these past few weeks, the only time the veils they'd held between them had fallen away was when they'd been intimate.

Now, they didn't even have that.

It worried him. Something had happened to change her and he had no idea what it was or how he could fix it. Talking to her elicited no more than a polite response and when he tried to probe deeper, she just shut him down by changing the subject. Short of holding her down and refusing to let her up until she admitted the truth about what bothered her, he had no idea of what to do next. What he did know was that he was losing her, and that was unacceptable.

He went through to the garage to double bag the trash sack to avoid any leakage, and put it in the trunk of his car. It was easier to transfer his waste to the massive trash bin at the apartment building in town than to leave it on the appointed day at the rubbish collection area here. Sometimes being remote from the city had its drawbacks but this was one he could live with.

Nate was picking up the bag and easing it into the second one when a tear suddenly appeared in the plastic and garbage spilled onto the garage floor. Cursing under his breath he scooped up the offending articles and pushed them back into the bag. As he did so, he noticed a small cardboard box that had been twisted up. The lettering on the box was not completely obscured, though, and he saw enough to pique his interest.

He separated it from the rest of the trash and unraveled the packaging. A pregnancy test? There was only one person here who could be responsible for this. He fished the used pregnancy test out of the package, but frustratingly, it was probably too long since it had been used to still show the result. But the fact that she'd taken a pregnancy test at all was enough to have his heart racing.

Every cell in his body demanded he march right up to her and insist she tell him the result of the test, but he forced himself to remain exactly where he was until he could recover some semblance of calm.

Nicole, pregnant? The very thought sent a wave of longing and warmth through his body. He couldn't think of anything he'd like better than watching her ripen with his child. Of sharing each special milestone along the way until they could hold their newborn son or daughter in their arms. Of having a family of his own, a family that included Nicole at its very center.

His heart pounded in his chest at the thought. A family, together, forever. It was everything he'd ever wanted and yet denied himself because he'd been unable to trust, unable to let anyone close enough to have the chance to hurt him since he'd been so twisted by the pain his father had undergone. And now he had the opportunity to put all that bitterness behind him. To forge forward with something new and right and special.

No wonder Nicole had been distant all weekend. She was probably worrying about how to break the news to him, about how he'd take it. He would have to take extra pains to reassure her he would take care of her and the baby, and that she had nothing to worry about, ever, while he had it in his power to take care of her.

Nate forced himself to put the pregnancy test box back in the trash bag and tied off the sack. A few minutes later, as he washed his hands, he thought about what he would say. There was no easy way to approach this. How did you tell the woman you had blackmailed into being with you that you wanted her to spend the rest of her life with you?

Back inside the house, he looked for Nicole. Through the windows he could see her out on the beach, her clothing buffeted by the wind. She was just standing there. Alone. Contemplating the life she carried within her, perhaps? How could he reassure her that everything was going to be okay? That she could trust him?

He reached a decision. He'd just come straight out and tell her. He'd learned a long time ago that occasionally you had to take risks—especially when something was as important as this.

Without taking another moment to think, he pushed open the massive sliding door and headed down the stairs that led to the beach. Nicole must have sensed him coming because she shifted her gaze from the seagulls wheeling on the air currents and turned to face him.

"Nicole, we need to talk."

"We do? What about?" she asked, her long hair whipping around her face in the stiff breeze.

Nate shoved his hands in his jeans pockets. "I know what's bothering you and I want you to know it'll all be okay. I'll take care of you. Once we're married, you won't have a single worry in the world, I promise."

"Married?"

"Of course. There's nothing stopping us. We know we're totally compatible. You can even keep working if you want to, I won't stand in your way. I know how important your career is to you."

To his surprise Nicole just laughed.

Nate frowned, somewhat less than pleased with her reaction. "What? What did I say?"

"Why on earth would I marry you?"

"Of course you'll marry me. We owe it to our baby to provide a united front. You, of all people, know as well as I do what it's like to grow up with two parents who aren't together. Our situation is not ideal, but we can make it work. I know we can. I swore an oath to myself that, no matter what, when I had children I'd be married to their mother, and that's what's going to happen now."

"What makes you think I'm pregnant?" Nicole asked him, taking a step back.

"You've been different these past couple of days and now I know why. I saw the box, Nicole. I know you've taken the test."

Nicole stared at him in horror. He'd found the test? What had he done? Trawled through the rubbish bins? Was he so determined to control every facet of her life? No, she pushed the idea aside. If she was being totally honest with herself, deep down she knew he wasn't like that.

"So, what? You think that if I'm pregnant that we must get married? That's being very old-fashioned of you, don't you think?"

She watched as his face changed, becoming harder, more determined.

"Old-fashioned or not, Nicole, my baby will not grow up illegitimate."

"Of course it won't," she flung back at him.

How dare he be so dictatorial? Didn't her thoughts or feelings factor into this equation at all? Just because he said something was a certain way, didn't mean it had to be so. Even if she was pregnant, marriage to a man who patently didn't love her would be the very last thing on her mind.

The fact that she was totally peripheral to his entire proposal was borne out by his assertion that his baby—*his,* not *theirs*—would not grow up illegitimate. Did he give her any consideration as an individual at all? There was no way she was marrying Nate Jackson. Absolutely no way.

"Good, then it's settled. We'll get married. It doesn't have to be anything big. I'm sure we can sort something out within the next few weeks."

"You can't treat me like some possession to be ordered about. I'm a human being. I've already had quite enough of that kind of treatment from my own father and I certainly won't put up with it from you." She drew up short as a new thought had occurred to her. "My father…is that what this is about? Do you want to get married to rub it in his face? Is this the next part of your revenge?"

"No!" His protest was immediate, and almost seemed instinctive, but how could she believe him? He'd been following his plan of payback right from the start. How was she to know this wasn't his next step?

"Really?" she drawled.

"Look, I know this wasn't the most romantic of proposals—"

"Romantic?" She laughed again, a harsh sound that came from a place deep inside her. A place that hurt with an ache that throbbed through her entire body. "Sort out what you like, Nate, but I'm not marrying you. There were two possible outcomes when I took that test. One, that I was pregnant, the other, that I wasn't. I'm not pregnant, and I'm not marrying you, so you can shove your proposal right back where it came from."

She pushed past him and strode on up the beach toward the house. She thought he couldn't hurt her any more than he already had done. She'd thought that perhaps they'd found a workable solution to their situation. She did enjoy her work at Jackson Importers. She had a freedom there that she didn't have at Wilson Wines and she loved the opportunity to spread her wings and to brainstorm her ideas with others who were on the same wavelength. And she couldn't argue that she and Nate were exquisitely compatible in the bedroom. It had been about the only thing that had kept her sane these past weeks. Knowing that she could seek, and find, oblivion in his arms at night.

But right now she was so angry she could barely see the steps in front of her. She went inside the house, sliding the glass door closed so hard the panes inside it wobbled. Through the window she saw Nate standing on the beach, his hands still in his pockets as he faced the house.

Childishly, she wanted nothing more right now than to flip him the bird, but she wouldn't lower herself to that level. Instead, she turned away from the glass and tried to bring her roiling emotions under control.

Damn him. Damn him for asking her to marry him that way. For asking her to marry him at all! She didn't want to marry, she just wanted to be able to do her job. A job was something she could measure herself by. It had no feelings and only relied on her showing up every single day and giving her very best. A job wouldn't hurt her when the going got rough.

And yet, she couldn't help wondering how she would have felt if the situation had been different. If she had been pregnant, after all—if Nate's proposal had come from a different angle where he'd expressed a desire to have a family with her, even expressed affection or maybe even love for her—would she have been so quick to turn down Nate's suggestion? Nicole knew in her heart her response would have been "yes." She felt the same way he did about raising a child in a unified relationship. In a stable and loving environment. It had been a dream of hers from when she was a little girl. She and Anna had played families, both of them pretending their respective man-about-the-house was at work while they cared for their doll-babies with infinite maternal care.

No, she had to be honest with herself. No matter her feelings for Nate—feelings she couldn't quite put into words—with no mention of love spoken between them, they would only have been setting themselves up for failure. It took a committed parent to raise a child and parents who were not committed to one another, and yet still lived under the same roof, only created a divisive and, in the long term, unhappy home.

And that, sadly, left her right back where she'd started. A pawn in a game where she held none of the moveable pieces. Waiting for the inevitable checkmate when Nate reached his goal against Wilson Wines.

She wanted out of this horrible situation. She wanted out, right now. But how?

Eleven

Nate lay in the bed listening to Nicole breathe, her back as firmly presented to him as it had been when they went to bed. She had barely spoken more than a handful of words to him since the beach and he could hardly blame her. He'd been careless and stupid—thinking only of himself and what he wanted.

He'd used her shamelessly for weeks and expected her to simply roll over and agree to his demand without a single consideration for what it meant to her.

One thing he'd learned from this was that his feelings for her went far deeper than those of revenge. Far deeper than he'd ever wanted to acknowledge. Understanding had struck when she'd accused him of proposing as part of his revenge. That's when he'd realized that her father hadn't even crossed his mind when he'd found the pregnancy test. All he'd thought of was Nicole, and the child they might be having together.

He knew, now, that everything that mattered in his life was tied to the woman who lay in the darkness beside him—beside him yet not touching him and not allowing him to touch her. The woman who'd rejected him most emphatically on the sandy shore outside.

Nate wasn't the type of person who took no for an answer, yet in this he had to. He had no other choice. He'd messed things up between them, well and truly, and he could see no clear way to fix them.

He still had her here in his life, would continue to do so while he could hold the DVD over her. But what did that prove? Nothing. It only proved that, given the choice, she wouldn't be with him and that truth was the most painful of all.

He knew now that he loved her. He didn't want to imagine a life without her. These past weeks had been an eye opener for him. From the start he'd been attracted to her, but that attraction had very rapidly gone far deeper than merely a face-to-face—or skin-to-skin—appreciation of one another. He hadn't wanted to admit it to himself but her rejection had forced him to be honest.

Nate didn't just want to marry her to provide for her and their unborn child—the child that had existed only in his imagination. He wanted the whole shebang. He wanted to love Nicole and spend the rest of his life loving her. And being loved by her in return. He wanted to marry her, for *her*.

Problem solving had always come naturally to him. It was one of the things that made him good at his job—being able to see solutions before anyone else even fully understood the problem. Yet in this he was helpless.

How on earth could he convince her that his intentions toward her came from his heart? He'd tried to lay it on the line on the beach, but he'd gone about it in entirely the wrong way. Had told her, rather than asking her, how things were going to be. With each syllable he'd destroyed every last chance of creating the reality he had really wanted all along.

This was his mess. And for the first time in his life he didn't have a plan for dealing with it.

He pushed back the bedcovers and rose, leaving the room on a silent tread. Streaks of moonlight lit the rest of the house, cold and gray, just like the future that stretched ahead of him without Nicole willingly by his side. It was no better than he deserved for the way he'd treated her, but he didn't want to accept that. Couldn't accept that this was all over. Somehow he would find a solution. It was what he did. And this time, his very happiness depended on it.

They'd remained civil to one another, at least that was something she could be grateful for, Nicole thought as she studied the distribution reports that had been sent for her perusal. Civility was one thing, but how on earth would they continue to live together? Already she could feel the strain between them. She'd had no appetite for anything all day and she knew that food would not ease the hollow that echoed inside her.

Nate had told her to bring her own car into work today as he would be working late entertaining overseas clients. She hadn't suggested she assist him as she was only too grateful for the excuse to put a little distance between them. Leaving the office was a relief.

At the apartment, she'd barely had time to put her laptop case down when the phone began to ring. She let the answering machine pick up but hastened to lift the receiver when her mother's voice could be heard through the speaker.

"Hello?"

"Nicole, darling, I was hoping to catch you at home. How was the rest of your weekend?"

"It was fine. We went out to the beach house."

"I see. Have you thought any more about what I said to you about the Jacksons? I really don't think it's a good idea for you to spend any more time under that man's roof. Seriously, my dear, nothing good will come of it. Surely you can see that."

Another person telling her what to do. Nicole fought back the sigh that built in her chest.

"I'm an adult, Cynthia, and I'm long used to making my own decisions."

"I know, but allow me a mother's care in this instance. I know I wasn't there for you growing up, but trust me when I say I do know better in this case."

"Was there anything else you rang me for?" Nicole asked, struggling with a desire to hang up before she was bossed around again.

"Yes, well, there is, actually."

Was it Nicole's imagination or did her mother sound a little upset? She waited, saying nothing, until Cynthia continued.

"Things haven't really worked out here the way I'd thought they would and I've decided to go back to Adelaide for now. I'd really love it if you could come with me. I'm leaving in the morning and I'll leave a ticket for you at the check-in desk."

"I really don't think—" Nicole started, only to be shut down by Cynthia's voice talking over her.

"No, please, don't make a decision right this minute. Take the evening to think it over. We really haven't had a chance to get to know one another, have we? After all, one lunch together does not a relationship make." She laughed at that, the sound ringing false to Nicole's ears. "At The Masters' we could just spend some time learning to understand one another a little better and you would have the chance to meet up with some of your cousins—get to know your extended family. After all, you're a Masters by blood, and you have every right to be there with me. It's your heritage, too."

Nicole felt a throbbing pain start behind one eye. Did Cynthia instinctively know all of Nicole's hot buttons? But to leave, now, just like that? With her father still direly ill in the hospital and with Nate still holding the DVD over her head?

"Okay, I'll think about it," she conceded.

"You will? Oh, that's marvelous." She gave Nicole the flight time and details. "I'll expect to see you in the departure lounge, then. I can't wait."

Cynthia hung up before Nicole could say another word and Nicole replaced the handset of the phone on its station, a sensation of numbness enveloping her body.

Her life was in tatters. Could her mother's offer be the new beginning she really, desperately, needed? Could she just walk away and say to hell with the consequences of what would happen when Nate gave her father the DVD? She had no doubt he would do it. If she'd learned anything about Nate in this time, it was just how far he was prepared to go to get what he wanted. He wouldn't rest until he'd pulled her family down from its pedestal. She'd already done her part—he didn't need her anymore. When you got right down to it, she was as disposable to him as she was to her father.

Was she prepared to let him hurt her father like that without even trying to interfere? Was she ready to end their affair, once and for all? Could she really, in all honesty, walk away?

Nate woke to an empty bed. Nicole had been sound asleep when he'd come in last night, a little the worse for wear after a few drinks with his hard-drinking clients. His head gave him a solid reminder that drinking on an empty stomach was not conducive to clear brain function the next day. He felt across the bed. Her side was stone cold. A glance at the bedside clock confirmed it was much later than they usually rose. Obviously she'd left him to it and gone into the office already.

He dragged himself from the bed and through to the kitchen where he downed the better part of the liter of orange juice that was in the fridge, then grabbed a banana from the fruit bowl. It was all he had time for. He'd have to make up for it later in the day.

Showering and dressing took more effort than he wanted to admit and, concerned he may still be over the safe driving limit, he caught a taxi to the office. Nicole had her car there so they could travel home together at the end of the day.

"Is Miss Wilson not with you this morning?" April asked as he entered the office.

Nate felt the first pang of warning. "Isn't she already in the office?"

"No, she left a note for me saying she wouldn't be in. I thought she would be arriving with you."

Nate felt his blood run cold in his veins. She'd been into the office already?

"Let me know if she calls, will you?" he directed as

he strode through to his office and rang the concierge of the apartment building.

Five minutes later he had confirmation that her car had left the parking garage a little after five this morning. Another call confirmed she'd swiped in at the office block parking floor shortly after, but that she'd left again within ten minutes. Which begged the question. Where the hell was she now?

He punched the redial on his office phone for the seventh time this morning, only to get the same automated message—that her phone was either switched off or outside of the calling area. He thought about his own cell phone, which had been damnably silent all morning, and reached into his pocket.

Sometime during the night he'd turned it off while he was out and hadn't turned it back on again. He must have been more intoxicated than he'd realized. Nate thumbed the on button and waited for the phone to power up. The instant it had connected to its service provider the screen flashed up—one missed call, one message. Cursing himself for all kinds of idiocy, he hit the numbers required to play the message. Nicole's shaking voice filled his ears.

"I can't stay with you anymore, Nate. It's slowly killing me inside. Do what you like with the DVD. I don't care anymore. I just know that if I don't get some distance, from you, from everyone, I'm going to go insane. All my life I've tried to be everything for everyone. I even had to do it with you, but I can't do it anymore, not now, not ever again. It's all too much. I need to take care of *me* and to learn to put myself first for a change. In fact, I need to find out who I really am, and what I want. I'm sick to death of being told.

My mother has asked me to go with her to Adelaide. Please don't bother trying to contact me again."

She'd left the message at about six o'clock this morning and it sounded as if she was crying toward the end, as if she was teetering on the edge of a breakdown. Nate felt every muscle in his body clench as the urge to protect her fired through him. He had to find her, needed to find her. As vulnerable as she was right now, she needed a champion. Someone to watch over her while she got her act back together. Someone like him. Certainly not someone like Cynthia Masters-Wilson.

Nate remembered the GPS device in her phone, the one that could track where she was at any given time. He called through to his IT guy, Max, who promised to get on it and let him know within the next few minutes where her phone was. In the meantime, Nate hit the search function on his desktop computer and keyed in Auckland International Airport's departures. Hopefully he wouldn't be too late to stop her from leaving on the flight for Adelaide.

Hope died a swift and sudden death when he saw the only direct flight to Adelaide that morning had departed at eight o'clock. The time she left the apartment, the time she'd left the message for him—it all fit with her being on that flight out of the country. The flight with her mother.

Anger and frustration vied for dominance as he weighed up the idea of booking the next available plane to Australia and making his way to Adelaide to get Nicole back. He wouldn't put it past Nicole to refuse to see him, though, nor her mother to prevent him from making any contact with her. Even if he could track her now it wouldn't be much use to him.

His phone rang on his desk and he swept the receiver up.

"Nate, the tracker shows this address for the phone. Are you sure she's not hiding in your office somewhere?"

Nate bit back the growl of frustration at his computer geek's humor. He reached across and opened a drawer where Nicole had often put her things during the day. There, in all its totally specced-up splendor, lay her cell phone. A sticky note on the screen said, *I won't be needing this anymore,* in Nicole's handwriting. Nate slowly slid the drawer closed and thanked Max for the information, then hung up the phone and, propping his elbows on the desk, rested his head in his hands.

The headache he'd woken with was nothing compared to how he felt now. He closed his eyes for a moment and thought hard about what he should do next. Flying to Adelaide was a definite option, but before he did that he needed some ammunition behind him and what better ammunition than her brother's support?

Nate went to grab his keys, then cursed anew as he remembered he'd left his car at the apartment. Not to worry, there was a taxi rank near the office block. The fare to Parnell and Wilson Wines would be a short one but he'd make it worth the driver's while.

"I want to see Judd Wilson," he demanded as he walked past the reception desk at Wilson Wines about fifteen minutes later.

"Mr. Wilson isn't taking appointments today," the girl behind the desk stated very primly, her expression changing to one of outrage as Nate totally ignored her and started to climb the stairs that led to the management offices of the two-storied building. "Wait, you can't go up there!"

"Just watch me," he said, ascending the stairs two at a time.

At the top of the stairs he caught sight of a woman he recognized as Anna Garrick. Raoul's reporting had been spot-on as usual. The woman was attractive, not unlike Nicole in coloring, but her hair was a little lighter and she was a bit shorter, too.

"Mr. Hunter?" she asked, a startled expression on her face before she pushed it back under a professional facade.

"Where is Wilson? I need to see him."

"Mr. Wilson is still in hospital and visitors are restricted to immediate family only."

"No," he huffed in frustration, "not Charles Wilson, I want to see Judd Wilson, right now."

"Well, then," she said, now appearing completely unruffled. "If you would like to take a seat I'll check if he can see you."

"I'm not waiting. Just show me where he is. This is important."

"Is that so?" Another male voice sounded across the carpeted foyer. "Don't worry, Anna, I'll see him in my office."

Nate couldn't help but intercept the look that passed between the two of them. Questioning his presence, for sure, but there was something more between them. Something that made him feel very much on the outside.

"Where's Nicole?" he demanded, not taking time for introductions or finesse.

"Why don't you come into my office and we'll talk, hmm?"

Judd Wilson gave him a cool blue stare, one that reminded him that he was on their turf right now and in no position to be making demands. With ill-concealed frustration he moved into the room Judd had gestured him into and seated himself in a chair opposite a large mahogany desk. If Jackson Importers was everything that was modern and current, Wilson Wines was the opposite. There was a sense of longevity about the fixtures and fittings, even about the building itself. As if they'd been here awhile and they would be here for quite a while still to come.

The sensation that filled him now was not unlike envy. This should have been part of his father's business, too, part of his legacy. But he didn't have time to dwell on old bitterness and recriminations. Right now he had one priority. Nicole, and her whereabouts.

"Now, how about you tell me what it is you want?" Judd said from the other side of the desk, his gaze still unfriendly.

"Nicole's gone. I need to find out where she went so I can get her back."

"My sister is a big girl now, Hunter. I think if she cannot be reached by you, then perhaps she simply doesn't want to be."

"She's not herself at the moment. She's been under immense pressure and I don't think she's capable of making a rational decision right now. Please, you must help me," Nate implored, shoving pride to one side for the sake of the woman he loved and cared for more than anyone else in the world.

"Must? I don't think so. Not under the circumstances. She left us to be with you. Now she's left you, too. What makes you think we'd do anything to help you get her back?"

"I think she's gone to Adelaide with your mother."

Judd leaned back in his chair, the lift of one brow his only expression of surprise at the news.

"No, she wouldn't have done that," Anna Garrick's voice came from the door.

"Why not?" Nate asked, confused. Nicole had made the point quite clear in her voice message that her mother had invited her to leave New Zealand with her.

"Because she couldn't, that's why. Her passport is still here in the office safe."

Nate felt all the fight drain out of him. Now he had no idea where Nicole could be. Searching for her would be like looking for a needle in a haystack. He had no rights to find out where she was. She'd left on her own accord, severing all ties with him.

"Thank you," he said brokenly, getting up from his seat and making for the door.

"Hunter, can I ask why you're so desperate to find her?" Judd asked from behind the desk.

"Because I love her, and I've done the most stupid thing in my life by letting her go."

Twelve

The look of shock on Judd's and Anna's faces had been little compensation for the empty days, and nights that stretched ahead. By Friday night Nate was a mess—his concentration shot to pieces, his temper frayed. He'd never been this helpless in his life. Well, at least not since his father's fallout with Charles Wilson, when his whole world had turned upside down.

It didn't help that everything around him reminded him of Nicole. From the lotions and perfume on his bathroom vanity, to the items of clothing that were mixed in with his laundry. Even in the office there was the constant reminder of her phone in his drawer, her laptop neatly sitting on the top of the desk.

Every day since she'd left he'd asked himself where she could be. He'd toyed with reporting her missing to the police, but he was quite certain he'd have been laughed out of the station. After all, she was an adult.

They'd had a fight. The separation that had come next was a natural progression. Except it felt unnatural in every way, shape and form.

Someone had to know where she was. She was a gregarious creature, one who got along with people. A pack animal rather than a loner. He wracked his brains to think of who she could have been in touch with. Only one name came to mind.

Anna Garrick. She'd said very little when he'd been at their office on Tuesday morning. Mind you, he'd been an over-reactive idiot—making demands and being belligerent. Hardly the way to garner respect or assistance. It was possible, too, that Nicole may not have even been in touch with her at that stage, but who was to say she hadn't been in touch since?

The time between making his decision to speak with Anna and arriving at the Wilson home became a blur. As he directed his car up the driveway he couldn't help but admire the enormous replica gothic mansion that loomed at the top. It had taken a hell of lot of hard work to build all of this and then to hold on to it, he knew, and he found himself experiencing a begrudging respect for the man who had held it all together.

He went to the door and lifted the old-fashioned knocker, letting it fall against the brass plate behind it.

A neatly suited man answered the door.

"I'd like to see Ms. Garrick, please," Nate said, after he gave his name.

"One moment please, sir. If you'll just take a seat in the salon, I'll see if she's free."

Nate didn't know if Anna was playing games with him or if she was simply genuinely busy, but he didn't like having to cool his heels for a good twenty minutes before she came into the salon to greet him. He had to remind himself more than once that he needed to keep his impatience in check if he was to find out if she knew where Nicole was.

When she finally deigned to see him she was composed and solicitous, probably more so than he deserved after the last time he'd seen her. She offered him a drink, obviously comfortable in her role as hostess. Nate declined her offer, too filled with nervous energy to do anything but pace the confines of the room. She composed herself on an elegantly covered antique two-seater sofa and eyed him carefully.

"What can I do for you, Mr. Hunter?"

"Nate, please call me Nate."

"Nate, then. What is it that you want?"

He swallowed and chose his words carefully. "Have you heard from Nicole?"

"If I had, do you really think she'd want me to tell you?"

He sighed. "I take it you have, then. Is she—"

"She's fine, but she doesn't want to see you or anyone else right now."

Nate lifted his eyes to Anna's, searching her calm hazel gaze for any sign that she was worried about her friend.

"I need to see her," he said, the words blunt and filled with an edge of pain he couldn't hide.

Anna shook her head. "Isn't it enough to know she's okay?"

"What do you think?" he asked her, letting every raw pain of loss show in his eyes. "I love her, Anna. I have to tell her I'm sorry, and I need to see if she'll give me another chance."

"I would be betraying her trust if I told you where she was. I've already done that once, recently, and I have to tell you that I'm not prepared to do that again. It nearly destroyed our friendship."

"Don't you think I know that? I'm begging you here."

"I can't. She needs to know she can trust me."

Nate felt as if a giant ball of lead had settled in his gut. Anna had been his only hope. "I want her to know she can trust me, too," he said brokenly as he rose to his feet and headed out the room. At the doorway he turned, "Thank you for seeing me. If you talk to her soon, please tell her…ah, hell, don't worry, it wouldn't make a difference, anyway."

The pity in Anna Garrick's eyes cut him straight to his heart. Nicole was lucky to have a friend like her, he told himself as he forced his feet toward the front door and headed down the stairs toward his car.

The heavy tread of rapid footsteps followed him down the stairs.

"Hunter, wait up."

It was Judd Wilson. Nate turned to face him.

"Yeah," he said, without even the will to fake a politeness he certainly didn't feel.

"I know where she is."

Nate felt something leap in his chest. "And you'll tell me?"

"Anna will kill me for this, but someone needs to cut you a break," the other man said. "Anyone can see you're hurting. The two of you need to work this out one way or another. You both deserve that much." He gave Nate an address about a two-hour drive north of Auckland. "Don't make me regret this, Hunter. If you hurt her again, you'll be answering to me."

Nate proffered his hand, and felt an overwhelming

sense of relief when Judd took it. Their shake was brisk and brief. "I owe you," he said solemnly.

"Yes, you do," Judd replied just as gravely. "We can talk about that later."

Nate gave him a nod of assent and headed for his car. He needed to swing by the apartment before driving up to see her. There was something he needed to collect. It was late, but maybe Nicole would still be awake by the time he made it to where she was staying. And if she wasn't, well, then he'd just wait until she was.

Nicole brushed the sand off her feet with an old towel she'd been keeping on the edge of the deck for just that purpose. Late-night walks along the sandy shoreline of Langs Beach had become a habit as she tried to do what she could to exhaust herself into sleep every night.

Since making the decision to leave Nate, and risk the consequences, she'd hardly slept a wink. So far Nate hadn't sent the DVD to her father, she knew that much. Anna had been keeping her up to date on her father's progress and it looked as if he'd turned a corner health-wise. Of course, that could all change if he viewed the thing. And while that preyed on her mind, when she was honest with herself, she knew she wasn't sleeping mostly because she missed Nate. Missed his strength, his solid presence beside her at night.

She sighed as she made her way across the deck, her feet frozen in the frigid night air. She could have worn shoes, probably should have, but she loved the feel of the squeaky white sand beneath her feet and, at this time of night, she could enjoy the sensation completely on her own with only the stars above her for company.

The aged French doors groaned as she opened them to let herself inside the rather decrepit holiday home she'd rented. After she'd left her laptop and the phone Nate had given her at the office, she'd just driven north—stopping only long enough to pay for the toll charge on the Northern Motorway and to pick up a cheap prepaid cell phone from a gas station on the way.

She didn't know what had drawn her to the area, aside from the fact it was near the sea and it was nothing like the west coast beach that Nate's house overlooked. Of course, if her goal had been to avoid reminders of Nate, then she'd failed. She hadn't been able to stop thinking about the man since she'd gotten here.

Nicole secured the door and went through to the kitchen to put on the kettle. Maybe a cup of chamomile tea would make the difference tonight and help her to sleep. She stiffened as she heard the sound of a car's tires rolling along the gravel driveway that led to the house. No one knew she was here but Anna, and she wouldn't have come without calling Nicole first.

The walls of the cottage were thin and she could hear a heavy measured tread come toward the house. A tread that seemed to hesitate on the wooden steps that led to the front door before she heard a solid one-two-three knock on the peeling painted surface.

Her heart hammering in her chest, she moved closer to the front door.

"Nicole, it's me, Nate."

How had he found her? More to the point, now that he had, what was she going to do?

"Nicole, please. I'm not here to hurt you or to argue with you. I just want to talk."

She hesitated a moment before reaching a trembling

hand to the lock at the door and swinging the door open. Shock hit her when she saw him illuminated beneath the bare bulb that lit the front porch. As much as she tried to harden her heart against him, she couldn't help but be concerned at his appearance. He looked as if he hadn't slept or eaten properly in days. Probably much as she looked herself. Except when she looked at him all she wanted to do was comfort him.

She fought against the urge to hold her arms out to him, to offer him respite from the demons that had obviously ridden him this week. Demons that might be similar to those she'd been wrestling with herself—unsuccessfully, too, if her instinctive reaction to him was any indicator. She took a deep breath and forced her hands to stay at her sides.

"You'd better come in," she said stiffly, standing aside and gesturing toward the open-plan living room/kitchen.

The place was basic. One bedroom, one bathroom and everything else all there for anyone to see. The property's saving graces had been its proximity to the beach and a modern lock-up garage where she'd stowed the Mercedes.

"Can I get you a warm drink?"

She didn't want to offer him any alcohol before sending him back on his way again, especially not looking the way he did right now. The last thing she wanted to be responsible for was him having an accident.

"No, thanks," he said, his voice ragged. "How are you, really?"

She poured boiling water over the tea bag in her cup and then took it over to one of the chairs in the lounge. Nate sat down on the sofa opposite.

"I'm okay. Look, I don't know why you're here but you won't change my mind. I meant what I said in my message."

Nate reached inside his jacket pocket and took out a flat case. A case she recognized with dread. He tried to hand it over to her and when she didn't take it—she couldn't risk touching him—he placed it on the scarred coffee table between them. She could see her refusal to take the case had surprised him, perhaps even hurt him.

She looked at the case, lying there, inert on the tabletop. So seemingly nondescript, yet so potentially damaging at the same time.

"It's yours," he said.

"What? A copy?"

"The only copy," he said, lifting his face so his eyes met hers. "I couldn't send it to your father—I couldn't do that to you, Nicole. I want you to know that. I could never hurt you like that. I know I threatened to, more than once. But even if I hadn't fallen in love with you I couldn't have abused your trust of me that way."

A fist clenched tight around her heart. Had she heard him right? Or was this just another ploy to get her back where he wanted her?

"You seemed pretty determined. Why should I believe you've changed your mind now?"

The voice that came from her mouth didn't sound like her at all. It was harsh, unforgiving.

He hung his head. "I don't deserve for you to believe me but I hope that you can find your way clear to understand where I'm coming from." He lifted his head again, his eyes filled with anguish. "I know I've been a total monster. I should have told you from the beginning who I was. I should have left you in the bar that night. But I couldn't. Even then I was compelled to be with you. I wanted you and I had to have you."

Nicole gripped her mug tight, mindless to the heat that stung her fingers. Just hearing him say the words about wanting her had her body beginning to light up in response. The old familiar coil of desire tightening deep inside her, craving his touch. Craving him.

"And once you had me, you used me," she said bitterly.

"I'm sorry. I know it sounds trite and empty and worthless, but please believe me. I am so sorry I treated you that way. If I had the chance again I would do everything differently."

And so would she, Nicole thought. For a start she wouldn't have left the house that night. Wouldn't have stormed away and wouldn't have lost herself in the one man who could hurt her more than any other. The man she'd fallen painfully in love with. Her heart beat faster in her chest as she acknowledged the painful truth for what it was. Hopeless. She couldn't trust him. He was a master at manipulation, he'd borne a grudge against her father for most of his life. How could she even begin to believe his words were anything more than another tool to control her?

"Is that everything?" she asked coolly. She held her body so rigid that she was afraid she'd shatter into a million pieces if he so much as reached across the table and touched her.

"No, it's not everything. I could spend the rest of my life telling you how much I regret treating you so badly and it would never be long enough. I love you, Nicole. I'm ashamed that I had to lose you to admit it to myself, but there you have it. On the beach that day I asked you to marry me. I'd fooled myself into thinking it was for the baby's sake, and hurt you by asking you for all the wrong reasons when I should have just asked you for you. Will you give me another chance? Let me make it up to you. Let me love you the way you deserve to be loved."

Nicole shook her head. It was a slight movement but Nate saw it and recognized it for what it was. He tried one more time.

"Please, don't make your mind up right now. Give it a few more days. Come back to the city, come back to me. Let's try again and this time I promise I'll get it right."

"No," she said, feeling as if her heart would break with verbalizing that one syllable. "I can't, Nate. I can't trust you not to hurt me like that again. Me or my family. I just can't." And she couldn't trust herself, either. She loved him too much. If she went back, if she let herself be with him again, she'd find herself falling back into his plans, for better or for worse. And she wasn't going to do that again.

Nate looked at her for a full minute, her words hanging in the air between them like an impenetrable shield. Then, slowly he nodded and rose from the sofa. She didn't move as he crossed the room and moved down the short hall toward the front door. It wasn't until she heard the snick of the lock as the door reseated in its frame behind him, that the shudders began to rack her body and the sobs rose from deep within.

He was gone. She'd sent him away. It was what she wanted, wasn't it?

Nate walked to his car wrapped in a blanket of numbness. She'd refused him. It was his worst-case scenario come to living, breathing, painful, life. He settled behind the wheel of the Maserati, and switched the wipers on only to turn them off again as they scraped across the dry windscreen. It was only then he realized the moisture he felt on his face had not been from any rain outside, but from his own tears.

He started the car and eased it up the driveway, away from the house, away from Nicole, swiping at his cheeks and eyes as he did so. He felt as if he was leaving his soul behind, as if he was just a shell now. An empty shell. She'd completed him and he hadn't even had the good sense to know it or appreciate it until it was too late.

At the top of the driveway he looked back, hoping against hope that she might be silhouetted in the doorway, that she might beckon to him to come back. If she did, then together they could find a way to work past the damage he'd wrought. Instead, he saw the outside light extinguish, and with it his last remaining hope.

He blinked hard. He'd lost her. He'd abused her trust, he'd threatened her family. He had gotten exactly what he deserved.

Nate turned the car onto the winding road that would eventually lead him back to State Highway One, back to Auckland. Back to a life lived alone with his grand, empty plans for revenge.

His eyes burned in their sockets by the time he crossed the Auckland Harbor Bridge and turned off toward the Viaduct Basin. Weariness dragged at his body as he let himself into the apartment, a place that felt empty without Nicole inside. As exhausted as he was, sleep was the last thing on his mind. Somehow he had to find a way to convince Nicole she could trust him and that his love for her was real. There had to be a way, there just had to be, because he couldn't imagine the rest of his life without her by his side.

It simply wasn't an option.

Thirteen

Nate straightened from his car outside the Wilson family home. He hadn't slept all night and was running on pure adrenaline right now. He hammered at the front door and stood back in the portico waiting for someone to respond.

It took a while but eventually the door swung open to reveal Judd Wilson dressed in pajama bottoms and a robe. His hair was rumpled, as if he'd run his fingers through it in an attempt to tidy it before answering the door.

"Good grief, man, have you any idea what time it is?" he grumbled at Nate.

"Look, I know it's early but I had to talk to you. This is too important to wait."

"You'd better come in, then." Judd gave him a hard look. "Have you seen yourself this morning?"

Nate grimaced in response. He knew he looked

about as rough as he felt. He hadn't shaved or combed his hair and he was still in the clothing he'd worn last night.

"Judd? Who is it?" Anna's voice came from the top of the staircase.

"It's Nate Hunter."

"And Nicole? Is she all right?"

Anna came down the stairs, a dressing gown wrapped about her and tied with a sash at her waist.

"Nicole was fine when I left her," Nate ground out. "She doesn't want a bar of me but I'm hoping that we can change that, together."

Judd and Anna exchanged a look before Judd spoke. "You need to fight your own battles, Hunter. My sister is responsible for her own choices."

"I know, but I have a proposal I think you might find worth listening to. Something that will benefit you and Wilson Wines, and that just might show Nicole how much I care."

"Sounds like something best done on a full stomach with a decent cup of coffee inside you," Anna said. "Judd?"

"Sure, come through to the kitchen," Judd agreed.

"We gave our house staff the weekend off, so I hope you don't mind if things are a little more basic than we can usually offer," Anna said as she pushed open the swing doors that led into the spacious modernized kitchen.

"Food is the least of my worries," Nate said, lowering himself into one of the kitchen chairs and pulling a sheaf of papers from his coat pocket. "Please don't go to any bother on my account."

As Anna began to make coffee, Nate started to outline his plan. Judd remained silent through most of it, only stopping Nate every now and then to ask him to clarify one point or another. By the time Anna slid plates of French toast and bacon in front of them both, and topped up their coffees, he was wrapping up.

"So, to sum it all up, I suggest that we amalgamate Jackson Importers and Wilson Wines and go forward as one powerful entity for the future, rather than two companies, which are absorbed in competing with one another. It's how it was meant to be all along, it's up to us to make it that way again."

"Why?" Judd asked. "I mean, the idea is definitely worth exploring, but why now?"

"Because I don't see why we should continue to be victims of our fathers' falling out."

"Your fathers?" Anna asked. "You're—?"

"Yes, I'm Thomas Jackson's son."

Judd leaned back in his chair and gave Nate a hard look. "You're certain you want to do this?"

"I've never been more certain of anything in my life," Nate said emphatically.

"You realize I can't do anything without discussing this with my father and with Nicole."

"I understand that. If possible, I'd like to be there when you talk to your father. I think it's time that the past be firmly put to bed. That all the bitterness be dissolved once and for all. It's hurt too many people for too long. It has to stop."

Nicole missed Nate with an ache that went painfully deep. Nights were fractured with dreams of him, days were filled with trying to forget him. But try as she might, she failed miserably. If only they could have met under normal circumstances, without the stupid feud between their families. If only she could trust that he loved her for herself and not out of some twisted sense of revenge. A person didn't let go of that much animosity easily.

She'd thought that getting away from him, getting away from the city would help. But it hadn't helped a bit. If anything it had only served to magnify her feelings for him. Without anything else to distract her, he was all she could think about. Especially after he told her he loved her—and she'd had to send him away.

Maybe she should get a dog, she pondered as she sat on the deck outside the cottage in the watery sunshine and watched a local resident throwing a stick for his dog on the beach. Even as she considered it she knew it couldn't replace the hole in her heart loving Nate had left. Loving him? How could she love him? He'd virtually kidnapped her, had held her against her will, had forced her to work with him instead of where she rightfully belonged. She made a mental note to look up Stockholm syndrome as soon as she could access a computer. She had to find some reason for this irrational attachment to the man.

But was it so irrational? Their attraction that night at the bar had been mutual and instant. Fierce. At least it had been on her side. His? Well, the jury was still out on that one. He'd been following an agenda, hadn't he?

Seeing him last night was tough. Had their circumstances been any different, had he not been so bent on revenge for what her father had done, she'd have dragged him to the tiny bedroom and laid him bare upon the covers of the double bed and taken her time in punishing him slowly for his behavior.

Her body flushed with heat at the thought. Heat that was rapidly diminished by the cool breeze coming in off the ocean. Exercise, she needed exercise. Anything to wear her out and distract her from her thoughts. She grabbed her puffy jacket from inside the cottage and pulled on a pair of sneakers before heading north up the beach. The wind had risen by the time she reached the end and started to walk back, bringing with it the scent of rain.

By the time she got to the cottage the rain was driving across the sand. She hastened inside, taking her jacket off in the tiny bathroom and hanging it over the shower rail to dry. Making her way to the kitchen, she put on the kettle for a warming cup of tea, as she did so she noticed her phone flashing that she had a message.

Not just one message. Several. And several missed calls, as well. All of them from Anna. What could be so important on a Saturday morning? she wondered. She knew it wasn't her father. He was making steady progress at the hospital and they were even talking about him coming home soon. Dialysis would be a major part of his future but at least he had a future. The messages were all the same—Anna asking Nicole to call her back right away. Her friend sounded excited, but not upset, Nicole noted. She poured her cup of tea and took the cup and her phone over to the sofa where Nate had sat last night, the stuffing so worn that the imprint of his body was still there.

Before she could stop herself, Nicole reached a hand to where he'd been sitting, as if she could somehow sense the man in the impression he'd left behind. A particularly strong gust of wind drove against the beachside windows of the house, making her jump and shaking her from her reverie. She had a call to make. She didn't need to be thinking about Nate. Not now, not ever.

Anna answered the phone on the first ring. "Nic, Judd needs to speak to you. Hold on and I'll put him on."

Judd's warm deep voice filled her ear. "How's it going?"

"It's okay. The weather's rubbish but aside from that I'm doing all right." Ironic, she thought, one of the few conversations she should have with her brother and it should be about the weather.

"Glad to hear it. Look, I'll cut to the chase. I have some important Wilson Wines business to discuss with you but I don't want to do it over the phone. Can you come into the office on Monday? I'd really rather do this face-to-face."

Monday? She could do that. It wasn't as if she had any other pressing social engagements on her calendar, she thought cynically.

"Sure, what time?"

"Let's say eleven. That should give you plenty of time to get down here, shouldn't it?"

"I'll be there."

Judd wasted no further time on any pleasantries, severing the call almost immediately after her confirmation. Well, it wasn't as if they had a normal brother-sister relationship. They hadn't ever had the chance. She wondered what it was he wanted to discuss. Hopefully it would have something to do with her coming back to Wilson Wines and reassuming her position there. Then, maybe, she could undo some of the damage she'd done with her work for Jackson Importers.

Monday morning rolled around slowly and Nicole was on the road earlier than she needed be. After another night plagued with dreams of Nate, she couldn't wait to have something else to distract her. The traffic heading into Auckland was that and then some.

Pulling into her usual car park at Wilson Wines felt strange, but that was nothing to what it felt like walking back into the building. Everything was still exactly the same. She didn't know why she'd expected it to have changed in any way, except that she had been through so much since the last time she'd been here that she felt that time should have marked its passage here somehow.

Their receptionist told her to go on upstairs and that Judd was waiting for her. Anna met her at the top of the stairs and gave her a quick hug.

"Do you know what this is about?" Nicole asked.

"It's better you hear it from Judd," she said with a smile. "He's waiting in your dad's old office."

"Old office? So he's not coming back?"

"It's unlikely. Even though he's a lot better he's not up to the day-to-day demands of business anymore."

Nicole was shocked. Her father had always been invincible. A powerhouse. They'd butted heads over his unwillingness to accept her ideas for advancement but, that said, she couldn't imagine the company without her father at the helm.

"Is that what Judd wants to talk to me about?"

"Go and see him," was all Anna would say.

Squaring her shoulders, Nicole walked toward her father's office. Judd's office, now, she supposed. He got up from behind the desk when she knocked and pushed open the door.

"I'm glad you could come," he said, first holding out his hand and then drawing her into his arms for a swift embrace. "We haven't exactly been able to get off to a good start, have we?"

"No," Nicole said, a nervous smile on her face. Considering she'd pretty much been pouting like a spoiled brat when he'd arrived, followed a few days later by her storming out of the house, his comment was a mastery of understatement.

"Hopefully we can amend that, if you're willing?"

"Sure. Who knows, we might even like each other."

Judd flashed her a smile and in it she could see a hint of their father's humor. It made her instantly feel more comfortable with him. It was a comfort she clung to as he started to talk about what he'd asked her in to discuss.

"You mean this was Nate's idea? That he *wants* to amalgamate the businesses?"

She got up from her seat and walked over to the window that looked out over the city. Nate? Merge Jackson Importers with Wilson Wines? What ever happened to his passion for revenge? By his own admission it had driven him since he was a child. Why stop now? They both knew that the deal was to Wilson Wines's advantage. The company was in a weakened managerial position with Judd inexperienced with the firm and her father incapable of reassuming his role. If Jackson Importers wanted to put them out of business, now was the time. Why was Nate throwing them a lifeline, instead?

"It was his idea, and after discussing it with him and going over the figures, I'm inclined to accept. It makes sense. Not only that, but it closes a door that's been open too long. It gives both our families a chance to heal."

Nicole shook her head. She couldn't believe it. "Are

you sure he doesn't have some ulterior motive behind this?"

"We stand to gain far more than he does at the moment. I'm sure you're even more aware of that than he is. You've worked with him. You know how strong they are in the marketplace, here and overseas. He's done that. With him running the whole company, they're poised to grow even stronger. Of course, Wilson Wines brings a respected name and established reputation to the table—but unless we modernize and expand, our company will grow weaker while his grows stronger. This is just what we need to get back on track."

She sat back down in her seat. Could Nate have been telling the truth when he came to see her on Friday night? Was he really letting all that resentment and hostility toward her family go, just like that? Was this a chance to finally mend the gaping rifts in her family life and allow her to feel whole again?

Was this the chance for her and Nate, after all?

"And you want an opinion from me today? Really, I need some time to think about this," she said.

"Look, I know it's a lot to take in. Goodness only knows Anna and I have made the most of having the past couple of days to begin to get used to the idea. But it's not just my decision to make. It affects you, as well."

Nicole felt the old acrimony rise in her throat again. "No, it doesn't. You have the controlling share in Wilson Wines. Dad holds the balance. It's your decision, Judd, whether you want that or not."

Judd lifted an envelope from the top of the desk and handed it to her. "Here, maybe what's inside will help you make up your mind."

She took the envelope. "What is it?"

He laughed. "Nothing that'll hurt you, Nicole. Seriously, just open it."

She slid a nail under the flap and ripped the envelope open. Inside was a single sheet of paper. A company share transfer, to be exact. Her eyes widened as she read the terms of the transfer. Judd was giving her everything their father had given him. Not half, not less than half. All of it. If she signed this paper she would have the controlling share and the decision as to how Wilson Wines would go forward.

"Have you lost your mind?" she asked.

"No, if anything I've found it. I learned the hard way that a life bent on revenge is no life at all. I think that Nate has recently discovered much the same thing. I nearly lost Anna over my need to make our father pay for abandoning me and our mother. For denying me my birthright until it suited him to get Anna to bring me back. I don't want to lose out on anything else. Neither does Nate.

"We've all been hurt, Nicole. But we deserve to be happy—*really* happy. I know I'm doing the right thing in giving this to you and I know you'll do the right thing in return."

"And are you happy now, Judd?"

"With Anna, yes. I'm going to marry her, Nicole. I know you two are close and I want you to know I'm going to look after her."

Nicole sat back in her chair and looked at him, and smiled again. Her first genuine smile since she'd arrived today. Maybe her first genuine smile in a long, long time. "You'd better, or you'll answer to me."

"Noted," he said with a nod. "Now, how about you take the next day or so to think about things? Anna has a folder ready for you to take with you so you can analyze Nate's proposal in depth."

Nicole sat in her car in the car park still shocked by the news Judd had given her today, especially his intention to marry her best friend. When pressed, Anna had admitted her love for Judd in return, but said they weren't going to make a public announcement until Charles was home and settled again. They'd already sought his blessing, which had been rapidly forthcoming, apparently. Which left Nicole exactly where?

She had plenty to think about, she realized as she started the car and backed out of the car space. It wasn't until she'd headed for the motorway interchange that would lead her back up north that she made a sudden decision to turn around and drive back the way she'd come.

The Auckland City Hospital car park was pretty empty given the time of day, and it didn't take her long to find a space. In no time she was in an elevator, heading for her father's ward. She only hoped that he'd agree to see her. If, as Judd had said, they all deserved happiness, then it was time for some truths between her and her father, especially the truth about her more recent behavior. Only with everything out in the open could the wounds—both old and more recent—finally heal.

She fought to hide her shock when she saw him lying against his pillows, his eyes closed. The ravages of illness had made him lose a great deal of weight and his skin held an unhealthy pallor. She could have lost him. Would have never had the chance to make amends. And all for what?

"Dad?" she said tentatively as she closed the door to the private room behind her.

His eyes shot open and Nicole was relieved to see they were full of their usual fiery intelligence.

"You came back."

His tone of voice gave nothing away but she caught the telltale tremor around his mouth. And was that a hint of moisture in his eyes?

"Oh, Dad. Of course I came back. I miss you."

"Ah, my little girl. Come here," he said, his voice shaking as he parted the side of the bed and opened his arms.

Nicole shifted to his side and let herself be enveloped by his hug, mindful of the monitors and tubes he was still attached to. But all that was peripheral to the fact that she was here, that he hadn't sent her away again.

"I've missed you, too. I've had plenty of time to think, lately, and I know I owe you an apology. Several apologies, actually."

"No, Dad, it's okay," she protested. "I've always acted first, thought second. I should have stayed. We'd have worked it out."

"No, it's not okay. I never gave you a fair shot, did I? I was so angry with you for defecting to the enemy after Judd came home that the sight of you in the emergency department just made me see red. But I was wrong. When all is said and done, family comes first. I should never have pushed you away in the first place. I should have included you when I decided to approach Judd about coming back home. It was wrong of me to make those decisions, decisions that affected you, without any consultation as a family."

"It's okay, Dad, I understand. It hurt me, but I do

understand. You never got the chance to raise Judd the way you wanted to. All of that was stolen from you."

"Stolen with a single lie," he said sadly. "Did you know that? Your mother told me Judd wasn't my son. To my shame I believed her and when she named my best friend as Judd's father, I stupidly believed that, too. So many years lost, so much time wasted."

"But you can make up for that now," she urged, shocked at the way his body trembled and happier than ever that she had chosen not to run away from her problems to Australia with Cynthia. She did want to meet her family at some point—get to know her cousins and uncles and aunts, but cementing things with her family here took priority.

"For what time I have left," Charles replied. "You know, Nicole, pride is a terrible thing. Because of pride I lost my wife, my son, my best friend and my health. If I had my time over again, I'd do so much differently. Maybe then I could have been the husband Cynthia needed. I've made some bad decisions in my life, not least of which with you.

"I know you think I was holding you back at Wilson Wines and, yes, I suppose I was. But I could just see so much of myself in you. You were so driven, so determined to grow the business to the exception of everything else in your life. I've always wanted the best for you but when I saw you going down the same road that I went, I had to do something to hold you back. You deserve more than just a business. You deserve a life enriched with a husband and children and steadiness at home—not all your energy driven into work and serving the mighty dollar as I have done."

"But I love my work at Wilson Wines, Dad. I've missed it."

"I thought limiting your requirements at work would push you to invest more of your time and energy into relationships. I shouldn't have made that decision for you. I'll wager you had more freedom with that Nate Hunter than you had with me. Don't bother denying it. He saw a good thing and he took advantage of it."

"Dad, there's something you should know about him."

"Beyond the fact he's a fearsome business opponent? Can't help but admire him for that, if nothing else."

She didn't know how to phrase this carefully, so she just came out with it. "He's Thomas's son."

Her father closed his eyes briefly before giving a deep sigh. "That explains a lot," he said quietly. "Another life harmed. Clearly I owe him an apology, too. It can't have been easy for him growing up. Are the two of you an item?"

Nicole shook her head. "We were. But I ended it. He wanted me for all the wrong reasons."

"And what are those?" Charles urged.

"Revenge against you, for one thing," she admitted. It sounded so pathetic when she put it into words to the man it had been directed against. But that's pretty much what it all came down to in the end, wasn't it?

Charles chuckled. "A chip off the old block, hmm? Well, I can't say I blame him. He had just cause."

Nicole could barely believe her ears. All his life her father had spoken in derogatory terms about Thomas Jackson and now he laughed about Nate's vendetta?

"Aren't you angry?"

"Not anymore," he said with a deep sigh. "There's a lot to be said for facing your mortality. It makes you see things differently."

"Judd gave me his controlling share of the company," she blurted.

"Did he? Well, that was his choice to make. I should never have created such a divisive position between you two but it was so important to me to bring Judd home, and I really did want to force you to create some balance in your life."

By the time she left the hospital it was growing late. Despite a few dark looks from the nursing staff, she'd been allowed to stay at her father's side all afternoon and they'd talked to one another as they'd never talked before. As she clipped her seatbelt across her chest she recognized that the feeling inside her now was one of happiness and acceptance of her position in her father's heart. She held all the cards now. She was no longer a pawn, she was the player.

Which left her only one last thing to do.

Fourteen

Her headlights picked out the possum ahead of her on the winding curve of road. Thankfully she avoided it without incident and could focus her attention to the confrontation she had ahead. Nate hadn't been at the office when she'd called, nor had he been at the apartment when she'd stopped in there. Which only left the beach house.

How appropriate that this would end where it had begun.

She cruised through the bends in the dark ribbon of tarseal slowly, more familiar with being a passenger on the journey than the driver. It was an interesting analogy for her life. Despite her efforts to get ahead and to be noticed in her life, she'd always allowed herself to be acted upon rather than to take charge and be fully responsible for her own behavior.

The idea that she was free of her previous constraints, constraints she'd allowed even into adulthood, was intensely liberating. Even so, she felt as if hummingbirds danced in her stomach as she neared the driveway to Nate's house. She pulled up outside the garage door and walked around to the main entrance, pressing the door bell several times in quick succession.

The door opened.

"Nicole!"

Nate looked stunned to see her, but she felt his eyes roam her as if he were touching her. Her traitorous body responded in kind. She dropped her eyes from his, hoping he hadn't seen her reaction reflected in her gaze.

"We need to talk," she said brusquely. "May I come in?"

He stood aside and gestured for her to take a seat in the living room. "Can I get you anything?" he offered.

"This isn't a social visit," she said firmly. It was important to her that she set the parameters right from the start. "I need to know something."

"Ask me. I'll tell you whatever I can."

"Are you still playing some game with my family with your proposal to join the companies together?"

He looked surprised. "You know about that already?"

"Judd called me down from Langs Beach to discuss it. He's given me a written report, which I haven't read yet. I needed to talk to you first so I can decide whether to read it, or whether to use it to light a fire, instead."

He gave a disparaging laugh. "It's not a game—it's anything but."

"So this is really what you want?"

He looked her square in the eye and she could see

the truth burning there in those sherry-brown depths. "Yes."

"And you're not doing this to somehow undermine my family or to hurt them?"

"No, I'm not."

She took a deep breath. "Or to hurt me?"

"Never to hurt you, Nicole. That was *never* my intention. I wanted to give you every opportunity to succeed all along."

"Why are you doing this, then?"

Nate sighed and leaned forward, resting his elbows on his thighs and clasping his capable hands in front of him. His gaze was fixed on her face, as if he was willing her to believe him.

"I made the suggestion for three very good reasons. The first is that it makes sound business sense. If we stop competing with one another we'll be in a stronger position when it comes to securing new business—one less player in the market should give us an edge on pricing. It's all in the report, when you read it you'll see what I'm talking about."

Nicole nodded. "Okay, so that's one reason. What about the others?"

"It was time to stop the feud. It's hurt too many people for too long. One of us had to make the first move. I decided it was time for me to let go of my grudge. Sure, I had a tough upbringing, a lot of kids did. I still had more advantages than most. Even while my mother and I were living hand to mouth my father was ensuring that I still had the best education that he could provide for me. And having to struggle a little made me tough, it made me determined. It made me the man I am today. Flawed, sure, but I know what's right, and letting go of the anger, letting go of the pain—it all had to happen so we can move forward.

"Pride can be a killer. I didn't want it to destroy every last thing I held dear."

Nicole nodded. Hadn't her father spoken along the same lines? She said as much to Nate.

He nodded gently. "You know, I want to see him if he's agreeable. We have a lot to talk about."

"I think he'd like that. I told him today about you. I was sure he was going to tell me that he'd be quite happy to carry on the competition between Wilson Wines and Jackson Importers indefinitely, but this latest illness has changed him, too. It's altered his perspective on things."

She paused for a moment, reflecting on the things her father had said, then reminded herself she was here for a reason. "What's the third reason?" Nicole pushed.

"The third reason? You already know that one."

She looked at him, puzzled. She already knew? When she said nothing, Nate continued.

"I love you."

"That's it?" She felt her skepticism rise.

"Yeah, that's it," he said with a deprecating chuckle. "Although I never quite expected to get that response."

"That's not what I mean—" she started to protest, but he cut her off.

"Nicole, I knew that after what I'd put you through, for you to believe that I love you would take an action on my part to prove it, beyond any shadow of a doubt. And I was already working at a disadvantage, because of the mistakes I'd made in our relationship. When I asked you to marry me on the beach out here, when I thought you were carrying my baby, I was prepared to do whatever I could to protect you and provide for you and our child, but I know I went about it all wrong. You have to understand. I grew up illegitimate. Sure, I know that wasn't the worst thing that could happen to me and I certainly wasn't the only kid in class from a single-parent family—but I wanted more for my child than I had."

He got up and began to pace the room, shoving his hands through his hair and sending it into disarray before pushing them deep into the pockets of his trousers. Nicole could see the outlines of his fists through the fine wool of his pants, could sense the tension in every line of his body.

"Go on," she urged softly. "Tell me the rest."

He stood where he was, staring out the window toward the dark shoreline, to where the moon and stars lit the foam of the waves that curled and raced inexorably onto the sand.

"I wanted to ensure that my child never wanted for anything the way I wanted, but at the same time I wanted him or her to know they were loved. You see, even though we struggled, even though I had to put up with the bullying at school because I was different—because my mother was seen shopping at the local thrift store or because one of the boys' mothers delivered our food parcels while doing her bit for the community—through all that I always knew I was loved. Always. I will never be an absentee father to my children. I will be a part of their lives and I will be there when they need me."

Nate turned and faced Nicole again. "That's the way I love, Nicole. With everything I am. It's the way I love you. I asked you to marry me without even fully understanding just how much a man could love a woman, but I learned that, and more, when you left me. You're everything to me and I knew that I had to prove that to you, even if it meant letting go of everything I'd always believed while I was growing up.

"That's it. I love you. Pure and simple."

Nicole sat there, stunned. What he'd just told her was anything but pure and simple. It showed the depths of the man before her. The man she'd rejected and who hadn't given up.

This wasn't the same person who'd calculatedly brought her back here on that fateful night just over a month ago, a man who was prepared to blackmail her over an illicit weekend of wild pleasure just to hurt her father. He'd changed. The old Nate would never have dreamed of combining their two businesses together to form one perfectly strong whole.

This was a man who loved her. Truly loved her. And she'd changed, too, into someone who wasn't afraid to love him back. She pushed herself to her feet and moved to stand in front of him.

"I believe you," she whispered, her voice shaking with the depth of her own love for him. A love she could finally acknowledge to both herself and to Nate. She raised one hand and cupped his cheek. "I love you, too."

The sound he made was part human and part something else. He turned his face into her hand, pressing his lips against her palm.

"It's more than I deserve," he said brokenly.

"We deserve each other. We're neither of us perfect, but together, maybe we can cancel out the bad and be nothing but good. Love me, Nate. Love me forever."

"You can count on it."

He pulled his hands from his pockets and swooped her up into his arms, carrying her to the bedroom where they'd already created so many special memories. This time they undressed one another slowly, painstakingly—taking their time to kiss and caress every part of each other as they bared skin. As if it was their first time—a voyage of discovery.

When neither of them could wait any longer, Nate covered her body with his own, pausing only to reach for a condom. Nicole stayed his hand.

"No condom," she said. "I want whatever naturally comes next in our lives and I don't want any more barriers between us."

"Are you sure?" he asked, his body rigid beneath her hands as she stroked his buttocks with a featherlight touch and then traced her fingers up the muscles that bracketed his spine. She relished the strength of him, loved that he was all hers.

"Certain," she whispered as she lifted her mouth to his, claiming his lips in a kiss that imbued everything she felt at that moment, and when he slid inside her she knew she'd made the right decision. Nothing had ever felt as good as this contact between them, heat to heat, nothing but him and her.

Nate started to move and she met him, stroke for stroke, her cries of pleasure intensifying as he pushed them over the edge of sanity and into another realm where only the two of them existed.

Afterward, they lay still locked together as one. As their breathing slowed and returned to something approaching normal, Nicole lifted a hand and traced the outline of Nate's face. He had never been more precious to her than he was at this moment.

"Do you think we'd have ended up like this without our parents' falling out?"

Nate smiled. "Who knows? I'd like to think so. I

know there's no one out there in this world for me, but you."

She snuggled against him. "Why do you think she did it?"

"She?"

"My mother. Why do you think she lied to my father for all those years? She drove a wedge between everyone without a second thought."

"You know that for sure?"

"Dad didn't tell me all of it, but he did say that her lie was responsible for what happened."

Nate shifted onto his back, pulling Nicole with him. "I suspected she instigated it all. I couldn't imagine anyone else but her having that power over them. Maybe she resented the time Charles put into the business—who knows—but it's no wonder he reacted the way he did to what he perceived as the ultimate betrayal from his best friend."

"But for her to have let it go on this long...I just don't understand it. Why would she do that?"

Nate closed his arms around Nicole and held her tight against him, making a silent vow that nothing would ever separate them again. "She was obviously a very unhappy woman. I'm sorry she never got to have what we have, but we can't let her spoil it for us, either."

Nate pressed a kiss to the top of Nicole's head. "I'm so sorry for everything I did to you, Nicole. I kidded myself that if I gave you everything I thought you wanted that you'd be happy to stay with me. I should have realized you deserved so much more."

"Good thing you got it right this time, then, hmm?" Nicole murmured as she shifted and raised herself above him. "Because I'm going to expect a whole lot of this loving."

"I think I'm man enough for the job." He smiled from beneath her, his body hardening inside her as she rocked gently against him. He gripped her hips with his hands, stilling her motion and his eyes grew serious. "Nicole, I mean it, though. Can you forgive what I did to you?"

"Of course I can, Nate. I already have. We both did things we regret."

"There's one thing I'll never regret," he said, continuing to hold her still. "And that's meeting you. You taught me to open my eyes and to love with all my heart. No conditions, no strings. You will marry me, won't you?"

"Yes," she replied. "I love you, Nate Hunter Jackson, and I will marry you."

"That's good," he replied, "because I'd hate to have to kidnap you all over again."

She laughed, her inner muscles tightening around him as she did so. She'd never felt this happy, or this complete before in her life. She belonged with him, as he did with her. All the security, love and recognition she'd craved all her life lay here with this incredibly special man. Their road together hadn't been smooth so far, but nothing worthwhile in life came easily. She knew that to the very depths of her soul. She also knew she loved him, and that her future would be all the better for having him at her side.

* * * * *

ML